THE
IRON
ORCHARD

THE
IRON
ORCHARD

a novel

TOM
PENDLETON

TCU
Press

Fort Worth, Texas

LIBRARY OF CONGRESS CATALOGING-IN-PUBLICATION DATA

Names: Pendleton, Tom, author.

Title: The iron orchard / Tom Pendleton.

Description: Fort Worth, Texas : TCU Press, [2019] | Originally published by
McGraw-Hill in 1966. | Present publication is copyrighted by the Estate of
Edmund Van Zandt, LLC.

Identifiers: LCCN 2018046161 | ISBN 9780875657134 (alk. paper)

Subjects: LCSH: Oil fields--Texas, West--Fiction. | Fortune hunters--Texas,
West--Fiction. | Texas, West--Fiction. | GSAFD: Adventure fiction. |
LCGFT: Action and adventure fiction.

Classification: LCC PS3572.A55 I76 2019 | DDC 813/.54--dc23

LC record available at https://urldefense.proofpoint.com/v2/url?u=https-3A__
lccn.loc.gov_2018046161&d=DwIFAg&c=7Q-FWLBTAxn3T_E3HWrzGYJrC4
RvUoWDrzTlitGRH_A&r=O2eiy819IcwTGuw-vrBGiVdmhQxMh2yxeggw9q
lTUDE&m=tT7UAwm97mQhfvMc36BSs_ooeZ5Fomjr7ezn6zW8MNQ&s=J_2
VOe7Qs89dZs7Ki93cFXFEJCwaxb4grZMOejw7jpc&e=

TCU Box 298300
Fort Worth, Texas 76129

817.257.7822
WWW.PRS.TCU.EDU

To order books: 1.800.826.8911

TEXT AND JACKET DESIGN BY ALLIGATOR TREE GRAPHICS

For F. D. A.

FOREWORD

I THINK OF MYSELF AS A NOVELIST, BUT I'VE published some nonfiction of mostly regional interest, and I've also written (or mostly cowritten) nearly forty hours of television/cable/streaming content. It was in the latter capacity that I met with some indie movie producers in Austin about two years ago who were aware of my past association with oil fields and wanted to know if I could consult on their adaptation of *The Iron Orchard*. The what, I asked? What in God's name is *The Iron Orchard*? And as they explained the history of Tom Pendleton's novel to me—that it had been a cowinner of the Texas Institute of Letters's fiction award (with Larry McMurtry's *The Last Picture Show*)—I felt my viscera twist like it had been cross-threaded. How the hell could this epic Texas oil field novel exist and I know nothing about it? I shut down discussions and hunted down a copy of my own. I didn't care so much about their movie as I needed to see what this man had written and, mostly, how it compared to what I had done over three decades before.

It may help to understand that I invested over five years of my youth in domestic and foreign oil fields. I knew, understood, and was quite comfortable with its culture as I had encountered it. My first drill crew was led by a Mississippi man in his early sixties, a dead ringer for Bull Conner, who had broken out on the drill floor during the Great Depression. My earliest toolpushers (rig superintendents) were older, more experienced, and manifested even bigger personalities than my driller's. They carried the noble bearing of men firmly in command as easily as they wore their stained company coveralls. Underneath those crusty exteriors they bore the scars of countless injuries and the inevitable self-medicating substance-abuse issues detected perhaps by their lumbering gait, the Camel cigarette butts that perpetually dangled from their lips, and the gravel in their voices. They lived hard and didn't give a damn if it showed.

A roughneck does not simply work with his crew. He *lives* with them. As far as I was concerned, I had proudly twisted myself into one of them. I felt safe in my insular assumption that I alone had earned the chops to represent a global industry that had been decisively shaped into a work of fiction by my home state. To me, the oil and gas industry, no matter where the kelly turned, was a *Texas* thing. I am a Texas writer. I wrote *The Empty Quarter*, the best book within me.

The Empty Quarter went out, created an impressive ripple in the literary stock tank, and was promoted by people who had very few resources and even less sense. It had enjoyed a customary three-month run on the featured fiction shelf of bookstores, then disappeared the day after I appeared there. *The Empty Quarter* would be, as Elmer Kelton privately forecast along with his pre-publication endorsement, my least commercially successful title.

We all learn to take a punch in this business.

But, I received reader letters and emails that I still cherish. The international oil field of the 1980s—before the era of satellite television, internet streaming, and the avalanche of entertainment "content"—was a community of devoted, if captive, readers. Some of them happened upon my novel, and they *knew* it had been written by one of them. Their approval was the one redeeming consolation for the many years of painful effort required to write any book. This one failed (for now). In time, I moved on to new challenges and disappointments, content that I had done with *The Empty Quarter* what I had set out to do.

We flash forward to 2016, when West Texas filmmakers first made me aware of *The Iron Orchard*. A hardcover copy of McGraw-Hill's 1966 edition exceeded $300 in the used book market. I don't sleep well owning a pair of cowboy boots in that price range, so I made do with a mass-market edition featuring ridiculous promotional copy suggesting, among other things, that I could barely handle a novel as wild and dangerous as this one; that I should be wary of its author should he appear in my town (I live in Austin, and have learned to be very wary of authors); and also that it was soon to be a major motion picture, with none other than Paul Newman "attached" to play the lead role.

I should've focused on helping these people make their movie (spoiler: they didn't need me), but I lapsed into a state of deep conflict and misgivings.

I suspected that my franchise on Texas oil field literature had been long ago usurped. When I read the novel by Tom Pendleton—a pseudonym for the late Edmund Van Zandt, a Fort Worth native and longtime oil industry executive—my envy morphed into dismay. I came to understand that I was dealing with a born writer, who had mixed with the best literary minds in Texas of his time and place (the deeply cultural city of Fort Worth), and included among his close friends the accomplished John Graves and the civic leader Amon Carter. This author (Tom Pendleton), and this flesh and blood man (Edmund Van Zandt) drew from a deep well.

More remarkable to me was how Tom Pendleton delivered a West Texas story in a working Texan's cadence so distinct you can hear their spit hit the dust and still captured the essence of an evolving global industry in very human terms, all in a *timeless* voice that has, at various times in our literary history, belonged to writers from Rabelais to John Steinbeck to Larry McMurtry. We all hope to tap into something greater than ourselves. In *The Iron Orchard*, Edmund Van Zandt, writing as Tom Pendleton, did it.

Yet even his timelessness is still not what drew me to his work. Van Zandt—from an established family well known among Fort Worth's social, economic, and cultural elite—chose for his protagonist Jim McNeely, an orphan whose biological parents were of solid stock but of short, tragic, brutal experience. As we first encounter a teenaged McNeely, he is already a perennial outsider. White trash. He did not belong in the oil fields. He was banished there in the hopes it would bury him. He was not welcomed by his crew. He was soon savagely victimized by most of them.

A wise therapist once told me that at the root of all male anger is a terrible sadness. McNeely is formidable in the pursuit of his goals, but he is also deeply, terribly wounded. Those two polar states of mind, hopelessly conflicted and dangerously volatile, drive the middle and end of McNeely's amazing fictional journey. Edmund Van Zandt was a child of affluence, a UT frat rat, who mixed readily with the money folks of Fort Worth, who earned an officer's commission in the Marines during World War II and later rose to become one of the highest-ranking executives of Gulf Oil (being groomed, he was told, to serve as its CEO). How he created such a gifted yet tragically flawed protagonist from the mean side of the tracks just astounds me. How could he have understood McNeely's hunger and rage so well?

Van Zandt broadens his canvas by capturing the eccentric culture of the oil field. He perfectly portrayed its mood, its spirit, its ugliness, and its ability to mangle men more easily than transform them. To pull that off in a four-hundred-page narrative requires skill, similar to that perhaps of a young Stephen Crane, who portrayed Civil War soldiers in *The Red Badge of Courage* with astonishing authenticity, or of Herman Melville, who captured the eccentricities of New England's whaling crews down to their acrid stench in *Moby Dick*. You come to know men like that only when you sweat and bleed beside them; when you've seen more than your share of them break in two. Reading *The Iron Orchard* convinced me that its author had travelled this terrain.

Even more remarkable is that Pendleton also created in Jim McNeely a protagonist who resonates personally with an old roughneck like me. I have known many McNeelys. Labored beside a few as brothers. Battled some as rivals. Drank whiskey with as many as I could catch on pay day in those rowdy pubs off Union Street in Aberdeen, or on that wild, nearly all-male Aramco charter that blew out of Houston International around midnight for Dhahran, Saudi Arabia. Seen far too many fade moaning from this world. Had I remained in the oil patch, there's little doubt that my fate would've been the same as McNeely's. I'm attesting that Van Zandt's narrative is an inside job.

Of greater interest is the scope of Tom Pendleton's cautionary tale. As the narrator of his novel casts himself more and more as the objective oil field philosopher, he teaches us perhaps more than a novelist should. In editorial terms, these omniscient sequences are sometimes known as "narrative stalls"—a point in the novel where the writer chooses not to propel the story forward for a page or two in order to expound upon what he knows to his readers. And Tom Pendleton knows plenty. For those plot-driven enthusiasts, this seems like a rookie mistake. That this Pendleton fellow is too much in love with his own expertise. We encounter such flaws often in historical fiction. I commit them every chance I get.

In the case of *The Iron Orchard*, however, Pendleton's objective narrator enriches the reading experience, just as William Makepeace Thackeray did so eloquently in *Vanity Fair*, where the human story at the heart of his novel is profoundly impacted by the Napoleonic Wars and the economic chaos that followed them. Almost forty years have passed since I read Thackeray, and I *still* hear the bells toll in London's financial district for yet another merchant ship lost at sea, making it known to all that someone's just been ruined. Such detail didn't quite fit in the novel; it just informed it—perfectly capturing the volatility of the characters' tragic times. Pendleton accomplishes the same feat, which is to say that, from the beginning, he aspired to the classic style of the novel that we inherited from the British, and then made our own in America. And we made it better, too.

But Tom Pendleton was born a Texan, and Americanizing his narrative wasn't good enough. The roughneck protagonist turned wildcatter, financier and huckster, with an insatiable appetite for money, status, beautiful women, and whisky neat, is as big as rancher Bic Benedict in Edna Ferber's *Giant*, and just as lost and tragic as Ferber's rags-to-riches antagonist, Jett Rink. Throughout Jim McNeely's journey, his rage burns brightly, and his restlessness propels him deeper and deeper into a web spun of his own dysfunction. For those of us who've knocked around the Lone Star State some, I don't know anything more Texan than that.

The Iron Orchard's sex scenes are racy as hell for the mid-1960s. I hope that sort of thing wasn't happening to the folks in my congregation. I remember sneaking a copy of Mario Puzo's *The Godfather* (from an unwary Methodist, no less) and being enthralled by Sonny's behavior in the opening scenes. Puzo's got nothing on Tom Pendleton.

The novel exhibits an incredibly enlightened treatment of homosexuality (seen in both a negative and positive light) at a time when most writers and readers chose to completely ignore it. McNeely's most loyal lieutenant, shrewdest strategist, and truest friend happens to be gay. Few writers of Pendleton's era would dare assume the risk of what today might be termed *tolerance*. He never blinked.

For as much as Edmund Van Zandt inhabited the oil field of his day, watching it evolve from the boardroom to the global energy industry of today, the born writer in him cannot refrain from biting the hand that has nourished him and his family. Pendleton's novel makes it obvious that he admires the drillers, the wildcatters, the lease men, and the humanity that tended to recklessly converge on the great oil/gas discoveries of West Texas, but he takes a dimmer view as wildcatting gives way to a corporate culture that, I believe, he views as tedious as it is tragic. The fictitious Bison Oil, whose Dead Lake installation conspires to break the young McNeely, circles back at middle age to destroy him as he risks his remaining resources to drill one last wildcat well. In the writing business, we refer to that depiction as artistic intent. Van Zandt personally witnessed some of the great mavericks of his day, whose ambition, guile, and daring created an industry as bold and restless as they were. But the author seems to disdain the fact that by the end of Van Zandt's professional career, the major oil companies and their efficiency-driven managers controlled every aspect of it.

The Iron Orchard has the subversive quality we feel in Joseph Heller's brilliant *Catch 22*, or Salinger's *The Catcher in the Rye*, or Melville's last work, *Billy Budd, Sailor*, and especially Ken Kesey's tome of 1960s alienation, *One Flew Over the Cuckoo's Nest*. Once you've worked in the patch, you just can't bring yourself to trust an "office worm," a person who controls your life but believes it's a little too shabby to share it with you. I never overcame my distrust of my corporate overlords. I gather from reading *The Iron Orchard* that Edmund Van Zandt never really did either—and he became one of them.

Van Zandt saw the future. Since my own novel was first imagined in the 1980s, I was looking at things twenty years later than Van Zandt. My prognosis (solitary groupthink, I guess) missed things by a continent. Van Zandt, on the other hand, nailed it. He bailed out of top management at Gulf Oil to work in his family's bank in Fort Worth (the antithesis of his lifelong ambition), but banker's hours meant more time and repose for writing. He understood that oil and gas were here to stay for decades to come. Dead of a heart-attack at fifty-six, Van Zandt would not live to see the production of America's vast shale oil plays—including Texas's Eagle Ford, Barnhart, and Reeves County fields—that would finally blow past the 1970 peak of US domestic production and return the nation that had invented the oil industry back to prominence as the world's largest exporter of oil and gas. Edmund Van Zandt would not have been the least surprised.

I don't deny that *The Iron Orchard* suffers from weaknesses inherent in many first novels. Supporting characters tend to show up only when the plot needs them, and one of them shows up in a particularly ridiculous scene. The dialogue is sometimes dated, and sometimes so stilted it creaks. Its redneck slang is sometimes undecipherable. I've never seen any sort of a woman melt down like McNeely's star-crossed flame, but if I did I damn sure wouldn't go out with her.

But the artistry is there. The language (mostly) rings true. The plot moves. These characters are wild as hell but we understand them. America will never tire of watching its rich, famous, and notorious wreck themselves—only stories of a rogue's redemption and perennial whodunits are revisited as often. But Tom Pendleton tells us the story of a lifetime, as only he can tell it, having been nurtured by the best writers and academics in Texas, and having earned such professional success that the prospect of living and working as a writer must have seemed absurd. Yet he orchestrated his life such that he wrote what is, beyond a doubt (*gulp*) the very best novel about the Texas oil and gas industry, and the kind of people who thrived in it, even if it ate them alive and spit them out in the slush pits. Van Zandt himself would perhaps seem like yet another casualty of oil men who lived too hard, enduring too much pressure and stress, for way too long. And like the rest of his maverick kind, he smoked and drank a little too much, too. Dead at fifty-six, with so much left undone. We will never know where his talent, drive, intellect, and humanity would've taken him.

The Iron Orchard should never have been left behind. We should all be thankful first to Ty Roberts and his development team for reinvigorating this epic tale by way of a two-hour feature film, and now to TCU Press for returning it to print. This edition saves you all about $300, and plugs you back in to a book that barked like a blowout in its day, with a feature film with Paul Newman "attached" in the works. And Paul was the right guy. Had a director come along back then who had the passion and artistry to render *The Iron Orchard* as starkly beautiful as Peter Bogdanovich adapted *The Last Picture Show*, we would never have needed this introduction. Even if *The Iron Orchard*'s not quite on par perhaps with *Lonesome Dove* or *All the Pretty Horses*, it's still right across the river, has no equivalent in the literature of Texas, and TCU Press just knocked down the fence. No one's claiming *The Iron Orchard*'s a perfect novel. But it held its own when it was first published in the days of drugstore blockbusters, and it's survived as a literary feast from a bygone era that few understood as well as its savvy Fort Worth oil-man-turned author.

Trust every word he wrote.

—David Marion Wilkinson
Austin, Texas
December 2018

David Marion Wilkinson is the author of *The Empty Quarter*, *Not Between Brothers*, and *Where the Mountains Are Thieves*, among other books. He is a member of the Texas Institute of Letters and of the Writers Guild of America, West.

THE
IRON
ORCHARD

PART
I

1

OUT ON THE OLD ANDREWS ROAD WHERE IT passed the Gulf station that in those days was the last outpost on the north edge of town, the young man stood with his back to the norther, rigid and shivering, his bony shoulders bunched against the driving wind. He wore no overcoat—that had been pawned to buy the train ticket to Odessa—and his old blue serge suit with the coat collar turned up gave little protection from the weather. He strained his eyes through the swirling dust for the truck, but he could see only the dim outline of the low buildings of the town.

The wind made a dry, desolate sound as it swept by, whipping at his dark hair. Sudden sand flurries stung his cheeks. His ears hurt numbly with the cold. With his hands thrust deep into his pockets he took a quick inventory of his wealth. The sum of it, identified and totaled in his fingers, added to his misery: an old bone-handled pocket knife that had been his father's, the stub of a chair-car ticket, half a dozen coins. There was nothing in the old wallet on his hip but a couple of cracked and faded snapshots and an identification card, the part telling who to notify in case of accident long out of date. But that didn't really matter, any more than it mattered that he didn't have the price of a return ticket. There was nothing to go back to.

Every few minutes, driven by the cold, he retreated into the filling station and hovered closely over the stove, shivering like a freezing dog, scrubbing his dry hands together until the shaking stopped. But he was afraid to linger in the gassy warmth for fear he would miss the truck. If he did, he would have to hitchhike to the Bison camp. Few cars were passing in the bitter, dust-palled afternoon. The camp lay miles north of the town and away off to the west of the highway, out in the gauzy wasteland of mesquite and shinnery that ran all the way to the New Mexico line and beyond, and he might end up having to hoof it if he missed the truck. It would be dark soon, and a stranger in the country could wander off on a wrong fork of an unmarked ranch road and get lost and freeze to death before morning. The ranch houses were twenty miles apart, and when the wind was blowing in this featureless brush country it was impossible to see a hundred yards in any direction.

His eyes filled suddenly with the stinging water of anger. When they found his body, sprawled stiff and cold by the lonely ranch road, nobody would give a damn! Oh, well sure, there was somebody who might shed a couple of dainty tears about it—this thought came as bitter as the wind—but a trip to the beauty parlor and the prospect of a new dress to wear to the Kappa Sigs' winter formal would make her forget her grief in a hurry. Then that would be that. No one would mourn. No one would even claim the frozen corpse. The sheriff or the rendering plant or whoever took care of such petty details would see to burying him. He turned a shivering sob of self-pity into a string of general cursing, directed at no one in particular, and at everyone in general. The hell with 'em—all of 'em!

He was startled from this wretched trance by the shriek of metal on metal and the throb of a big engine as the truck loomed out of the down-wind dust, braking fiercely. He grabbed his suitcase out of the way as the heavy-loaded White slid to a stop directly before him, seething like a monster. He stared up at the big green B in the red triangle on the cab door, emblem of the great Bison Oil Company. Grateful, yet apprehensive, he reached up and opened the door and flinched at the squalled greeting that spilled out upon him.

"Haaawee haw! You 'sleep stan'in' up?"

He drew in his chin. "I'm not asleep. Just froze my ass off waitin' for you, is all."

"You the new hand fer Bison?" the driver shouted over the drumming engine.

"That's right."

"Well, climb in, f'Chrissakes! Flang that grip on the back an' git aboard! Godamighty, we ain't got all night!" The man's voice was rough as a saw, but there was no anger in it. The young man swung his suitcase onto the short bed behind the cab alongside the spare tire and toolbox in front of

4

the tandem trailer which was stacked deep with drill pipe boomed fast to the bed with chains. He climbed up into the cab, and before he could close the door the driver jerked the gear stick into low-low and poured the power to the engine, which took hold with a fundamental roar, straining against the tonnage of the load.

"Cold enough fer ye?" yelled the driver over the noise, leaning onto the big steering wheel as if to help the truck into motion. Without waiting for an answer he shouted encouragement to the engine. "Come on, ye wore-out ol' sonofabitch! Take a country mile t'git you outa grandma!" He double clutched into second and third. As the gears whined to a crescendo and the heavy load gained momentum, he eased the stick expertly into high. Then with the load rolling nicely on the highway he pulled off his glove with his teeth and thrust out a bony, work-broken hand.

"Pucketts is the name, son. Y. Y. Pucketts. You kin call me Mister Pucketts."

The passenger received the gripless country handshake—it was like grabbing a handful of sticks—and gave Mr. Pucketts a suspicious once-over. He was a small, scrawny man with a neck like a turkey and an Adam's apple that elevatored wildly when he talked. His nose resembled a squeezed, purple-veined lemon. Under the bill of his stained duck-hunter's cap his little black eyes darted back and forth like a monkey's. He was bundled against the cold in layers: union suit, two khaki shirts, sweat shirt, faded blue jumper, all outcropping at the throat under the sheep-lined outer coat. He sat high and straight, with elbows out, as if to stretch his small stature to fill the importance of the job he was performing.

"Mine's McNeely. Jim McNeely," said the young man.

"McNeely . . . McNeely," Mr. Pucketts mused loudly. "Seem like I knowed a McNeely. Back in Ranger. Naw, his name were McKeeters. Sorry bastards, all them McKeeters. Pipe thiefs. No reflection, son. You a weevil?"

"A what?"

Mr. Pucketts cackled. "If you don't know what a weevil is, you're one fer shore! Boll weevil! Ain't been to the oil patch before. A kid they send to fetch the left-handed monkey wrenches and all."

Jim McNeely drew in his chin again and his voice became stiff, as if he had been challenged. "Ssshuh! I'm no college boy. I've made a payday or two."

Mr. Pucketts cackled again, but with a friendlier sound. "It don't mean nuthin' *agin* yuh, son. Everybody got to start out in the oil patch sometime. If they ain't got better sense, that is."

After a mile on the highway Mr. Pucketts braked the truck lightly and veered off onto a caliche road that angled to the northwest through the brush. He fought the wheel as if steering a schooner in a storm, then cleared his throat roughly with satisfaction when the truck was moving ahead again. He made a very important thing of truck driving.

"How old'd ye say ye was?" Mr. Pucketts said.

Jim McNeely, who hadn't mentioned his age, replied, still stiffly, "I can vote."

"A-yelk?" said Pucketts dubiously, cutting his small eyes at the passenger. "I taken ye fer about eighteen."

"Sshuh!" Jim McNeely said.

"You bin in the CCCs?"

"Hell, no, I haven't been in no CCCs." This was an insult.

"Well, this yere oil field work ain't no CCC camp, son. It's rougher'n a cob." He cut another glance at the slender passenger. "Separate the men from the boys outchere in a hurry."

"It don't scare me," said Jim McNeely.

"No?" The truck driver rolled down the window, whacked up a good one and spat expertly into the rushing wind. "Not to change the subjec', my reg'lar work is surveyin'. I only taken this truckin' job as a favor to the Comp'ny, because I knowed the road layout. He-e-ll, I know this oil patch like my old lady's boody, son. *Sur*veyed most of it. A new man'd spind half his time comin' back from gittin' lost."

"Yeah?" said Jim McNeely.

"He-e-ll yes! Why, I *sur*veyed this very dang road right chere. Look at it, son. Straight as a' arra. Thim fellers what surveyed it from Penwell made a road like a dog's hind laig. Y'got to know what you're a-doin' in the oil patch, son. 'Spairiance! Hit's one thing they ain't no substitute fer, an' that's *'spairiance*!" (Ort Cooley enlightened him later: "That Pucketts? He were a surveyor, all right. Usin' a mule's ass fer a *compass*! That little pecker-neck wasn't nuthin' but a muleskinner in a road gang!")

They traveled rough miles into the dust-shrouded brush. The world outside the cab was a swirling globe of brown fog with a fringe of naked mesquite branches swaying past on either side. Once, off to the right, Jim McNeely caught a glimpse of a great skeletal structure looming high into the haze, and he felt rather than heard the clanking, pounding commotion of giant machinery at work.

"Sinclair wildcat," said Mr. Pucketts importantly. "They been on her two months now. Three fishin' jobs in a row. Ever see a strang o' rotary tools before?"

"Oh yeah. Sure." The young man said it trying to sound offhanded. It wasn't necessarily a lie since he didn't have any more idea than a spook what a string of rotary tools was. Suddenly he didn't feel too good. The chill had worked into his bones. The gloom of the afternoon and the strangeness of everything and the unknown future ahead rolled together in a wave of loneliness that washed out of him all the cockiness and belligerence that were his reliable defenses and left him suddenly on the edge of panic. He clutched for an ally. His tone was meeker, almost friendly.

"Sand blow like this much, Mister Pucketts?"

"Blow like *this*? He-e-ll, this ain't no blow! Man, we *had* a blow las' week. I seen a prairie dog goin' by scratchin' out a hole 'bout sixty feet up in the air!" Pucketts switched his eyes at the youth, frowning for a moment, then burst out with laughter. "Naw, this ain't no real blow, son, but you'll git use to 'er. Git to where if it don't blow, you'll go out an' git you a handful of sand an' spread it in yo' bed so you kin sleep!"

Jim McNeely knew this was supposed to be funny and gave a half-hearted chuckle.

"Reckon what they'll put a feller to doing?" he said, again trying to sound casual.

"Start you out with a idiot spoon, likely. In one of the gangs. Diggin' ditch fer a flow line. N'en 'fore long they'll have you on the end of a pair of pipe tongs buckin' up fo'-inch pipe. Six month o' that an' you'll never git you no boy-babies. Strains the boy-baby jizzum right outa you." He shook his head and reflected sadly on this for a moment. Then he went on: "They's two gangs. Bishop's gang an' Bruner's gang. Bishop, he's all right, but that Bruner, well, he's got a little shit in his blood. You git in his gang an' watch out! He got a lead roustabout name of Drum. Big squash-headed sonofabitch thinks he owns the place. Him an' a little pissant name Dendy. They orta pinched *his head* off when he was *borned*. He grapes up to Drum and Drum grapes up to Bruner, an' you gonna grape up to the three of'em if you git in *that* gang, or they'll run yo' ass off 'fore you make a payday."

This brought an automatic surge of the old belligerence. Jim McNeely said darkly, "I don't grape up to anybody."

7

"A-yelk?" said Pucketts. "That bein' the case I sho'ly hope you take on with Mr. Bishop's gang."

The Bison Oil Company's field camp was a ten-acre square of alkali hardpan scraped clean of mesquite and greasewood, fenced with barbwire and lost in the vast cartographer's quadrangle of dry and unlovely wilderness known as Ector County, Texas. It lay on the edge of the Dead Lake oil field, discovered less than two years earlier, and a mile and a half down a road of recent origin from a place called Coker City, which wasn't a city or even a town but a fresh eruption of shacks and trailer houses and tents surrounding the filling station, the cafe, and the honkytonk which supplied the essential needs of life to the assorted humanity who had come to this godforsaken corner of the earth to develop the new petroleum reservoir.

Arching above the cattle guard at the Camp entrance, a welded sheet-iron sign proclaimed in foot-high letters that this was the nerve and muscle center of Bison Oil Company, Dead Lake District. An oiled road ran from the entrance down into the Camp area between two rows of box houses, four on each side, all painted the same dispirited gray, each with an identical concrete stoop at the front. These were the homes of the Company's married men. Beyond the houses the road passed a mess hall on the left and a long, low bunkhouse for single hands on the right, then ran down to a big corrugated-iron building that was mainly warehouse, with a small office in one end, then to the truck park and pipe yard beyond at the far end of the compound. Dead patches of last summer's bermuda grass and dry remnants of petunias and zinnias in tiny beds around some of the houses were the only signs that women lived here.

With a mighty grunting and breathing Mr. Pucketts wheeled the big White under the sign and powered it rumbling over the cattle guard and down between the row houses toward the pipe yard.

"That there's my house, son," he said proudly as they passed. "Number six. Ol' lady'll be up at Bishop's jawin' an' smokin cigarettes. She'll run like hell when he hears the truck. Knows I'll beat tar outa her if supper ain't on the table." He cackled gleefully. "Ma-a-n, we have some good uns!"

Looking out through the windshield Jim McNeely saw nothing in the barren scene to cheer him. No warm lights lit the windows in the early dusk. No children played in the yards.

Pucketts rode the brake, grinding the truck to a noisy halt at the corner of the warehouse. "This here's the end of the line, sonny boy. That there's the office. Field clerk inside name is Paxton. The Lord made some queer ones. Guess he knowed what he were a-doin', but I don't."

"Well, I sure thank you for the ride," Jim McNeely said, trying to sound grateful and hearty but sounding hollow and apprehensive in spite of himself. He got out of the cab and took down his suitcase and stood watching the truck as it pulled off toward the pipe yard, and he couldn't hear Mr. Pucketts saying, "Whooee! Thank me fer nuthin'. Pore little boll weevil. That Bruner'll have yo' ass workin' buttonholes 'fore sundown t'morra. Run you off inside a week. But t'ain't none o' my never mind. Whoopeedoo, Sadie Jane, 'nother day, 'nother dollar. Whoa-down, truck, le's go to supper."

"Hello," Dent Paxton said. "Been wondering when you'd show up."

"My name's McNeely—"

"I know. The whole operation's been practically shut down waiting for you to get here."

Jim McNeely looked hard at the pale blond youth sitting behind the table top cluttered with typewriter, stacks of run tickets, a scatter of time sheets and payroll forms, an adding machine, a half-eaten apple, and an open copy of *Seven Pillars of Wisdom*. The old defenses rose in him and he was instantly prepared to hate and fight this new smart aleck, with his sarcastic greeting, as he was prepared to hate and fight all human beings whatever. But there was no venom in the new one's voice, and his thin, bantering smile had a blandness that said, "I am Denton Paxton, a friend to all men, so long as they don't ask anything of me."

Jim McNeely said, "Well, I'm here. What do I do?"

"First of all you fill out these two stupid forms. You can write, I guess. Silly question, but some can't."

After a second's hesitation the new arrival sat down in the chair opposite, worked his cold fingers, and picked up the pencil that Denton Paxton tossed across the table to him.

"You're assigned to Cap Bruner's gang, God help you, and you'll stay in room four in the bunkhouse, bunk three," said the young clerk. "That's the same space occupied until recently by the late, lamented Ham Brockett, another genius who tried to mix pop-skull and gasoline. Rammed his

9

Model A into a Halliburton truck between here and Odessa, and now sleeps with his fathers."

Jim McNeely glanced up, sniffed uncertainly, still trying to figure out what manner of bird this Paxton was, then started in on the form.

Dent Paxton continued, "The mess hall is open for breakfast and supper, and they'll fix you a sack lunch to take out on the gang truck. Tasty, if you happen to like horse-cock and stale bread. Your credit is good till payday. The Company furnishes you a tin hat and a pair of safety shoes, which will come out of your first paycheck." He glanced at the old suitcase. "You got any work clothes?"

"I got some old suit pants and a shirt."

"Won't last a day." The young man behind the table hesitated a moment as he studied the dark, angular face frowning over the forms. "Mm. I'll scrape you up some khakis and a sweat shirt and jumper till payday. And you'll need gloves—my God, have you got any money?"

Jim McNeely looked up. "A little."

"Oh, never mind. I'll promote you some gloves from somewhere." He rocked back in the old swivel chair and fixed his light blue eyes on the frowning head across the table.

"Now for the free lecture. Welcome to jolly Camp Dead Lake of that great octopus, the Bison Oil Company, owned and controlled by a bunch of third-generation panjandrums back in Philadelphia, P-A, who never saw this fleabitten paradise and aren't likely to.

"Our local high Pooh-Bah is Mr. Scofield, the field superintendent. You won't have any dealings with him, unless you get in trouble. Our sole and only reason for existing out here is to get that stinking crude oil out of the ground and moving down the pipeline to where it can be made into gasoline and lube, and dollars." Denton Paxton talked in a clipped staccatto, like an automatic firearm of small calibre.

"Bishop runs the roustabout gang. They do the general oil-field house-keeping. Bruner's gang, the one you'll be in, is the connection gang. They lay the flow lines that tie the new wells into the tank batteries, and do the oil-field plumbing, *big* plumbing. Big pipe, big fittings, high-pressure stuff and heavy as hell. Teach you how to sweat at ten above zero."

When he finished the forms, Jim McNeely put down the pencil and shoved the papers across the table.

"Don't sound too bad," he sniffed.

Denton Paxton glanced at the forms, then looked hard over them at the new man. "Buddy, I don't know what you've been doing, but whatever it was I'll guarantee you it was better than this. My advice to you is to cut and run like hell, while you can. I mean just pick up that old suitcase and go out through that door and don't come back, and I'm not joking." He looked at the forms again and winced. He shook his head and winced again. "You didn't even finish high school."

"I would have finished," Jim McNeely said defensively. "I was due to graduate but my ma got sick. I had to quit and go to work."

"I'm sorry about that, but that's not the story. Suppose you graduated. You still wouldn't have a chance out here. You can't go up in this Company without a college degree. They're nuts about degrees. If you had a diploma from a barber college you might get to be president, but without a degree you'll never make assistant foreman. You'll either get banged around and run off in a week, or what's worse you may think you have to prove you're a tough character and stick it out. That's how you'll get indentured for life, buddy. A life of stretching your guts out for enough to eat, with a little left over to get stacked and shacked with some honkytonk pig on Saturday night!" His narrow face became intense and a glint of genuine anger flashed into his pale eyes. "That lousy bunkhouse is populated with people like that! Is that what you came out here for?"

Jim McNeely frowned uncertainly at the blond boy. He was not accustomed to having people take an interest in his welfare, at least not unless they had some private motive of their own. He kept expecting Dent Paxton to break out laughing at him. But the other one was serious. Jim McNeely said, "I don't aim to get run off or become a slave, either one. I got some plans of my own."

"Oh, have you really?" said Dent Paxton with a scalding little laugh. "You realize where you've come to? The sinkhole of the universe—only here they phrase it less delicately. And they're not kidding, buddy. All hopes and illusions are finally blasted to pieces here. There's no future in Dead Lake for you, McNeely. None. I'm telling you what the Lord loves—the truth!"

Jim McNeely studied the other narrowly, suspiciously. "If it's all that bad, what are you doing here?"

Relaxing suddenly from his tirade, a sly smile crackling across his thin face, Dent Paxton said, "That's different. I haven't got a degree myself, to be sure. But I'm not going out on one of those gang trucks. They couldn't get me on one with a winch." He waved his hand and turned his gaze to the window against which the wind rattled in cold, sandy gusts. "I'm here by choice. For me it's a good place." What he meant but didn't say was that it was a good place for Denton Paxton to escape from certain things that ride most men like demons clamped to their backs with fang and claw. From ambition and responsibility and mainly from the necessity to work hard for a living. He cut his eyes back at the other youth, glowering again. "But it's not a good place for you, buddy. I'm warning you. Go back where you came from."

Jim McNeely stood up and hitched at his pants. He hung on to these last words for a moment, uncertainly, then he picked up his old suitcase and moved hesitantly toward the door. He felt suddenly very much more like a boy than a man and very lonesome. All the cocksureness was gone from his voice. The faintest shrug of apology lifted his shoulders.

"I got no place to go back to."

Dent Paxton had returned to his book and apple, his feet on the desk, as if he had suddenly lost interest. He didn't even look up. His remaining words were a curt dismissal. "OK, buddy, good luck."

Jim McNeely walked across the hard scrabbly ground to the bunkhouse in the olive dusk. The wind had let up, but dust still hung thick and clogging in the air so that he tried not to breathe much. He stepped up on the long porch of the deserted building and went down it, his footsteps sounding hollowly on the boards. When he came to room four he went in. It was nearly dark inside and he groped around in the air until he felt a string and pulled. The naked bulb threw a hard, swinging light into the corners of the room and he stood in the center and looked around his new abode. It smelled of working men—bitter sweat and sweet soap. There were four iron cots made up with army blankets, two on each side. An unpainted wooden table stood under the light. A deck of worn-out Bicycle cards lay scattered across the grimy top. The room's other furnishings were four cane-bottom chairs and a cast-iron stove rigged with a drip-oil burner, which, after inspection, he left alone because he didn't understand how it worked, though the room was like an icehouse and he felt an aching shakiness in his limbs that he knew meant he was coming down with flu or something.

A double closet of bare boards with a door on each side jutted into the room from the north wall, forming two narrow alcoves where two of the beds stood. He found a white numeral 3 stenciled on one of these beds and swung his suitcase on top of it. This, he thought bleakly, was his new home. Opening the closet door on his side he found it full of clothes. He walked around and looked into the closet on the other side. The sudden stench that met him when he opened the door almost made him gag. The bottom of the closet was piled knee deep with sweated-out, oil-soaked work clothes and old shoes, suppurating with the bitter fecal smell that men leave behind when they convert their life-force into dug ditches and laid pipelines. He was glad he didn't sleep on this side by this stinking closet from whose dark interior the abominable odor seeped, even when the door was closed. He returned to his side and wedged a place among the clothes on the pipe and hung his coat on a wire hanger.

By now he was feeling sick and weak. He hadn't eaten anything since breakfast except a Baby Ruth, and the adrenaline that had kept him going through the past hateful days had finally played out. He guessed, with a small flutter of apprehension, that the other men, the unknown faces and bodies that occupied this room, would be coming in soon, and he hoped they would welcome him as a friend and fellow wayfarer. He pulled out the light and sat down weakly on the bed, then lay back and stretched out. Being an outsider he didn't know what else he could do to establish himself in his new place of residence until the others arrived. A chill ran through his body and he was feeling sicker by the minute, so he got up and pulled back the blanket and got under it with his clothes on.

2

AS HE LAY THERE LOOKING UP INTO THE COLD gloom of the room, his confused memory returned for the hundredth time to his interview with Madelon Wales, Mrs. Dr. Waldo B. Wales, as she called herself, clubwoman, civic leader, socially prominent Mrs. Dr. Waldo B. Wales. Each time he thought of their meeting he improved on the cutting, destructive things he could have said to her, wished he had said to her. Oh, he should have given it to her good. But he hadn't said any of them. Hadn't even thought of them until it was all over. He had just sat there like a dumbbell while she all but destroyed him, in her composed, assured, great-lady manner.

"I do appreciate your coming to see me, Jim," she had said in her gracious, melodious voice. She prided herself on her graciousness with lesser folk, no matter what their station. She sat in a brocaded wing chair in her living room, knees sideways, her beautifully manicured hands resting easily in her lap. "With the holidays here and Mazie coming home from the University I thought it would be well if you and I had a little visit."

For a few idiotic moments young Jim McNeely experienced a rush of joy that left him almost giddy. Mrs. Wales had called him to come and talk about plans for the Christmas holidays, maybe a surprise party for Mazie or something, or maybe even to invite him to take Christmas dinner with the family. The sudden sense of belonging, of being a part of holiday plans and everything gave him a feeling of inner warmth and well-being that he had seldom known. He loved this house and this big, elegant room, though he had been in it but a few times. The carved marble mantel with the great gold framed mirror over it, the big couch with down cushions in front of the windows that looked out across the lawn to Bryan Drive, the faint smell of prime roast beef that whetted his appetite as he went down the hall toward the kitchen, all reminded him of the good life he had read about in books but had never known—and of Mazie. He felt a sudden wave of affection for Mrs. Wales, though he had always been a little afraid of her. She was truly a beautiful woman, in her pink lace dress, smooth pink skin, smooth ropes of taffy-blond hair so perfectly coiled about her head that she looked as if she had just this minute come from a beauty parlor, or, he thought, tickled, a candy kitchen.

The warm inner glow so emboldened him that he ventured a light-hearted swagger. "Glad to get your call, Mrs. Wales. Any mother of Mazie's is a friend of *mine*."

In the following moment of silence no smile crossed Madelon Wales's face. The chill in her voice was unmistakable. "Jim, I gather you think you are in love with Mazie."

"That's not a thinking matter, Mrs. Wales," he said with eager, still happy enthusiasm. "I *know* I am."

"At your age I'm afraid it *is* a thinking matter," she said. A ripple of hostility cut the smoothness of her tone. "You can't possibly understand what love means, or the very great responsibility it entails. Crushes are normal for youngsters. You get over them. They're sort of the measles of adolescence."

"I guess you're right about that, Mrs. Wales, but I'm nearly twenty-one," Jim McNeely said, trying to keep the light confidence in his voice, though his dark brows clouded as he began to sense, from far off, what was coming. It was as though he had suddenly seen a haircrack pop out in the far corner of the ceiling and begin to snake its way toward the center of the room, branching and spreading as it came. He looked intently at the woman, as if trying to head off what was coming next. A hot prickling of mortification spread over his face and up into his scalp.

Madelon Wales's voice moved ahead implacably. "We weren't too concerned when you started dating Mazie last spring, Jim. A high school girl's head is an utter mess of impractical romantic notions. But I knew she was going to camp in the summer and on down to the University in the fall. Such things usually run their course." She shrugged as she said this, almost parenthetically, as if to excuse her own laxity, then she came firmly to the point. "Now Mazie has written me that you have asked her to three of the Christmas dances. This puts a different light on things, Jim.

It places me in a very unenviable position." She frowned with irritation as her foundation garment began suddenly to gouge her ribs. The composed, gracious facade tottered. It was obvious that this duty, though inescapable, was unpleasant to her. "The position of having to be a realistic, responsible parent—and intervene." The crack in the ceiling shot forward in multiple branches and began to run down the walls, and the whole room began to crumble in slow motion above Jim McNeely's head.

He blinked at her. "I don't know what you mean, Mrs. Wales," he said, though he did know, knew it in his bones as of old. He was again, and still, the outcast, the unacceptable, the rejected.

"Jim, the kindest thing I can do in these circumstances is to be perfectly frank. I don't think it's for the best that you and Mazie go out together this Christmas."

"But she wrote me and said she would."

"I know. Unfortunately, I had already accepted dates for her for those dances. She didn't know that, of course, when she wrote to you. It isn't your fault. But that's not really the point, Jim—"

"Mrs. Wales"—he sat forward, elbows on knees, fingers fanned out in sudden tension—"she said she would go with *me*. I can show you the letters!"

"My dear boy, you're making this very difficult for me. And for yourself. I hardly know how to put it. Don't—can't you see this is an impossible thing?"

"But we're not going to run off and get married or anything, if that's what you're worried about, Mrs. Wales." He was struggling to head off the disaster that was already upon him. "I promise you! I mean, I do plan to marry Mazie when I'm making enough money and she's through school and all. But not now, gosh! We, I mean we . . ." His voice trailed off miserably, catching at the air.

Madelon Wales pushed at her constricting inner garment and steeled herself to her painful necessity. Then she laid it out for him, cold and stark. "Jim, what do you think you can offer Mazie? Have you ever thought about that? The kind of life? Do you think you could make her happy? You didn't even finish high school."

"That wasn't my fault, Mrs. Wales. I can explain about that. My mother—you know what happened." The old dogged anger started up in him.

Madelon Wales truly did not want to be unkind. But she knew what she had to do, and she would be as ruthless as a lioness defending her only cub if she had to. "I do know about that, and I'm very sorry. The fact remains that Mazie lives in a different world, Jim. In any case she's not going to be married for a long time. She's going to travel. Doctor Wales and I are already talking about her European tour summer after next. Then she will make her debut. She probably hasn't even met the man she is going to marry, yet." In a stroke of attempted mercy she added, "Nor you the lovely girl you'll eventually marry."

"She said she would marry me."

The pink lady paled and the underlying granite came out in her voice. "Did she now? Well you can forget that right now." She saw now that the kind approach was hopeless. There was no alternative but to terminate the interview quickly. "Look at this house," she said coldly. He looked. It seemed to be falling in around him. "Would you take Mazie out of an environment like this, where she was brought up? Would you take her away with you to live in some cheap roominghouse, or whatever you could afford to give her? Is that your idea of love, Jim?"

Hot blood rushed into Jim McNeely's face. "No ma'am, I would not take her to any roominghouse. I'm practically assistant manager at the store now. I'm gonna get somewhere, Mrs. Wales. You can believe that, or not, but I am." He was veering wildly between pleading for mercy and wild, insolent defiance.

"Oh, Jim, face facts! You're a checker in a grocery store, wearing an apron, and that's all you're equipped by background or education to be. At this time, in any case. Later, if you—at any rate—oh, well!" She gave up. Her voice was hard, all flint now. "You leave me very little choice. I must speak plainly. You're not welcome in this house any longer. You're not to see Mazie again. Here or anywhere else. Is that perfectly clear?"

Her last words rocked him as if a beam from the crumbling ceiling had struck him on the head. A storm of angry blood congested in his chest and in his throat and ears, and when he spoke his voice trembled and was so low as to be almost inaudible.

"We'll see about that."

Mrs. Dr. Wales arose. "Very well then, we shall. But please take my advice and do some clear thinking about this, Jim. Also, please don't underestimate me." She stood above him, now slightly flushed, but unyielding as quarried stone. "There is one thing more. I have nothing against you personally. Surely you understand that. Doctor Wales has very important friends in the business world. He and I would like to help you. He can help you get a good job somewhere, perhaps in the oil fields. If you care about making anything of yourself but a grocery clerk, go by his office and have a good talk with him. After Christmas. Good-bye, Jim. And please *do* do some levelheaded thinking about what I have said—for your own sake."

With the house falling to dusty shambles about him, his face burning like fire, his mind churning with unreasoning fury, he got up and stormed out of the room, dumbly, blindly, out through the vile roast beef odors of the hallway and out the front door into the crisp December air and the stately, hateful vistas of Bryan Drive.

When Mazie Wales came home from the University for the holidays Jim McNeely sent a note to her by Udalia, the Waleses' Negro cook who was his good friend and confidante, and Mazie met him just at dark when lights were beginning to come on. She wheeled the family's big black Buick up into the vacant lot across the side street from Grayford's Pharmacy—the rallying ground of the upper-middle-class young of Winfield.

As he slid into the seat beside her, perspiring with anxiety, his joy was blunted by the plaintive, bee-stung pout on her childish face, for it surely meant that her mother had got to her first. She fended him off with shy, feminine expertness as he tried to embrace her, and gave him the barest peck of a kiss. Still, her tumbling blond hair, the wide, liquid child's eyes, the baby cheeks, and the fragrance of her that reminded him of pink cotton candy sent a flutter of tenderness and desire through his belly and a fierce surge of masculinity through his nerves and tendons that made him feel at this moment that he could wrestle down the world with his bare hands and make it cry for mercy.

He held her small, warm hands, and they talked closely in the dusky light, conversing with intense, almost savage tenderness. Several times, overcome by his hunger for her, he tried to kiss her, but each time she shivered away and said someone might see them. The light on the drug-store sign across the street came on and began to flick off and on, casting a pale red glow over the cars in the lot and lighting a cherry halo around Mazie's fluffy hair.

"There's not but one thing to do," Jim McNeely said firmly, trying to fix her in the eyes in the darkness. "We got to get married. *Now.* It's not the way we wanted it. But she's tryin' to bust us up, and she sure as hell will if we let her. I got it figured out. I can swing it on what I'm making. There's an apartment on Bowie Street, a block this side of the creamery. It's not too big, but it's real nice. I can get it, furnished, for twenty-five a month. Your folks are bound to come around when they find out they can't keep us apart. This is not like the old days, Mazie. This is the twentieth century, USA!"

Mazie began to cry. She cried softly and squeezed his fingers in her moist hands and they talked in hushed, desperate tones, and she kept resisting his attempts to get close enough to kiss her. What she couldn't see was how *could* they get married? She was pledged to the Pi Phis and hadn't even been initiated yet. And they were so *young*. They didn't even have a car of their own. And he obviously didn't *know* her mother. No telling *what* that woman might do. And to each objection Jim McNeely gave the same answer: "If you love me, it's the only way." Of course, if she didn't really love him . . .

She countered fervidly, almost frantically, "I do love you! I do! But we're so inexperienced, and sometimes people *change*, and you might not even love me at all in any little old apartment on Bowie Street!" And then he said flatly that he would love her anywhere, any time and for as long as he lived, and that that apartment would seem like a marble palace to him with her in it, but he guessed maybe she didn't love him that much. And then gradually as the hot whispered words flew back and forth in the closeness of the car, the hopeless, excruciating love scene turned agonizingly into a quarrel. The hands dropped apart and she said he must not really love her as much as he said he did to put the pressure on her this way, with Christmas here and everything, and besides she had to get the car home. Then in the heat of anger and of hurting and bitter disappointment, he found himself getting stiffly out of the car and standing outside in the cold air looking in at her and saying that no doubt she would prefer to go to the dances with somebody else, anyway. Then he slammed the door, and to his sinking amazement she started the engine and gunned the car, gravel flying, out of the parking lot, sobbing furiously.

That night Jim McNeely got drunk. He had never cared much for drinking, but this night he got drunker than he had ever been in his life, and when he woke up it was Christmas Eve afternoon, and he was very sick. The sweetish musty smell in his nostrils, and the torn window shade and gray airshaft through the dirty window slowly told him that he was in

19

a walk-up whorehouse of local fame called the Ajax Hotel. The rush of old and recent memories crowding in upon him filled him with utter desolation. His head ached excruciatingly. He dressed himself and stumbled down the dark stairs and went into the dismal cafe next door and ate half a bowl of soup. He barely made it outside to the curb before the soup came back up, and he sprayed it explosively over the turtle-back of a parked coupe into the street Then he walked unsteadily around the corner and bought another pint of Old Quaker and went back upstairs to the Ajax, and that is where he spent the Christmas holidays, drunk, and shacked up with a girl named Velma, a big, two-toned blonde, about thirty-five, who got drunk, too.

Velma became very sentimental and tuned in Christmas carols loudly on the table radio, and kept asking him what he was going to give her for Christmas, and when, giggling, he showed her, she started bawling and said it was sacrilegious to offer anybody anything like that for a Christmas present, and she kept it up, sobbing boozily until he became so depressed that he got up and dressed again and walked, weaving, down the cold, Christmas-decorated streets. He had begun to feel a little weepy himself. This was the first Christmas in his memory that he did not have a present to give someone, and that no one had a present for him.

When he found an open drugstore he went in and jostled his way through the last-minute shoppers, and bought Velma a three-dollar bottle of Coty's Houbigant, with some of the money he would have paid to redeem the Christmas gift for his love, which was waiting, still in layaway, at the jewelry store down the street.

When his money, all of his money in the world, finally ran out, it was December 29, and he was no longer welcome at the Ajax. He emerged into the bright day with frost crystals sparkling on the sidewalks. He was pale and sober and weak, as if he had just got up from a bout with the scarlet fever. He knew there was no use going back to the grocery store. The job would be gone, and he didn't want it, anyway. He wouldn't be able to face it again after Madelon Wales had put the bad-mouth on it.

He wandered aimlessly around town for a while in a kind of washed-out daze, the physical misery of his stomach mercifully distracting him from the pain in his mind. During the afternoon he went into a pawnshop on lower Main and exchanged his overcoat, the one his mother had given him the Christmas before—at a sacrifice that made him want to cry when he thought about it—for a pawn ticket and a five-dollar bill. Later, without consciously planning it, and after first walking all over town, he ended up at Veteran's Park and headed slowly across its unlovely concrete geometry, past the statue of the World War doughboy with bayonet at the ready, past the big community Christmas tree whose tinsel decorations rattled coldly in the breeze against the pale blue sky, toward the Physicians and Surgeons Building.

As he crowded into the elevator with the assortment of sick people and their kin, most of them middle-aged and older, country-looking people, the sick ones holding themselves, the color faded out of their faces from fear and pain, he wondered angrily why people couldn't just go on and peaceably die when they were worn out, why they clung on and fought so for life, clinging to the last measly scrap of it, as though it was good. Like his poor pitiful mother.

He got out on the tenth floor and went down the antiseptic-smelling corridor to a door on whose frosted glass was lettered WALDO B. WALES, M.D. EYE, EAR, NOSE AND THROAT. Several patients waited inside. A nurse in a starched uniform at a desk ordered him to sit down on the chair opposite her and began cross-examining him crisply to find out what was wrong with him and how long he had had the symptoms. He had no intention of trying to tell her. It pushed him almost to the point of exasperation to shut her off so he could explain that he wanted only to see the doctor on a matter of personal business.

When Jim McNeely was finally admitted, Dr. Waldo B. Wales sat at his desk looking half mean, half amused and all-wise, his round silver reflector with the peephole still on his head. He was a handsome man in his mid-fifties, with iron-gray hair and a firm jaw. In thirty years of practice he had peered at enough wormy tonsils to think he understood much about life and what made men tick, and he was not unduly disturbed by the presence of this young visitor whose business he knew must in some way concern his daughter.

He had repeatedly assured his wife that this coltish thing between Mazie and the McNeely kid would burn out of its own accord if she would just keep her bloomers on; whereas if she made an issue of it, given the hardheaded nature of the human beast, she might blow it up into something really big and end up with a real problem on her hands. But Madelon Wales was very upset and said it was absolutely necessary to get this boy out of town before something terrible happened. And so the doctor, growling with annoyance, but with his usual complaisance when she put her foot down, said that he would see what he could do. Madelon Wales had the important money in the family—her separate property inherited from her father she had never quite let him forget—and he knew he wouldn't have any peace until he did what she wanted him to.

He looked at the miserable youth across the desk and a sudden flood of memories crowded into his mind. Not a bad-looking boy. In fact he would be almost handsome if he was fed up and filled out and didn't have that bolshevik look on his face. Surely looked as if he'd been on a binge. Chip off the old block, all right.

The faint hackles of old desire prickled at his forehead as he remembered the boy's mother, that—what was her name?—Margaret Schuler, the fair Maggie, fresh-faced young schoolteacher with raven hair and a figure that inspired sinful thoughts in every buck in town. She could have done better than that Hulen McNeely—a *lot* better, the doctor thought, still, after all these years, savoring the bitter aftertaste of having been among the also-rans. Well, she wanted Hulen and she got him, and it served her right that she chose that handsome, charming, liquor-loving purveyor of hot air, when she could have done a lot better.

The doctor had a special taste of bitterness in his memory of Hulen McNeely for another reason, a hard tangible spot of bitterness over a thousand hard-earned dollars that he bad been conned out of—well, it wasn't quite fair to say conned, but talked out of—when he was a young struggling doctor, by a fast-talking, equally young promoter, to back a scheme to build a furniture factory that would put Winfield on the map as the Grand Rapids of the Southwest and make its backers rich. The doctor still had the rather oddly contrived ladderback chair in his study at home, which he referred to as his "thousand-dollar chair," and which was all he had to show for his investment in Hulen McNeely's collapsed furniture venture. He had been tempted at times, in anger, to refer to Hulen as "that crook." But the doctor was essentially a fair man and he knew that Hulen wasn't a crook. He hadn't really conned him or the other unfortunate citizens who had been gullible enough to put money into that or one of Hulen's other high-flown dreams. Hulen hadn't made any money out of any of those schemes, either—most of the time he couldn't even pay his bills. He was just a glib, Irish, overenthusiastic visionary, and very talented along those lines. And if he hadn't been so fond of the bottle and had lived longer, one of his wild ideas might have struck fire and made him rich.

The doctor's hard memories were softened by a fairly recent one, a chance one, of seeing the name Margaret McNeely on a ward chart during one of his hospital rounds, and of walking down between the beds and seeing there under the white sheet, shriveled and dying, the remains of what had once been a beautiful, vibrant woman, and of a slender, black-haired boy sitting in a chair by the bed, keeping vigil, slowly turning the pages of an old magazine. It seemed to the doctor that there was, somehow, justice in all this. That and the present fact that here across the desk from him, obviously miserable and obviously a supplicant, sat the seed of that ill-starred union. But it was strange justice, and the doctor couldn't find much satisfaction in it all.

Giving Jim McNeely his patented half-stern, half-bantering philosopher's smile for which he was famous in the sore throat trade, he said, "All right, son, Nurse says it's not your gullet. What's your problem?"

Glancing painfully at the imposing white-jacketed figure Jim McNeely knew he did not have the heart in him to reopen his case about Mazie. He simply said that he needed a job and that Mrs. Wales had said that maybe the doctor could help him find one. Then he sat dumbly while the older man gave him a lecture on how hard it was to find a good job in these times, and how many men with families were out of work, and how a young fellow who did land a job ought to thank his lucky stars and make the most of his opportunity and so on and on. Then the doctor suddenly picked up the telephone and made a call as if he had known all along he was going to, and talked to somebody on the other end named Si about the young fellow he's been telling him about, a fine boy, studious, bright, strong, no bad habits, hard worker, willing, all-around fine lad, and when the call was finished he told Jim McNeely that it was all set and where to go and whom to see and that he would skin the hide off of him if he didn't make a go of it.

The ease with which this man of affairs had brought about this major change in his destiny made Jim McNeely feel his own insignificance all the more. He had no way of knowing that Si, who was Dr. Wales's golf partner on Wednesdays and Saturdays, was also vice president of Bison Oil Company, or that he happened to be advising the doctor from time to time on the investment of some of Madelon Wales's money in wildcat royalty. That arrangement had turned out to be quite profitable on both sides. Nor could Jim McNeely guess (as the doctor could and did with a chuckle) that the vice president, having angrily banged down the phone, was even now dictating a memorandum to the Bison production superintendent in Odessa, telling him to find a spot somewhere for a raw kid named James McNeely, another one of Doc Wales's miserable protégés, and never mind reminding him they weren't hiring anybody, just find a place for him and work his tail off and if he couldn't cut the mustard, can him and send in a report.

And so in five minutes in two high offices overlooking the town and the river that snaked languidly into its tree-shaded neighborhoods from the grassy prairies to the west, Jim McNeely's future was set in motion, and all because he was callow and presumptuous enough to try and court a girl from a higher stratum in the local caste system, like Mazie Marie Wales.

3

JIM McNEELY WAS AWAKENED BY A LOUD CLOMPING of feet, a burst of light in his eyes, and the sound of strange voices, voices of men, tired men smelling of sweat and oil. For grasping moments he did not know where he was.

A huge, breathing shadow blotted out the light and a querulous voice from somewhere behind the shadow said, "What the hell's that there layin' up in yo' bunk, Buster?"

A hand ripped off the blanket covering him.

"Well, kiss my ass!" The shadow boomed and stepped back. "Lookit him! Got his fuckin' *shoes* on in my *bed*!"

The first voice gave a high pealing giggle of delight. "Ooowee! Somebody done took over yo' bed, Mister Drum. Better look out, now! He might fight! He looks like a mean 'un!"

"Shee-ut!" said Buster Drum, contemptuously. The shadow blotted out the light again. A big, greasy hand hooked itself under Jim McNeely's belt. Another clamped onto his ankle and he felt himself lifted and swinging through the air, as if on a crane. Lights wheeled and he was dumped in a dignity-shattering heap against the wall onto the bed across the room. He fought dizzily to his feet. Staggering, eyes reeling, he tried to focus. He stood for several seconds clawing back to the place and the time, looking dumbly around him.

There were three men in the room besides himself, all in filthy, mud- and oil-caked khakis and jumpers. The tremendous hulking one was brushing angrily at the bed which Jim McNeely had recently occupied. "Goddamn dirty clodhoppers on my bedsheet!" he muttered. The small one, bobbing up and down as if on a string, slapped himself in a fit of laughter. The third, a haggard, gray-faced man who was all bones and knobby joints, was sitting in a collapse of exhaustion, sunk down over his greasy shoes, slowly unlacing them, as if he saw and heard nothing.

"Look out, Buster!" the capering idiot cried. "He's got fight in him!" In a state of outraged shock Jim McNeely said, "What the hell—what the hell's the idea?"

Buster Drum straightened to his giant height and breadth and turned a sullen-mouthed look upon him. "You don't need to worry 'bout no idea 'less you pile yo' ass up in my bunk again, then I'll give you the idea." He was an enormous young man with a small face, grimy with oil to the line of his hat sweatband, then dead white in the forehead to the lank, light brown hair that was roached straight back over his flat skull. His shoulders were as thick and sloping as a bull's and his eyes were set deep and too wide apart in his face. It was a child's face, the face of a playground bully, fixed onto the body of a giant.

Jim McNeely advanced toward his assailant, his quirted glands charging his body with fresh adrenaline. Then the instinct of self-preservation, reacting to the size of the man, reined him in time.

"That sure looks like a number three on that bunk to *me*," he said. The words sounded almost girlishly ineffectual in his own ears.

"Look out, Buster, he's gonna swing on you!" crowed the capering clown, who had the head and sharp nose of an opossum. This was Peaches Dendy.

"The clerk at the office told me to take bunk number three," Jim McNeely persisted, doggedly. "Well, that's bunk number three and you got no call to come pulling me out of it when I was asleep. Ask me to move. If I got the wrong bunk, I'll move."

"Clerk, shit! Ask, shit! Just keep them big dirty feet outa my bunk." Buster Drum dismissed him as of no further importance and began to rip off his oily jumper and shirt and undershirt. Presently he stood naked by his bed, searching for soap and towel in the closet. Massive muscles writhed like boas under skin that was white as skim milk to the neck and wrists where the olive staining of crude oil began. His buttocks were like rounded blocks of concrete. The sight blunted Jim McNeely's anger with animal fear. He had learned from hard lessons in the past to know when he was faced with insuperable odds.

Peaches Dendy, also undressing, was not content to let the matter drop.

"This here must be the boll weevil come to take ol' Ham's place, Buster.

He sho' do look *strong* to me. Mus' be one of them college athaletes. Boll weevil, you one o' them college boys?"

Outgunned and in strange waters, Jim McNeely slid away from battle. He caught his open suitcase by the handle and dragged it angrily across the room to his new bunk and bent over it, ignoring this new thrust.

Peaches Dendy wouldn't let it ride. "Don't seem like ol' boll weevil want to talk to us, Buster. Guess he don't care 'bout 'sociatin' with us ignorant no-college boys." Wrapping a soiled towel around his naked waist, Dendy hopped to the door and headed out for the shower room down at the end of the porch. A second later he stuck his head back in the door. "He ain't said what his name is, neither. Must have a name, Buster. What you reckon we gonna call him?"

Clinching a big towel around the muscle coils of his stomach, the gigantic Drum said, "Dendy, you little bastard, you better not use no hot water til I git there, or I'll frog yo ass." He walked heavily to the door on his big, bare simian feet then stopped and turned his sunk-eyed child's face on Jim McNeely and said, " You kin call him ever what you want to, but he looks like a two-bit hot-shot to me."

In a storm of rage, sickness and helplessness Jim McNeely pawed blindly at the clothes in his suitcase, then he kicked it under the bed. His face and eyes stinging with ignominy he groped, as if in gravityless air, for a thought, a course of action, help from any quarter, anything. It was as if he were a small boy on the schoolground again, knocked down, searching for a big rock. He threw a hot, fevered glance at the only other man left in the room, assuming that he, too, was an enemy.

Ort Cooley slowly finished unlacing one shoe and sat awhile, drawing deep, labored breaths, resting, before starting on the other. His knobby elbows on his knees and his sparsely thatched head, down between bony shoulders, were like an old featherless vulture's. If he also was an enemy, clearly he was not a formidable one. He had given all he had to the day and sat quietly, physically defeated, beginning the slow recovery process which with the elapsing of twelve hours would put him in shape to go again tomorrow. Now there was no strength left, to rush like the others, and no need to. The hot water would be gone, and there would be a long wait for more. He had long ago given up trying to compete with youth for the first water. He seemed to be unaware of Jim McNeely's presence in the room.

In a haze of fury Jim McNeely flung open the door to the stinking closet and began to drag the sour soggy clothing and shoes out into the room. The stench raised a gorge in his throat as he threw the filthy garments into a pile in the center of the floor.

Ort had now removed both shoes and sat in his underwear and dirty socks, taking measured breaths as if pumping air back into an old inner tube. When the closet was emptied, Jim McNeely transferred his coat from the other one, then stood wiping greasy fingers on his hip pockets, exhaling defiance through distended nostrils.

Without moving or looking up, the older man said, "Ort not make too free with them clothes what you don't know who they b'long to, sonny. Feller *could* git hisself harelipped that way."

From this manner of speaking, Ort Cooley had acquired his name. He prefaced nearly all he had to say with "ort"—"You ort to do this" or "you ort not a'done that."

Jim McNeely glared at him. "That big ape had no call to go pulling me out of a bed when I was asleep. The clerk in the office told me to take bunk three. I don't give a damn if it's bunk three or eighty-three or five thousand and three, a bed's a bed! But he had no call to do that! If it's his bunk, and he asked me, I woulda moved!"

Ort nodded at the stack of clothes and kneaded his grimy forehead. "I'm talkin' 'bout them dirty khakis, sonny. Ort not tuck 'em outa that closet without findin' out who they b'long to."

"Hell, man!" Jim McNeely cried with exasperation. "I'm not gonna sleep with my head in any damn stinkhole! Does this closet go with this bunk, or don't it? It's full of clothes and they're not mine!"

"I just said you ort to find out who them clothes is," was all Ort Cooley said. He was trying to be helpful, and it was an effort he was almost too tired to make.

By the time the newcomer had unpacked his suitcase and stowed its meager contents in the closet on the bare plank shelf, and hung his other pants on a wire coathanger on the pipe rod, the door to the room flew open and Dendy danced in, shivering. He saw the pile of filthy clothes on the floor and fell back in mock horror, bumping into the giant Drum coming up behind him. Drum shoved him into the room ahead of him and slammed the door. He rested his big hands on his hips and stood looking in puzzlement, first at the clothes then at Jim McNeely, then back again, his small eyes almost clicking in his head. "Hey! You, hot-shot," he said, not fully comprehending the significance of what he saw. "What you call yourself doin' with them clothes?"

Jim McNeely ignored the question and kept fiddling with things in the closet, but his pulse quickened, raggedly.

"Like I tol' you, Buster," Peaches Dendy said. "This dude don't talk to us no-college boys."

"You, hot-shot. I'm talkin' to *you!*" Drum's tone deepened menacingly and promised immediate action.

Jim McNeely said, "I answer to the name of McNeely. Not hot-shot."

"*Do tell.* Well, hot-shot, suppose you sure 'nough *git* hot an' put them clothes back in that closet."

Half-afraid but incensed, Jim McNeely swung around. He threw out his arms in exasperation. "What's the matter with you guys? I done nothin' to you. I got a right to closet space same as anybody else, haven't I? What's eatin' you guys, anyway?"

In exaggerated quavering tones Dendy said, "He done tuck over the runnin' of the room, Buster. Guess we better do what he says."

"He shit!" said Drum, advancing on Jim McNeely, kicking the pile of clothes toward him. "Put 'em back, hot-shot. Jest like I said."

"Not in this closet. Not by where I sleep—"

Jim McNeely could never clearly reconstruct in his mind exactly what happened next, what Buster Drum did, or what he did, if anything. But in a quick flurry that was over in seconds he found himself upended, with his head buried deep in the pile of stinking clothes, unable to breathe, his feet kicking helplessly in the air and one arm cranked high up behind his back by a steel grip that caused him such excruciating pain as he had never felt before, as though his shoulder and elbow were being unjointed. With his lungs clutching for air he fought the wet clothes aside with his head and sucked in a breath and let out a yell of agony, in spite of himself.

In the following humiliating two minutes, which he would long remember, with Buster Drum one-handing his arm up between his shoulderblades he picked up the soggy shirts and pants and shoes with his free hand and in utter humiliation transferred them all back into the closet, like an obedient monkey on a chain. When it was done he was released and sank heavily, squeezed out, on his bunk and sat kneading at his twisted arm, which was white and numb and dead as old wood.

"Now, you leave them clothes be, hot-shot," said Buster Drum, not even breathing hard. "When us fellers take a notion we'll blow 'em out in a steam barrel at one of the rigs, and then we'll start over." He went to his bunk and half turned only to add, "And long as you stay in this room, don't git no more bright ideas. You understand that, hot-shot?"

Almost retching with fury and desperation, Jim McNeely peered through burning, watering eyes at the great, muscle-mounded back, then did the only thing possible in his abject defeat. He fled.

He propelled himself out the door and headed up the board porch, not knowing where he was going or what he was going to do. The night air was sharp. Through the settling dust the jeweled spires of drilling rigs winked faintly far off in the distant oil field, but he did not see them, and his half-wild cursing was measured by the rapid beat of his feet on the hollow boards.

At the end of the porch he saw a lighted window and Dent Paxton inside. He tore open the door and burst in upon him.

"What number's my bunk, by God?" he said in a shaking voice. "Three? OK. You tell that to that big sonofabitch, you hear? *Go tell him!*"

Dent Paxton sat in a canvas chair with his feet on a bed, beside a table stacked with books. He looked up in mild surprise. There were books scattered all over the room, in orange-crate shelves, on the beds, on the floor. The room had the musty smell of a library, flavored with the sweetish tinge of sour mash whiskey and cigarette smoke. A bottle of bourbon, half gone, and a glass were at his elbow, on the table. He wore clean khakis and his shoes were off.

He put his book down and studied the distracted youth before him.

He shook his head. "Well I'll be goddamn. Already?"

"You go tell that big hame-headed sonofabitch that you assigned me to bunk three, and if I don't get the bunk, at least, by God, I get a closet! *You go tell him!*" shouted Jim McNeely, weaving with sickness and uncontrollable rage.

"Wait, wait, wait," said Dent with patience, dog-earing a page in the book and tossing the book on the table. "Tell who what?"

"Drum! That big, pig-eyed bastard that acts like he owns the place! He can't shove *me* around! We're gonna set that gentleman straight! Come *on!*"

"Now, wait," Dent said. "Take it easy."

"Go tell him, goddammit! I guess he thinks I'm lying!"

Dent shook his head slowly and sat back, propping his thin fingers together. "I guess you already told him. Making him is something else, buddy. I'm not the policeman here, just the field clerk."

"Well, by God, I want to talk to the *man*, then! That Mister—what's his name—Scofield! Where's his house? That big ignorant horse's-ass Drum can't shove *me* around!" Jim McNeely grasped wildly for any support he could think of. He shouted, "I'll tell you one thing! Doctor Wales will damn sure take it up with the bosses in Winfield when he hears about this, and then there'll be some people out here hear about it too, and I don't mean maybe! Where's that Scofield's house?"

With a wince Dent got slowly to his feet. He pulled around a chair. "Why don't you sit down, buddy? You're all shook up."

"That sonofabitch!" Jim McNeely's voice fairly screeched.

"Oh, sit down, for Christ's sake!" Then in a more placating tone that was almost laughing, Dent said, "Look, I'm on your side, buddy. But we're outnumbered, so sit down and tell me what happened." He scratched his head. "Man, you really are shook up." He uncorked the bottle and poured an inch of whiskey into the glass. "Try a little jolt of this. It'll help take the strain off."

During the next hour, with Dent's bourbon whiskey seeping into him, caulking the cracks in his shattered pride, and with Dent's calm, half-amused words of youthful wisdom cooling the heat in his head, Jim McNeely slowly cooled down. He gradually unwound and regained enough of his native caution and balance so that he was saved from rushing out into the night crying up ridiculous alarums.

"You better not go and see Mr. Scofield," was the first thing Dent told him, "unless you take along a fast walking stick. Because that man will send you right on down the road and tell you not to bother about coming back. This camp runs, buddy. I'm not saying it runs right, but it runs. It puts the oil in the pipeline. Scofield don't give a damn what happens down here in the bunkhouse so long as the crude keeps moving out and he's not bothered. Buster Drum is a top hand. He gets the work done. Some new boy that don't know his ass from a ratchet—hell, you think Scofield is going to listen to him or take his side? I told you I didn't know why you came to this godforsaken hole in the first place. But that's your business. And if you want to stick around awhile the only way you can do it is *fit in*. I'll put it this way: you've got two alternatives: you can win Mister Drum over by your charming personality, which means kissin' his ass—grapin' up, as they call it—or you can go back down there and beat hell out of him. Either way, you got a problem, because you're dealing with an ape. A physical and mental anthropoid. Can you whip him? Hell, you couldn't whip his baby sister. He cleaned out the Tascosa in Odessa a couple of Saturdays ago. Put two rig builders in the hospital. The contractor they were workin' for came stormin' out here mad as hell. Scofield just laughed at him. That's the way it is, a world apart, an animal world with its own animal code. You make like an animal or you don't make it. Muscle and meanness count in this bunkhouse, not brains or good looks or fair play. You look fairly sensible. Well, just do your work and find your place, or get out. Nobody's going to take up for you or give a damn if you leave. Unless, of course, you're some big-shot's boy out here getting experience. Which I can tell you're not. You got hungry written all over you, so you got no choice but to conform. That means you've got to do whatever Mister Buster Drum says, because he's bigger than you are. It's tough-titty, buddy, but that's life in the oil fields."

As the hour passed, the level dropped in the bourbon bottle and the pale, half-joking sympathy of Dent Paxton's words reached the knot of fire deep in Jim McNeely's chest and cooled it. It didn't put the fire out, or solve his problem, for he did not, would not, accept the inevitability of humbly debasing himself before the giant tyrant of the bunkhouse. But the burning was made bearable, just barely. And Dent Paxton, who took extreme pains to insulate his private little world against intrusion by the crude denizens of Dead Lake, found himself getting involved with the troubles of this new boy, Jim McNeely, counseling him like an older brother, trying to keep his wild, raddled, youthful fury from blowing him out of the job before he began it. Dent Paxton didn't understand why he did things like this, and he was extremely annoyed with himself. The strange, awkward, intense, brooding young man sitting across from him, gulping down his whiskey, was as unpromising a specimen, with as little prospect of survival, as he had seen come to Dead Lake. A natural-born loser if there ever was one. He frowned and shook his head and told himself irritably that he was a fool to get mixed up with him. But before the night was over, there in the bunkhouse room, over a bottle of whiskey, he put together with this Jim McNeely the fragile beginnings of the first real friendship that either had ever known.

4

OR ALMOST AS LONG AS HE COULD REMEMBER JIM
McNeely had lived with his mother on Antelope Street,
in a small frame house that had once been white. It sat on
the corner of an otherwise vacant, weed-choked block at the edge of
Bryan Heights in an area known as No Man's Land. To the west of it,
in the creek bottoms where the railroad ran, no self-respecting white
man would have his home, and to the east no Negro in his right mind
would aspire to live. This was the house to which Jim McNeely's father
had moved when his fortunes were at their lowest ebb, and in which
he had suddenly sickened and died, the house where his mother had
continued to live, partly because the rent was all she could manage on a
teacher's pay, and partly because, after Hulen McNeely died, she never
found heart again to try to do better. People waited and speculated
about when she would blossom again and whom she would marry when
she married again, for she was young and beautiful, even in the dark,
uncomprehending mask of tragedy that she wore from the hour she
returned from the cemetery. But she never blossomed, and she resisted
all kindly and self-interested attempts to bring her out. Then her health
and her robust, black-haired beauty began to fade, and in a year or two
the animal attraction was gone, and the men, one of whom might have
been Jim McNeely's stepfather, lost interest.

Jim McNeely remembered his mother as a patient, rather detached
person who always seemed, while attending to him with kindness, to be
vaguely preoccupied with thoughts of other places and other times. And

sometimes when he came in from playing at dusk, he would find her sitting in a darkened room; and when he turned on the light he could see that she had been crying.

Though a slender, bony boy, he grew with tough, close-knit joints, and his thin muscles were wiry and strong. His hair was the last deep shade of mahogany before black, and the cast of his eyes and skin was dark. It was perhaps inevitable that being thus "dark complected" and living on the edge of the colored settlement, he was called, from his first day in school, Nigger Jim.

The first time the epithet was hurled at him, he promptly took exception; and for his pains he had his face scrubbed into the schoolyard dirt by a larger fourth-grade boy. The next time it happened, when the same bully tried to shove him out of line and cause him to lose his turn on the swings, taunting "We don't allow niggers here!" The seven-year-old Jim McNeely, instead of retreating, adopted the weaponry he had learned from the little colored boys down the street from his house. He picked up a good-sized rock and bounced it off the larger boy's head. This caused great excitement on the schoolgrounds and great consternation in the principal's office, since the wound drew blood and required stitches and the stitchee was the son of prominent parents. Stern warnings were promptly issued to the miscreant's mother, who taught at another school, and plainly implied loss of employment if there should be a repetition. The heartache which this caused his mother capped Jim McNeely's ignominy.

One of the few happy remembrances of his childhood was his recollection of his mother holding him in her lap on the little porch of their house, rocking him and crying and telling him that he ought to try to get along, but if any bigger boy tried to beat him up, when he wasn't at fault—when he honestly knew in his heart that he wasn't in the wrong—then it was all right with her if he stood his ground and defended himself with a rock or a club or anything else he could lay hands on, even if it meant she would be fired from her teaching job. This was one of the very few times that his mother emerged from her vague, tragic shell and showed the warmth and mettle of the spirited young woman she once had been. He could only remember this when he tried, vainly, to remember his father.

He was a troublemaker in school from the beginning, for he had only to be called Nigger Jim to fight, and he knew more than once during those grim, scrambling days of grade school the utter vanquishment of watching his own blood trickle from his nose into the dust, and of hearing the exultant voice of his oppressor taunting him to make him "take it back" if he was man enough. Each defeat only intensified his truculence, and with each he became a wilier, more experienced adversary, capable of inflicting stinging punishment with his small fists upon opponents of his own size, and quick and ready to resort to rocks when he was overmatched. In the process he became a marked individual, and he was as lonely an outcast as only a small boy without a single friend could be, for even the few children who seemed to like him deserted him when a crowd took up the hue and cry of "Nigger Jim!" It was not an uncommon sight in those early days on the grounds of Fourth Ward School to see a ring of small boys dancing around a dark, defiant boy clutching a large rock in each hand, glaring at the crowd all screeching the hateful name at him, shoving him from behind and showering him with dirt.

Under the hammer of these trials he became a sullen, silent boy. Though equipped with more than sufficient intelligence to make good grades, he was not an attentive or a desirable pupil. At the end of the year one teacher would say to the next, "Well, I'm sending you a bad actor this time."

He cast a thin, solitary shadow walking home from school, taking a roundabout way down by the cotton oil mill, cutting through alleys and across vacant lots to avoid meetings and inevitable clashes with other homegoing boys. There were times when his yearning for someone to be with, to play with, was so intense that he would break into a jog-trot down the rutted yellow road that ran by his house and down through the bottoms and through colored town and over the railroad track and out into the open country, and he would keep on running until he was out of breath. He played always, if it could be called play, by himself, shunning the companionship of the Negro boys down the road, who could have been his friends. To play with them would only have confirmed and justified the insult that daily was hurled at him on the schoolground.

It would have been easy to put an end to being an outcast if he had been capable of playing the proper role. He could have found his place in the nearest neighborhood gang on the white side of Bryan Heights if he had been willing to be the Boche every time "war" was played, or the runner of errands and doer of menial tasks for the gang leaders, or to caper and giggle and act the fool when he was called Nigger Jim, accepting his inferiority as right and natural, wearing it like a clown's suit. But these things he could not do. He never thought about why he could not. It was just impossible. On the day he was conceived an unyielding pride had been fused into him as an integral part of his structure and grew with him, from microorganism to man, and no matter what pain and longing his solitude brought him, the pride would not bend.

5

THE LAND BETWEEN THE COLORADO AND THE Pecos Rivers lies like a yellow, dusty cowhide stretched on a Comanche drum. Burned dry by the white sun of summer and raked by the hot sandy winds of what in other climes is called spring and fall, it lives in a permanent condition of drouth. When the rare rains come they tear at the earth with a violence that seems almost malevolent, and then for a short space the land takes on a faint greenish tinge that keeps cattle and men's hopes alive through the long dry spells that are sure to follow.

Yet it is a beautiful land, in the way that hard and stark things can be beautiful. Perhaps by contrast with the desolate land, the sky seems a higher and a cleaner blue than the piney-wood skies to the east, where the humidity can close in around a man's neck like a warm towel. But here in these desiccated plains, when the wind is quiet, the early light falls across the land with a serenity of colors that flow imperceptibly from a star-specked blue-black just before dawn into pale spreading yellows and melon pinks, and then the whole sky seems to open up into a depthless shimmering light that makes a man feel he can breathe better.

By the end of his fourth day in Cap Bruner's gang, Jim McNeely was totally insensitive to this stark beauty of his surroundings—in fact, to everything but the aching of his body. He was ready to quit. To quit and slink back to his job in the grocery store, any job in any grocery store, anywhere. Anything would be better than this, and nothing could be worse. He lay on his back on his bunk, fully clothed in the now filthy borrowed khakis. He was utterly exhausted, unable to move, too bone-tired to notice or care about the odors seeping out of the loathsome closet by his head. Every muscle and tendon in his body ached deeply as though beaten and bruised and swollen with infection. Every attempt at movement drew an involuntary mutter of pain in his throat. This was the fourth night that he had been unable to drag himself to the showers or the mess hall, and this would be the fourth night that he would sleep in his grimy underclothes, his sweat-salted body unwashed, his matted hair uncombed, his belly empty. The primordial animal agony in his body occupied his entire consciousness like a dull red fire, and he was beyond reacting to the jibes of Peaches Dendy who, toweling himself vigorously, giggled, "What you reckon's the matter with ol' hot-shot, Buster? He must of went to a hog college, 'cause he sho' don't like to wash!"

If he had known on that first cold morning when he climbed into the tin doghouse on the back of the gangtruck and seated himself on hard boards with the glum, silent men, tight-lipped and drawn into themselves as they set out upon the cheerless day's labor, if he had only suspected the havoc which that day and the next and the next would wreak upon his poor, soft-muscled body, he would never have started out. How right, how wise was Dent Paxton!

After a jarring ride of twenty minutes, during which a frigid wind sliced like a knife through the cracks in the doghouse, the truck stopped and the silent hands climbed stiffly out, Ort Cooley among them looking remarkably renewed. They dropped cheerlessly to the ground, the impact paining their freezing feet, and the day's work began. This was to be the laying of a four-inch flow-line of steel pipe from Bison's newly completed Well Number 44 in the field to the battery of stock tanks nearly half a mile away. The men began the day bone-cold. They beat their arms across their chests as they hit the ground and breathed great plumes of frost smoke from their mouths, but they would not stay cold long.

Cap Bruner, a large scowling man, emerged from the cab of the truck, followed by Buster Drum, who always rode on the soft spring seat beside him, and then by Cap's other squire and favorite, Peaches Dendy, who drove the gang truck. Cap was a powerful man, almost as big as Drum, but gone to fat in the middle, with a belly that overhung the belt of his pants. His squinted eyes were cold and his large jaws were sooty red with a two-day beard. He wore a big sweat-stained Stetson which set him apart from the tin-hatted gang hands and was his badge of authority. He had come to West Texas from over around Carthage, and had earned his foreman spurs "working niggers," it was said, and so it was considered natural that that was the way he ran this gang, by verbal abuse and fear.

Training a bleak stare upon Jim McNeely, who stood gawkishly beside the truck not knowing what to do, Cap growled something audible about "them compounded swivel-chair operators" in Winfield who had sent him another sorry boll weevil to break in when what he needed was men. Then in his flat unpleasant voice he said, "All right. I 'low you hands har'd out to work. If you never, you can draw your time right now. If you come to work, then git the lead outa your ass an' *com*mence to makin' up some pipe."

This was all the orientation or instruction that Jim McNeely received for the first important work in his life. It was the same spirit-deadening charge with which Cap Bruner sent his men to their work every day. It never varied, was never omitted. No one answered him back or wise-cracked, for Cap was not one who understood that the hands were, after all, men and human beings, just like him.

When the tools were unloaded from the truck the men fell to, a pair of them raising the end of the long black pipe which snaked back into the mesquite brush, taking up the work at the point at which yesterday's work had ended. Another man shoved the battered lazyboard under the lifted pipe-end which was dropped heavily upon the board by the straining pair, one of whom then pulled out the wad of rags which had been stuffed into the pipe opening to keep rabbits and rodents from crawling into the line during the night.

"You, Cooley!" Cap grunted sharply, for he spoke customarily in grunts. "Take that boll weevil an' git to pissantin' them joints over here. An' by God see if you can keep up today. If you can't, there's plenty wantin' work as can."

Ort Cooley crooked a gloved thumb at Jim McNeely and started off through the naked bushes in a westerly direction. Jim McNeely followed dumbly, obediently, not knowing where he was going, or why, but deter-mined to move smartly, as directed. After a few paces he caught up to Ort, who he sensed, or at least hoped, was, if not a friend, at least not an enemy ready-made, like Drum and Dendy.

"What'd he say?" he said in a low, anxious voice. "What're we supposed to do?"

"See them joints?" said Ort as he stalked ahead, pointing to lengths of unconnected pipe which now came in sight strewn haphazardly along the ground, roughly end to end like a great black python hacked into

39

segments, running off into the brush as far as eye could see. "You an' me gonna pissant them joints from here—over yonder—to the gang, so's they can make 'em up in the line."

"How're we gonna do that?" said Jim McNeely, naively, eyeing the thirty-foot lengths of pig-iron and envisioning dollies, hand trucks or the like, clearly not in evidence, for moving them.

"Ever see a pissant work?" said Ort.

"Don't guess I ever did."

"Well, he totes it, piss-piece at a time, kid. That's what you and me gonna do. So suck up yer gut an' let's git at it." Ort put out a hand for Jim McNeely to stop at the near end of the first joint. "Jest hook yer hand in the bell an' do like I do." He glanced at his slender partner dubiously and frowned, then shambled down the length of the pipe to the other end. "When I say *hump*," he said, "you jest heist her up an' take off. Ain't nuthin' to it but back an' guts. An' fer God's sakes don't drop it!" Ort hesitated a moment, shook his head again and sighed as the thought of the long day ahead, then he said, "Hully-gully! Here we go."

Jim McNeely bent over the pipe, hooked a gloved hand in the open end, just as Ort did, and when he heard the *hump!* he gave a jerk and to his amazement the pipe came up on his thighs, then to his waist, and then he had it cradled uncertainly in his forearms. The weight of the steel pipe shocked him. It was a profound, dead force that seemed to be pulling him into the earth. Then he realized that he was expected to carry it across thirty yards of brushy ground to the gang, with only old Ort on the other end. He could scarcely believe it. With every muscle and tendon in a tight, quivering strain he heard Ort's tense command, "Step out!" and he set himself into compressed, wobble-legged motion.

When they reached the gang and delivered their ponderous burden into waiting hands which seized it and began immediately to spin it into the line, Jim McNeely felt light all over, as though he had suddenly grown an inch. A momentary exhilaration sped through him. It had been a hard and satisfying experience and he stood puffing, pulse pounding, brushing gloved hands together and feeling that in spite of all it was a fine thing to be, at last, doing real man's work.

"Boll weevil!" Cap Bruner's explosive voice right behind him lifted him to his toes. "*Git* the lead outa yo' ass! You think you done done yo' day's work?"

Already Ort Cooley was heading back toward the strung-out pipe. He looked over his shoulder at Jim McNeely and gave him a motioning jerk of his head.

When they had carried the third joint to the gang and Jim McNeely's tender, overtaxed muscles were already beginning to cry with pain, and the sweat was starting down his temples in the icy wind, the appalling realization came over him that he was expected to go on doing this incredible thing over and over, perhaps all day, less than ten minutes of which had now elapsed.

On the walk-backs, since talk was impossible when they were loaded, Ort informed him, "You kin thank that goddam fool Pucketts fer all this here pissantin'. Him an' his swamper strang this pipe las' week. That little turkey-neck bastard calls hisself a surveyor! Shit! He couldn't *sur*vey his way back from the crapper if you drawed him a chalk line!"

It seemed that Mr. Pucketts, in stringing the pipe, had aimed his heavy-laden truck straight as a "arra" from the newly completed oil well to the tank battery, while his swamper, in the accustomed manner, had rolled the pipe joints off the moving truck one at a time, so that they would be in proper position to be made up into a flow-line by the connection gang.

Unfortunately Mr. Pucketts had aimed at the west end of the battery. Since the battery was quite a long affair of four five-hundred-barrel cypress tanks inside an earthen fire wall, this placed his point of aim a considerable distance from the east end where the manifold and gas separator were located and where it should have been, since it was there that the end of the flow-line had to be connected. As a consequence the course of the strung pipe gradually diverged from the path along which the pipe had to be laid, making it necessary to "pissant" the joints from the Puckett line to the true line. Since there was a kind of unspoken mutual support among the camp aristocracy, those who lived in the houses, Cap Bruner would make no mention of the error other than giving Pucketts a private "ass-eating," and only the unfortunate individuals assigned to the "pissant" detail would ever know the difference.

By 3 p.m. Jim McNeely was a staggering wreck. His limbs had turned to lead, and his mind had ceased to function, except to concentrate on the extreme effort of will, far beyond mere muscular capability which had long been surpassed, to make just one more joint.

Ort Cooley, being an old man of forty-five, had been spelled at noon, changing places with a rawboned, taciturn man named Luke Odum, who, being taller than Jim McNeely, made the pipe weight run downhill and increased the torture of his travail.

Twice Jim McNeely had stumbled and dropped the pipe, and was flung sprawling to the ground. Both times the infliction of a hernia or ruined shinbone on the man at the other end was narrowly escaped. On both occasions Cap Bruner lashed him with merciless abuse.

"God damn all sorry-ass boll weevils! *You*, boll weevil! Tryin' to kill somebody? Break a workin' man's leg fer him? Them bosses got a lot to do, sendin' me a bunch half-ass kids, an' I'm supposed t'git a day's work done! You git me a lost-time accident agin my record an' I'll make yo' ass suck wind sho'nuff, you boll weevil you! Now pick up that pipe an' git the lead outa yo' tail!"

In his top-hand position as stabber, spinning the new joints into the line until the tong men took over, Buster Drum was Cap's second in command, and he felt it incumbent upon himself to pick up the harassment of the new man where Cap left off. In the intervals between Cap's outbursts he rode Jim McNeely with harsh ridicule, making no allowance for his newness to the job or the greenness of his muscles.

"Now this weevil thinks he's mighty smart. Act like he been takin' smart pills! Shhuh! He don't know his ass from his lef' foot. Like Peaches said, he's a real athalete. Bet he was captain a' the girl's basketball team!"

Cap Bruner echoed his assent in grunts. He harbored a deep and dark resentment over what he considered an unacceptable infringement of his prerogative, as gang pusher, of hiring new hands for the gang. The ability to hire and fire gave power and prestige, and it was rumored there were emoluments—Christmas presents and loans that were somehow forgotten—which attached to the pusher's job. It thus had become an obsession with him to demonstrate quickly and conclusively that a man hired out of the head office was incompetent, unreliable, and totally incapable of performing the assigned work. Of course the big-shots' kids, sent out for a few months' seasoning, were tolerantly excepted from the Bruner treatment. But the rank nobodies, in which category Jim McNeely obviously belonged, were marked to be ground up and eliminated as quickly as possible.

Few of these unsponsored weevils survived as long as a month, and those who did were the prideless ones adaptable enough to "grape up" and make themselves Cap Bruner's men, capable of adopting the attitudes of complete subservience of those who had been hired, and consequently could be fired, by Cap himself.

Jim McNeely showed no early sign of possessing this happy, adaptable faculty. Even in his agony he was distant, self-contained, and, as the day wore on, obviously and increasingly defiant. Cap Bruner thus marked him for early destruction, and Drum and Dendy, as dutiful lieutenants, laid in their verbal blows to make it a quick kill. As the new line crawled forward toward the distant tank battery the divergence between the line and the strung pipe increased, and there was increasing pressure for the pissanters to hurry, to keep the gang from having to wait for the next joint after the last had been bucked up tight.

"Lookit ol' hot-shot blow!" cackled Dendy, who was working as collar-pecker. "Look like his eyes gonna bug outa his fuckin' head. Oh, that's a mighty strong boy, that hot-shot!"

At this moment, when all attention was focused upon him, Jim McNeely caught his foot on a mesquite root and stumbled again, pitching helplessly forward. His end of the pipe hit the ground with a dull *whong!* The impact tore the other end from Luke Odum's grasp and Luke lurched backward with a shouted curse.

Echoing the profanity, Buster Drum flung his wrench aside and strode angrily toward the fallen youth who was struggling to his feet. Grasping Jim McNeely by the shirt he jerked him roughly aside, then he stalked to the midpoint of the pipe, picked it up in his two hands, as easily as if it had been a length of wooden two-by-four, then carried it, almost effortlessly, the rest of the way to the gang by himself.

Turning on the boll weevil, who had doggedly got to his feet and was following behind, Buster Drum said, "Go set down, Shirley Temple, afore you hurt somebody! Whoever told you you could do a man's work, anyhow?"

Beyond caring, his mind as raw and inflamed as his whole body, Jim McNeely said, "You take a flyin' bite at my ass!"

Cap Bruner had been off in the brush answering a call of nature. At this exact moment he reappeared. Seeing all work stopped, all hands frozen, awaiting the explosion of Buster Drum's wrath, he boomed furiously, "God *damn*, boll weevil! I can't turn my back. You har' out to work? Well, *move!*" His instinct of self-preservation still barely functioning, Jim McNeely moved, and thus what could have resulted in a quick and violent end to his career in the oil fields was averted, at least temporarily.

That he made it through the rest of the day, and the three incredible days that followed, was a miracle of youthful corpuscles driven to perform

43

impossible tasks by a strong and prideful spirit. The remembered last sight of Mazie's blonde head as she gunned her mother's Buick out of the parking lot, and the cool, powdered tones of Mrs. Wales calmly dismissing him from polite society spiraled in his head—and kept him putting one leaden foot in front of the other. He would not give *her* the satisfaction of saying she had been so right about him. He would prove that she was dead wrong. A lot of other people had to be proved wrong, too—all those who had Nigger Jimmed him. He had a lot of getting even to do, and this was where it had to start.

6

EVEN ON THOSE OCCASIONS IN EARLY YOUTH when he wished with all his heart to shrink back into obscurity, Jim McNeely's pride had propelled him forward into trouble, though it meant going to the extreme of publicly asserting his right to be considered as good as Roger Keene or Teddy Neighbors, when Roger's father was a lawyer and ex-State Senator, and Teddy's was a leading banker of the town, whereas his own father had been something darkly referred to by other children—doubtless parroting their parents—as a "promoter," a word which became in his mind a calumnious and unjustified insult.

In the third grade a game was played on Friday afternoons in which the teacher would call out an arithmetic problem, and the first child to raise his hand with the right answer could choose a partner of the opposite sex, and the two could take erasers outside and dust them on the shady concrete steps at the back of the school building. Intuitively and almost invariably the social stratification of the community was nicely observed by the children in the pairing off for this game. Starched frocks called out tweed knickers. Overalls called out cut-down gingham dresses.

On this black Friday, which Jim McNeely would never forget, he was somehow fatefully quicker than the rest, and something, perhaps the still stinging humiliation of a recess defeat, drove him to do what he knew was freighted with peril. There would be no trouble if he called out the dull little creature with the white eyeball and the frosted lens in her glasses. He chose, instead, to call out Mazie Wales, the beautiful child with the lustrous taffy-colored hair and pouting cheeks—Mazie Wales, idyl of his wakeful nights, fair daughter of one of the fine old families of Winfield, whose physician father was also president of the School Board.

Acutely aware of the inappropriateness of this selection and sensing trouble ahead, the teacher stammered and gave him a second choice. "Now let's be sure to let everyone have an opportunity to go out. Pass the fun around. You don't all have to choose the same girl or boy. Now let's think *who* we would like to choose, Jim."

"I already chose," said Jim McNeely stolidly. "I chose Mazie."

The class felt the small shock of excitement in this decision. Titters ran around the room. Suddenly little Jim McNeely felt panic and wanted to sink into the floor, but he could not retract his choice. It was impossible. The exquisite child with the candy-colored hair and the face like a fresh peach flushed a fiery pink. She looked plaintively, pleadingly at the teacher. She started to rise, then she plopped back down in her desk, burying her fluffy head in her arms, sobbing, "I won't go out with *him!*"

In a moment of choked indecision, during which she pushed nervously nine times at her hair and got it all out of shape, the teacher debated with herself the principles of fairness and democracy and decided in favor of the president of the School Board. She abandoned the game and set the class abruptly to work on Monday's geography lesson, and Jim McNeely sat staring unseeing at his book for the rest of the day, his face tingling as if bathed in acid.

The wound which this afternoon gashed in his nine-year-old ego took a long time to heal, and it left a lumpy scar. He survived because he was armored with the toughness of youth, and he did not change because he was stricture-bound with pride. At the same time he was sensitive enough to know, and ache for, what he was missing, for the warm inner knowledge that he was accepted, as the psychologists say, by his peer group. How he longed to walk scuffling along the downtown streets with a bunch of boys under the store awnings and have some man single him out and catch him up and playfully scrub his head with his fist and call him "Rusty" and "Buttonhead," as the men did the other boys, and ask him how his old man was. But he was ignored, for he had no father, and he knew he was not one of these people. He became ever more the loner, and between him and the beautiful world of companionship, of belonging, of going out to dust erasers with girls with taffy hair, was a dead father who had been a "promoter" and a home on a square of ground called No Man's Land on

46

a rutted yellow street which separated the white men from their darker, disfranchised brothers.

At the end of his fourth day in Cap Bruner's connection gang, Jim McNeely knew he could not go on. On top of the utter depletion and failure of his hemorrhaging muscles, he was sick—really sick from a bug that would have put him in bed, even under ordinary circumstances. And now the pride of spirit which was all that had kept him going this last day when the youthful reservoir of animal strength had been drained dry was playing out on him, too. What was the use? What did it matter? Suppose he could go on, what was the point of it? Who cared? Dent Paxton was right. The future here was hopeless. For him it was nonexistent.

A long time after the men had gone to supper Jim McNeely lay a sick, drained wreckage in the darkness of his bunk. Finally, somehow, he scraped up his last resources of strength and struggled off the bed to his feet. Out in the cold air he shuffled down the porch to Denton Paxton's room. The light was burning, and he could see Dent inside through the window, feet up, reading a book, sipping his nightly bourbon.

Shoving open the door Jim McNeely stood framed like a gaunt and grimy scarecrow, with matted hair, and dead white pallor beneath the grime.

"I've been expecting you," Dent said, closing the book and looking up. "The only thing I didn't know was when."

The wraith moved unsteadily into the room and leaned back heavily against the door. In a hoarse voice he said, "You win. I quit. Make out my time."

For almost a minute Dent sat studying him. A play of amusement in his eyes was crossed by a flickering frown. In another it might have passed for compassion.

"You sick, buddy?"

"I'm beat, man. Ever' whichaway."

"Mmhm," Dent Paxton mused, tapping his finger ends together. "I been hearin' what Cap's been doin' to you. That insufferable sonofabitch!" He waited another while, then he said, "Well, I don't think this is the time to quit."

"I've had enough," Jim McNeely heaved a big painful breath. "You said it right. There's nothing here for me."

"I said it right," said Dent quietly. "You should have quit before you started. But you didn't. Now it's different. If you quit now, you're a flop. They beat you and ran you off. And they proved you couldn't take it and didn't have anything to you to begin with. No, I don't think you better quit now."

He got up and forcefully guided the shaking youth into a chair. Standing above his bent shoulders, lips compressed, he said, "Now you've got to stick it out awhile. Six months, maybe. Then you can quit. Then you can thumb your nose at 'em and tell 'em all to go to hell. That'll show 'em you can take it. It'll show you, too, and that might be pretty important, buddy."

"I can't do it." Jim McNeely shook his dark head that had sunk down between his shoulders. "I sure enough can't."

"The hell you can't!" Dent made an impatient gesture, his voice ringing with asperity. "You've got to! Here—" He uncorked the bottle on the table and poured a third of a tumbler of whiskey and splashed in some water from an old crockery pitcher. "Take a swig of this and listen to me. Go on, dammit, drink!"

He paced back and forth eyeing the revulsion with which his forlorn friend faced the drink, then gagged it down and fought several seconds to keep it down.

"Now understand me. I don't give a damn, personally, whether you quit or not. It's completely immaterial to me. That clear? But I hate to see you give those Neanderthal bastards the pleasure of running you off. Now listen. I *know* you can get through this. You're just a little sick. If you weren't you'd make it through the soreness in a few days and Cap Bruner couldn't bust you out if he—" He stopped pacing and said sharply, "Quit shakin' your head, goddammit! Listen to me! You can and you will stick!"

He drew himself up and pointed an imperious finger at Jim McNeely's bent head. "I said you can, and by God you will! Take another swig."

Later, he sat knee to knee with Jim McNeely, talking earnestly, persuasively, to him. "I got a little stroke with Mr. Scofield. I'll ask him to tell Cap to put you in the warehouse tomorrow, and he'll do it. Scofield owes me a thing or two. Anyway, the warehouse has gotten in a hell of a mess and we're overdue for an inventory. That'll be better than reportin' sick, because they'd figure you couldn't take it and were gold-brickin'. Then after tomorrow is Sunday and by Monday, hell, you'll be a new man." He walked around on light feet, slapping the back of his neck with his slender hand, thinking rapidly. "Later on you'll have to figure out how to get that hulking Drum off your back. I can't help you with that, but you can do it. Anyway, we can't fight but one fire at a time. What you need right now is another little swig of booze and a bath and bed. There'll be hot water by now, and—my God, you look like a sewer rat! Come on!" His tone was still imperious, but there was a vein of tenderness under the sharpness. "I'll show you how to undress yourself. It appears you have forgotten how."

Thus, a second time, Dent Paxton saved Jim McNeely from defaulting on his young manhood.

7

A S LONG AGO AS 1540, WHITE MEN CAME HERE, questing for gold. Perhaps they were spurred by the thought that the Lord, in His divine justice, must have hidden riches within this land, since he had so clearly deprived it of all visible evidences of His bounty. Francisco Vasquez de Coronado, armored and beplumed, led his conquistadors clanking and sweating up its dry reaches in search of the fabled Gran Quivira, never dreaming that he passed within a league of riches greater than all the plate and bullion carried by all the Spanish galleons to swell the treasuries of Castile. Nor would he have known how to get at this loot, or what to do with it, if some seer had told him where it lay, for it was straight down, beneath the measured drum of his horses' hooves. It was imprisoned in great layers of porous rock. It was oil.

In old time when the earth was young, this wasteland was covered by a shallow, tepid sea. A hundred streams spread their silts and sands in dreamy whorls over its bottom. Upon and between these soft layered sediments sank countless generations of dying sea creatures, brachiopods, cephalopods, foraminifera, their tiny carcasses rotting and mixing with dead seaweed, their shells building with infinite slowness, layer upon layer, limy mantle upon limy mantle, above and between and below the blankets of mud and sand.

As the soupy sea began to fill and dry and drop its salts out of suspension, the shell beds were covered by other layers of anhydrite, other silts and sands; and as the time-wheel turned in thousands and then millions of years, the process repeated itself, countlessly, changing with the primordial seasons as new seas spread and ebbed, one stratum building upon another, compacting the lower beds under unthinkable weight, as new species in the evolution of plant and animal life added their debris to the stratigraphy. Pressure and time changed mud into shale, sand into sandstone, loose shells into limestone, compressing and cooking the fermented animal and herbiferous garbage as the years fled by the thousands, into a gaseous noisome brew, which retained in its reformed molecules the energy which its plant and animal origins had taken from the sun.

In the cycling of the deca-centuries, as the earth shifted its shoulders and mountains were melted down and washed away and others rose, and the seas dried and resurged and the thick layered old sea bottoms cracked and warped, slipped and bowed under tremendous pressure, the petroliferous ooze in the porous rock layers began to migrate up the tilted beds, separating particle by particle from the heavier subterranean waters, to collect slowly in the buried high places, in the gentle arches and domes of old sea beds and faulted traps of sandstone or vuggy limestone, until, when a fill of droplets had collected in one place or another and could move no farther, an oil field was born.

This, at any rate, is roughly what the geologists say took place, though even the most authoritarian of that recondite brotherhood will confess that theirs is not an exact science. There is room for argument about the details, but in the broad this is probably what happened.

The winter had blown itself out with the last angry sandstorms of March, and April into May brought a brief respite of fair weather before the heat of summer. The air was clear and sparkling. White cotton clouds blew down a clean blue sky, and the sun was pleasantly warm on Jim McNeely's back as he swung the pick, and the pick-point glinted into the caliche rock that lay brittle and crumbly just below the surface soil. He worked steadily, with a new economy and directness of strength, and the ditch took shape, inching forward slowly into a long, narrow grave for a future flow-line. His newly hardened muscles of shoulder, arm, back, thigh, and buttock were taut, swollen with good blood pumped by a heart that was young and sound. He functioned now with a native skill, thus newly and quickly boned, that made it difficult for Cap Bruner or Buster Drum to find the smallest excuse for complaining of his work, though from start-up to quitting time they watched him like goshawks and were silently, grimly alert for the slightest opportunity to catch him in a fault. Jim McNeely felt this. He knew that his status in the gang was perilously insecure. Though he had done nothing to deserve their hatred, it was clear that Cap Bruner and Buster Drum were his implacable enemies, and his young mind was steadily troubled.

Just as Dent Paxton had said that he could, he had survived the trials of those first critical days. Thanks largely to Dent's shrewd manipulations and to his stern, demanding exhortations, Jim McNeely had stuck it out on the job. He had quickly regained his strength and resolve and bearings, and since then had accepted every hard and dirty task which Cap Bruner had thrown at him. In the process he had done all well enough, learning fast, getting better each day, so that Cap, with the gang as mute witnesses, had been unable to find a legitimate excuse for running him off. He was the first to hit the ground when the gang truck arrived at the day's work site, the first to grab the heavy end of any object to be lifted, the first into the ditch bending his back when it was picks-and-shovels, generally displaying an alacrity and industry that should have warmed any pusher's heart, but only deepened Cap's unreasoning fury toward him. His very eagerness to do well had, in fact, been taken as an unspoken challenge by the pusher, and there began a silent, uneven contest between the two which had in it the seeds of violence and destruction.

Finding himself thus in the frustrating position of having no reason to complain of Jim McNeely's performance, Cap Bruner delegated the task of his elimination from the scene to his anthropoid lieutenant, Buster Drum, who being uninhibited by the need for apparent fairness, took upon himself, dutifully, and with relish, the assignment of driving Jim McNeely out of the camp.

If the newcomer had been gifted with a more adaptable set of genes he might have found a way to flatter and bribe his way into the graces of this pair of small-brained, brute-bodied men. But to Jim McNeely this was an impossibility. It would have been a worse defeat than to have washed out, broken physically, in those very first days. As a consequence he now faced in Buster Drum an adversary, who was like an evil, unreasoning force of nature, a force with which he knew not how to cope or compromise, but which he must inescapably meet and defeat, or die.

He also recognized that it was impossible to go on indefinitely accepting the insults which Buster Drum hung upon him, like wet verbal garbage, on the slightest pretext, on the job, in the bunkhouse, and even when their paths crossed in Coker City. One who continued to tolerate another's calling him "hot-shot" and worse in the contemptuous and challenging tone which Buster used, could not long retain that minimum of self-respect that makes it bearable to live and work and eat and wash with other men. He knew that Buster was purposely and methodically whip-sawing him, taunting him to a breaking point at which he would finally lash out, irrationally, in physical combat. And he knew that this was a trap into which he must not fall for even in his new and growing strength he was no match for the man. Buster would pop him as easily and as mercilessly as he would a cockroach or a dog-tick under his foot. Jim McNeely knew this would finish him at Dead Lake, and there was no place else to go.

A crisis was approaching, and both men knew it. Cap Bruner and the whole gang knew it and waited for it. In the evenings after supper, when the bunkhouse inmates were settling down to their various pursuits of penny-ante, or reading pulp westerns, or just shooting the wind, Jim McNeely would walk off by himself, partly to avoid Buster Drum and partly to think. Down through the shadowy pipe yard among the dark silent shapes of trucks and stacked machinery, he walked, swinging absently, distractedly at the rocky ground with a stick. Under the new moon he could see the sparkling derricks far across the mesquite flats where the rigs were working, sinking their slender holes into the earth, around the clock. They were too far away for him to hear their clank and hiss and grinding roar, and he heard only the soft flow of the wind across the cheeks, and the turmoil in his head. Many nights he walked here, following the line of the barbwire fence around the compound, until the lights began to go out in the bunkhouse, and sometimes he would stop at a post and strike it with his stick with hard, steady, increasingly furious blows, as if trying to beat some sense out of the post, about his predicament, and some solution to it.

When the thing finally happened, it was not by Jim McNeely's design, for he would have rejected it, had he thought of it, as too fantastic, too fraught with danger. The climax came suddenly, without warning. His reaction was as direct and natural as reaching for a rock on the schoolground, the simple instinct of self-preservation. In a hard moment of clarity he knew that he could take no more abuse from Buster Drum, no matter what the consequences.

On this afternoon Cap Bruner had broken the gang into several small work groups to clean up a number of odd, unrelated jobs in various parts of the field. The truck had dropped Buster Drum and Jim McNeely to dig a ditch and lower a new flow-line below the surface where it crossed a lease road. Cap paired the two together, ostensibly to have a green hand working with a skilled veteran, but his real and steady purpose was to afford every opportunity for the tension between the two to build to the expected breaking point.

When the truck had disappeared down the road the two set to work, in tandem, with pick and shovel, driving their picks into the chalky caliche rock, then scooping out the rubble with their long-handled "idiot spoons." Drum worked in front, making the ditch, and Jim McNeely followed behind at a safe distance, deepening and trimming the trench as it inched across the oiled dirt road.

After half an hour's hard labor, when the crossing was nearly made, a fateful collision of slashing steel and dumb rock sent a rock, like a bullet, straight for the taut buttock of Buster Drum, just as he bent his back to lift his loaded shovel. The sting of the rock as it struck his tender part straightened the giant with a grunt.

Enraged, Drum threw his shovel aside and, rubbing his stinging buttock, turned, as if answering a long-awaited cue. Without haste he stalked down the narrow ditch. With neither a sound nor a flicker of his pale-china eyes he reached out a simian arm, caught the front of Jim McNeely's jumper in a gloved fist and jerked the slighter youth's face to within inches of his own. His voice was a flat twanging of fury.

"You hit me in the ass with one more little rock, hot-shot, an' I'll pop yo' head like it was a flea 'tween my fingernails."

Still holding him, tethered tight in one hand, Drum placed the oily palm of the other glove full in Jim McNeely's face and forced his head backward until his tin hat fell off and clunked to the rocky rubble. Helpless, Jim McNeely was thrust down heavily in the ditch. Standing above him like a great shadow, Drum strewed a slimy string of obscenities upon his bare sweaty head. Then the giant turned with utter contempt and went back to work.

Jim McNeely recovered his hat and put it on, automatically. Then he slowly got up. There could be no mistake now. The time had come. If he did not meet this challenge, without further excuse or postponement, the whole direction of his life would be turned, back, away from where he wanted to go, down toward second-rateness. Toward docility and ignominy. The big man in the ditch ahead blocked the only road into the future that he cared to travel. Jim McNeely did not think those things in a logical sequence of thoughts. But he felt them, all at once, clearly, like an unbearable pain in his head.

Strangely, he felt no anger. The broad back before him was now only an inanimate phenomenon of nature, like an avalanche, or a storm at sea, and he knew simply that he must now overcome it, or succumb to it.

His pulse was fast but steady. He took up his pick as if to resume work, but he did not go back to digging. Instead, he jarred the hickory handle straight down against the ground, sharply, then once again, harder. The steel pick-head broke loose and slipped down the handle and fell free. Grasping the polished shaft Jim McNeely hefted it like a baseball bat, as though he were stepping into a batter's box. He did not hesitate. The danger of what he was about to do was clear, but that was academic, for he was faced with the choice between survival and ruin, right here, right now. And he would not have another chance. He moved silently up the ditch until he was directly behind Buster Drum's massive bending back. As the big man straightened and dumped a shovel of rocky debris onto the ground, the pick handle arced swiftly upward. The motion was crisp and true. The thick end of the handle clipped the rim of Drum's safety hat and sent it spinning and flashing through the air. As the handle reached the top of its arc Jim McNeely, heart hammering, brought it swiftly downward, breathing an instant's prayer that the force was hard enough, but not too hard-squarely against the flat top of Buster Drum's head. Hickory met living bone, with a solid whack! The big man flinched, trembled a moment, arms akimbo, then sank slowly to his knees in the ditch.

Shaking all over, licking at dry lips as he stared at the fallen giant, Jim McNeely stood faint and dizzy in the ditch. In that instant he was certain he had killed him. He had hit him too hard, fractured his skull, murdered him!

But there was a great thickness of bone in Buster Drum's head. He began to twitch, then he sprawled around in the rubble like a stalled ox, his head wagging on his neck, his eyes rolling senselessly. The next moment he was staring up at Jim McNeely, slowly working his vision into focus. Then he hooked his elbows on the sides of the ditch, rested a moment, a quizzical expression crossing his flat face. Then, as his scrambled consciousness returned in a rush, he rose straight out of the ditch and launched himself at his assailant, emitting a great gasping roar of rage.

There was no alternative left now but to finish the job. Setting his teeth together, Jim McNeely raised the pick handle above his head and brought it down again swiftly, harder this time, in a short solid stroke against the slope just above Buster Drum's ear. The big man fell heavily into the ditch on his face and lay still.

With a shudder, the weapon still clutched in his hands, Jim McNeely sank slowly to the edge of the ditch. The monstrousness of what he has done sent successive waves of horror through him. Now, now he had really killed a man. They would give him the electric chair. Everybody would know they had been right about him. It was the fear of shame more than of death that strapped itself upon him. Nobody would understand. Nobody would understand that he had to do this. He thought he was going to cry, and he could not bear to. An impulse to jump up and run, flee wildly through the brush grew in him.

Then Buster Drum stirred in the ditch. He moved one leg, spastically. Then an arm. And then the whole complex internal chemistry of Jim McNeely reversed itself and began frantically to manufacture secretions from a different set of glands, to meet the new situation.

He moved quickly away from the man, as if from a stirring snake. Gingerly he poked the great body, once, with the pick handle. The great body moved and groaned.

It could hardly have been better. With a flood of relief Jim McNeely sat back. He felt a sudden almost hysterical impulse to laugh. In a shivery voice he said, "If you got a minute, Buster, I'd like to talk to you—*you low-life sonofabitch!*"

In a wobbly motion Drum lifted his head. Ropy saliva drooled from his mouth into the dirt of the ditch. He spat and moaned. Then, instinctively, he began to struggle toward his feet. It required a full minute for him to raise himself to a sitting position. He leaned heavily against the edge of the ditch, his head swaying, eyes swimming. As Buster Drum thus looked out over the flat landscape, wondering where he was, his senses seeping slowly back into his head, Jim McNeely spoke to him. He spoke slowly and deliberately, as if instructing a child.

"I coulda killed you, Buster. I still can." He raised the pick handle and slapped it solidly against the cut bank of the ditch. "I could bust your head like an Easter egg, right now."

As Buster Drum's brain slowly cleared and his ears and eyes cleared and focused on the tense words and the fateful form sitting above him

56

outlined against the sky, club in hand, a pallor of wild panic blanched the remaining color from his face. He sat frozen in sheer animal fear.

In a voice serious as a blade Jim McNeely said, "Now you listen to what I'm gonna tell you, Buster. And listen good, because you won't have another chance to hear it." He jabbed the pick handle in the man's chest. Buster listened. The words echoed down the bony corridors of his brain.

"I haven't done anything to you, Buster. Not a damn thing! But somewhere you got the idea that you got to break me and run me off. Well, you're not gonna do it. Understand? You're gonna leave me alone, from now on—if you want to live, Buster. And don't think I'm gonna fight you fair. I'm not crazy. Are you listening, Buster?" He prodded the semiconscious man again with the pick handle.

"Listen to this, too, big man. If you so much as put your hand on me again, or tell Cap or anybody about this, I'll kill you, sure. That's a promise, Buster. You may think you can catch me and bust me up before I can do it. Well, you better do a good job when you start, because if I live I'll come back and get you. And you won't know when it'll be, or what hit you. But I'll be waiting for you, sometime, somewhere out there in the dark, and you won't ever know who's walking behind you. You'll be afraid to go out after night, because just as sure as I'm looking at you, Buster, I'll come back and get you. And I won't care what they do to me, because if I get run off from here I got no place else to go. You better believe that, Buster."

When he had said these simple words, Jim McNeely got up and recovered the loose pick-head, slipped it back down the hickory handle and jarred it tight against the ground. He felt a sudden washed-out calmness of spirit, the utter tranquility of a man who had just passed a point of no return in his life and was committed irrevocably, come what may, good or bad, to a perilous, unknown future.

He no longer hated or even feared Buster Drum. The only feeling he had toward him was something closer to pity than contempt. He looked down at him draped like a giant, slow-witted baby over the edge of the ditch and added one final word of advice.

"Any time you got anything to say to me in the future, just call me by my name. That's McNeely. Now get outa the way. I got work to do."

That night when they came in from the field Jim McNeely emptied the soiled work clothes from the stinking closet by his bunk. When Peaches

Dendy returned from the shower and saw them piled high in the center of the floor, he let out a yell.

"Buster! Looky what ol' hot-shot done gone an' done agin!"

Jim McNeely walked over to the bristling little man and fixed him in the eye. He stuck a straight finger against the plate of Peaches's bare, bony chest.

"Dendy," he said, "the next time you 'hot-shot' me I'm gonna kick your little ass right up between your shoulder blades."

"*Bus*ter!" cried Peaches in disbelief.

At this moment Buster Drum entered the room from the porch, girdled in his towel, his flat head swollen on top to a more symmetrical roundness. He shoved Peaches Dendy roughly out of the way and stalked heavily to his bunk.

"Shut up, you little rat," he said. And that was that.

8

THAT REMOTE GRANDFATHER WHO FIRST STOOD UP
on his hind legs and began to walk about on this planet must, in
time, have wandered across some surface sign of this great force
laminated into the rock layers beneath his feet. Throughout the millennia
of the earth's springtime, long before this grandfather appeared, infinitesimal quantities of oil and gas had begun to seep slowly upward from
the imprisoning reservoirs, through cracks in the overburden, and some
of it eventually found its way to the surface where it collected in isolated
springs and bogs. This distant direct ancestor must have rubbed the sticky
stuff in his fingers, tasted it, spat, and puzzled dimly about its origin. He
soon must have found it to have a passing usefulness as an insect repel-
lant when smeared on his hairy limbs, or as an effective, if rather violent,
cathartic, or, later, as a passable caulking for his boat, or even as fuel. Later
still the discovery of a burning gas seep, ignited by chance lightning, must
have served as a terrible confirmation of the fate awaiting souls consigned
to the underworld.

Yet it was only seconds ago, as the geologic time-clock runs, that his
grandsons dared to plumb the Devil's furnaces and siphon off some of
his fuel for the use of comfort of inter vivos sinners. An odd, stovepipe-
hatted Yankee named Drake, in a mid-nineteenth-century year of our
Lord, reasoned that if there was a little of the stuff bubbling to the surface
here, there ought to be a lot more down below. And that if there was, and
he could tap it, it might be a pretty good substitute for whale grease and
make a little money for himself and his Yankee backers who put up the
money to sink the well. He drilled it out in Pennsylvania, or up or over or

down in Pennsylvania, depending on where you happened to be sitting, in an area rich in surface signs of oil.

A few romantics have tried to make out a case for Drake's indomitable explorer's spirit, for his insatiable curiosity and deep burning altruistic urge to probe the unknown for mankind's use and betterment, and there were trace elements of those noble motives beneath that stovepipe hat, without a doubt. But the inescapable probability is that the prime mover of this first wildcatter, and certainly of his backers, and of everyone who has followed them down the wildcatting trail since then, was the even more insatiable Yankee urge to turn a good profit without having to sweat too much for it. Some even aver that this much-maligned motive has been responsible for *most* of the world's material development, which passes for human progress, and which has resulted in the almost hilariously complicated predicament that man finds himself in today.

Whatever his reason, Drake drilled his well, sixty-nine-and-a-half-feet deep, and the oil came up gurgling. It was very good oil, good for fueling lamps when refined to kerosene, good for easing the squeak of wagon axles and the clash of steam-engine gears. But there was a great deal of this rock oil and it took a while for people to get on to what it could do for them, and so oil didn't create a major stir in the world's economy right off. But gradually the civilized world awakened to the fact that it had come into possession of a new substance that had the power locked in its molecules to heat and illuminate a man in his cold darkness, and a new and specialized business of trafficking in the stuff came into existence and began to spread. Then a few decades later when a fellow named Olds tinkered an invention called the internal combustion engine into a contraption that ordinary people could climb on and go like hell all over the landscape in, using one of the light, refined ends of this oil as a propellant, and another fellow, named Ford, made a simple and reliable machine in mass quantities that lots of people could afford to buy, the demand for oil zoomed suddenly upward, and it became a very big thing. As one certified philosopher put it, when the sparrows began disappearing from the streets of New York, it was clear that oil was here to stay.

Thus, almost overnight, as the geologic time-clock runs, man found himself the owner of a new natural resource which changed the way the world ran, one that could make a man rich if he could find it. And so men began to hunt for it everywhere. They didn't find it everywhere, but they found it in many places, and they found a lot of it. They chased it from that first discovery in Pennsylvania following the surface signs, down into West Virginia and out into Ohio, then down through Oklahoma to Texas and into Mexico, and in a matter of years, mere ticks of the geologic clock, oil was spouting up in odd places all over the world, and in the process, without anybody especially noting it, a new, distinctive and tough-minded breed was born, called oil man.

He was part gambler, part adventurer, part hardheaded businessman and do-it-yourself practical scientist. On the average he wasn't any better or worse than any other breed. There were saintly oil men and crooked oil men, flamboyant big spenders and quiet home-loving types, but the big spenders made better copy than the rest, and somehow the whole breed got spattered with the same brush in the public eye. Possibly it was because this was one of the few Horatio Alger dreams left in America, which let a poor boy with a sixth-grade education and guts and luck turn out to be a multimillionaire, almost overnight. Enough of the lucky ones made public jackasses of themselves that a kind of aura of crudity and flashy irresponsibility attached to the whole breed. This troubled the respectable, successful oil man some, and he worried about it all the way to the bank.

"A man ort not never *whistle*," said Ort Cooley positively, "comin' outa no dang dice hall." The words had an aphoristic ring of wisdom and experience, as if they might have fallen from the lips of Confucius or, at the very least, Bat Masterson. They were spoken, apropos of nothing, to Jim McNeely and Dent Paxton, who sat opposite each other in a booth, to the end of which Ort had hitched up a chair which he straddled backward, in the greasy atmosphere of the Oub Cafe of Coker City. It may have been some vaguely bitter taste at the bottom of the sixth bottle of beer just finished that brought this thought to Ort's mind, or it may merely have been that the loose machinery in his head at that moment trolleyed the thought around like one of the immortal ducks in a shooting gallery.

"I bound ye," he said, shaking his head emphatically. "An' don't fergit it. Don't *never whistle!* I never seen such a run of luck. Them cubes was really listenin' to me that night. 'Star-green, one half a' fo'teen!'" Reliving his triumph he blew on his fist, shaking the imaginary dice in his ear and sending them scampering wildly across the table with a pop of his horny fingers. "Whap! Out come a seven! I say, 'Oh, Jimmy Leroy, the clap-doctor's son, caught him a dose an' away he run!' Whap! Out come a 'leven! Nine straight passes before they cooled on me. Bound ye! One hunnert an' thirty-two dollars is exactly what I taken offa that table, an' it weren't good Saturday night yet. So nacherly I get to thinkin' about a little poon-tang. Well, I cashed in. So I'm a-comin' down them dark dice-hall stairs, whistlin' like a god-dang idiot. Man, I mean I'm advertisin'! Ker-*blam!* Next thing I know I'm a-comin' *to*, layin' on the steps, a knot on my head the size of a turkey aig, an' my god-dang pockets turned wrong side out!"

He took the last swig from the beer bottle and mused reflectively for a moment. "The sorry devil never even lef' me the price of a bowl o' chili." He gave a happy chuckle. "But he weren't all bad. He *did* leave me his ol' dirty sock with the bar a' laundry soap crammed down in the toe, what he brained me with. Printed the name a' the soap right on top a' my god-dang skull! So there I am, settin' there in the dark , rubbin' my noggin' an' cussin', when I hear this *next* idiot comin' down the steps, an' *him* a-whistlin' like a god-dang fool. Now boys, you *know* don't *no*body whistle comin' outa no dice hall if he done lost his ass. He *bound* to won *some*thin'."

He rapped his empty bottle loudly on the table for service. "Well, I lef' this cotton-picker the sock an' the soap, same as my man lef' me. Laid it right across his chest. Figured that were only fair. Ort not a' done it, though. The sorry bastard never had but thirty-three dollars on him. He likely doubled his money on the next one. I bound ye he did!"

Jim McNeely gave a sharp crackling laugh of unfeigned mirth. Dent Paxton said, "Ort, you liar. Don't you know you'll go to hell for lyin' same as stealin'?"

Ort slapped a palm emphatically on his thigh. "I'll take a paralyzed oath! One hunnert an' thirty-two dollars I winned—exactly! Nine straight passes! I mighta invested it an' been a rich man by now. Mighta har'd you sorry boys to work for me. Mighta married a purty woman with a Marmon automobile, hadn't been I taken a notion to *whistle* comin' outa that god-dang dice hall." He gave a slap-happy cackle and a wink and dug Jim McNeely in the ribs with his thumb.

The waiter, a tubercular-looking little man with a wrinkled face, approached the booth, wiping his hands on his dirty apron. "What you boys gonna eat?"

"What you got good tonight, Slim?" said Dent.

In a bored voice the waiter said, "Ham, lamb, ram, beef, bull, and pork. All the same. All good."

"I'll try the chicken-fried steak and some shoestrings," said Jim McNeely.

"Oh, God," said Dent. "I guess I'll have the same."

"Jus' bring me a Pearl an' some more a' them god-dang strawberries," said Ort, pointing to the empty bowl on the table.

"Them ain't strawberries," said Slim. "Them *was* reddishes, an' I don't serve but one bowl to a settin', an' you done had it."

"Hell, I don't give a god-dang!" cried Ort expansively. He fished a quarter from his pocket and slapped it grandly on the table. "Bring two bits' worth! Fresh ones! Them little bandies'll put lead in yo' pistol. They got a bite!" He dug Jim McNeely another one in the ribs. "Might be better'n Spanish fly!"

Jim McNeely laughed again and said, "Ort, you're headin' for trouble tonight. You better eat some groceries and come on back to camp."

Ort Cooley was dressed for Saturday night on the town. He wore a clean white "dress" shirt, open at the collar, with cuffs rolled up two turns on his bony forearms. His brown satin tie, bedizened with a hand-painted hula girl, was made more festive by a large imitation ruby stick-pin stuck squarely in the hula girl's navel. His gray serge "dress" pants were sharply creased and his square-toed "dress" shoes were of calfskin shined to a brilliant tan that was almost yellow. His sparse hair, which later would hang like dead grass into his face, was still pasted carefully across his narrow pate. In his eyes there was the old glitter of excitement that still came like a recurring fever of youth when it was Saturday night.

Ort's weekends followed a pattern. All through the week he would vow loudly to anyone who would listen that he was through with all that "rattin' around," and *this* Saturday night he was going to stay in camp and start saving his money. Buy himself a farm back in Archer County, where he came from, go in the hog business, and get out of this sorry oil-field work and start living like a white man.

As the Saturday afternoon shadows lengthened and the bunkhouse emptied itself of its tenants, setting off one by one for the cool draughts and beguiling sensations of the pleasure palaces of Odessa, he would stand on the porch, leaning against a post, and watch them go with furtive eyes, shaking his head and mumbling, "Naw, I ain't lost nothin' in Odessa."

Long about sundown he would dress himself and announce to any stragglers left that he was going into Coker City to get himself some cigarettes and have himself *one* beer and a bowl of chili and come home and go to bed.

Invariably it seemed he ran into a situation in Coker City that made having just one beer a virtual impossibility. "A man buys you a beer, you got to buy him one. Well, ain't that only right? Then he buys you another one. What the hell you gonna do? Act a horse's-ass an' not treat him back?"

By nine o'clock, nine beers later, the old fever was hard upon him and he was looking for a ride into Odessa. Sometimes he caught a ride with a late-returning mud hauler or maybe an acid truck just coming off a new well. He sat high in the cab beside the driver swigging en route from a new bottle, talking loud and palpitating like an old gasoline engine to the excitement of the night, eager for the bright lights of Odessa as a boll weevil with nothing on his mind but women.

Somehow, some time between sundown Sunday and break-out time Monday morning, Ort would make his way back to camp, broke, dead drunk, and more often than not, badly scratched about the face, battered and bloody. With lank hair hanging in his watery, red-rimmed eyes, his "dress" clothes torn and dirty, he looked a breathing, staggering Sunday school example of weak man addicted to the fleshpots of life.

Jim McNeely's Saturday nights followed a pattern as fixed as Ort Cooley's, though as different as possible. To Jim McNeely the weekend was a wasted time, a time of impatience. He took care of his personal housekeeping, carrying dirty work clothes to the nearest rig for laundering in a steam blow-out barrel. He sent his paycheck off to the bank when it was payday, the endorsing, the filling out of the deposit slip, and the mailing of these with the little red savings book and stamped, self-addressed envelope, performed with the care and precision of a young priest celebrating the mass. When it was possible he lined himself up to accompany one of the company engineers or geologists on a Saturday or Sunday morning job out in the field, seeking always to learn something. Or if nothing was going on, he sat and jawed with Dent Paxton, sitting in Dent's room, with the wind blowing softly through the screen door, talking idly, as if life would last forever, trying, usually without success, to get Dent off his behind to go into Coker City to eat supper, just because it was Saturday night, and because it was a fair chance to escape the unvarying boredom of camp boardinghouse fare. If Dent wouldn't go, Jim McNeely sometimes went alone, and sometimes he didn't.

It hadn't always been this way. In his early days at Dead Lake, three and a half years ago, Jim McNeely had yielded to the vague, restless desire to go and taste the honeysuckle, to seek the solace of a woman's feel and smell, and immerse himself in the excitement of a thronging Saturday night town where cold-eyed men made a profit from providing commercial temptations of the flesh that helped a working stiff forget for a few hours the hardness of his life. The pull was very strong. But it also meant a week wasted. It meant that all the money he had sweated for since Monday morning went down the drains of pleasure on Saturday night.

And then came this miserable Saturday night at the old Tascosa. He had gone there, pleasure bent, and soon embarked upon a project of buying sweet-wine for a plump, steely-eyed little honkeytonker named Sybil. He sat in a booth shelling out his money for shot-glasses of diluted Coca-Cola at twenty-five cents a shot, speculating as he watched her toss them off how many more he would have to buy before he could rightly proposition her for something worthwhile. When he figured she was about primed, somebody called her away from the booth. A few minutes later he heard a great commotion and a screaming outside the front door. He got up and went with everybody else to see what was happening.

Outside in the graveled parking lot under the glare of the naked light bulb over the entrance he saw a big roughneck working Sybil over vigorously. The man was drunk and cursing violently. He slapped the girl's chubby face, backhand and forehand, hard and repeatedly, all the while calling her a cheating little whore and worse, and she screaming and spitting and kicking at him. When he finally slapped her down, she grabbed his leg and sank her teeth in a fleshy part and he let out a roar and fetched her a kick in the ribs that sent her sprawling and shrieking in the gravel with her skirt up around her waist.

Jim McNeely had a natural sympathy for anyone who was getting beat up, and when he saw his investment being thus maltreated he moved out of the crowd and stepped in front of the roughneck just as he was getting ready to belt the girl again. Shoving the big man back with both hands Jim McNeely measured him carefully then drove a fist, hard as he could, straight into the man's stomach. In return he received a vicious roundhouse blow high on the forehead. It stung but didn't hurt him, so he set himself and triggered a short left that had all of his shoulder and forearm behind it, a clean blow that caught the roughneck flush on the jaw. The big man hung in the air for a second, then went into a slow half-gainer and piled up in the dirt on his head, out cold. When it was clear that he was finished for the night two of his buddies who were not looking for a fight themselves loaded him into the back seat of their car and drove away.

It was an exhilarating, if ridiculous and somewhat troubling, experience for Jim McNeely. Busting a total stranger over a honkytonker, who probably had it coming to her anyway, bothered him considerably. Yet it made him aware of his new strength, and at the moment it heightened the animal urge of Saturday night which was already tickling its little fingers into his groin. He immediately became Sybil's champion, and she immediately became his woman. She attached herself to him like a passionate female leech, fiercely tender, possessive, and in a little while she took him off with her to one of the cabins out in the back of the honkytonk and proceeded to show him her gratitude, by giving him the clap.

It required three months, and most of his paychecks after the stinging started, before the doctor gave him a clean bill of health. To say nothing of the pain, inconvenience, and mortification which the malady, oddly called social, cost him. Three hard months shot! Everything set back ninety days, timetable, saving schedule, plans, ambition—just to get rid of an infection which, when he reflected on it, hadn't really been much fun to catch.

He never again voluntarily went honkytonking in Odessa after that, except on very special occasions, like Ort Cooley's forty-seventh birthday or Pluto's departure, and then he gave the sweet-wine pigs a wide berth.

9

OUT OF THE SEARCH AND THE PROFIT FEVER AND through years of trial and a few successes and many failures, oil men slowly learned that oil was most likely found in "highs" or arches in deeply buried sedimentary marine rocks, formed by the deposition of silts and sands and limy shells on the floors of ancient seas. And so, out of necessity, a new sub-breed, a practical scientist offspring of hard-rock geology called a petroleum geologist, came into being, a fellow who could read rocks at the surface and make a little better guess than a blacksmith-turned wildcatter about the nature and conformation of the rocks at depth.

These geologists identified and catalogued the old rock layers by name and age and began to understand them a little better with each hole that was drilled. And when, scattered across the country, pecking with their pick-hammers at the outcrops in dry creek beds and cliffs, they discovered an area of old marine sediments, they diligently mapped the surface with plane table and alidade, and if they found a surface swell, they said, "Drill here," figuring that if it was "high" on the surface, it might be "high" down below, too. And often enough to earn their keep they were right, and in time they became a kind of priesthood to the growing young economic giant that came to be called the *oil business*.

The wells the oil men drilled didn't go very deep at first, because the drilling tools were primitive, by modern standards, and they could pierce and tap only the shallow beds. But with ingenuity sharpened by the prospect of more profits from the growing demand for more oil to fuel and lubricate the spawning population of tin lizzies, another new subgenus, called petroleum engineers, soon devised new techniques and equipment that could drill deeper and get at the more deeply buried oil and bring it to the surface, once the geologists had found it.

When most of the obvious surface expressions of subterranean "highs" had been drilled—and not all of these produced oil by any means—some bright, profit-motivated minds reasoned that there must be oil traps down below that weren't reflected in any way at all on the surface, and so an even more sophisticated sub-breed was born, a mixture of practical geologists and engineers and earthquake seismologists, who came to be called "doodle-buggers," and, more properly, geophysicists.

With secretive cunning this new hybrid learned how to create miniature earthquakes with dynamite, and to record the resultant shock waves that rebounded from deeply buried rock layers, and to make from the recorded wiggles on a paper tape some kind of an educated guess about how things set down below. And often enough to make it profitable for the oil men and oil companies to hire them and pay their keep, they too were right, though even when they were right and found a "high" in the buried rocks where oil by rights ought to be, the oil, irrationally and expensively, often as not was not there. In the end it was only the drill that could tell for sure.

This drilling cost money, and, as the holes searched deeper, it cost big money. The failures were many and costly, but the rewards of success when it came were great, and in a few short years the business of finding and producing oil became a serious factor in the economic metabolism of that part of the world called civilized.

In the process a few men got big rich, and a lot more went broke, wildcatting for the stuff. And that, roughly, is how after several hundred millions of years of geologic and evolutionary preparation of mineral, vegetable, and animal, the oil business got started and in less than a century grew into a major aid or distraction, depending on how you looked at it, to poor old sapient Homo in his wandering quest for salvation.

It was another Saturday night and Ort Cooley sat in the Club Cafe pulling on beer number eight and regaling Jim McNeely and Dent Paxton with a continuous line of chatter as they consumed their supper of chicken-fried and shoestrings.

"The reason I'm so pore an' measly," said Ort, setting his bottle down and wiping the back of his hand across his mouth, "Is because my daddy was such a tight ol' sonofabitch. Tight as the bark on a tree." He shook his head. "I bound ye! He use to give me ten cents not to eat supper. Then th' ol' bastard charged me a dime fer my breakfast! Meanest man that ever lived! It's a wonder I growed up at all."

"Pity you did, you old liar," said Dent Paxton, forking the last bite of meat from his plate.

"I ain't lyin'! I'll take a paralyed oath!" said Ort, jabbing a crooked-jointed finger at Dent. Suddenly he broke off. His head swiveled sharply and he almost fell out of his chair. He gave a quavering falsetto cry. "*Ma-a-an!* Looky yon-der!" Jim McNeely and Dent stopped chewing and followed his gaze in respectful silence.

The young woman who had suddenly claimed the focus of six eyes had just got up from a booth at the rear of the cafe and was passing along the counter toward the cashier's stand.

"Shee-hoo!" Ort exclaimed again. "Boys, all I want fer Christmas this year is a little piece o' that!" He gave a couple of sharp yelps like a moon-crazed Indian.

"You moron!" hissed Dent. "Shut that big idiot mouth! You know who that is?"

The only sound Jim McNeely made was, "Mm-*mmh!*"

All three continued to watch as the young woman took her change from the cashier, then put it in her small purse and went toward the door. Their eyes followed her through the window as she turned down the board sidewalk and disappeared in the direction of the drugstore.

"Man!" said Ort, religiously. "Ma-*an!*"

"A real athlete," murmured Jim McNeely.

"If they cut you bastards' heads open," said Dent Paxton, "wouldn't anything come out but cockroaches!"

Yet for the moment all three sat in a kind of subdued tribute, as if they had seen a moving work of art. The young woman truly was a thing to watch. It was as much the easy unself-conscious grace with which she carried herself as it was the full, perfectly proportioned, narrow-waisted figure with which she was endowed. She walked straight, but easily rather than primly or proud, under perfect control, yet obviously unaware of herself.

She was neither short nor tall. She wore a simple wash dress with a narrow belt, and her slender stockingless legs and firm bare arms were brown from the sun.

Jim McNeely caught only a glance at her face, but his impression was that she was not pretty. Not as Mazie was pretty. She had an almost Italian look. The look of a young Italian beauty who has spent her life in a villa by the sea, and lived much in the sun. Her brows were dark and thick and her nose definitely aquiline. Her short, nearly black hair had the slightest wave in it. No, she definitely was not pretty.

"Man!" sighed Ort finally.

"You illiterate sex maniac," said Dent Paxton. "That happens to be the wife and private property of our new field engineer, Clyde Montgomery. He's on a well up in Andrews County tonight and when he gets back he ought to whip your ass for what you're thinking. That goes for both of you!"

"How do you git to be a engineer?" said Ort. "I'm puttin' in fer engineer tomorrow!"

"She's worth looking at. That's for sure," said Jim McNeely.

"Yeh, but you can't look at too much of that," said Ort. "It's too strong. Rot yer danged eyeballs out."

Jim McNeely stretched his chest and drew a deep breath. "Thinkin' about it ain't gettin' any. Let's go to camp, boys."

Ort Cooley pushed back from the table and stood up. "Now you fellers jes' go on ahead. I got a little business to transack over at Odessa." He winked slyly at Jim McNeely. "An' whilst I'm there I might jes' look me up a little. Feller needs a little now an' then to take the strain off hisself." With that he strode to the cashier's stand, the beginnings of unsteadiness showing in his gait. Then he paid for his beers and disappeared through the door into the night.

Dent Paxton shook his head. "There goes a man," he said, "that's got all of his brains in the head of his pecker."

The two friends walked slowly down the nameless street of Coker City in the late spring night. The town had grown older and uglier since Jim McNeely first cast dismayed eyes upon it three and a half years ago. The street was now a wide, rutted road full of chug holes that could break an axle and was periodically sprayed with slush-pit oil to keep the dust down. Low banks of oily dust lapped against the buildings on either side, where it had been wind-drifted, like brown snow.

For a quarter of a mile the road was lined with corrugated iron buildings and wooden shacks. Only a few had been prettified with paint or board sidewalks. The best of them were semi-portable establishments of the oil-field sutlers, who migrated from one boom to another. Besides the Club Cafe there were two other grease-stained eating houses, a couple of clothing and general dry goods stores, one run, inevitably, by a Mr. Cohen and the other by a Mr. Weinberg. There was also a dusty drugstore and a picture show currently featuring Bob Steele in "Outlaw Code." The only hotel was a long two-story structure thrown up in haste out of number three lumber and tar paper, with profit rather than comfort or architectural beauty in mind. The street petered out into the prairie with two welding shops, a mechanic's garage, a filling station, a grocery store, Tyrone's Barber Shop, and a few buildings with glassless windows like sightless eyes, already abandoned by business failures.

Behind the central street to the east lay the residential district, a disordered array of dwellings that followed no recognizable pattern of streets. There were several apartments that resembled large packing crates with doors and windows cut in their paintless sides. But for the most part, the citizens of Coker City lived in trailers and tent houses. These were the homes of the drillers and roughnecks and tool pushers who would sink their wells in Dead Lake and move on to new fields. Home could never mean more to these migratory yeomen of the oil patch than a place to get in out of the wind, out of the heat and cold, a small place of privacy from the world in which to sleep, to eat, to make love. It never failed to amaze Jim McNeely to see parked in front of these meager dwellings new and shiny Buicks and Packards, and occasionally, even a Cadillac. The glossy surfaces of their cars reflected the roughnecks' pride. They returned from their daily labor mud-spattered and oil-stained, and their toilets were privies out in back, but they rode in the carriages of bankers and tycoons. This, at least, they could do to make up to their women for the hardness of their lives.

Walking unhurriedly along the slatted sidewalk toward the filling station at the end of the town, where they would, in a while, catch a ride back to camp with some late-returning pumper, the two young men passed the open door of the pool hall and heard the click of balls and saw the men bending over the green baize under the coning light. They breathed the cool night air flavored with the rich, meaty smell of casing-head gas drifted in from the field.

As they moved in and out of the lights along the way Jim McNeely was filled with a comfortable, if temporary, sense of well-being. He felt almost at peace. For he sensed that he was working in a necessary phase of his life, and working well in it, and that the phase was not yet at an end. And so at this moment he was not tormented by the old restlessness and impatience and urgency to move ahead, nor yet by the fear and uncertainty which would come again when the time to move arrived.

It would arrive, inevitably, in good season. But now, in this plateau of time, there was no pressure to worry about that, and he would come to look back upon these months as the best time in his life, when, for a while, he had been able to enjoy just being young and strong and alive, hopeful and innocently confident, ungnawed by the buried worries that come when a man's affairs grow increasingly complex and increasingly important to him, and his powers and influence increase and spread with age, and he cannot stand still but must keep pumping furiously forward, like a bicycle rider with feet chained to his pedals, who knows that when he stops he will fall over. Jim McNeely would never in his life smell the gassy aroma of raw petroleum on the wind without feeling a pang of nostalgia for these days of his life. They savored of the wine of youth, and of hope.

Later, the two sat on the porch at the bunkhouse, leaning back against the posts, looking out through the pleasant spring darkness at the winking spires of the lighted rigs in the field, not talking much. Jim McNeely this night felt a vague physical restlessness, not altogether unpleasant, that arose from the long unanswered call to love deep in his body. The after-image of the stirring young woman he had seen in the Club Cafe still lingered in his head.

He considered an idea that persistently pushed itself to the front of his thoughts; that there was still time to get into Odessa tonight and do some fundamental things with a woman, then firmly rejected it. Yesterday he had made a deal with Bud Shirley, one of the well-sitters, to go out on a job with him about midnight when a new producer would be ready for testing.

The men who worked through the long lonely night hours, often sitting up with a sick well, liked his company and were glad to take him along. These outings distracted his mind from the youthful heat in his groin, and they kept him out of the honkytonks, and out of trouble, and saved his money. They helped to fill the long, lonely Sundays, too, because he usually didn't get to bed til daylight, and Sunday could be used up in sleep. Monday mornings he would be fresh and ready to go again in the gang.

It was funny, and satisfying, too, to look back over three and a half years and see how he had come to be the lead hand, the stabber, in Cap Bruner's gang. What made it funny was that Cap had hated his guts every step of the way, but hadn't been able to keep him down. In the process Cap's personality had changed from merely ugly to that of a man who lived in a state of black, constant fury. The reason Cap hadn't been able to deny him was that Jim McNeely was a better lead hand than Buster Drum had ever been. The men worked with him and not against him. Cap knew this, and beyond merely infuriating him, the knowledge made him uncertain and afraid. He had to get the work out to survive. It made him dangerous, too, because Cap wouldn't admit this, even to himself.

Jim McNeely still thought of Buster sometimes, and when he did, he felt a kind of vague guilt about him. Buster had never been the same after the showdown in the ditch. It was as though something had been broken in him that didn't heal right—his confidence in his physical dominance of life, his essential animal courage. After that encounter he became a kind of sullen, addled giant of whom nobody was afraid any more. Jim McNeely saw this, and felt a certain uneasy responsibility about it—for spoiling something that was really kind of magnificent, even if it was bad, in this world. And sometimes he felt almost sorry about it, though he didn't know why he should, and told himself that he had had no choice, because he had been fighting for his life.

The accident that happened later was possibly the most fitting and humane way out for Buster Drum, and also for that pitiful and insignificant litter-runt, Peaches Dendy. It was ironical that what happened to Buster and Peaches was Cap's doing. It was he who had given his favorites the cool job on a sun-blistered day of going into the well cellar to bolt a Christmas tree on top of a casing-head flange of a new well, while the rest of the gang sweated in the naked August sun a mile down the road, back-filling a flow-line ditch.

No one understood, in those early days in the Dead Lake field, how poisonous the well gas really was. Moreover, it was not reasonably foreseeable that the valve on the casing head would have a leak in it, or that the escaping gas would accumulate in the cellar on this unusually humid and windless day. And so a slow-witted man like Cap Bruner could not, in justice, be held accountable for the tragedy, though it didn't help his standing with the "Comp'ny" any. When the gang truck returned to the well to pick up Drum and Dendy at quitting time, the two were found curled up like children gone to sleep around the iron base of the Christmas tree, and they were as lifeless as yesterday's catch of crappie.

After the first shock of excitement, and the momentary, truly regretted elation had worn off, Jim McNeely found himself feeling very bad about Buster's death. Though they had been enemies in life, Jim McNeely had been deeply involved with Buster. They had been engaged together in solving the gigantic, mercilessly complicated riddle of how to live on this earth. And the experience of helping to carry Buster's lifeless form, like a cooled-out carcass of beef, up out of that cellar had shaken him. The fact of death itself, here, in his hands, chilled his warm inner coils and made him think about things he didn't like to think about. He had seen his mother die. But she had lived her time, and had been old and sick. She had wasted away slowly, slipping out of life in a stupor of agony. In her case, death had its reasons. But Buster Drum was young and filled with the vital tension of life, just as he, James Albert McNeely, was filled with it, and this death troubled him, and turned his thoughts to the consideration of ultimate purposes and reasons, which was distracting and debilitating. It got his mind off of where he was heading, and of how he was going to get there, and the importance of it.

He was scantly consoled in his unease of spirit by Ort Cooley, who mused that night when they were alone, after the Odessa undertaker's "meat wagon" had carted the bodies away: "I always wanted to live longer than Buster. So I could call him a *dead son-of-a-bitch!*"

After the tragedy Jim McNeely had succeeded naturally and inevitably, and without Cap's counsel or encouragement, to the position of lead hand left vacant by Buster Drum. With his natural physical dexterity and quickness, and his far better than gang-level intelligence, sharpened by the lessons of his apprenticeship, and his driving desire and newly grown into manhood strength, there could be no other choice. That this came to pass despite the open hostility of Cap Bruner, whose hatred for him had not diminished but deepened into a twisted obsession, was the source of satisfaction and growing self-confidence to Jim McNeely. He had not made the slightest gesture of reconciliation or compromise toward the pusher. He made it perfectly clear that he was not "his man" and never would be.

He had proved Cap's predictions about him to be patently absurd, and had shown Cap's pronouncements about the incompetence of the head office to "har' a man worth his salt" to be ridiculous.

Cap had to get the work done, and Jim McNeely was one of those born-competent people who could take hold of a job and push or drive or wrestle it through to completion. And so Cap went along with the inevitable, his hatred sulling and festering in him, biding his time, waiting out his chance, his excuse to wreak his vengeance and justify himself.

Dent Paxton went through the screen door into his room and a few moments later came back out into the light-and-dark patches of the porch, swirling a drink in his hand, sipping it tentatively. With a puckering frown he uttered a short sound of distaste. This was directed not at the drink but at his friend who was leaned back against a post, one thigh drawn up, the other foot resting on the ground. He was studying a small red savings-bank book by the light that came from the room. "It seems to me," said Dent testily, "that a young man with any juice in him would be in town on a Saturday night pleasurin' the girls instead of sitting out here counting his money. What's the matter? You queer for money?"

"Screw you, buddy."

"How much have we got now?"

Jim McNeely canted the book to get the light. He said, "Three thousand two hundred and twenty-one dollars and twenty-one cents. Got a little interest last time. Twenty-nine sixteen. They wrote that down in red. I guess that's because it gives 'em the red-ass to have to pay out that interest."

Dent sat down and backed up against the next post and worked himself into a comfortable position. He set his glass on the porch, took out a cigarette and tapped it against his wrist watch. The flaring match lighted his pale narrow face. He flipped the match out into the darkness and drew carefully on the cigarette.

"Tell you what let's do, buddy," he said. "Let's you and me take that thirty-two hundred and go down to old Mexico. I been there. We'll get us a big house with plenty of tequila and some cute little *muchachas* to fetch it, and man, we'll have us a time. On what you got in that bank book we can live like a couple of hi-larious *hidalgos* for a year. Maybe more. Sleep on silk sheets and eat chicken *mole* every day."

75

"And when it's gone what'll we do?"

"Why then you come back out here and save up another thirty-two hundred and we'll go again."

Jim McNeely gave a derisive laugh. He closed the little bank book and slipped it back in his shirt pocket and buttoned the flap.

"I reckon not," he said. "This dough is for a one-way ticket outa this place. When I got enough."

Dent was silent for a while, and when he spoke the banter was gone from his voice. "A ticket to where? What's the next stop?"

"I'm not a hundred percent sure yet. I got some ideas."

"What's enough? How much?"

Jim McNeely didn't answer for a while. This was a question he had asked himself many times. He had a number in mind, but it was different from the one he had been thinking about last winter, and both were different from the one he had had in mind a year ago. He kept upping the figure, and he had begun to wonder if he would ever arrive at a sum that would satisfy him. And he had even begun to wonder if he didn't keep raising the number because he was afraid to break off and take the plunge. At this moment he was not ready to commit himself, to himself or to Dent.

"More than thirty-two hundred," he said. "Less than thirty-two million."

Dent sat another while in silence, slowly sipping his drink, giving his friend a long narrow-eyed look across the darkness.

"The next thing I'd like to know," he said at length, "is what do you plan to do with that little bitty fortune that you've dug out of the big money-mountain? Grub-stake yourself for a great business enterprise, I presume. Get your start up the ladder of life, to where you can hack out a bigger chunk of this marvelous geetus. Come to think of it, that's a silly question. You got Horatio Alger written all over you. Sickeningly. Well, what do you aim to end up with? Where? What are you really going for? Have you ever thought about that? Can you tell me?" He put down his glass and looked at Jim McNeely, his head cocked like a small sardonic owl.

Irritated, Jim McNeely said, "The hell with you and your silly questions. Let me ask you some. What have you got to show for all the dough you've made out here and pooped off once a year, going to New York and all, making out like you're a rich bastard? In two weeks it's all gone. What are *you* gonna end up with?"

"Fun, while it lasts. Pleasant memories of a happy time. Anticipation of another year to come."

"Where's that getting you?"

"Depends on where you want to get *to*, buddy. That's what I'm asking *you*. What are you working your tail off for? What are you driving at? You tell me that and we'll have a basis for understanding one another. Tell me. You must have something in mind."

"Oh, bullshit!" Jim McNeely threw up both hands in a gesture of irritation. He didn't like to be pinned down and examined like a bug under a microscope, and he did not like being pressured into thinking about things in this asinine analytical manner.

"OK. O-*kay!*" said Dent defensively. "Don't face facts. I don't give a damn. You've hung on here in this godforsaken spot for a long time now. It must be for some reason, and it surely isn't because you like it. You've put up with a lot of crap and broken your back for *something*. How come? What's your goal? What's your ultimate destination, buddy?"

Jim McNeely got up and gave Dent a contemptuous look. Then he turned down the porch as if he were leaving. After a few paces he stopped, kicking at the floor, angrily. He wheeled around and walked back, scowling at Dent. With one hand he unbuttoned his pocket and took out the bank book. He looked at it a moment, then shook it, emphatically, right at the tip of Dent Paxton's nose.

"All right, you smart, inquisitive little bastard. Since you asked me, I'll tell you. I want more of *this*. Money! A hell of a lot more just like it. All I can get my hands on!"

"A-ha!" cried Dent, rising to the challenge, thrusting up his glass, as if in a toast. "There we have it! The skeleton totters out of the closet! We are come to the heart of the matter. You are going to corral yourself lots and lots of green stuff, federal lettuce, crisp and cool. That's what it's all about. Now, at the risk of seeming puerile and impertinent, may I ask you—*why?*"

"Oh, hell," breathed Jim McNeely with sudden resignation. "You're really full of hot air tonight!"

"Are you real sure it's hot air, buddy?" said Dent tenaciously, getting up and warming to his subject. "Why do you want money? You're intelligent. You don't do things without a reason. If you've got a reason, you're bound to know what it is, provided you've got guts enough to face up to it. You want money. But it's clear you don't want the pleasure money will buy you, because you're hoarding it instead of spending it, now, while you're young, in the good-time part of your life, when you could get more pleasure out of money than you will, ever again, as long as you live. Why? Why do you really want money?" Dent stood staring at him, aroused, wide-eyed, his arms out from his sides.

Jim McNeely returned the stare. In a level voice edged with anger he said, "Because, you stupid horse's-ass, money makes you somebody. Because when you've got money you're something. And not any half-assed, insignificant philosophical field clerk that plays like he's somebody-come, for two weeks out of fifty-two. And because when you've got it in the bank people respect you, and they're afraid of you, and you carry some weight, and nobody runs over you, and you've got a place in the world and nobody's gonna shove you out of it. Does that answer your stupid goddamn question?"

They stood staring tensely at each other for several seconds.

In a queer voice Dent said, "That's a reason?"

Glaring back at him Jim McNeely said, "It'll do until you come up with a better one."

Of a sudden Dent's tension seemed to collapse.

"I just thought I'd ask," he said meekly, and turned and went into his room.

10

HOW IT CAME TO WEST TEXAS WAS THAT A COUPLE of men named Haymon Krupp and Frank T. Pickrell came into possession of some oil and gas permits covering 431,000 acres of drouth-ridden sheep range belonging to the University of Texas, way out in the middle of nowhere west of San Angelo. That was 1919. Knowledgeable people in the oil business would laugh at you in those days if you tried to sell them any kind of an oil deal west of Ranger, because there wasn't any chance of finding important oil out there. Everybody knew that. But Frank Pickrell, who was the gall and go-ahead member of the partnership, was a man with more than his share of imagination, and a real talent for stimulating the easy-money instinct in his fellow man. So he went all the way to New York and set about exerting his persuasive abilities in order to raise the financing for a well. It took a while (the well was not drilled until 1923), but he finally promoted the wherewithal from a group of Easterners who some oil men said obviously had more money than brains. It didn't turn out that way.

There are several versions of how the Santa Rita Number 1 came to be drilled where it was drilled. Most of the versions have been vigorously denied by the people involved. But the tradition is strong and persistent, and the country out there is so big, with such a sameness and such a dearth of surface geologic features to base a location on, that there is room at least to wonder if maybe Saint Rita, the Patron Saint of the Impossible, didn't have something to do with the success of the wildcat, as well as the geologist who claimed it was drilled right where he drove the stake.

In any case, there are still old wrinkle-necked tool-dresser types around the cafes in Big Lake and McCamey who will tell you that they know what happened, and that it was Santa Rita, or blind-luck one, and not any geology that brought in Frank Pickrell's gusher. What they say is that the flatcar on the freight train bearing Pickrell's drilling rig westward out of San Angelo was dropped off on a siding some miles from the place Pickrell planned to drill. The rig was immediately loaded on wagons and headed for the location because the permits were going to expire if Pickrell wasn't making hole by midnight of that day. The story goes on to say that long before he reached the appointed place Pickrell's transport broke down, and that since he was fast running out of time, he unloaded and set up and started digging right there on the spot. Long after Santa Rita Number 1 came in, flowering green oil over the crown block, the old-timers will tell you, another well was spudded where the first one was meant to be drilled, and turned out to be as dry as popcorn.

If that first well had been a duster, the opening of the Permian Basin as a major oil province would probably have been a long while postponed. Sooner or later somebody would have stumbled onto it. Wildcatters are a stubborn and hungry breed. But Frank Pickrell was the one who did it, whatever the true story is, and all those big limestone buildings on the University of Texas campus are a monument to his daring and his vision and his luck.

It is not unfitting to consider it so, because Frank Pickrell was a great adventurer and a gambler, cut from the same tough cloth as Columbus and Drake and Vasquez de Coronado. It may be that if he hadn't run out of time to get that first well started, nobody would remember him, and he would take his place among the nameless men who gambled their lives for a rich dream and lost. But as it turned out he was responsible for starting a chain of events that changed the character of a sizable piece of the earth.

It was another Saturday night, or rather it had started out as Saturday night and was now into the dark early hours of Sunday morning, and Jim McNeely was out at one of the drilling rigs with a geologist named Wakely, who had driven out to Dead Lake from the district office in Midland to supervise the taking of a drill-stem test. The well was a mile and a half west of the nearest production in the main field, and was referred to as a semi-wildcat, because the geologists weren't sure the field extended out that far. They thought it did, based on the angle of dip of the producing horizon in the field, but there were also indications that there might be a fault, or displacement of the beds at depth, along the west side of the field. But they weren't sure, and the company's leases in this area were due to expire before the end of the year unless production was established on them. The only thing to do was drill a hole and find out what was down there.

Jim McNeely stood in the iron doghouse a little distance from the rig, looking over Wakely's shoulder as the geologist drew schematic lines on the back of an old driller's log. Outside, across a space of cold, bare ground, the battery of boilers had up a full head of steam, and up on the rig floor the draw works chuffed mightily as the drilling crew, moving like trained athletes under the ghostly glare of floodlights, went about their business of lowering forty-two hundred feet of drill pipe back into the hole.

The crew had been standing by, waiting for them when they drove up to the rig just after midnight. The drill pipe stood racked in the derrick in ninety-foot thribbles like giant black stems of spaghetti. When Wakely gave the word, the driller and the two floor men and the derrick man on his thribble-board high overhead had swiftly gone into action, picking up the first stand of pipe with the steam-powered traveling block, making up the testing tool and rubber packer assembly on the bottom of it, then letting the tool, packer, and attached pipe slide into the mud-filled hole. Then, stand at a time, they began to screw the remaining thribbles into the lengthening stem of pipe, rapidly lowering four-fifths of a mile of the hollow steel tube, dry, toward the bottom of the hole, in preparation for the test.

"You see here," said Wakely, sounding like a schoolteacher as he sketched out the situation on paper at the rough stand-up desk called the "knowledge box." "We pick up the top of the pay over in the field at about 4215 feet. That's the top of the San Andres formation, a limestone of Permian age just below a dense black shale body. Over there we get a forty-foot oil column in the lime and below that the ocean. That's roughly speaking, of course. What I mean is that the San Andres, which is very porous over there, is like a thick layer of more or less spongy rock with oil in the top forty feet floating on the heavier salt water underneath. So we normally run casing and cement it in the hole when we hit the top of the San Andres. Then we drill about twenty-five feet deeper into the pay formation and complete. That way we don't get down into the water, and the water won't break in until the reservoir is well along toward depletion—maybe ten or fifteen years from now, depending on how fast it is produced.

"The San Andres formation dips, or gets deeper, to the west, whereas the oil and water levels in it are horizontal, so the oil column in the formation gets thinner and will gradually play out as we go west. Normally we would just keep moving the rig west one well at a time until we ran out of the oil and then call it quits. But because these damn leases way out here on the west side will expire before we have time to do that in an orderly fashion, we've had to step way out here and punch this well down, to save the edge leases, if we can.

"That's just one of the many headaches in this business. If we don't drill, and these west-side leases expire, it'll cost the company fifty bucks an acre or more to renew 'em. And somebody else might outbid us, at that. These old ranchers have really smartened up about the oil business. They're mighty sharp traders. So we figure it's cheaper to drill this hole and run the risk it'll be dry than to have to try to renew the leases."

The geologist shrugged. "Well, we've cut the damn hole now, and we'll soon find out how smart we were, or how dumb. The immediate problem is whether we ought to spend *more* money to try and complete the well. That'll depend largely on what this test shows. But I'm getting ahead of myself."

He picked up a bulging linen sack the size of an apple from a cluster of similar string-tied sacks on the wooden bench at his side. Loosening the drawstring, he shook into Jim McNeely's hand a small mound of cuttings that looked like coarse gray river sand.

"In this well we picked up the top of the San Andres at 4242. You can see a little oil stain in these cuttings. Here, take a look through the microscope." Jim McNeely bent and peered into the eyepiece of the instrument on the desk-box, and though his untrained eye saw nothing that looked like oil to him, he grunted appreciatively. "There's a faint oil odor, too," said the geologist. "Smell." Obediently the younger man sniffed at the chat in his hand and nodded his head, though he smelled nothing at all.

Wakely continued. "Now you figure it out. Back in the high part of the field we hit the top of the San Andres at 4215 feet and salt water at 4255. Out here we hit the top at 4242. So, assuming the surface elevation is the same here as in the field—which it is—how much oil column should we have here, taking into account that the dip is normal—that is, the fault, or break in the bed, wasn't there after all?"

Jim McNeely twisted his ear and thought briefly. "Thirteen feet," he said.

"Well, I'll be damned," said Wakely, glancing curiously at his new young friend. "I went to college four years to learn how to do that. Hmm. You ought to be in geology. Well, anyway, thirteen feet of pay ain't so hot. Especially since those cuttings look pretty tight. Not near the porosity we've got back in the field. It won't make the company much money at best because the oil this well can ultimately produce depends on the thickness of the oil column and the porosity and permeability of the formation. And it'll cost a lot more money than has already been spent on the well to set casing and try to complete it. That's my worry right now.

"However, this is oil country, and if there's a fair chance this well will be commercial, that is, get our money back, we probably ought to go ahead and complete it, because of the deeper possibilities.

"What I mean by that is, there may be better pay zones down below the San Andres. We don't know too much about that yet, but there's no telling what deeper drilling in the future might uncover. There might be a regular layer cake of oil fields here, one on top of the other. It's happened in other places."

Jim McNeely hefted the sack of cuttings in his hand. His brow furrowed in a thoughtful frown.

"Who's gonna decide whether this well is a keeper or not?"

Wakely glanced at the young man sharply again and grinned. He was still a young man himself, less than thirty. With his metal-rimmed glasses he looked like a schoolteacher indeed, despite his rough khakis and mackinaw. Yet there were wrinkles of responsibility around his eyes and mouth.

"Me, I guess. Or me and this test we're about to take. I'll turn in the results and my recommendation. My bosses will make out like they're making the decision, but in the end they'll probably do what I recommend. If I'm right, they've made a smart decision. If I'm wrong, they've got somebody to blame. They're just human. If I'm wrong two or three times they may put me back to washing samples, or else I'll be hunting a new job. Come on, let's get some coffee."

They went out of the doghouse into the dark and walked in the cold, biting air of the early winter night to the boilers, which stood like four black locomotives without wheels, hissing and singing in a row a short way from the rig. Gas fires roared in their bellies and the lights flickering through their stokeholes made dancing squares of yellow light on the ground.

The pot-fireman, a wizened little man named Charley Vick, was moving busily along the catwalk in front of the boilers checking the pressure gauges and adjusting the gas and water valves. The heat of the boilers could be felt far out in the chill darkness as the two approached.

"How about a shot of coffee, Charley?" Wakely shouted over the singing of the imprisoned steam. The pot-fireman nodded and pointed to a large pot setting on a row of steam lines leading from the boilers toward the rig. Jim McNeely and the geologist poured themselves tin cups of the smoking liquid and moved a ways down the catwalk where there was less roar but still enough heat for comfort. They sipped gingerly at the blistering brew for a while, then Wakely said, "Y'know, since the last time you came out with me I've been thinking. How come you don't go to college? You pick this stuff up pretty fast."

Sitting with elbows on knees, swirling the hot coffee in his two hands, Jim McNeely looked at the ground and said, "I'm too old. Twenty-four is too old to start college. Anyway I'd have a year of high school to do before they'd let me in any college."

"Hell, you're not too old," said Wakely. "There was a fellow in my graduating class that was thirty-five."

Jim McNeely shook his head. "I'm too old. I got to take another route."

Wakely said dubiously, "You can't go anywhere in this company without college, my boy."

"So they tell me. So I got to make out some other way."

"You gonna quit the Company?"

"I'm not saying. Not yet, anyway. But I'm too old to go to college and start from scratch. That's for sure. Take too much time."

"Yeah," said Wakely, pushing at his high forehead with two fingers. "Maybe so. I've thought a lot about taking the plunge, myself. I mean about going out on my own. It's tough when you've got a wife and baby. But damn! I see a lot of possibilities."

Jim McNeely rocked back and grinned. "You keep those possibilities in mind. If you know where some oil fields are that nobody's found yet, maybe you and I can go find 'em one of these days."

The geologist grunted. "Fat chance a couple of broke bastards would have, trying to compete with these companies. To buy a halfway prospective lease block and drill a well on it would cost fifty, sixty thousand dollars. It keeps me in a hard strain trying to save fifteen dollars a month. Maybe in a hundred years we could get together enough dough to take a flyer as independent operators."

"Maybe, maybe not," said Jim McNeely. "There's bound to be ways. But you got to be willing to take a gamble. 'Course, that wife and baby—I don't know about that. If I had dependents I guess I'd think twice before I cut loose from a regular meal ticket. On the other side, I don't reckon you'll ever get rich sniffin' rocks for any company. Unless you figure on being a vice president one of these days."

"Nuts. I'm not the vice president type. You've got to be mean and smart and ambitious as hell. And have an extraordinary talent for ass-kissing without showing it too much. And be halfway unscrupulous. I'd never make it. I've got all those attributes except I'm not mean enough—I'm just a nice guy who wants to get along and do his job and serve his fellow man." He winked at his younger friend. "Let's go run this test. They're going in with the last thribble now."

Jim McNeely got up and followed the geologist up the steel ladder to the rig floor. As they came onto the drilling platform the floor men were making up the last stand of pipe with the floating tongs, powered by a rope wound around the cathead of the draw works. Then the tongs were disengaged and the driller hit the throttle and the fundamental power of the steam turbines compounded through the wire cable strung through the crown block high overhead and the massive traveling block, lifted the imponderable weight of the near mile of pipe hanging in the hole, then the floor men jerked free the slips which had clamped the pipe in the rotary table, and the driller, riding the brake, cut the throttle and let the traveling block come back down through the derrick pulled by the gravity power of the long string of pipe as it slid into the hole toward the bottom.

As the last stand of pipe disappeared beneath the floor into the well head in the cellar below, the driller leaned his weight carefully onto the brake handle, his eyes glued on the weight indicator on the derrick leg until the pipe was sliding into the earth slowly, inch at a time. When the arrow on the weight indicator flickered, then swept rapidly around the dial toward zero, the driller jammed his arm down on the handle and the pipe jerked to a stop.

"On bottom," he said curtly to the geologist. "Packer ought to be set OK."

Wakely nodded. One of the mud-spattered roughnecks clamped the jaws of the floating tongs onto the pipe with a piercing clang. The driller nodded and the roughneck leaned against the tongs and the pipe slowly turned, a quarter, half, three-quarters of a turn to the right. "Tool ought to be open OK now, Mister Geologist," said the driller, snubbing down the brake handle with a small chain.

"Very well, gents," said Berry Wakely crisply. "Let's go down to the slush pit and see if this baby is going to pee a little. We'll leave the tool open an hour, driller, unless she gets to snorting and raising hell, which I doubt very much she's going to do."

Jim McNeely followed the geologist and a roughneck down the steep stairway to the ground and picked his way over pipes and around machinery to the shallow diked pond where the drilling mud was mixed. An open-ended pipe extended from under the derrick floor and stuck out across the dike over the slush pit.

Wakely explained carefully and in detail to his friend as they waited how the formation four-thousand-plus feet below was now opened into the drill pipe so that any oil or gas trapped in it could come rushing to the surface. He took pleasure in instructing Jim McNeely, for he felt his words were not wasted but were being stored away to be put to good use in some future time.

Kneeling on the dike, his shadow under the cold floodlights stretching far across the mud pit, he held his hand over the open-ended pipe. "Feel here." Jim McNeely knelt beside him and felt.

"Just a little blow of air."

"You are so right, unfortunately. If this was gonna be a bitch-kitty it would be blowing a lot stronger by now, and in a few minutes we'd get some gas, then the oil would come. Some of the good wells over in the field flow a solid four-inch stream of oil, halfway across the pit five minutes after the tool is opened."

They sat on the dike and talked and every few minutes they felt the blow coming out of the pipe. The blow settled to a soft steady stream of air.

"Well, she sure ain't got much life," said Wakely, rising. "We'll leave her open an hour and give her every chance. Meantime there's no point sitting out here in the cold. Let's go to the fire and take on a little more of Charley's boiler acid."

They went back to the boilers where the entire drilling crew was now gathered, sitting or reclining on the catwalk in easy relaxation, drinking coffee. Among them was Jinks Gilbert, the derrick man, who had climbed the ninety feet down the steel derrick ladder to spend the hour in warm, comfortable repose and companionship rather than waiting in the icy solitude aloft. As the pair walked up he was giving the pot-fireman a ribbing that had more cruelty than humor in it.

Cutting his badger's eyes in Charley's direction, Jinks was talking, in laughter: "All I'm sayin' is that a man is entitled to *worry* some when he reaches a certain age, if his wife keeps having kids. 'Specially if he works *nights*. Afore he can feel comfortable a man needs to be sure he kin still git kids *hisself*. And stay around home nights to do the gittin'. That's all I'm sayin'."

Over by the number two boiler Charley Vick was peeling an apple with his pocket knife. When the derrick man's words sunk in he cut into the apple with the sharp blade, lopping it in two. Then he threw the pieces away angrily without eating them. Charley had a young wife, young enough to be his daughter. He also had two small children. He also worked nights. The young men of Coker City, cruel as children, took delight in deviling the old man about this. The cruel inference maddened him. Someday, people said, he would kill somebody over it. Wiping the apple juice off his knife against his pants leg, as if preparing the blade for warmer stuff, Charley walked toward the derrick man, his face a mask of fury.

"You oughta know better than to talk like that, Jinks," he said. Jinks whistled a silly tune and cast his eyes owlishly at a small cloud passing the moon, controlling a laugh and tensed to spring out of harm's way.

"One of these days you liable to git cut, Jinks," Charley said, in his frozen voice. "If you don't git to jigging around up there on that monkey board scratchin' your crabs and fall down and bust your fuckin' empty head open first. If you do, it won't be no loss to nobody but the crabs."

The derrick man decided to take the returned insult as a joke. A look of mock fright came on his face and he winked at the driller. At this point the driller thought it was time to break in. He was a big, amiable man, and while he didn't object to a good healthy fist fight among the boys now and then, cutting was something else. "Not to change the subject," he said, "did you all hear about that derrick man over at Hobbs fell outa the derrick las' Thursday night? Was a cud'n of Tom Gentry's wife. They say he cussed and squalled all the way to the ground."

The derrick man, still carefully watching Charley's knife from the comer of his eye, was glad enough to see the tension ease. He said, "You work derricks long enough an' that's the chance you got to take. You might fall. But I don't worry none about the fallin' part. It's them last two feet. That's what kills you."

The two other members of the drilling crew looked on with morbid interest, grateful that if there was going to be a cutting, they had ringside seats. With a sharp sense of timing and a natural desire to head off a senseless clash between men who had no real reason to hate one another or shed blood, Jim McNeely walked up to the pot-fireman and said, "Charley, how about another shot of that Arbuckle. Your coffee makes that messhall java taste like it ain't even trying."

Charley blinked with pleasure at the unexpected compliment, and the glass-hard tension was broken. The drilling crew drifted back to the floor and the hour passed. Then they closed the testing tool and began to draw the pipe out of the hole, the traveling block drawn upward by the steel cables and the power of the roaring steam engines lifted the glistening column up into the strained derrick where the pipe was unjointed and racked back stand at a time by the derrick man perched once again high on his monkey-board. As the drill stem emerged from the hole one of the floor men began a rhythmical jingling tattoo on the empty pipe with a ball-peen hammer in order to know when they reached the column of fluid trapped inside. When most of the pipe was out of the hole and stacked in deep rows in the derrick, the sharp ringing of the hammer turned suddenly to a dull clunking. Then the driller stopped the engine and they measured the place where the ringing stopped and the clunking started, then went on pulling the pipe, and after that when they unscrewed a stand of pipe the liquid inside sloshed down onto the floor, spattering everybody around with gray drilling mud at first, then as the pipe pulling continued, with greenish-black oil, smelling a little like rotten meat, only different, because there is no other smell exactly like the remains of sea anemones and vegetation and trees that have been cooking together for a hundred and twenty or thirty million years, when the kettle is first opened.

When it was all over, Berry Wakely, the geologist, wrote up the results in his little black book under the garish white light in the doghouse: "DST 4242-52 feet; open 1 hr.; fair blow of air in three minutes, diminishing in six minutes to weak blow which continued throughout test; recovered 30 feet drilling mud; 225 feet oil, no water. Rig now waiting on orders."

As they bounced over the caliche road in the early morning darkness toward Coker City, Jim McNeely said, "What you reckon you'll do now?"

Behind the wheel of the company car, Wakely didn't answer right away, then he said, "This kind separates the production geologists from the boys. I'm damned if I know. Haven't made up my mind. Anyway, between here and Midland I've got to decide what to recommend. A good swabbing might make this baby pick up, but it might bring in the ocean, too. I mean, we're pretty close to the salt water. What'd you do?"

Jim McNeely said, "Hell, if it was mine and my lease was running out and I had a shot at some deeper pays, I'd tease that baby into some kind of an oil well, any way I could. That is, if I had the money to gamble on setting pipe."

"Yeah, that's the hell of it. The money. The Company's got plenty of money to gamble. But if most of their gambles poop out they'll go as broke as a snake-bit wildcatter."

"Well," said Jim McNeely, grinning. "I reckon that's why they pay you experts fifty thousand a year. To make the right decisions."

"Horse-apples!" said Wakely. "I sweat over these blamed wells like they were my own, and I haven't even finished paying the baby doctor yet, and Kathy's near a year old."

They stopped in the all-night cafe in Coker City and ate breakfast in the last hour of darkness before sun-up. They talked, tired, satisfied, feeling a sense of camaraderie in having spent a meaningful night together, whatever its outcome.

Mopping up the last golden nectar of two fried eggs from his plate with a piece of light bread, Jim McNeely said, "This oil is funny, the way it lays. Here we are, sitting here. There's a good oil field less than a mile south. Gulf has a field of some kind about a mile and a half north. How come the two fields don't join up? Seems like we ought to be sitting right on top of some oil right here."

"No reason why not," said Wakely, giving his younger companion that close, quizzical look again. "The most successful money geologists are trend players. If you get an oil field that indicates some kind of a direction, that is, with a long axis, follow the line of the axis, and the hell with the theories. I've thought about this town area right here, myself. So have other people, and more than one company has tried to lease it. But old man Coker is a kind of a maniac. He owns this quarter section the town is on, but he just leases out the surface to the store and cafe and house-trailer and filling station owners. He hates the oil companies' guts, and oil men in general, with a passion. He says they've messed up the cow business out here. He won't even talk to our lease men. He runs a ranch spread over in Jarrett County and tells it around town he'll shoot the next oil company land man or broker that comes out to his place trying to lease any of his land, 'specially this piece. Bison doesn't give a damn. Gulf either. They'll drill up to the line of this little old quarter section, and if they can't lease it, they'll drain it, if there's any oil under it, with their offset wells. Oil isn't stationary in the formation, you know. The books call it a 'fugacious substance.' You put a straw down on two sides of a pan of water and suck, and you'll get what's in the middle, too, whether you put a straw down in the middle or not."

When Wakely let Jim McNeely out at the bunkhouse it was breaking first light. Purple shadows softened the hard lines of the familiar, ugly buildings of the Camp. Yellow light burned in a window of one of the row houses. Some early riser making coffee. There was no wind and the air was sparkling cold. Jim McNeely felt tired, and good. The night had been well spent and he was ready to sleep.

"Thanks for the company," said the geologist. "I'll let you know next time there's a job coming up on a weekend."

"Don't forget what I said," said Jim McNeely, winking, but more than half seriously. "If you figure out where there's a little old stray oil field laying around loose, you let me know. We might think up a way to latch onto it."

"Right," Wakely said, smiling. "Save your money and I'll call you up about ninety years from now."

After the geologist had gone, Jim McNeely went down the porch of the silent bunkhouse to his room. It was deserted. None of the Saturday night revelers had returned. He took a shower, raised the window by his bunk and went to bed.

As he lay stretched out between the coarse sheets, relaxed, waiting for sleep to come, his mind wandered over the surface of a hundred thoughts. Something made him think of Mazie, perhaps the hungering of his loins, unrequited these many months, sublimated but ever present. He had not heard anything about her in a long time. So far as he knew she was still in college. She would be a senior this year in the full bloom of her radiant young womanhood, a debutante, gay, laughing, excited by her youth and beauty and desirability. She probably hadn't even thought of him in months. The vague aching he felt when he thought of her never failed to come, but it was centered perhaps more nearly in his pride than in a sense of loss or of longing for the person of Mazie Wales, and the thought faded and shaded into a mental image of the dark-haired, full-bodied young woman with the sun-kissed skin and features of an Italian, who would be sleeping now, tawny, tender-warm in a bed not a hundred yards from where he lay. There was a woman. Lee Montgomery—he had learned her name now—and though he had never met her, he had seen her enough times that he felt entitled to nod and speak when they passed on the street in Coker City or when he saw her watering her tiny patch of grass in the evenings as he walked down the road past her house. It was the way in which people isolated together in camps gradually came to know one another and began to feel a kind of kinship, without being formally introduced. His imagination, dwelling upon her graceful sleeping form, excluded the light-haired, fuzzy-limbed man who undoubtedly was sleeping beside her. How a non-entity like Clyde Montgomery, even with his engineering degree and promising, steady future with the Company, had ever landed a woman like that was the Lord's mystery to Jim McNeely.

Yet as he sighed and stretched his broad smooth chest under the army blanket, he realized that the steady ache in him for a woman, a good woman like that, like Lee Montgomery, was just something he had to live with for a while, maybe a long while. He didn't like it, but he didn't know anything he could do about it now. He consoled himself with the thought that when he *could* do something about it, he would damn sure make up for lost time.

In the meantime there wasn't any use in indulging in mental masturbation about it. He swung his thoughts back to the disappointing well he had watched the geologist run the test on during the night. It had opened his eyes some. It made him see that sinking all of your money in one wildcat well was like putting your life's savings on the nose of a long shot at the race track. He would have to play it another way. A faint, hazy design to the business was beginning to form itself in his mind. The beginnings of some ideas of how he could somehow fit, squeeze, elbow, force, his way into the picture were beginning to emerge. He knew he had to gamble. But there were ways, being smart, that you didn't have to bet your whole life on one race. His two weeks' vacation the past summer had been enlightening.

11

STRANGE THOUGH IT SEEMS NOW, NO BIG BOOM HIT
West Texas after Frank Pickrell's well came blowing in. Not right
away, at least. West Texas was too much country, and most people
figured this Santa Rita strike was just a blind lucky stab into an isolated
puddle. But oil is oil. It draws men like blood draws flies from far off, and
soon the oil company scouts and geologists began to buzz around over
the broad dry plains to the west, and then a few more wildcatters and
promoters and hungry-eyed lease hounds began to drift into the area, and
a few more wells were drilled at widely scattered places, most of them dry,
and the ones that had any oil weren't anything to brag about. But some of
the dry ones cut a reservoir-type marine rock that set a few sharp people
to thinking.

One was a major company geologist named Ben Belt, a big bear of
a man who had blooded his spurs in oil down in the Golden Lane of
Mexico. He began to study the logs and samples from as many of these
scattered dusters as his company could lay hands on. He pondered the
broad, empty map of West Texas, scratched his lantern jaw, and pondered
some more. He spent days and weeks driving up and down the ranch
trails that snaked across the barren reaches, pondering and puzzling as
he followed the insignificant-looking Cretaceous outcrop, a kind of low
chalky ledge that ran like a faint scar up through the dry sameness of the
wasteland toward the New Mexico corner, trying to get some meaning
out of the country, trying to make the fragmentary bits of subsurface evidence and this surface outcrop, and his knowledge and experience gained
in other places, and the imaginative geologizing of the area that had been

done by some able young associates with such names as Harper, Dono-ghue, Fuqua, and Closuit, all add up to a picture that would hang together, of what was down there three, four, five, ten thousand feet below the bat-tered tires of his dusty old Dodge touring car.

Then all of a sudden it went together in his head, and he was taken by a conviction that had been all these weeks building up—that this was a giant geologic basin, a great synclinorium with buried structures in its depths, and that it could be a rich incubator of oil fields. When the con-viction firmed and held, he climbed in his car and drove all night into Fort Worth. The next morning, haggard and unshaven, he confronted his bosses and told them in a voice that must have been imperious and pro-phetic to get a crew of lease men the hell out there fast, with checkbooks in their pockets and authority to lease everything they could buy for four bits an acre in the vast area he outlined on the map.

It is said that Ben Belt had to do a lot of ranting and arm-waving before he got his point across, but he carried considerable weight with his company, and in the end his bosses proved themselves to be men of imagination and gall, too, and before the clock rolled around many times, a team of leasers headed by a top landman named Lourcey was on its way to West Texas. In two weeks' time they had slapped oil and gas leases on an expanse of range land big as a respectable-sized kingdom. Many of the drouth-ridden cowmen were deep in debt to their banks in that time and the four bits an acre kept more than one from going under.

Oil men "spook" easily, and when the other companies got wind of Ben Belt's lease play they joined in the leasing spree, more because they didn't want to be left out, in case Belt had something, than because they were really sold on the oil prospects of the area themselves. They called it taking "protection" leases. The result was that when all was done Ben Belt's company had bought the heart out of half a dozen giant oil fields, and some of the others ended up with sizable pieces of them just by playing follow-the-leader.

It was quite a spell before the picture fully developed and all this was revealed, because the Depression set in before too long and money was scarce, and so it was near the end of the ten-year primary term of the leases before the definitive wells were drilled and the story was finally told.

In any case, West Texas made Ben Belt's company from a merely big, reasonably successful enterprise into one of the giant companies of the world. And it was here that some of the middleweights that followed

Ben grew into heavyweights, too. Ben Belt did a lot more good work and eventually retired and died a respected pillar of his company and community, though he never was generally credited with being a kind of Cortez who sacked up the riches of a great subterranean continent after a kind of a wildcat-gambling Columbus named Frank Pickrell had run onto it.

Dent, good, silly old Dent, had taken off in a flap of almost feminine excitement for New York City, where he would blow the savings of a year's labor in one week of living like a scion of ancient wealth at the Plaza Hotel, riding taxicabs and eating raspberries and clotted cream for breakfast served in his room. Dent had done his best to get his single-minded friend to join him in this feasting time at the luxurious fleshpots, but Jim McNeely, with sardonic thanks, had declined the invitation and set out to find a vacation job that would add an extra two weeks' pay to his savings account.

Failing in this he had settled for the next best thing, which was to go to the cheapest place he could find and spend fourteen days of enforced idleness, meanwhile observing anything and everything he could that would, hopefully, add to his knowledge of the oil business, and advance his cause. Beyond his uninspiring associates at Dead Lake he knew not a single soul in the world outside of Winfield, and he had no desire to see anyone in that place of bitter defeats and depressing memories. Not yet.

So he went to Midland, Texas, thirty miles to the east, because he had heard that that was where the deals were made, and because that is where the cigarette salesman who picked him up at the gate of the camp was going, anyway.

Hot, dusty Midland was the last place on earth that an inmate of Dead Lake would have thought about as a vacation possibility, but that dry, spare town was, by accident of fate, the medulla oblongata of the oil business in the Permian Basin. While Odessa, a short distance to the west, was the work center, headquarters of the tin-hat breed, home of the supply houses, the service companies, the drilling contractors, Midland was the place where the trading in leases and royalties, all mysterious and incomprehensible as Arabic to Jim McNeely at this point, took place.

It had slowly dawned on him that this, somehow, was where men got rich by their wits. Out here at Dead Lake, in the oil patch, and around Odessa, men labored and sweated and dug holes and pumped oil out of the ground, and nobody got rich. There were no rich drillers or rough-necks. They merely traded their labor, their life force, and their simple competence for beans and beer. Jim McNeely meant somehow to break into the mystery of how the real money was made. He had no entree, no introduction to anyone, but he went to Midland. It was by instinct, perhaps. He took a room in a boardinghouse whose carefully lettered sign with backward Ss advertised clean beds with electric fans at five dollars per week, payment in advance.

He walked along the glaring, dust-powdered streets free in mind and body as thistledown floating in the hot air, past the sleepy courthouse with its patch of green lawn, along the main street which was also the straight track of US 80 as it arrowed westward toward Pecos and El Paso. A little later, he drifted into the Scharbauer Hotel coffee shop and sat at the white marble counter under the ceiling fans that turned slowly overhead. He made his late breakfast of coffee and doughnuts. Next to him, two wind-burnt men in faded levis and stained Stetsons supped blistering coffee and quietly deplored the price of steers on the Fort Worth market.

Later in the morning he sank into a worn leather chair in the lobby and passed an hour glancing through the Winfield paper and watching the tempo of the day build as ranchers and lease brokers and oil company scouts drifted in and out of the lobby, exchanging greetings and talking in little groups, unrolling their land maps and plats. A line of ranch types, some masters of desert cattle kingdoms, some thirty-dollar-a-month cowhands, with no visible difference between them, squatted on their bootheels along the wall of the corridor leading to the glaring street. They smoked, laughed, and hollered at late arrivers.

Jim McNeely folded his paper and stuck it beside the cushion for the next loafer, then got up and strolled slowly around the lobby listening in on snatches of the close talk of the little groups, straining to hear some-thing significant, something that would open his eyes and instruct him in the mysterious art that was being carried on here. He had heard it said that on a good day a million dollars or more would change hands in this hotel lobby.

Toward noon he found a vacant seat on a couch next to a fat, flabby man wearing a sweated-out pongee shirt and panama hat pushed back from a glistening forehead. The man was talking intently to an old rancher. The rancher, dressed in khakis that had been washed almost white and a stained buckskin Stetson, listened with weathered, expressionless face.

Poking a pudgy finger at the unrolled map in his lap, the fat man was saying that three dollars an acre bonus for a lease was more than the going rate and more than the land itself had been worth a couple of years ago. On top of that, the lease would pay an annual delay rental of twenty-five cents an acre until there was drilling or production. This was more than a rancher could count on making out of the drouth-ridden cows that grazed on the land, and the lease wouldn't interfere with the ranching operations anyway. The old man responded to each forceful sally of the lease broker with a barely audible grunt, his arms folded, his light blue eyes peering off into the dim recesses of the lobby as if he were only half listening.

After nearly an hour of talking, the lease hound sank back against the couch, exhausted.

"Is that a fair offer, Mr. Dodson?" he said plaintively, almost pleadingly, his bald pate beaded with sweat. "You want me to open my veins so you can sign with my blood, or will pen and ink do?"

After a long wait, without a change of expression, the old man merely grunted again. Then after another while he hauled his stiff old frame up from the couch and looked sternly down at the fat man. "I'll have to think about it. I'll let you know." He went stalking off in a stiff-legged walk on his dusty, high-heeled boots.

The broker lay back against the couch, his arms slack at his sides, and blew out a slow breath. He glanced at the young man beside him. "He'll let me know. Yes, he will. But that old sonofabitch will shop my offer to every broker and oil company in town, first." He added bitterly, "I should have short-fused him. Shoulda told him to take it or leave it right now. But I know these old cockle-burrs. He'd have told me to take my three dollars and stick it up my ass. You got to work 'em up slow, just like a woman. But I'll nail him yet. You wait and see."

When he had rolled up his map he looked at Jim McNeely again, more closely now, and with some interest. The slim, strong-looking young man with dark hair and intent eyes seemed to be taking in every word he said, and this flattered and interested the man. Whereas he had been merely talking to himself, he now had an attentive audience. He spoke directly to the young man beside him, and as he did Jim McNeely caught the faint, sweetish smell of good whiskey on his breath.

"First that old rascal's got to go and sound out all of his neighbors on what *they* leased for. Hell, he don't know from straight up what a lease on his land is worth. But he'd rather lay down and die than to lease for less than some old codger that owns the ranch next to him. Pride is a funny thing. You have to take it into account in this business almost more than anything else. I'm offering him sixty thousand cash and I happen to know he's got a past-due note at the bank. But he'd rather have 'em foreclose on him than sell a lease for three dollars if his neighbor got four. Well, his neighbor hasn't got four. Not yet. And nobody's ready to pay him that much, because they don't know what I know—"

He stopped himself and pursed his lips, frowning at Jim McNeely with an expression of sudden caution.

"My name's Hennery. What do you do, boy? You a scout? A company man?"

With open-faced seriousness that was obviously honest and consequently disarming, Jim McNeely said, "My name's Jim McNeely, Mister Hennery. I work for an oil company, but I'm not a scout. I'm just a field hand over at Dead Lake. I'm on vacation."

"Hell of a place to spend a vacation," grunted Hennery, who obviously wanted somebody to listen to him. "Now you just wait and see. I'll sack up that old rawhide before sundown. I'll ease out to his place long about four or five o'clock. He'll have time by then to check with his cronies and feel out the company offices. Somebody might offer him two, maybe even two-fifty. But not four, so he'll be ready. He'll sign my lease, just about dark. You wait and see. I know these dried up old bastards like a book."

"You gonna give that old gentleman sixty thousand dollars cash, for a lease?" said Jim McNeely in a tone of wonder.

With a look of innocence Mr. Hennery swung his gaze around the lobby. Then he leaned his face close to Jim McNeely's so that his warm, whiskeyed breath was almost too rich to breathe. "Well, not exactly cash, son. What we'll do is just put that lease in the bank on a thirty-day draft, subject to title examination. His lease, and my thirty-day draft for sixty thousand. You see, I tell him that I need thirty days to check his title to see that it's good. Which I do, I *do*. But hell, I know his title's good. Anyway, that's not the idea." He unrolled his land map again, a renewed glint of enthusiasm sparking in his eyes. This young eager-faced squirt was obviously a safe and callow youth, and appealing to boot, and the urge to talk was upon Mr. Hennery. His red-rimmed, faintly rheumy eyes were liquid with the excitement of the chase.

"Look here, sonny boy." He smoothed out the map with his puffy hand and tapped it with two of his fingers. "Here's old man Dodson's spread right here. Thirty sections. Each one of these squares is a square mile, six hundred and forty acres. Now look down here to the south." Jim McNeely looked, straining to comprehend. The geometric pattern of lines on the unrolled paper represented the ownership of that scrubby patch of the earth's surface known as Andrews County. "See these little black dots? That's the Pharr Pool. Every one of those spots is an oil well. Everybody thinks that's the end of the line right here where the spots stop, three miles south of Dodson's south line. That little circle with a line through it right there on the edge was a dry hole, or they claim it was. But I know it would have made a well. It wasn't low on structure. The sand might have been a little tight, but what the hell. What really happened was they fucked up the completion and nobody wanted to admit it. I talked to the tool pusher. He says they can still make a well there, but that's the way companies are. Nobody wants to admit a mistake and take the rap. OK. Now look up here twelve miles due north. Straight north of the Dodson ranch. Philmac is drilling a wildcat on the Carruthers ranch. It's a tight hole and nobody gets the dope on it except the Philmac management, of course, and yours truly." He gave Jim McNeely a knowing smile. "Now it just happens that yours truly is acquainted with a roughneck on the graveyard tour on that well, and this roughneck, who happens to be married, has got a young single lady in a family way and needs a little financial assistance. Which, it happens, yours truly is able to provide. To make a long story short, yours truly just happened to learn last night that they pulled twenty foot of core that looked like a honeycomb and was bleeding live pipeline oil from the top of the San Andres." He closed his eyes and blinked them, smiling at Jim McNeely. "Now what does that add up to, sonny boy?" He tapped at the map again. "Here's an old field here. And here's a new discovery here. And the trend of the fields out here is north and south."

"Looks like that country right there in between those two would be mighty promising," said Jim McNeely, tracing his forefinger back and forth over the Dodson Ranch.

Mr. Hennery smiled benignly. "Smart boy. Promising is the word."

"But it looks like to me that Philmac, or whoever you said was drilling this wildcat up here, would get after old man Dodson and try to lease his place as soon as they pulled that bleeding core."

"Ah!" said Mr. Hennery. "They will. They undoubtedly will. After the geologist makes his report to Midland, and the Midland supervisor makes his report to Tulsa, and the head knocker in Tulsa calls the vice president in New York and they have a big powwow on the telephone, and then they reverse the whole process back down the line, then maybe somebody will go out to see old man Dodson about next Tuesday, with authority to pay him up to seven dollars an acre if they have to. A big oil company is a creaking giant that reacts in slow motion. Most of 'em, anyway. That's where us little old poor boys have a chance. If the Lord is with me," Mr. Hennery crossed himself and glanced piously at the ceiling, "I'll have that lease in the bank long before Tuesday, and Philmac will pick up my draft and give me four dollars an acre on top of my three, and a thirty-second override to boot."

"A thirty-second override?" Jim McNeely said with a frown. "That means that out of every thirty-two barrels they produce, you get one free, don't it?"

Mr. Hennery grinned broadly, "Button, you look like you really understand what I'm talking about. C'mon, let's go up to my room and have a little toddy and then I'll buy you some groceries. I got a feeling you're good luck for me."

That is how Jim McNeely picked up his acquaintanceship with Mr. Horace Hennery, who before the day was over was insisting that they call each other Hoss and Jimmy. As predicted, Hoss Hennery drove far up in the country in the afternoon to call on Mr. Dodson, and Jim McNeely went with him. Almost, but not quite as predicted, a lease was signed, nearer midnight than sundown. And the price was not three but four dollars an acre, and the delay rental was fifty cents and not a quarter.

At Hoss's invitation Jim met the older man the next morning and thereafter stayed close to him, eating and drinking and talking with him in the exciting days that followed. Hoss had taken an obvious liking to this young and eager chance acquaintance, and began to talk in terms of taking him on as a junior partner and teaching him the oil business. He needed somebody, he said, to chase down deals for him. He was getting too old to run so hard and so fast. He could really teach a young feller a thing or three, and hell, they could make a single deal that would bring him more in a day than he could save out of his salty sweat at Dead Lake in a whole year.

"Look at that feller comin' yonder," he said as they sat in the lobby once again. "T. P. Yandell. Don't look like much, does he? Hello, T. P." He waved and nodded as the man passed. "Two years ago he bought half the royalty, undivided, under the Crabtree Ranch for a dollar-fifty an acre. He could sell it now for a thousand an acre, if he was a mind to, which he's not. And he's not a damn bit smarter than you or me."

In the days they were together he pointed out the various other notable figures of the oil world that were drawn to and moved in and out of the Scharbauer lobby, the current focal point, the unofficial exchange of the red-hot play in the Permian Basin. Hoss knew them all, and, among others, he introduced Jim McNeely to the fabulous and flamboyant J. E. (Big Jim) Wilfong and to Boyd Hallam, a quiet, boyish-looking fellow not many years older than Jim McNeely, who Hoss described as a "real comer."

Jim McNeely found the thought of joining up with Hoss intoxicating, though it never entered his mind to wonder why Hoss should take such an interest in him. Hoss was a friendly, interesting man, full of funny stories and worldly know-how that Jim McNeely soaked up like a blotter. He began to think he might not even go back to Dead Lake at all, except to get his last paycheck, though he felt vague, uneasy reservations about the ethical propriety of Hoss's giving Mr. Dodson a draft for sixty thousand dollars, a mere order to the bank to pay that amount to the rancher, when it came out that Hoss had less than two thousand dollars to his name.

"I mean, well, won't he want you to show you got the money to pay off with?" Jim McNeely said as they sat in Hoss's room, their feet on the bed, both puffing Hoss's good cigars and swirling glasses of bourbon and water.

"Aw, hell no," said Hoss. "These old buggers have too much hospitality. Code of the West. Their word is their bond, and they don't question anybody else's. I mean if a man looks decent—until he falls down on 'em, he's OK. Hell, I knew a rancher out in Jeff Davis County that took in some people whose old car broke down on his place, a family of pure no-count trash from New Jersey headed for California. He put 'em up for three months. Finally the only way he could get rid of 'em was to send their car to El Paso and get it overhauled and then give 'em a hundred dollars to see 'em on their way. They're like children, these ranchers. They'll smarten up some as time goes on. But right now is the time to get to 'em—I mean," he chuckled, "to do business with 'em."

"Well, what if you can't sell this lease to Philmac for more than the amount of your draft?" said Jim McNeely, his dark brows knitting on the older man, who was draining his glass of water-paled bourbon. "Tut-tut-tut," said Hoss wiping his mouth. "You can't be a pessimist in this business and make out, son. But just as an academic matter, if the lease won't sell, I will surely find something wrong with the title. Every title has something screwed-up in it, way back along the chain. Anyway, he'll get his lease back and I draw down my draft. Nobody'll be hurt."

"But you agreed to pay sixty thousand dollars."

"So I did," said Hoss arching his brows, his voice suddenly harsh and unfriendly. "I never welshed on a deal yet. What are you, one of these natural-born crepe-hangers?"

"No. OK. I got it," said Jim McNeely, though he was not completely satisfied with the explanation.

Before the week was out, after many conferences in the Scharbauer lobby and in the offices of Philmac and two other companies, which Hoss tried to tempt with his prize, his lease was assigned, not to Philmac, who turned him down cold for some reason known only to themselves and later regretted, but to J. E. (Big Jim) Wilfong, and not for seven dollars an acre, as Hoss had predicted, but for four-fifty and a sixty-fourth instead of a thirty-second override.

"Big Jim," said Hoss, still complaining bitterly as they sat in the lawyer's office where they had repaired to close the deal and sign the papers, Hoss and Jim McNeely and Big Jim and a couple of Big Jim's retainers who looked like retired race track touts, "this is like stealin' from an orphan. It ain't right and you know it. This lease is worth twice what you're payin'."

"Well now, Horace," the big independent intoned, sitting back and fixing him with a steady gaze. "I know a man in travail when I see one. You visualize great wealth slipping through your fingers, and I wouldn't deprive you of it. I don't really want this lease, nohow. And it pains me to see your disappointment. I reckon we better just call the deal off. My labors in the oil vineyard are for the glory of the Lord, and I would not do unto ye as ye would not be done by. Mister Lawyer, just tear up them doc-u-ments, and tell me what I owe you for your trouble."

"Oh-ho, now, Big Jim, you old fox," said Hoss quickly, smiling broadly. "You know you want this lease and you know I got to sell it to you. It just looks like you'd have a little more charity for an old broke lease broker."

"Proceed, Mister Lawyer," said Big Jim. "The gentleman has repented of his intemperate remarks."

Big Jim Wilfong was a large and imposing man, well padded with the flesh of good living. His physical stature was enhanced by the big gray beaver fedora which he wore indoors and out over his flowing senatorial locks, and by the beautiful hand-tooled cowboy boots on his feet. His double-breasted suit was of the most expensive tailoring and his shirt was of tan silk. A ten-carat diamond in a heavy mounting sparkled from the finger of one beefy, dexterous hand.

Big Jim had started out as a small-town Oklahoma barber but soon turned to professional gambling. Then, finding the stakes higher and more enticing in the oil business, he switched to promoting oil deals through the mails. It was common knowledge that the federal authorities who were soon hot on his trail would surely have nailed him for mail fraud if the wildcat in which he had sold shares to widows, schoolteachers, and other gullible citizens had been a dry hole. It turned out to be the "sure-fire gusher" that he had promised in his advertisements. Nevertheless, it was an uncomfortable experience for Big Jim and he never tried this route to riches again, and never had to. Others who did had time to contemplate their bad luck and his good in Leavenworth.

Being a lucky gambler he had an instinct that told him when the odds were right and he went from success to success. He projected himself into the big time when he got in early and leased up what turned out to be nearly a third of the fabulous Maypearl Field in Starnes County, a massive up-tilted block of saturated Ordovician dolomite that would still be flowing oil when his grandchildren were old men.

Like many gamblers, he had been strictly reared in his youth by God-fearing, church-going parents, and the fear and wonder of the Lord had stayed with him. As he had an insatiable weakness for flesh, both of horse and woman, and a predilection for the strong waters of Kentucky, and knew all of these to be sinful, he early made a pact with himself to devote as much of his burgeoning income to the Lord's work as to the Devil's, just in case there was, after all, something to this hell-fire business. It was a smart gambler's way of laying off the odds. Since he was fundamentally a softhearted man and could not bring himself to dispose of either a worn-out race horse or lady friend who had performed well, and since he was constantly adding fillies of both types to his stables, the Lord's portion became considerable.

He was at least sixty when Jim McNeely first saw him, but still much of a man. His wife of many years was an addled little woman with deep rose-tinted glasses and a hat that seemed always slightly askew, and whom he placed in charge of his "tithing." She wore a pained, apprehensive expression as if she had just been goosed and was momentarily expecting another as he catapulted her around the country from church conference to fellowship union to interfaith brotherhood meeting, partly to spread his pious bounty and the public recognition thereof, and partly to keep the little woman so engrossed with God's work that she would not have time to fret herself about his dalliance with Aphrodite and the bang-tails.

As a result the little lady was widely recognized as one of the most churchly women of the faith, and though persistent rumors of Big Jim's weaknesses gave some ministers pause, he was credited with being, at heart, a truly Godly man and he would without doubt, when his time came, be handsomely buried from one of the dozen churches that his oil wells had paid for.

When the assignments and bank drafts were all signed and exchanged, Hoss Hennery sat back laughing, relieved and expansive. Blowing the ink dry on his check, he said, "Big Jim, you done made yourself another ten million sure." He turned to Jim McNeely. "Here, boy, take care of this pittance. We'll go down to the bank and see if it's any good, as if I didn't know. Big Jim, this young friend of mine is named Jim, too. He thinks he wants to be an oil man. What do you think? Reckon we ought to disillusion him?"

Big Jim Wilfong rose from his chair, smoothed out his great double-breasted coat and gazed benignly on the young man now standing awkwardly before him.

"Do you love the Lord, son?" he said in his deep resonant voice.

Jim McNeely, not knowing whether he was being kidded, stammered, "I—well, I guess I do."

"Do the Lord's work and your own will be easy, son," said Big Jim, closing a ham hand around Jim McNeely's hard calloused fingers. "Come see me if I can ever help you." With that he turned and, followed by his retainers, moved grandly out of the lawyer's office. Jim McNeely was greatly impressed by it all and he filed Big Jim Wilfong's invitation away in his mind for future use.

With a ten-thousand-dollar cash profit in his pocket and Jim McNeely in tow as his knightly squire, and a belly full of bourbon whiskey, Hoss Hennery became the king of the hour in the Scharbauer lobby, reveling in his triumph. His young friend and understudy, completely enthralled by this exciting new realm of high finance and fast dealing, accepted on the night of victory, and imbibed more of Hoss's bourbon than was prudent. Later he found himself in a half waking, half drunken state in Hoss's bed in the deep stale darkness of the hotel room, dreaming of a new and fabulous future as Hoss's junior partner. It was an exciting prospect, somehow vaguely, strangely erotic. Good old Hoss. Like a father or a big brother, he was. There was money, big money to be made. With plenty of women and expensive cars and clothes and diamonds in his future. Ah, women . . . Mazie, Lee Montgomery. And old Hoss was going to show him how.

With slow-dawning awareness prickling at his scalp he realized where he was—in Hoss's hotel room in bed. It also seeped slowly into his drugged consciousness what was happening to him. The delightful erotic dream of success and of beautiful women dissolved slowly and focused downward upon the chubby fingers of the fat man next to him gently stroking the stalky erectness of—Jim McNeely!

In outrage and shock he leaped straight up from the bed like a stricken deer and landed wide awake on the floor, groping for the light switch. In the first shock of light his instinct was to drive his fist into the slack, quivering mouth of the man who had defiled him, now sitting upright staring at him out of puffy eyes like a bloated owl. In fierce, befuddled haste, still unsteady from the whiskey, he grabbed up his clothes and hopped around on one foot, yanking on his trousers.

Hoss Hennery got nimbly out of the bed. He was quite naked.

"Now just what are you doing, Jimmy boy?"

"I'm gettin' out of here, that's what!" said Jim McNeely furiously through gritted teeth.

Following him around the room as he dressed himself, Hoss tried to make a joke of it. "Now, Jimmy, you must have been dreaming or something."

"I don't have those kind of dreams!"

Hoss went to the door and leaned back against it, like a large obscene kewpie doll.

"Aw, don't rush off, Jimmy. I already made up my mind to take you in as my partner, as of tomorrow. And you know the first thing I'm gonna do? Buy you a brand-new Chevy company car to ride around in."

"I'm not interested!"

"You could change your mind, Jimmy. I think we'd make a swell team."

"You got another think comin', mister! Now get outa my way, because I'm goin' through that door!"

Hoss Hennery eyed the wrathful, strong-muscled youth for a moment. A hard smirk came on his face and he did a little mincing step to one side then swept him out with a grand bow.

"OK, big boy," he said. "Toot sweet and olive oil."

Jim McNeely lurched through the opened door and fled stumbling down the dim hotel corridor, buttoning his trousers as he went, groping his way toward the fresh air.

That was the sorry end of his vacation in Midland. Yet, in spite of the shock and disappointment and disgust of having Hoss turn queer on him, it had undoubtedly been an enlightening and profitable experience. Some of the mystery enshrouding the oil business had been ripped away. Now he understood, in a degree, the mechanical manipulation of legal papers and of property rights by which poor men, who were lucky and bold, became rich ones.

As he lay in his bunk, once again at Dead Lake, on the ragged edge of sleep, thinking back over the Midland interlude of his young life, the strange, warm thought, half dreamed, came over him that somewhere hidden deep within the laminated crust of this earth, unknown as yet to all but God there was a great, tumescent oil field, waiting for him. Waiting to make him rich. And some day he would be guided, unerringly, to find it.

Yes, somewhere there was an oil field with his name on it, and he would surely claim what was his own. And mixed with his feeling of revulsion toward the warped, disgusting Hoss Hennery was a strange accompanying feeling of gratitude, almost of youthful compassion, for the sad old geezer whose wires had got crossed somewhere but who had showed him how a man with nerve and savvy and little else might carve out for himself a chunk of the earth's treasures. Hoss Hennery's way of doing this and Big Jim Wilfong's were only two ways, but they opened Jim McNeely's eyes to the fact that there were surely many other ways—many other variations that could be woven about the same ancient, elemental idea. One of these variations, one day, would work for him—when he went to find his oil field that was there, somewhere out there, waiting for him.

Late on Sunday afternoon he was awakened by a commotion at the door. He cracked his eyes the slightest slit and lay motionless, for he knew at once what the hard grunting and scuffling and the sounds of cursing imported. Still savoring the deep pleasure of a long, healthy sleep, he did not wish to become involved in what was sure to be thankless effort.

The trio of wheezing men jammed and struggling in the doorway blocking out the slanting afternoon sun were clearly of two minds and purposes. Ort Cooley, bloodied, hair down in his eyes, dress shirt filthy and torn, opulent satin necktie soiled and turned around so that it hung forlornly down his sweat-stained back, was striving manfully and with the dogged singleness of purpose and total dis-coordination of a man magnificently drunk, to avoid being put to bed and to escape into the open air. His two companions, only a little less inebriated than he was, were striving with equal earnestness to pen him into the room.

"You ort not a' messed wiv me, boys," Ort argued in explosive breaths as he struggled. "I had that big sumbitch just about wore down. Lemme 'lone! Whaddyou doin? Goddang it!"

"We *ort* to of let them fuckin' bulls cart you off to the stout house is what we *ort* to done, you ol' crock-head," said one of his companions, under tight breath. "Come *on*, Ort! Git in the goddamn bunk and sleep it off!"

"Leeme *be*, boys, goddang it!" Ort cried. "Ah'm gonna go git me a woman!"

"Sheh-tt!" cried the other, blowing with exertion. "Wouldn't no woman have nothin' to do with you if you was slicked up and sober—lest it was a woman *goat!*"

One of his friends caught him from behind by the waist and pulled while the other hammered his fingers clinging to the door frame until his grip was broken. The pair lurched backward into the room as if dancing a wild hornpipe on a pitching deck. Then the other friend grabbed an arm and the two propelled Ort headlong across his bunk so that he battered his head into the wall with a force that jarred the furniture. Wheezing great sighs of relief, the two good Samaritans then departed, leaving Ort spread-eagled across his blanket, out cold.

Jim McNeely, who had watched it all through cracked eyelids, gave a grunt of disgust that was half a chuckle. Then he turned over, punched his pillow and went back to sleep, dreaming of two beautiful women, one dark and one fair.

12

WHEN DRILLING ACCELERATED IN WEST TEXAS and discoveries began to pop up all over the place, the oil business moved west in a great migration. The companies, the independent wildcatters, the lease brokers, the drilling contractors, the equipment and material suppliers, the lawyers, they all came, and with them the working stiffs who could turn their sweat into more money in the oil fields than they could back east as thresher hands or hod-carriers, and with them the storekeepers and cafe owners and honkytonk impresarios and whores, not all in the same class, of course, but they all flocked in as necessary support troops to the big effort of strong men engaged in serious enterprise in this area that had little comfort to offer except a few dusty whistle-stops on the railroad where the ranchers bought their staples and rope and tobacco.

And so in short years what had been a vacant, drouth-stricken wasteland became a populated drouth-stricken wasteland, made tolerable only because there was important work to be done here and important money to be made doing it. Something significant was happening here on this hitherto insignificant patch of the earth's haunch, something bigger than an ordinary man could see all at one time. What it was was power stirring, power flowing out of the ground in a volume that was accelerating the world's material and technological progress at a dizzying rate. And the money and power that were produced here bought comfort and importance and influence for the lucky ones. And if there was a philosopher among all of those that came, a single man who was concerned over what the ruckus was really all about, and how it fitted into the big picture, and how, if any way, it was all going to help men in their wandering, stumble-footed march toward their ultimate high destiny, it was purely an accident. But altogether it made a hell of a show.

Lee Montgomery stretched with such violent intensity that she quivered all over. Then, as suddenly, she relaxed and lay gazing wide-eyed at the ceiling. What to do? She was face to face with the blank wall of another day. The sameness of another day at Dead Lake. It would be yesterday all over again, and yesterday she had thought she would go out of her mind before the day finally dragged itself out. And the day before that. And the day before that, and for weeks and months before that, that seemed years. The worst of it was that tomorrow would be the same. And the day after tomorrow. And the day after that. Nothing was in sight that would be different, ever.

She felt an impulse to clench her eyes tight shut and scream like an Apache. A very young Apache squaw of twenty. She had, after all, some Indian blood in her. Not much, but some. One great-grandmother had been Indian, and something had to be done to release that narrow steel spring which she was sure was right there, under her rib, winding tighter and tighter with each passing day and was now beginning to kink and curl, dangerously.

With a small, explosive movement she raised herself to her elbows, her chin drawn in on her chest. She looked down the length of her naked body. Pointing her toes, she tensed the muscles of her smooth thighs and slowly raised one brown, golden leg until it pointed like a finger at the corner of the ceiling. Then she lowered it as slowly, in tension, and began to roll her body slowly, sensuously, first on one hip then the other.

"What a pity, what a waste, what a pity," she murmured, feverishly, to no one.

She marked with approval that there was no trace of bulge or puffy flesh about her. Her body was tawny and firm and lithe, Indian-like, with just a hint of deeper tone from last summer's sun remaining to color her limbs and distinguish the parts of the torso which paleface convention required to be clothed. A stream of little sample emotions flowed through her, like alternating currents of heat and cold, as she looked down the smooth hills and valleys of her full breasts and flat belly and rounded thighs; anger, self-pity, disgust, disdain, lust, resignation, rebellion.

Dropping her head back on her pillow, she expelled a long breath through slender flared nostrils. Then she clenched her fists and set her even white teeth together and her whole body stiffened again. "Dear God," she muttered in a voice vibrant with indignation, "are you going to sit up there and let me starve to death?"

"Oh, well," she answered her own question with a deep sigh, "I guess you are." She slid one foot off the bed and let it swing down to the floor. Then she rolled quickly to her feet. She stood, thinking a moment in her slim nakedness, fists on hips, legs planted firmly apart. Her round, firm buttocks protruded slightly, like an athlete's.

The bedroom was small and over-warm, though the gas heater was turned down so that only the tiniest of blue tongues showed along the burner. A perfect little love nest, she thought sardonically. A very good place to sleep, as well. But she had slept and slept until she thought she could never close her eyes again.

Beside the bed there was a comfortable chair covered with bright chintz, also a standing lamp to read by, a compact metal chest of drawers with a man's military brush and comb set and a bottle of hair oil neatly arranged on top. Across the room stood a small skirted dressing table with mirror and stool and to the right of that a varnished wooden bookcase filled with books, bright-jacketed volumes from a book club, and engineering texts. Beautiful books filled with exciting adventures, intrigues and seductions, and precise empirical knowledge and formulas, dry as dust. But she was fed to the teeth with vicarious book-bound excitement, and the cold precision of engineering logic made her ill when she thought of it. If only someone would make her feel—even if it was only anger! She dug her nails into her thighs like a cat's claws. What a welcome change, what a relief it would be!

Suddenly she moved to the dressing table and seated herself before the mirror. With an impulsive motion she swept her thick hair from the nape of her neck to the top of her head and turned her face this way and that, surveying the effect. Not bad for a squaw, she thought. Her deep brown hair looked almost black in the filtered light of the room. The sprinkling of black pepper in the hollows of her armpits added to the exotic effect. She bared her even white teeth and clicked them defiantly at the image in the mirror. Then, quickly she grasped her swept-up hair into a flaring topknot and bound it tight with a rubber band. A kind of mirthful savagery swept through her.

Taking a lipstick from the table top she extruded its red phallus to its full length and contemplated it. Why, she demanded to know, must one put it only here? She touched it to her lips. Was there any law that said one should celebrate only the lips? Why not here? She made a jagged red line across the smooth expanse of her forehead. Or here? She drew a thick line down the aquiline bridge of her nose. The very act of code-breaking sent a delicious little shiver through her limbs. With an enthusiasm that was almost frenzied she rapidly completed the picture. Seizing an eyebrow pencil she drew her brows a thick and ferocious black flaring upward at the corners. Then she made black hachured slashes slanting across her high cheekbones. Digging furiously into the little jewel box on the dressing table she fished out a looping gold ear-ring and clipped it into the slender septum of her nose. Her heart now beating with excitement. She took up the lipstick again and drew three concentric circles on each taut straining breast, the first close around the puckered upturned nipple. Then she seized her hairbrush like a war club and arose from the vanity table, kicking over the stool as she stepped back to admire herself. The grotesquerie of her mirrored image was delightful.

Whirling, eyes ablaze, she glared dangerously around the cozy room. Her narrowed gaze fell upon the parchment diploma, neatly framed on the opposite wall. The dark look on her face took on an ominous shade as she strode, then fairly leaped across the room and crashed her hairbrush club savagely into the glass of the frame, showering it into a thousand flying fragments. The dented, denuded diploma, proclaiming that Clyde S. Montgomery in anno Domini 1932 had been laureled a Bachelor of Science in Petroleum Engineering, seemed to stare at her in addled, off-center shock. The naked savage, limbs akimbo, nostrils distended, glared back at the parchment as if it were an implacable enemy. For this effron-tery she drew back and struck it another blow, full on its crenelated seal, and sent it spinning and crashing to the floor.

A thrill of release raced through her body so swiftly that she was instantly covered, arms, back, belly, and thighs, with delicious gooseflesh.

With the excitement still ringing inside her, having at last cast off her civilized disguise and struck a devastating blow at the enemy, she strode almost prancing out of the bedroom into the small, drab, unheated dining room, a barbaric look of challenge gleaming in her face. The swift rush of cold, against, around, into her warm nakedness was keenly erotic. She circled the mail-order dining-room table belligerently, smacking her bottom hard with the brush, relishing the stinging sensation. This was revenge, rebellion against the diplomaed automaton who called himself her husband—the blocky, sand-colored, self-centered, self-contained nonentity whose notion of a wife was a female creature who could cook and wash clothes and clean house efficiently, and was useful for the purpose of relieving a man's periodic rutting urge, also efficiently and with as little romantic nonsense and associated folderol as possible. Ah, he was a sound, solid, no-nonsense man whose conception of the proper way to entertain his wife was to talk to her, or at her, interminably, and in great technical detail, about the merits of the casing program he had devised for the well he was currently supervising, until he got into bed and began his nightly leaden sleep of ten hours. Uughh!

Lee Montgomery did not hate her husband for anything he had done to her. She despised him for what he had not done. She despised him for starving her intellectually, emotionally, sexually. Yet she knew that she had no real cause to complain. No one forced her into this arrangement. She had made this bed with her eyes open, though in youth and ignorance and impatience, and now it was hard to lie upon.

Four years at CIA in Denton had brought her a teacher's certificate and just a faint taste of the goodness that life holds for the lucky and the talented. The desolation of returning to the colorless, motherless house of her father in McCamey, Texas; the boredom of teaching second grade children of uneducated itinerant oil-field workers in the cheerless shack that was called a school, filled her with such a deep and desperate sense of the futility and numbness of her life that she had looked upon Clyde Montgomery, with his college degree and his new khakis and slide rule and correct manners, as a knight in shining armor come to rescue her from this wasteland of life—from which in her immaturity she could see no other hope of escape, ever.

People told her how lucky she was, what a fine, hard-working, well-educated young man he was, what a bright future he had, and her belief in what they said had carried her a long way. Her father, taciturn old Lee Thomas, had raised the only momentary doubt when he said, just one time, "Lee, sissy, do you really, *you* know, get *along* with this fella?" Not knowing then what "get along" meant, not ever having experienced the fireworks that real physical or even intellectual rapport can shower into a young woman when she is fused by the right young man, Lee had answered, almost indignantly, that of course she got along with him; she was marrying him, wasn't she?

Lee Montgomery stopped her naked war dance around the dining room table and jerked at the roller shade masking the single window. It flew to the top and spun off in a wild, fluttering orgasm and was silent. She stood boldly in the window, breathing hard. The familiar scene outside enraged her. Six drab identical houses facing six drab identical houses on opposite sides of the oiled road. Feeble patches of winter-dead lawn. Identical clotheslines hung with inelegant garments, all of a depressing sameness. Down the road she saw the big tin warehouse and the rear of the bunkhouse and the mess hall, painted the same colorless gray. She stood patting her toes on the cold floor, shaking her brush nervously as if thinking, debating, her left thumb hooked on a jutty hipbone, slender fingers lightly tapping the top of the small springy delta that bloomed darkly at the top of her thighs. The whole senseless camp appeared to be a monstrous machine that drew people in and crushed the life out of them and ran on and on, fueled by their squeezed-out blood and hopes and spirit.

Her sudden impulse was to run shrieking out of the house, to dash madly down the road naked, screaming, brandishing her hairbrush. The great stupid machine would shudder and konk and fly into a million pieces, then the earth would open up, belching fire and brimstone and swallow them all and slam shut again, with nothing but a curling wisp of smoke to show they had been there.

"Fools! Fools!" she cried suddenly, almost sobbing, clutching a fist to her temple. "This is the only life you'll have! Don't let them do this to you!"

Then, suddenly, as she stood there, now shivering from the cold that had sunk into her body, the savagery, the rebellion went out of her, drained away like sand out of a slit sack. She realized that she did not know who "they" were who were doing this to them; and whoever they were, no one was keeping anyone, not even her, here by force. Her shoulders, her whole body sagged. The war-club brush hung limply from her hand, then slipped from her fingers, and the cold of the room seeped into her pores. She felt at once so heavy and lifeless that she could hardly support herself. The imponderable, inescapable order and routine of the world closed in upon her like a cold, miasmic fog, and shame came upon her, as if the walls were suddenly studded with eyes.

Slowly, sadly, she crept back into her warm bedroom and sat down blankly before her mirror. Her face was a pathetic mask of lipstick and pencil, now smeared with tears. Her mind began automatically to pick up the old routine like the ordered circuitry of an automaton returned to normal after an orgy of excess voltage. She would get lamb chops today. No, she had given him lamb chops day before yesterday. Sausage. Sun the blankets. Clyde had an obsession about blankets being sunned once a week. He would ask about it. Fix the tack in the chair where he had torn his trousers. Mend the trousers. All of this and an explanation of how she had broken the glass on his diploma while dusting. It would provide the substance of her day's conversation with her husband before he started talking to himself, with her as an audience.

With heavy, listless hands, as if rubbing out a last, fantastic hope of escape, she began to smear cold cream over her face and body.

13

THE MEN ON THE TONG WRENCHES BENT THEIR backs in violent, jerking rhythm, driving their weight and strength into the handles, grinding the long steel joint of pipe quarter-turn at a stroke into the steel collar, coupling it into and making it a part of the black tube that stretched off across the buckskin earth until it disappeared in the direction of the battery of oil tanks on the low horizon. Four hands on each wrench, four shoulders and backs together driving two tapering steel handles alternately up and down in steady rhythm paced by the endless, ear-piercing tang-tang-rattlety-tang rattlety-tang rattlety-tang of the collar-pecker's hammer beat upon the coupling, keeping up the tempo and keeping the threads from freezing in the collar before the joint was bucked up tight.

"Break in!" sang out Ort on the number one tongs, as the joint approached tightness, and without losing a beat the two pairs of backs ceased alternating and bent now in unison, four backs together, four weights, four strengths, up and down grinding the pipe tight into the coupling.

Cap Bruner, standing behind the tong men, thumbs hooked in his belt, called out in a grunting rhythmic drawl, "Hump now! Hit 'em now! Come on, lard-ass, hit them tongs! You ain't on no pension." The tong men, sweating in the cold wind, drove their arms and shoulders and neck and bellies into the tongs and the pipe began to give up tense, shrill shrieks as the male joint married itself home into the female coupling.

"Tight joint!" cried Ort, and on the upbeat the men jerked the heavy tongs from the pipe and carried them ahead toward the next joint of pipe lying loose on the ground. They were four big men, and they breathed heavily and walked slowly to let the blood drain from their heads back into their bodies while the next joint was being stabbed and made ready to go.

The pusher kept up a nasty nagging daylong commentary as a background chorus to this ballet of sweat, full of threats, belittlements, and abuse. "Better damn sure be tight. If there's airy leak in this line it's gonna be somebody's ass, and it ain't gonna be mine." The rough, grunting sound ate into the men's necks, worked through their thick hides as the day wore on, and finally got down to their deep-buried nerves. But nobody answered back. Nobody said anything.

Cotton, whose job it was to knock down the lazy-board that held up the pipe behind the collar, then carry it forward to support the open end of the joint just screwed into the line, tried always, with a working man's consideration for another, to shove the board down easy, because the open end of the newly made up joint was supported in hard tension on a steel-fingered jack, and the jack was braced against the jack-man's shoulder, and when the board was knocked down, the whole weight of the pipe hit the jack and went through the jack and smacked into a human being's shoulder and back and guts. Cotton knew about this because he ran the jack sometimes and when it was done wrong it hurt, and if it was done wrong all day it aged a man before his time. So Cotton always tried to let the pipe down easy. Sometimes this was hard to do because the board got wedged at an angle against the lip of the coupling and it took a little time to tap it loose easy. It was wedged now, and Cap began to bawl and Cotton pranced around hitting at the board, trying to hurry but still trying to let it down easy.

"God damn, some people'll be a boll weevil all their life!" Cap Bruner muttered. "I need men and they 'spect me to pipe-line with childring and old ladies. Get outa the way, buttercup!" Breaking into one of his vicious flurries of activity Cap brushed Cotton aside and drove a heavy heel into the board, dropping the pipe's weight sharply onto the jack and the jack-man, who grunted with the blow, but made no other sound.

"All right, you," said Cap to Cotton. "Grab a holt of that board and git your girlish ass on up there with the men!"

Face burning, Cotton grabbed the heavy board and flung himself forward with it. Cotton was only twenty-one, but he had a towheaded baby boy nearly three who looked at him with round adoring eyes, and Cotton thought of the day when his kid, with open mouth, would stand and see his daddy shoved out of the way by Cap Bruner or some other pusher, and hear him called contemptible names, and him just standing there and taking it, and Cotton's throat constricted and his eyes watered with shame and humiliation.

He dropped to his knees on the hard ground and slid the board edgewise under the pipe-end. As he did so his troubled eyes raised automatically to the immobile face of Jim McNeely, the stabber, as he waited for the stabber to lift the pipe from the jack and drop it on the board. Jim McNeely locked his fingers under the pipe, set his feet and took a strain. The pipe came up a half inch and the jack-man jerked the jack away and Jim McNeely dropped the tension-bound pipe-end with a tension-driven thud onto the edge of the lazy board. Another joint of four-inch flow-line had been laid.

Without a change of expression Jim McNeely glanced at Cotton and gave him a wink that made him feel almost good again, then the stabber turned and walked down to the far end of the next joint.

There was artistry in the way Jim McNeely worked now. He moved with an economy of motion that was graceful and sure. In his lean frame there resided a deep-corded strength made of sound bone and tough sinews under perfect coordination. Not an ounce of strength was spent that was not needed. It took a good man to stab pipe all day long without relief. Jim McNeely never asked anybody to spell him. His work was seasoned, precise, and certain. He never left a man in a strain; he never hurt a man working.

When he reached the far end of the next joint of pipe and saw that Cotton and one of the other men had struggled the other, threaded end, to their knees, he hooked his gloved hand into the pipe bell and with a swift motion snatch-jerked the pipe to his waist. Then the three men carried the joint forward as a team and stabbed the threaded end into the open coupling. Supporting his end in the taut crook of his arm, Jim McNeely moved the pipe until he knew by sight and feel that it was started straight, then he nodded to the jack-man who slipped the jack under the pipe so that one of its steel fingers supported the pipe in that precise position. Snapping his short-handled mahoney wrench into place around the pipe-end, Jim McNeely crank-spun the long tube strongly into the coupling until it stopped. Then he said, "Tong 'er, men." Sometimes those were nearly the only words he spoke all day.

Under the up-tilted brim of his aluminum safety hat, Jim McNeely's face shaded downward from tan at the temples to a deep-burned brown that masked the creases which had slowly etched themselves into his face these three and a half years, across the forehead, around the eyes and mouth. The slight cleft in his chin had perceptibly deepened. His eyes, now habitually squinted in the strong sunlight, were a steadier, deeper gray. It was mainly his eyes that gave his face the cast of seriousness and confidence, and of generosity. The men in the gang had come to glance at him, now and then, almost automatically, for reassurance and comfort. He had become a kind of champion to them, a man whose quiet determination somehow gave them renewed confidence that they could stand up to it, too. They took pride in the fact that their stabber never left anybody in a strain. His shoulders were angular still, but broader and thicker under his khaki shirt and washed-out blue jumper. It is said that the worth of a working man can be judged by the condition of his pants. The seat of Jim McNeely's pants was unsoiled, nearly as good as new, while the knees and thighs were worn and grimy.

The crew moved slowly, tortuously across the mesquite-mottled prairie, leaving in its wake a black line of pipe snaking back to the horizon. Cap Bruner stumped up and down behind the laboring backs, foul-mouthing, goading, muttering, grinding his authority into their necks.

It was a tribute to the excellence of Jim McNeely's work that only rarely could the pusher find any excuse for throwing his verbal venom in his direction. On those infrequent occasions, when the younger man made some minor mistake or small error of judgment on the job, the pusher would let loose a barrage of verbal abuse that sometimes lasted half the day before it abated. Cap took care never to curse the stabber directly, but he cursed all around him, and his hatred was so violent and so irrational as to stir hopes in some of the men that it would one day drive Cap Bruner actually and literally crazy.

The only levity that Cap permitted in his gang was the privilege of laughing at his own dirty jokes, on those rare days when he was in a good temper. These jokes were totally devoid of humor and were remarkable only for their filth, which was, in fact, the whole point of their telling. When he sprang one of these odious chestnuts Cap permitted the men to lean on their tools and laugh, which they dutifully did as he laboriously repeated the punch line, which he expected to, and which invariably did, draw another chorus of laughter—from all except Jim McNeely. The stabber, who was as interested as anyone in getting along with Cap, stubbornly refused, nonetheless, to debase himself in this fashion. He did not change expression even to smile but went about his work steel-brushing the threads of the next joint as if he had not heard a word.

This attitude, which Cap took as a flaunting of authority amounting to open disrespect, quite naturally got under the pusher's thick skin and galled him to renewed fury. The men looked forward to these jokes, and their laughter became genuine, for they were immensely tickled to watch the stoic expression on Jim McNeely's face and the apoplectic coloring that invariably rose in the pusher's face as a result. A break must surely come. Someday soon. It was bound to come.

There was a sudden stirring in a clump of mesquite bushes behind the gang and a stocky, grinning boy emerged. He had a shock of curly reddish hair sticking clownishly from under his hat. He wore khakis like the rest, but they were newer, and the only real wear had been in the seat of the pants. Clayton LeMayne III, called Pluto by the men because of the frequency with which he escaped the monotony and physical exertion of gang work by disappearing into the brush, always on the half-joking pretext of having taken a powerful physic the night before, was a charmingly oafish but shrewd young man. Cap Bruner tacitly ignored his labor-dodging maneuvers for the simple and understandable reason that Pluto was the nephew of Taylor B. LeMayne, the vice president in charge of all of Bison's producing operations. It was understood, and accepted by all as in the natural order of things, that Pluto, who was serving this brief apprenticeship as a "trainee" (because of some old-fashioned notion in his family that he should learn the business from the ground up), was not to be judged or treated like the other members of the gang—this in spite of his uncle's admonishment to the field superintendent that Pluto should be treated as an ordinary hand, and that they should "give him the works and make a man of him."

Pluto underwent this indoctrination tolerantly and in good spirit, more as a matter of humoring his elders than anything else. It wouldn't last long and was kind of fun anyway. He knew where he stood and so had no intention of straining himself.

He walked briskly, businesslike, back to the gang and sat down astride the pipe behind the lazy-board and resumed his duties as collar-pecker, beating a crisp, piercing tang-tang-rattlety-tang on the pipe with his ball-peen hammer, adding rhythmic embellishments of his own from time to time. He was quite accomplished on the trap drums. This talent, however, had the effect of infuriating the tong men rather than assisting them.

"Y'didn't go to sleep out yonder and fall back in it, did ye, Pluto?" said Ort Cooley under his breath, puffing it out between strokes on the tongs. Ort became a bitter man as the day wore on. Pipe-lining hurt him, slowly ate the temper out of his back muscles, and the unfairness of the difference between his estate and that of this whelp, Pluto, set a dull fire in his head.

"That old Pluto water is still giving me a fit, Ort," said Pluto grinning. "I been loose as a goose all week."

"You been loose as a goose ever since you been here, an' that's goddamn near four months," said Ort in an angry voice.

Cap Bruner strolled up behind. "Seems to me like they's a lot of goddamn runnin' off at the mouth goin' on around here. If you put some of that hot air into them tongs you liable to get along better, Cooley." Ort plunged down on the tong handle with such ferocity that it threw the other men off rhythm. For quite a while after that the tong men speeded up their strokes, running ahead of the collar-pecker's beat, taking out their anger on the tightening pipe.

The gang ground its way across the plain, leaving its extrusion of pipe behind, never slackening its pace, never stopping to blow. At the slightest sign of flagging or slowing down, Cap Bruner would open up his foul, torrential mouth. In a sense he was a good pusher. He got the job done, and the men under him worked through the dragging hours, sullen, silent, except for their rhythmic grunts and their periodic cries of "Bell 'er!" "Tong 'er!" "Tight joint!"

Sometimes Pluto, sitting on the pipe, resting the side of his face in his free hand would break into a singsong fraternity ditty—"Glorious, glorious! One keg of beer for the four of us"—singing from sheer boredom in time to the peck of his hammer. At length, after trying futilely to engage someone, anyone, in conversation, he would jump to his feet and cry in alarm, "Boys, I got another call. That blasted Pluto water!" Then he would bolt for the bushes with feigned haste and in a moment the outline of his hunkered form could be seen through the brush, marked by a streamer of cigarette smoke swirling away in the wind.

Pluto was not a mean or domineering boy but a good-natured, lazy youth, smart enough to get away with every bit that he could. He added very little to the work output of the gang. Around work he was, as Ort

Cooley put it, "helpless as a one-legged man at a' ass-kickin'." But he made out such a good case with Cap Bruner of being his uncle's favorite and heir that Cap never once risked calling him to task. In fact Cap openly courted him, treating him and addressing him in a confidential manner, as if they were equals, kindred beings of the bosses' world. He took great pains to explain things to Pluto that Pluto had utterly no interest in learning. "You'll need to know that when you go 'on up,'" Cap would say. "It'll help you to know about these things. It sho'ly will. They's a lot to gittin' a day's work out of a bunch of hands." Pluto would nod his head sagely and say, "Good point, Cap. I'll mention that to my uncle next time I see him." Then Cap would fall all over himself explaining other ideas of his that would "benefit the Comp'ny," and Pluto would purse his lips appreciatively and figure he was good for another peaceful fifteen minutes in the bushes.

It would have been impossible for Pluto not to know that he was deeply resented by the gang hands, and he was casually sorry that they felt this way about him. However, he was intelligent enough to realize that they did not hate him personally, because he knew that he was personally inoffensive since he bore no ill-will toward anyone. They hated him as a symbol of unmerited, inexperienced, unearned privilege as he sat playing with his hammer while they sweated out their bitter salt on the oil field pig-iron. They knew that they would spend the rest of their lives doing this, after he had gone "on up." Pluto regretted this, but there was nothing he could do about it. It was just one of those things. He didn't design the system, so he didn't make himself unhappy worrying about it.

He genuinely liked the men, and of them all he liked Jim McNeely the best. He admired the stabber's strength and skill and the taciturn imperturbability with which he did his job under the nerve-sawing harangue of the pusher. Around the bunkhouse he tried to work into a friendship with Jim McNeely, but the latter, though civil and never unpleasant, kept to himself, for he, too, felt and somehow hurt about the inequity between their respective positions. He knew that if he ever got out of Dead Lake he would have to jack himself out by his own sweat and raw strength and will and long-suffering patience. He also knew that if he buddied up to Pluto there might be something in it for him, some quicker easier way, and so he took a kind of perverse satisfaction in resisting his natural impulse to become friendly with this happy, oafish boy.

The powdery sun hung far to the south in the winter-whipped sky. It cast a thin, almost delicate light over the wide sweep of desert. Mesquite and greasewood and cat-claw, winter-bare and ugly, raised their twisted branches to the sky and clicked their claws dryly in the wind. Tiny drifts of snow gathered on the shady side of the dry grass clumps that mottled the alkali earth. A lone bird lost from its flight in the immensity of earth and sky streaked high down the wind, calling shrilly.

At intervals, as if to emphasize the privilege of his rank, Cap Bruner wandered away from the gang and disappeared through the broken thickets of brush. These periods of respite from the sawing of his voice were intensely welcomed by the gang hands, and when he was gone they heaved unconscious, grunting sighs of disgust and relief. But there was no slackening of the work tempo, for they knew that Cap would be watching. A glimpse of his big hat could be seen through the brush now and then, now fifty yards west of them, minutes later moving up softly on them from the east. He would walk a quarter of a mile circling the gang in an effort to catch them loafing, or to overhear some unwary hand venting his feelings against him. Though he rarely succeeded in this, most of the men being old hands wise to his ways, he never returned from one of these circumlocutions without harrassing them with angry, belittling deprecations, as if he *had* caught them, red-handed. "I'm a sonofabitch if it don't seem like I can't turn my back without they damn near quit workin'," he would say to the air. "It'll be a great day in my life when they give me some rightful *men* to work with!"

It irritated and depressed Jim McNeely to observe how these grown men in the gang would sneak in snatches of conversation under their breaths, almost without moving their lips, like frightened ventriloquists, during these periodic jaunts of Cap out of earshot. It made him ashamed for them, and this debasement of grown men was the one thing that made him feel hatred for Cap Bruner, upon whom he otherwise looked with nothing more than contempt and patient acceptance, as a necessary part of his unlucky lot, to be endured in silence during this time of waiting and getting ready. No decent, reasonable pusher would forbid men to talk on the job the way Cap did. Men needed to communicate, if only about trivialities. It helped the desolate day unwind. It made the creeping clock move ahead. It kept them from sinking deeper and deeper into their unhappy inner wells. But Cap said it used up air that the "Comp'ny" was paying good money for.

"You know what I think," said Cotton once, when Cap had disappeared into the bushes. He spoke seriously, quickly, and under tension as he struggled toward the bell with a new joint of pipe in his arms. "I think ever' man ought to have a suit." He made the pronouncement positively, as if it was the considered conclusion of long reflection. He broke off under the pressure of lowering the pipe and shoving it into the open coupling. The threads were buggered and Jim McNeely at the other end could not turn the joint with his monkey-tail wrench.

"Roll pipe," the stabber called out curtly. Cotton and two other men gripped gloved hands to the pipe and started turning to help the stabber get it started in the bell. Cotton continued with his thought, earnestly: "Yessir, this pusher done made me come to the conclusion that ever' man ought to have a suit. Just goin' along, a man don't need one. But you git out of a job and you ain't got a suit, you're screwed!"

"Shuh, boy," said the one called Otho, scornfully. "You ain't gonna be lookin' fer no suit job."

"Yeh, you won't be needin' no suit," said Ort, "till they lay you out in a box."

The pipe was well started, the tongs clanged on with their heavy jaws biting into the rounded metal. When the strokes got hard Cotton fell in on the handle of one pair of tongs and finished his say in puffs, with determination. "That's what *you* think. By God, I'm gonna start buyin' me a suit, come payday, an' I don't give a shit what *anybody* says!"

The hazy sun moved slowly down the sky and the light winter shadows lengthened imperceptibly. The unrelieved monotony of minutes dragged into hours. The work went on at the never varying pace. The brazen beat of the collar-pecker's hammer became fused in the ear, echoing down through the winding corridors of the brain.

"It wouldn't be so bad if a feller could rest at night," said Ort, his depleting sources of strength reflected in the sag of his angry voice. "All night long I lay pipe, an' I wake up wore out like I ain't been to bed."

"I don't have no trouble sleepin', but I'm sho' gittin' behind in my family duties," said Otho.

"How you doin', stabber-man?" said Cotton, proud at least of the youthful spring in his muscles. "How 'bout spellin' you awhile? I ain't hardly worked up a sweat today."

"Much oblige," said Jim McNeely, aiming and feeling and turning a joint straight into the bell. "Don't want you strainin' your milk, bud. Stabbin' is a man's job." His tone was half-hard but friendly, and Cotton didn't take offense. Jim McNeely wasn't any more used-up than anybody else this time of day, though his work was harder, and he took good satisfaction in never letting anybody spell him off. Anyway, he had seen Cotton trying to stab pipe, and he knew that Cap would tear up the ground if he came back and found Cotton slowing down the work on the stabbing end.

"Man's job, my ass!" said Cotton. "I got a three-year-old boy could stab pipe good as you."

"I can't git the goddamn ringin' outa my ears!" cried Ort. "I hear it all day, and I hear it all night!" His voice was edging toward exasperation. He turned a glare on Pluto. "You reckon the goddamn collar-pecker is tryin' to beat a *hole* in the pipe?"

Cotton's wary eyes cut toward the brush behind Ort. He hissed under his breath, "Shht! Yonder come the stud-duck!" But Ort didn't hear him. The latch was tripped on his anger and the words spilled out, bedevilled and caustic.

"Sho' 'nough, city boy, why don't you see if you can't beat a hole in the pipe? You got nothin' to do but set there on your ass and keep time. Why don't you git a bigger hammer and see if you can't *beat* a *goddamn hole* in the *goddamn pipe*? An' see if you can't make us boys *deaf* whilst you're at it? Ort to make it faster an' louder! *Beat yer fuckin' brains out!*"

There was a desperate, half-demented whine in his voice. Pluto frowned unhappily and looked uncomfortable. His hammering slacked off to an uncertain tap. He didn't mean anybody any harm. Then with a sickened sensation like a rising gorge, Ort felt rather than saw the presence behind him. For a full half minute Cap stood silently behind him, swollen in rage, dark color spreading over his red-shot face. He was an enormous man with great sloping shoulders and a huge belted stomach. He nudged his big Stetson back with a forefinger and his voice was dull and ominous.

"Did you har' out to work, old man?"

Ort stared at the tong handle and pumped furiously in silence.

Cap's voice erupted in a deep throated roar. "By God, you answer me! I ast you a question, old man, and I ain't askin' you for my health!"

The next moments stretched in strained suspension over the gang. Then, almost inaudibly, in a voice that was broken and submissive and unspeakably miserable Ort answered, "I har'd out to work, Cap."

"*All right*, then," said Cap Bruner. Having nailed the man's ears to the door, he proceeded to clinch the spikes. "When you git too old to keep up, you can git your time. Any day. Like right now. Jest ask for it. Won't nobody want you to stay." That was all he said. He didn't have to say anything more. He knew where this man's wound was. The fear of age. Of being cast off on a rubbish heap, worn out, to starve and die. It was enough to throw in the salt and let the wound burn.

Toward four o'clock the gang truck, having gone in to the warehouse for gate valves, came lumbering back, swaying through the brush. As it drew alongside the line where the gang was working, Jim McNeely held up his hand for it to stop. "Let's drink, men," he said. He stepped up on the running-board and loosened the top of the Gott can in its welded bracket behind the cab. Before he would remove the cap, Cap sprang forward light as a big cat and splatted his hand down upon Jim McNeely's hand and slammed the top back into the can.

"Jest a goddamn *minute!*" said the big man. Jim McNeely looked hard down at him and a sudden blush of color showed through the tan of his face. The men coming forward stopped in their tracks.

"Jest how much money are you drawin', *Mister* McNeely?" Cap said.

Jim McNeely regarded the man silently for a moment, and as he did the unnatural color faded from his face. His gray eyes narrowed and there was a hard twinkle in them. He didn't move from the running-board. Somehow he felt relaxed, ready for anything.

"You asking for information, Cap?" he said. "You know what I make."

"I ain't askin' fer a goddamn thing! I do the *tellin'* in this gang, an' I'm tellin' you you ain't drawin' enough money to be givin' no orders. Now supposin' you climb down from that truck until *I* say to knock off the work."

In the drawn seconds that followed the two men looked at each other, the younger one returning the other's gaze steadily, almost smiling. Ort and Cotton and the others stood unmoving in their tracks.

This could be the time they'd been waiting for. In this charged moment even breathing was suspended. Would he take it from Cap and step down and break, as Ort had done? Or would he come through for them? The unspoken question in the eyes of all didn't wait long for its answer. With a strong, unhurried motion Jim McNeely shoved the pusher's hand off the top of the water can. Then he pulled out the lid, took the tin cup from the wire book, and dipped out a cupful of water.

Still looking at Cap, he said, "The man don't live that draws enough money to tell me when I can drink." Turning his head aside he spat out a mouth of cotton. Then he drained the cup, then dipped out another and drank part of it and threw the rest onto the dusty ground.

Finished, he replaced the lid, hung the cup back on its hook, stepped down from the runningboard and walked back to his work.

Cap Bruner followed his motions with stunned disbelief, his mouth half open. Then he stalked after him, his shoulders bunched, and Ort, under his breath, said, "O-o-oh shit, here it comes!"

But Cap, in his fury, could not carry it through. He was a baffled man. He had made an indefensible move and he knew it. A working, sweating man has a right to drink when he's dry. The rule had almost the force of law. Cap knew this, yet his natural stupidity compounded by his anger was so great that his next efforts to regain control of the situation resulted only in making him appear more ridiculous.

"Now *that* is the most *inneresting* speech I've heard since Ma Ferguson ran for gov'ner," he said in a scalded voice, circling Jim McNeely, who had now dropped to his knees at the pipe-end and was wire-brushing the threads. "An' I guess maybe you think there ain't anybody here drawin' enough money to run your ass off! Well, you got another think comin'! I can git smart bastards to work in this gang a dime a dozen."

Jim McNeely cocked his head and pondered this a moment. Then he decided it was not a direct enough cursing of his personal self to make it mandatory for him to bring the issue to a climax. It was pretty close, but he decided to let it pass. He turned his head away, spat again, then resumed brushing the threads, quietly waiting to see if Cap's mounting fury would bring forth the words which a man could not duck or retreat from. Cap waited, too, breathing heavily through his big hairy nostrils, glaring down at the young man. And then he flatly could not carry it through. He had put himself in a maddening, impossible situation, and it was he who had to retreat. He made the most contemptuous sound of which he was capable and turned savagely upon the rest of the gang, now standing in a frozen tableau. "All right, you apes!" he shouted, "gitcher goddamn water!"

During the remainder of the afternoon Cap rode the gang with an eloquence of vilification that did proud to his reputation of having the foulest mouth in West Texas. Jim McNeely worked on steadily, smoothly, efficiently, as if he were deaf. In fact, as if the pusher did not exist, and the gang finished the day with a gusto that was almost hilarious.

In every working man is a hidden spring of bravado which begins to flow at the stroke of quitting time, and from which a man draws the balm to soothe his abraded pride, and energy to inflate his spirit for a go at another day. These men who were silent, cowed, and humiliated the live-long day were, from the moment they entered the shower room, instantly transformed. As if on signal they opened their throats and began to roar like disintimidated lions returned from the lion tamer's cage and whip. On this day, especially, their shouts rose above the rush of the showers, a clamor of outrage, unmitigated hatred for their oppressor, and renewed pride in their kind.

The shower stalls were in a long, windowless room at the end of the bunkhouse. One wall was lined with a double tier of wire lockers crammed with greasy, sweat-saturated work clothes, soggy towels, and cheap toiletries, all together exuding a smell so strong it could almost be felt and pushed aside with the hands. At the far end of the room stood the pitifully inadequate water heater whose blistering contents were exhausted in five minutes and whose inadequacy inspired the pell-mell, undignified race between the tired men who jumped down from the gang truck at the end of the day. For all but the swift the choice was either to wait an hour for a bath, or try and cut the accumulated grime with ice water.

Opposite the lockers the showers were nothing more than a row of open pipes spilling their scalding, then icy blasts down upon a slatted wooden floor.

In five minutes the room was packed with shouting naked men. Cotton, dancing on his toes, teeth chattering, lapped out handfuls of water onto his slick body and scrubbed himself furiously with a gray abrasive soap.

"Jest a ignorint sonofa*bitch* is what he is!" he yelped. "He's gonna crowd me a little too fur one of these days, an' I'm tellin' you, when he does, he's gonna git some wind tuck out of his sails, and that ain't just horse-hockey neither!" He sucked his lungs full of air and ducked under the shower, letting out a gasp at the icy impact of the water. Then he went into an orgy of arm-flailing as if he had already come to grips with his enemy.

Ort's cries, lacking the elastic braggadocio of youth, were more bitter, but still, this night, salted with new hope of retribution. He stood flat-footed, blue-white and trembling with cold, soaping himself. The muscles of his arms and chest were sagging cords. The hair on his chest and down his belly was streaked with gray.

"I've laid a heap o' pipe man an' boy, and I've worked for some certified sonsofbitches. But that man is the shittiest excuse for a human being I ever run up against in my life."

"That dirty bastard," said Otho. "Twenty minutes we got stuck today."

"Twenty-five! It was twenty-six after when I set down in the goddamn truck, an I got *railroad* time!"

"Sorry devil stuck us nigh ten minutes at dinner, too, don't fergit that."

"Oh, he's a petty thief, he is," said Ort, coming out from under the shower, gasping and chilled. "Stealin' a nickel's worth o' time from us rich roustabouts and givin' it to them poor millionaire sonsabitches in Philadelphia."

"One of these days that big ugly bastard is gonna make me really mad," said Cotton between his teeth, toweling himself savagely with a dingy towel. "Then I'm really gonna—"

"Horseshit!" said Carl, scornfully. Carl was a nondescript man who had little to say. Being a practical defeatist and coward himself, he was irritated by this windy show of after-work fortitude on the part of the junior member of the gang. "You like to peed in your britches today."

"Yeah?" said Cotton belligerently. "Well, you just wait and see. I ain't like myself when I really git mad. You ask some of them down at Crane! I'll take so much, an' then I won't take any more."

"Sho," said Carl.

"They's one thing I'm waitin' to see," said Tyson, the jack-man, opening the topic that was on all minds, the one which they had been saving back, savoring like children eating around the fringes of a cookie and saving the cherry in the center for the last tempting bite. "One of these days a sonofabitch that calls hisself Cap Bruner is gonna get his frame clumb. An' I mean clumb *good*. I'm talkin' about that stabbin'-man. I'd a'walked off this job six months ago, but they's one sight I don't want to miss, and that's when that stabber-man gits his belly full and tries on that pusher's ring."

It was clear that every man in the room had been holding back something he had to say on this subject, and they all tried to say it at once, in a deafening burst of talk.

"You ain't just a-wolfin'!" cried Cotton. "That Jim'll cream 'im!"

"Hoo-hoo, goddamn," said Otho gleefully. "Didn't ol' stud-duck git tuck down a notch about the drinkin' water!"

"When I was his age I never taken nothin' offa nobody, neither," said Ort. "Only thing is, he ort to of clumb him right then."

"Ain't he a perculiar joker, though, that Jim?" said Cotton. "Looked like he was about to unload on ol' blubber-gut, then he jest walked off."

"He'll unload one of these days," said Tyson. "With both barrels. Then that Cap, he won't be *able* to walk off."

"Oh, that will be a fight to see!"

"Be one o' them two-hit fights. Jim'll hit him, an' he'll hit the ground."

"Don't kid yourself, button. That Bruner's plenty man, 'spite his gut. He's got forty pounds on Jim, maybe fifty."

"He'll wish he had eighty when that Jim gits a-holt of him. Christ! That Jim'll ram him in a pipe collar an' spin him up to his ass like a joint of fo'-inch, 'fore he can git his fists balled."

Just then the door opened and Jim McNeely came in with a swirling draft of cold air. It was, perhaps, a part of the way the men felt about him that Jim McNeely never raced for the shower. He never engaged in that petty, futile scramble for the first few minutes of warm water. Entering now, late as usual, with a fairly respectable towel cinched around his hard, flat belly, his dark hair matted close to his head with drying sweat, he was greeted by the men, most of them years older than he, proudly, playfully, as if he were a big brother. He walked through the midst of the shivering, chattering men and they made way for him, chucking his rump, playfully ham-boning his shoulder. His chest had grown big and hard in three years and his long muscled arms were still swollen from the day's labor. He hung his towel on a nail and with a grimace went about the business of soaping himself.

"J'ever have frosty balls?" cackled Cotton, catching a handful of icy water and splashing the late arrival with deadly aim. Jim McNeely gasped and dropped his soap and in the same spasm of motion darted out and seized the youth by the neck and arm and shoved him under the frigid stream from a shower pipe and held him there until Cotton was yelling with joy and agony. The room rocked with shouts of laughter. They were all proud of Jim McNeely's strength and quickness and felt a special warm pride that he could take a joke. Especially Cotton.

When the ruckus had quieted, Tyson brought up the thing that was on everybody's mind.

"Looked like fer a minute that you and the stud-duck was goin' to fist city," he said.

Jim McNeely only grunted and finished soaping himself.

"Yeah, what about that, Jim?" Cotton said with anxiety that was child-like. "You think you can take him?"

Jim McNeely tossed his bar of soap quickly to Cotton and scrubbed his soapy hands over his face and hair. He said, "Aw, there's not but one thing wrong with old Cap. Like a fella told me a long time ago, he's just got a little shit in his blood. I guess he can't help that."

He stepped quickly under the sparkling stream, gasping and stamping and scrubbing in a paroxysm of motion until the icy water had sluiced the gray suds from his head and body and down through the wooden slats into the floor.

The winter died upon the gray and dry land, and the spring blew in and howled its sandy breath across it, then choked off at the end with a short, violent spasm of rainstorms. Then the summer began, early and hot. Jim McNeely counted his money in his sleep. The total in the little red bank book increased with such painful slowness that it hardly seemed to move at all. It was like the watched pot, and he wondered sometimes, when his spirits sank in the long dull evenings, whether he would ever, *could* ever, get together a stake big enough to do a man any good. Without a stake he didn't know what he would do if he left Dead Lake, except get another job, and jobs were hard to find—he had made inquiries from time to time—and even if he could get another one, it would just be another job, a better pusher maybe, but essentially no different from this one. A working man's job, in which you paid your sweat for the dubious privilege of just staying alive. No steady progress up a ladder to prestige and comfort and security. Just shelter and food to stay alive for this week, this month, nothing more.

Tonight he was feeling, as Ort often said, very "low in his mind," and because Ort had instigated the usual midweek poker game which was loudly in progress in the room, and because he didn't feel like drifting down the porch and getting into a long-winded conversation with Dent Paxton, which almost always ended up with Dent turning philo- sophical and cross-examining him imperiously about his basic aims and motives in life and him getting more than half sore and calling Dent a flea-brained dreamer and stalking off to bed so aggravated it was hard to sleep, he, this night, put on a fresh suit of khakis and struck out for Coker City. He went by himself, giving himself the reason that he needed some razor blades, though all he really wanted was a change of scenery and a little distraction.

As he walked up the camp road through the dark warm night to the gate his eyes strayed to the lighted windows of the house of Clyde Montgomery, the engineer. He couldn't see anyone moving inside, but Montgomery's company car was not parked in front and his personal car was in the garage, which meant to Jim McNeely that the one he was really thinking about was probably at home, alone, and this set off the tiny explosions in the tiny streams which flowed from his healthy, pent-up glands.

With the passage of time he had developed a casual speaking acquaintance with Lee Montgomery, as people did in time who lived together in the same camp, even though they never met socially. Once or twice—one time in Coker City and once in Odessa, he had caught eyes with her, and nodded. Each knew who the other was. He had been staring at her in a drugstore, that social center of desolate places, both times. She had glanced at him and looked away, then as if drawn by the unconscious intensity of his eyes she had looked back and a little thing had passed between them which was probably nothing more than a vigorous male's instinctive avowal of his desire, and the female's half-dismayed, half-flattered acknowledgment of the compliment.

The topic of conversation which in the bunkhouse was relished only slightly less than the long expected head-on collision between Jim McNeely and Cap Bruner was the sexual desirability, imagined prowess, and "hotness" of the District Petroleum Engineer's wife. In his usual philosophical approach to the subject, which swayed no one, Dent Paxton put it thus: most men, pitiful creatures, are attracted by the same shape, the same musk, the same vibrations, which are endowments of certain favored females of the human species. "You bastards all get your wicks up about the same woman. But that's all you get. Think how nice it would be if you could get excited about some babe like that no-hips cashier at the grocery store. You wouldn't have any competition at all. And in the sack, in the dark, you couldn't tell the difference. It's all in your stupid minds."

"That's just straight pussy you're talking about," said Ort, waxing a bit philosophical himself. "What I'm gonna tell you about is love. Love is when you sack up with somebody, and still want to kiss 'em when you git th'oo. I ain't loved many women in my life, but I'm really in love with that engineer's wife."

"Ort," said Jim McNeely, disgusted with the conversation, almost angrily, "you're just a randy old goat. Why don't you shut up. That girl's a married woman."

"*Ma-a-an*, is she a woman!" said Ort enthusiastically. "I bet she flangs that silly Montgomery around till he can't tell which way west is. An' he don't act to me like he got sense enough to know what to do with it."

Jim McNeely reached the cattle-guard at the camp entrance just as a pair of headlights whizzed down the road outside. He grunted, for he had missed an almost certain ride and realized that he would probably walk the mile and a half into town before another car came along. Today he was tired enough that he didn't relish the prospect of more exercise.

He had walked only a hundred yards down the dark road when another pair of headlights bore down upon him. As he glanced back and stepped to the shoulder the car slowed, its tires crackling on the tarry surface as it came to a stop beside him. He opened the door gratefully and got in, momentarily blinded by the lights.

"Much oblige," he said.

Before his eyes adjusted to the darkness he realized, perhaps by the faint fragrance, perhaps intuitively and with a pleasant rise of gooseflesh along his ribs, that the driver was young and female and, astonishingly, the very one he had just been thinking of.

"Hello," she said.

"Well, hello," he replied. "Thanks for the lift."

"I recognized you," she said, shifting gears as the car gained momentum again. "I don't make a practice of picking up strange men on highways after dark. Isn't it a lovely night?"

"I guess it is," he said. "I hadn't noticed til now."

"Maybe it's just the contrast. It was a real scorcher today."

Jim McNeely said, "It sure was. Fella out on a rig told me he saw a lizard crawl up on a steam pipe to cool off."

Lee Montgomery laughed with delight. "Did he really?"

"The fella really said it. I can't say about the lizard. Anyway, it was hot."

She laughed again and said, "I'm on my way to buy some candles. My husband told me the electricity would be off for a while sometime tonight. Is that what brings you to the metropolis?"

Jim McNeely said, "They're cutting a new pump station into the power line. The service won't be off long. I reckon I can make out in the dark. I'm just going to be going."

"My!" she said. "A big night in Coker City. You single boys really don't have much to do out here, do you? No YMCA. No ping-pong."

"Oh, I don't know. We can always go to Pinky's."

"Oh! I've heard about Pinky's," she said, with slightly horrified interest. "Sounds like a very wicked place. Soft lights and music and exotic dancing partners."

"Yeah. One light bulb painted red, a juke box and two—well, dancing partners. They say it's all right if you're blind and drunk. No, I'm really just going for razor blades."

They drove the rest of the way in silence and drew up and parked, head-in, in front of the Coker City Drug. It was such a short ride that Jim McNeely was sorry it was over. It gave him a funny feeling to be sitting this close to a pretty girl, something he hadn't experienced in a long time. He said, "Many thanks for the ride. Sure beats walking."

She said, "I'm glad I happened along." Their eyes caught for an instant, with the same little clash that he had felt when he had seen her before. Then they got out of the car and went into the drugstore.

He bought his razor blades and walked down the street, feeling troubled. He stopped in the Club Cafe and drank a cup of coffee, just to be doing something, then he went past the pool hall and decided he couldn't stay interested in a game of pool, then headed on down the main street toward the filling station at the end to catch a ride back to camp. He was walking around a pile of gravel and a cement mixer which forced him out into the road when the car pulled up beside him. Lee Montgomery called out the window, "You want a ride back?"

He got in beside her again, feeling unaccountably happy. He said, "I ought to be paying you taxi fare."

She said, "I ought to be paying you for the company. With this crazy drilling program my husband spends half of his nights on a rig somewhere. I'm practically a rig widow. It's nice to have somebody to talk to."

"Lots of leases expiring," said Jim McNeely, wondering quickly if he could read something provocative, some veiled invitation in her words, and deciding as quickly that this was silly. "They've got to drill 'em and they nearly always get to the critical point at night. At least it seems that way."

"It certainly does. But I'm sure it's all done for the good of the Company. I dread going back to that hot house, though. It holds the heat until two or three o'clock. I don't know why people don't sleep out in the yard. My husband thinks that uncivilized."

There was silence as they reached the end of the town and turned left on the main road leading to Camp.

On a rash impulse, Jim McNeely said, "A cold beer might make it seem cooler. How about stopping by Pinky's for one?"

Lee Montgomery took her foot from the accelerator. She turned and looked at him, and her tone was reproachful, almost cold. "Are you asking me to go to Pinky's with you?"

"Oh, no!" said Jim McNeely quickly, wincing at his ineptness. "I didn't mean *that*. I meant I could run in and get a couple of cans of beer, and we could drink 'em on the way to Camp." He tried to steer out of a bad moment with a bantering tone, "That way I could pay you back for the lift. I don't like to be under obligation to anybody."

The girl considered this silently for a moment as she let the car roll along under its own momentum, then she decided not to be angry, and laughed. It was, after all, a harmless suggestion. This young man was pleasant and attractive, and he apparently hadn't meant to be fresh. He was, after all, a neighbor, a fellow inmate in dear old Camp Dead Lake. They were all in this thing together. This rationalization was aided by the fact that a cold beer out of the can seemed at this moment almost irresistibly appealing.

"Well," she said. "If we go dutch."

"It's bad luck to go dutch," he said. "Sometime I'll run into you and your husband in Odessa and you can buy me one."

She hesitated. "Mm. All right. I guess so," she said, thinking it would be a cold day in August when she would ever try to explain to Clyde Montgomery why she owed a beer to this good-looking young roustabout.

Halting the car rather far out on the road in front of Pinky's, she left the motor running while Jim McNeely went quickly inside. Moments later he reappeared holding two cans wrapped in paper napkins in one hand. When she had started up again, he handed one of them to her. "Ice-cold Schlitz Blue Ribbon," he said. "Good health to you."

She drove along slowly, sipping from the little triangular hole in the can. "Mm! Divine! I'd almost forgotten how good a cold beer is. Reminds me of college."

Jim McNeely said, "If you had a million dollars you couldn't enjoy it any more."

"That's a happy thought."

"Not original. I'm quoting William Shakespeare Paxton."

"Oh, Dent. What a funny boy!"

"He's a character, all right. No, he's really a pretty good guy. Good for what, I don't know. Anyway, I like him."

133

"That's a feeling not shared by all, I hear."

"Oh, I don't know. He doesn't mean any harm. People just don't understand him."

"Do you?"

"Well—no, I don't guess I do. But I like him, anyway."

"Well, tell me, Mister McNeely, how are you enjoying your stay in Dead Lake?"

"Gosh, call me Jim."

She thought about this a moment. "If I do, then what will you call me?" she said, a sudden trace of coolness again in her voice.

"I'll call you Mrs. Montgomery," he replied with the slightest bantering twinkle in his tone. "Like I'm supposed to. But you can call me Jim, anyway. When anybody calls me Mister McNeely I feel like they don't like me." As this sounded a little presumptuous in his own ears, he added, "Not that I'm running for constable or anything."

Driving along with one hand, sipping her beer in the other, Lee Montgomery said, "That's pretty funny. If I call you Jim, you should call me Lee. It doesn't seem natural to call you Mister McNeely, and, well, I guess it really wouldn't be proper or something for you to call me Lee. What a world."

"That's right, it wouldn't be proper. I'm a peon and you're an engineer's wife."

"I didn't mean that. I mean, being a married woman—You know what I mean. Don't you?"

"I know what you mean. That's life. I'll tell you what let's do and settle it. You call me 'hey,' and I'll call you 'say.' Next time we meet you can say, '*Hey*, how are you?' and I'll say, '*Say*, I'm sure glad to see you.'"

She giggled so at this that a trickle of beer went down her chin. She wiped it with the back of her wrist.

"Very well, 'hey.' Look, you made me spill my beer." She waited a moment, then she said, "I don't think you'll be a peon out here forever."

"You don't? Well, anyway, I don't intend to be. I'm running an ad in the papers for a job as vice president of an oil company. I haven't had any takers yet."

"I'll bet you'll make it. Maybe not all in one jump. But from what I hear, you'll make it, if that's what you want."

He was silent as she slowed up at the Camp entrance. He took the beer can from her hand as she turned into the gate over the cattle-guard, then handed it back to her.

He said, "What do you want?"

It was a short distance to her house. She braked to a stop in front. She cut off the motor and switched off the headlights.

"I beg your pardon," she said, and her voice was definitely iced up now.

"Look," he said, feeling a sudden intoxication and boldness that the beer had nothing to do with. He knew that with his last question he had definitely taken a liberty, but he didn't care. Perhaps it was the closeness, the freshness of this young, beautiful woman from whom he was about to depart and to whom he would probably never again be close enough to smell the freshness of and feel—yes, almost feel—the alive animal excitement of. It was a moment of instinctive opportunity.

"Look," he said again. "We're living here together on a desert island. Don't think people don't see you and know you're here. You're on every man's mind in this camp. I got no right to ask it, but I've thought about it, and I've wondered what you're looking for. I'm serving my time here because I have to. I started from scratch or less. I don't know where I'm going, but I know the direction, and it's up, way up. That's why I wondered about you. You seem like you ought to be big-time. I don't know what a woman's ambition is. Raise kids? Partly, maybe. But I don't see you with a bunch of kids, living in a company house somewhere, or even over in Midland as a superintendent's wife." He began to trail off, losing force, losing his thought. "We haven't got much to think about out here. You're topic A amongst the single boys. I mean, I just wondered—"

"Yes?" said Lee Montgomery, her voice bristling with indignation. "How interesting. Is that all? Don't stop. Do go on."

"No, that's all. It's too much already. I'm sorry. Just charge it to desert fever."

Lee Montgomery sat stiffly for a moment, then drained the last drop from the beer can and cleared her throat sharply. "I must say you have gotten a lot of mileage out of one can of beer."

With an explosive laugh, feeling suddenly giddy and foolish, fighting off a spasm of boyish hysterics, Jim McNeely said, "I should have walked back to camp. Like I said, we get the desert fever out here. Don't take it wrong. Here—look." He shook his empty can, then gripping its two ends firmly in his strong hands he crimped it with his thumbs, then abruptly crushed the can together as if it had been a pasteboard carton. It was a minor feat which those who are strong can do, and he did it easily. "That's for luck." He handed her the crumpled can. "For you—whatever you want."

She looked at the can, amazed, momentarily distracted from this odd, outrageous conversation. Then she gripped her own can in her two hands and squeezed and strained until her fingers trembled, but she could not make the slightest dent. Jim McNeely took the can from her and in one motion crimped it and crushed it together. He said, "You got to hold your mouth right." He looked at her in the dim light that came from the bulb on her porch.

"You can have mine. I'll keep yours. I feel like it'll be good luck for me," he said.

Then he got out of the car and, still holding the crumpled can, walked down the oiled road in the dark, tossing the can lightly in his hand, toward the bunkhouse, leaving Lee Montgomery breathing sharply, queerly, between anger and amazement, staring after him in the car behind.

14

IT WAS LATE OF A FRIDAY AFTERNOON IN LATE SUMMER, not yet dark, though mauve shadows had begun to lengthen across the Camp compound. A cool sundown breeze whispered through the screen door into the bunkhouse room where Jim McNeely was shaving, after a late shower, clad only in the damp towel cinched about his waist. His roommates had showered and dressed with Friday night's usual urgency and had departed, scattering in pursuit of their respective weekend pleasures and consolements, leaving the room a shambles of clothing, old magazines, toilet articles, playing cards, dominoes, and other debris of single working men who have little pride of home.

Scraping the last whiskers from his neck Jim McNeely swirled the safety razor in the tin basin on the cold stove, then washed the remaining scraps of lather from his tanned jaw, pulled the towel from his waist, and dried his face. He walked out onto the porch naked, since there was no one to see him from the south but the jack rabbits. Sloshing the basin of water far out across the gravelly ground, he returned to the room. There he procured clean underwear shorts and socks from the old suitcase under his bunk, took down a fresh suit of khakis from a hanger in the closet, and began slowly and methodically to dress himself.

He had finished dressing and was standing spraddle-legged and stooped before the small mirror combing his wet, dark hair when Pluto came in.

Pluto opened the screen door tentatively and stuck in his head, grinning in his puckish, half-apologetic manner. Seeing that Jim McNeely was alone, he insinuated his chunky body fully into the room.

"Hidy, stabber. I come in?"

Jim McNeely saw him in the mirror and grunted noncommittally without turning. He finished combing his hair, then began filling his pockets with wallet, knife, change, bank book, and handkerchief, which lay spread out on his bunk. Pluto was accustomed to being ignored. He sat down on the bunk across the room and began bouncing up and down lightly. He had on a shapeless comical hat, pulled down over his dark reddish hair, and he wore an expensive but rumpled Palm Beach suit, two-toned shoes, and a shirt and tie, carelessly tied and open at the collar.

"Goin' in to town tonight, stabber?" he said after a moment.

"Hadn't figured on it," said Jim McNeely.

"Nope," said Pluto, nodding and frowning, as if he had expected to be disappointed. His manner of speaking was boyish and deferential. "I just wondered. Uncle—you know, my uncle—well, he sent out for me to come home an' work in the Winfield office, an' I thought I'd throw a little party, kind of, before train time." He paused hopefully. "That is, if you happened to be going in to Odessa." Jim McNeely didn't answer. Pluto went on, "I mean, man, I got the old moola. I'm loaded. They paid me off an' it's not even payday. I'd sure hate to take any of it home."

"I haven't lost a cotton-pickin' thing in Odessa," said Jim McNeely. There was a tone of finality in his voice.

Pluto's bouncing slowed to a stop. He got up and stood around for a moment in silent, awkward discomfiture, touching a finger gingerly to the cold stove lid to see if it was hot, taking off his comical hat and resettling it.

"Well, heck, sure," he said, then added, rather idiotically, "Anyway, thanks, just the same." Pluto LeMayne tried very hard to be a nice guy and he wanted very much to be liked by everybody, and especially by Jim McNeely. For another little while he stood fiddling with his hat, then he said, "Well, it's been nice knowing you, stabber." He half offered his hand. But Jim McNeely sat down on his bunk, ignoring the farewell gesture, and began to tie his shoelaces.

"Yeah, well—" Pluto stood tentatively for another moment or two, then said, "Well, so long, Jim." Then slowly and reluctantly he started making his exit, backward, through the screen door.

When he had gone Jim McNeely got up and kicked his suitcase fiercely back in place under the bunk. He rubbed his hands roughly over his razor-slick cheeks and walked to the door and looked out. He felt mean and a little ashamed of himself. He didn't hate Pluto. He just hated the way things were set up that made it possible for a helpless, half-assed kid like

Pluto to sit on his rear end all day and draw the same pay that seasoned men sweated their souls out for, and then after less than six months to go "on up," as they said, to soft office work and the good life that the rest of them could never aspire to, only because they hadn't been smart enough to be born of parents who could send them to college. Jim McNeely was not wise enough or experienced enough in the infinite complexities of life to realize that the best of social and economic orders, given ordinary men to work with, will inevitably have its creaking inequities. He allied himself completely with the unendowed who put pig-iron together with sweat and salt and heart, and he felt keenly, bitterly, the gross unfairness in the system that this funny, likable boy represented.

On the other hand, he also felt as though he had just kicked the wind out of a big, flop-eared puppy that had come bounding clumsily in to lick his hand and be petted. He remembered how hungry he had felt for friendship four years ago. Pluto's only crime was being born well-off. Wadding up an old pay slip into a tight ball he tossed it in his hand for a moment, then threw it angrily at the stove and went out the door looking for Pluto.

The honkytonk was not crowded, for it was early. Two men, clad in "dress" shirts and trousers, stood at the bar drinking beer from clear glass steins. The bartender, a fattish, sinister-looking young man with curly hair, was reading a newspaper spread out on the bar. When one of the beer drinkers rattled his stein on the polished board the bartender, without glancing up, reached into the icing vat and drew up a brace of cold bottles which he opened and emptied into the steins. Behind the bar crude chalky letters on the large mirror spelled out the basic terms of trade: TEXAS BEER—15¢. BUD—20¢. A smaller sign tacked to the wall on the right said:

YOU CAN'T BUY BEER IN NO BANK
YOU CAN'T CASH NO CHECKS HERE.

Beer cans, blue and gold, were stacked in artistic pyramids on each side of the mirror. On the wall over the cash register another little cardboard sign, silver lettered, said:

IF YOU BELIEVE IN CREDIT, LOAN ME $5.

Above one of the pyramids was a large poster picture of a creamy, golden girl with luscious limbs and popping breasts, fulsomely displayed in a bathing suit which appeared to have been applied with a spray gun. She was holding a frosty bottle of Grand Prize and she winked and smiled at you wherever you were, as if life was one grand frolic so long as you had a cold bottle of Grand Prize in hand. All around the dark shadowy building were similar posters displaying overripe girls wearing almost nothing but inane, happy smiles.

From the nickelodeon a coarse voice was whanging out a popular tune: "*Oh, sweet Corrina, whereja stay las' night*—" In the absence of paying customers and in a pitiful attempt to create the illusion of life and gayety in this dismal establishment, two pairs of honkytonk girls were dancing together, holding each other loosely around the waist, whirling mechanically, and hitting the floor hard with their feet, more or less in time to the music. All chewed gum and looked with boredom out of their mascaraed eyes at nothing. Whenever a new man came in the place one pair would dance over in front of him, dipping and wiggling their hips to the tune, advertising their wares, trying to stir up a little business.

Sitting in one of the deep-shadowed booths, drinking whiskey, were Pluto and Jim McNeely and a couple of women. Pluto drained the last of a pint bottle into a shot glass, then cut his fingers trying to open the metal cap of a fresh bottle. He swore, sucked his fingers and poured some whiskey into the small wound. Then they all took a drink and chased the whiskey with Cokes.

Pluto's girl was an imperfectly peroxided blonde named Boots, who had shaved off her eyebrows and drawn new ones higher up on her forehead, giving her the aspect of an exotic sheep. She leaned over and whispered something into Pluto's ear to which Pluto replied in a loud, thickening voice, "*Sure*, I'm gonna buy you another sweet-wine, sugar. Bartender! Bring this charmin' lady another goblet of mead!" He leaned his face close to hers and held a forefinger up between their noses. "Just as long as you take a drink of whiskey with me every time I do, I'll buy you sweet-wine til you bust, you ravishin' creature!"

The one called Darlene similarly approached the silent and somber Jim McNeely, but less confidently. She was a big brunette with large breasts and hips compressed in a sausage-tight dress. Her face was heavily painted, and where the rouge left off the skin of her neck was dirty. She was the simpering, refined type, and she was already drunk.

"Don't you want to buy *me* a sweet-wine, hon?" she said.

"No, I don't want to buy you a sweet-wine," Jim McNeely said flatly. He had no use for honkytonkers. It wasn't only the bad experience he had had with the one who had infected him with gonorrhea. He looked upon honkytonkers as harpies who preyed on lonely sex-starved oil-field hands and gave nothing in return. They weren't even honest whores. As long as a drunk was buying them sweet-wine he was a walking angel, but when his money ran out he was a bum. Then they wouldn't give him a free smile, much less the companionship and consolement he was pining for.

These two were all the more repulsive to Jim McNeely because Pluto appeared to be having a good time with them. For Jim McNeely knew that in a little while Pluto would be far away, sitting with another gentler girl in a chiffon dress on some country club terrace, telling her, to gasps and giggles of delighted horror, about his honkytonk experiences when he had been an oil-field hand. And he would make himself out to be quite a man of the world, and later he would take this nice girl out on the tenth tee and neck hell out of her. But Jim McNeely knew that when *he* got to honing for a woman, his only recourse would be the same as Ort's and the rest—get liquored up until a stained crepe dress looked like chiffon and a dirty neck looked pure and soft as swan's down. Honkytonkers were a passing adventure in Pluto's young life, but to Jim McNeely they were symbols of his inferiority, and he despised them.

"Hon, just one little sweet-wine?"

"You're wasting your time. I'm not buying."

"Well, hon, I can't just set here if you won't buy nothing for me."

"I'm not stopping you," said Jim McNeely. "Good-bye."

Pluto LeMayne held up both hands, as if he were about to give an invocation. "Stay! Cease an' desist this idle chatter. This is my party an' I'm buyin' the sweet-wine for *every*body. Darlene, you luscious peach, you just keep your seat. All you got to do is take a drink of whiskey every time my good ol' buddy does, an' soothe his dark and troubled brow with your tender womanly intuition an' everything's gonna be great! OK?"

He beamed at the girls and they giggled and punched one another, and Darlene said he ought to have been a preacher. Pluto whistled shrilly and cried, "Hey, Oscar! C'mere. Make it two *double* sweet-wines for the ladies!" The bartender came over presently with the two small glasses filled with ice and diluted Coca-Cola. Ceremoniously Pluto extracted a dollar from the crumpled wad of money he took from his pocket and handed it to the bartender, who gave each of the girls two sweet-wine tickets to be redeemed for a dime a ticket when they got off work.

Pluto poured whiskey in all of the shot glasses, spilling a good deal on the table. He arose unsteadily and held up his glass.

"Ladies an' gentlemen, I'm gonna give a toast. To the best damn pipe-liner in West Texas. I give you the man that ought to be the boss of the whole damn works out here. He knows more about pipe-linin' an' oil-field work than anybody, but he's not the boss because he won't rat on his fella coworkers, an' he won't grape up to nobody! I give you the man of the hour, the one an' only Jim McNeely!"

Boots and Darlene laughed and clapped and said, "Speech!"

Jim McNeely scowled tiredly at Pluto and grumbled, "For Christ's sake. You're drunk." He took down his shot of whiskey without chasing it and made a face and sat looking mean and glum.

For a long time they carried on in this fashion, putting away the whiskey, collecting sweet-wine tickets, Pluto doing most of the talking, belting himself with the warm bourbon and sloshing Coke down on top of it, pulling deeply on a cigarette and drooling and weaving a little more in his seat after each drink.

Across the table Jim McNeely drank quietly, turning the small oily glass between his fingers, holding the liquor in his mouth for a moment then swallowing and breathing out hotly through his nostrils. The first bottle had done nothing for him but bring a bitter edge to the dissatisfaction and anger that lay always in the back of his mind. He kept on into the second bottle looking and waiting for the old buoyancy of spirit, the bellicose confidence in himself, what he was going to do and be that in former times used almost always to come after the third or fourth drink. That was before he came to grips in his mind with the practical business of getting ahead in the world. But tonight the old feeling didn't come at all. The liquor seemed to burn like acid rather than fire. He sat staring into the darkness, oblivious of the hulking woman who sat beside him nodding and tittering at Pluto's broad, self-satisfied witticisms, she lifting each succeeding drink a trifle more unsteadily, but always with the little finger arched, the other hand meanwhile filing sweet-wine tickets away in her ample bosom.

Pluto was sloppy drunk now. He draped himself over Boots, blubbering in her ear, and kept trying to run his hand up her dress. Boots acted horrified and pushed him away and giggled outlandishly. Pluto took another drink and soon his passion rose to irresistible heights. His face was flushed and his hair tousled like an old broom. His whisperings in Boots's ear became more urgent and she kept teasing him, shoving his hands away, and giggling. After a while she gave in and Jim McNeely heard her coo, "Well, all right, hon, but you'll have to rent a cabin."

"I'll *buy* the goddamn cabin! How much is it?" Pluto said, fumbling in his pockets.

"They get four dollars for a short-time."

With a grand gesture of disdain Pluto drew forth a handful of crumpled bills and without counting them planked them down on the table. Jim McNeely started to stop the girl's hand when he saw it snake out for the money, but he didn't, and with disgust watched her punch the wad down into the cleft between her breasts. He shrugged tiredly. What the hell. It was this stupid boy's money. Pluto thought he was having a good time and money was no problem to him. The hell with him. But it hurt when Jim McNeely translated the dollars into hours on a pipeline gang.

"Don't follow me too quick, honey," Boots said under her breath, with feigned and unnecessary caution. "Just act like you was goin' to the johnny." She slid out of the booth and disappeared through the back door. Pluto held himself in check for ten seconds, then, giving Jim McNeely an exaggerated wink, he got to his feet and listed unsteadily across the floor, as if walking on a slope.

After a while, when her sweet-wine, demurely sipped, was nearly gone, the big girl Darlene launched a fresh assault upon Jim McNeely.

"Hon, what makes you so cold tonight?" she said in her most understanding tone. There was no response. Jim McNeely poured another drink and took it without relish, almost chewing the hot liquid, its deadening effect now penetrating to his deep centers and numbing his face and lips.

Darlene's voice grew plaintive. "Don'tcha wanta have a good time with me, hon?"

Jim McNeely set his glass down hard and leaned back in the booth and turned his full gaze on the woman. Then he gave such a sudden, loud, explosive laugh that Darlene jumped and started to get out of the booth.

"Damned if you don't have more bulldog tenacity than any bulldog I ever saw!" he said.

Darlene settled back down uncertainly and tried to focus her eyes on him. "*Hmm*, hon?" she said with stupid sweetness. "Well, that's better now. I was beginning to think you didn't like me."

"Oh, for Christ's sakes! Why'd you pick on me? I already told you, you're wasting your time. Your girl friend's got the gravy boat. I got no money."

"An' *who*," she demanded in an offended tone, "said I wanted any money?"

"I see," he said. "You love me for myself alone."

"Well, I guess if a girl likes a boy, why she's got a right to—" She groped for words to express the unmercenary character of her interest. "A right to—hell, I'll pay for the goddamn cabin myself!"

Just then Jim McNeely caught sight of Boots strolling in nonchalantly through the back door, returning alone, ironing out her dress with her hands. He pushed the big girl roughly out of the way and got out of the booth and went after Boots, catching up with her at the bar. He took a hitch at his pants and sized up the bartender, thinking he might have a fight on his hands. The girl had come back too quick.

"Where's the kid?" he said.

All the honey was gone out of the hard blonde's voice. "Aw, he's too goddamn drunk. He couldn't do nothin' tonight if you helped him."

Hanging on a moment of uncertainty, debating with himself whether it was worth the effort to try to recover Pluto's money, he finally said, "Oh, the hell with it!" and turned and crossed the room and went through the back door into the night air. He passed two dark cabins, and when he came to the door of the third, which was lighted, he went in. In a corner, opposite the iron bed with its sagging, beaten mattress, stood Pluto, wearing only his shirt. He was weaving wildly, bracing his hands against the walls, vomiting on the walls, on the floor and himself. Jim McNeely waited until the paroxysm had passed, then he caught Pluto by the shirt collar and straightened him up. Pluto looked at him through reeling, watery eyes. His face was mottled red, his child's mouth drooling long stringers of saliva. He started to speak, then wheeled abruptly and began to retch again in violent jerks. The pungent fumes of soured whiskey and half-digested food made Jim McNeely begin to feel a little sickish himself, but he supported Pluto by the back of his shirt collar until he began to gag and moan dryly. Then he wheeled him around and let him fall onto the bed. Taking up the white water pitcher from the washstand Jim McNeely measured Pluto's prostrate form, then let him have the contents full in the face.

For a long time they walked in the dark shadowy night, walking along the edge of the road in and out of light patches. Jim McNeely half supported

144

the younger man and relaxed his grip on him only to let him break away and gag futilely at intervals and spit and sputter into the dirt. The night was clear and still and the horizon to the north was tinged with the diffused light of gas flares in the oil fields. The meaty smell of petroleum, even here, was faintly present in the air. Headlights of cars on the road approached from both directions and whooshed by, bound for unknown destinations.

All the while Pluto burbled, incessantly, lugubriously. "A friend in need is a true friend like you indeed my old Jim friend . . . isn't everybody's got a true friend indeed . . . no, indeed, ooogoddamn I'm seck, Jim . . . I'm a seck Messican . . ." He stumbled along, falling over his own feet and his teeth began to chatter as if from cold. He was a big, sloppy, sick, and drunken boy. Jim McNeely walked along beside him, silently, holding him up. He steered him into a hamburger joint and made him drink a cup of black coffee which Pluto promptly went outside and threw up.

"Jim . . . ol' pal Jim . . . I'm a dizzy sonfabitch . . . I wanta go to bed . . ."

Gradually the cool night air and the walking cleared him up a little, but he continued to talk, without stopping. He turned and put his hands on Jim McNeely's shoulders and made a big effort to look him in the eyes.

"Jim, I jus' want to tell you this one thing. An' I don't want you to get any idea an' say, 'Well, ole Pluto's drunk an' he don't know what he's sayin',' because I know when I'm drunk an' when I'm not, an' I know I'm drunk, see, drunker'n a by-god, but I just want to tell you this one thing and this is what I want to tell you, see? OK?"

"All right. OK," said Jim McNeely.

"If I didn't like you I wouldn't be here right now, see? You know that?"

"Yeah. Yeah," Jim McNeely said.

"You goddamn right you know it . . . ole Pluto may be drunker'n a god-damn skunk, but when he says somethin' it don't jus' mean goin' in one ear an' out th' other, see. . . . *See?*" Pluto became almost belligerently insistent. He swayed around on his feet, holding onto Jim McNeely's shoulders and talking right into his face. "No, now wait a minute, this is no goddamn hock, see . . . you think I'm drunk . . . an' what if I am, I been around quite a bit for my so-called tender years, see, an' I know when I'm drunk an' I'm tellin' you that's no hock . . ."

"OK," said Jim McNeely. "No hock. You're drunk. Now let's get going."

"Now wait a minute, by God!" Pluto said, wrenching him around by the shoulders. "I don't wantohaveto think you're callin' me a dam' liar by your dang uncomplamentary tone a' voice . . . when I say no hock I don't mean I want any trouble about it, see?" Jim McNeely drew a deep breath, beginning to get a little exasperated. Pluto's momentary belligerence softened and he lurched against his friend and draped a heavy arm around his shoulder. The maudlin feeling of fraternity that alcohol infuses spread warmly through his whole body and even down into his feet.

"Lissen, Jim, you sweet sonofabitchin' ol' pipe walloper, you don't think fr'agoddaminute that ol' Pluto is gonna forget anything, see? We been through a hell of a lot together, you an' me, and don't think I don't know you been gettin' a dam' dirty deal . . . buckin' that stupid Cap Bruner . . . stupid ass . . . well, we got to have guys like Cap in this comp'ny t' keep most people in line, see, but not you. You ought to be *Cap's* boss . . . by God, don't you think framinute I'm not gonna set my uncle wise about some things. I'm goin' into Winfield an' I'm gonna talk to my uncle *straight* about you, see? *See?*"

"OK. OK, Pluto," Jim McNeely said shortly. "Let's go. You got a train to catch."

"Now wait a minute, by God!" Pluto jerked him around facing him again, and almost lost his balance. "I don't 'preciate you actin' like I'm just shootin' a bunch of hock an' won't giveitanotherthought, see? *I'm going to talk to my uncle*, see, an' I don't 'preciate you callin' me a goddamn drunken liar, see, because you an' me've been through the mill together. See? Well, if you don't believe it, go ahead an' call me a liar, by God!"

"Oh, for Christ's sake, I believe you, kid, now let's move."

"All right, just a minute . . . you say you *do* believe me, an' I don't believe I believe *you*, an' I want to hear you say it, by God! We'll have it out right here! Say, 'I believe ol' Pluto's goin' to talk to Uncle about me an' how I ought to be Cap's boss instead of him bein'—' . . . Oh, shit! Anyway, you say it! You're man enough to say it if you b'lieve it, an' I wanta hear it straight from you straight an' not from . . . not . . . say it . . . say, 'I believe Pluto's goin' . . .'"

Jim McNeely gave a sharp, exasperated growl and clasped his hands on Pluto's hot ears and shook him, not too hard, not angrily, but sharply.

"I believe you. I truly believe you, Pluto, you little bastard! Now, for Christ's sake, let's get the hell out of here!"

"Well, tha's more like it," said Pluto, pressing his ears back in place and starting off obliquely down the road. "That's the way I like to hear you talk. Now, le's *all* take a drink! Le's *all* take a drink an' get on the goddamn iron horse an' go to Winfield! Yeehoo!"

"Part of that's a real good idea," said Jim McNeely.

"Le's *all* take a drink an' go an' get Boots an' ol' what's-her-name an' go get on the goddamn *ferrocarril* an' go to Winfield! Where's Boots?"

"Oh, Christ, why don't you leave them old hides alone," Jim McNeely said.

"Ol' hides, sir? Ol' *hides!*" cried Pluto, stopping indignantly. "I'll have you know you're besmirchin' the fair name of the queen of my heart! The lady Boots! By God, sir, I owe her an apology . . . you want me to drag the fam'ly name in the mud . . . I got to apologize! By God, sir, a LeMayne never failed to raise a rail in the presence of a lady an' not apologize . . . by God, sir . . . !"

Jim McNeely turned Pluto over to the Negro Pullman porter, who accepted him reluctantly and kept whispering loudly, "You gen'a'men, they's folks already asleep in heah." They stood in the curving, mahogany-paneled passageway, and Pluto clung to Jim McNeely's hand and pumped it lugubriously, while loudly extolling his old friend's virtues to the porter.

Jim McNeely could see past Pluto down the long, dim-lit green-shrouded corridor. The Pullman car had the muffled, musty smell of privilege. It was a capsule of a rich and wonderful world that hurried, lights winking, through this desert in the dead of night, a small portable part of a world he had never known. He had never ridden in a Pullman. He felt vaguely bitter and faintly ill at ease.

The two girls who, hungrily, had picked up with them again, stood bulked together glassy-eyed and stupid just inside the door, like a couple of moulting birds automatically attendant upon any additional crumbs that might fall from Pluto's pockets.

"Ol' frien', you think I'm drunk," said Pluto, clinging to Jim McNeely's hand, falling against him. "But I jus' wanta tell you this one thing, an' no more hock, see? There's somethin' between you an' ol' Pluto tha's thicker than water, see? An' I want you t' know if you ever need anything atall why ol' Pluto'll always be there." His voice was getting soggy with tears. "You jus' call on him."

The porter started shaking Jim McNeely's sleeve, whispering insistently, "Boa'd, you gen'a'men, boa'd!"

"Don't think I'm hockin' ol' son, 'cause I never hadabrother, but if I did, you'd be him, an' I mean it."

"We's movin', gen'a'men!"

"When you need a frien' jus' remember you got ol' Pluto." He began to sob, hugging Jim McNeely around the shoulders. Jim McNeely felt the train jerk beneath him. The girls started scrambling wildly for the door. Jim McNeely freed himself, holding Pluto's wrists long enough to get out of his grasp.

"OK, kid. Take it easy. Good luck." He stepped down the passageway and swung out the door and dropped lightly off the moving train. After the last car had rolled past, dark and heavy, gaining momentum, leaving the bare rails glistening faintly red from the disappearing train lights, he stood beside the tracks following it with his eyes as it faded in the direction of the land where the green grass grew and the overhanging trees waved as the cars rushed past. Then he turned and started back toward the boxlike station house, crunching cinders under his feet.

As he walked through the dim patch of light that fell from the telegrapher's window he saw the two girls standing together by the road, waiting for him, and he grunted involuntarily with revulsion.

When he came up to them Boots addressed him in a hoarse, sleepy voice. "Hon, why don't you jus' give us six dollars and go and spend the night with *both* of us?"

"Not tonight, Josephine," he said, starting around them. Boots stepped in front of him and ran her fingers and hands up under his arms.

"We'll show you a *real good time*, sugar."

"Oh, come on. Get out of my way!" said Jim McNeely with sudden savage impatience, extricating himself and running squarely into the hulking Darlene, who embraced him in her big arms and began to love him up.

"Come on, Darlene," said Boots contemptuously. "Leave him go on home and play pocket pool!"

"Hon, I'll treat you right," said Darlene. "And for me, you don't even need any money."

"Look," said Jim McNeely, calling on a man's strength to get free from the entwining arms, "I'm not interested, see?"

"Hon, please. We'll give you something nice."

"No thanks. I don't want any souvenirs. I can't afford the doctor bills."

"Oh, izzat so!" said Boots, shaking her false blond curls right in his face, fairly spitting. "Well, let me tell *you* something! I wouldn't have nothin' to do with you if you was white!" As he stepped around her and started down the track she screamed after him, "An' what's more, if they wasn't a lady present, I'd tell you to kiss my ass!"

15

PLUTO'S DEPARTURE CAST A BITTER DEPOSIT IN THE mind of Jim McNeely, and it was many days before this was absorbed into his system and thrown off. Pluto had performed his token apprenticeship in the harsh fields of labor and sweat, where profanity and obscenity were as much a part of speech as breath, where art and beauty were absent or unrecognizable, where abstract, reflective thought was unknown and men's minds were almost wholly preoccupied with satisfying the elemental instincts to eat, to sleep, to rut, to become intoxicated, to escape from heat and cold and, to the greatest degree possible, from hard work. Pluto had returned to the world of softness and fragrance, of manners, fashion, clean women, books, polite language, where men worked with their brains instead of their backs, and the sex chase was played as a game more or less according to rules designed to heighten its subtle pleasures, rather than as a blind, blundering instinctive exercise of grunting, sweating animals.

Jim McNeely did not sort out and think all of these things rationally, but he felt them after Pluto had gone. And the vague, metallic cast of bitterness left him restless and irritable.

It was a Tuesday night and he had no reason whatever for going into Coker City, but he was in no mood to face a long evening of Cro-Magnon conversation with his roommates. Moreover, Dent was away for an evening meeting in Odessa to learn about some new, more efficient system of field accounting that was being installed by the Company in its constant, relentless quest for increased profits. And so, after supper, Jim McNeely headed down the oiled road from the mess hall toward the little town. He felt mean inside. He did not even turn his head to look at Lee Montgomery's house as he passed, to see what he could see, and imagine what he could not, for that was a fruitless exercise in self-flagellation, like staring at his savings bank book and imagining that the figures had three naughts behind each one of them.

It was a windy night. A light layer of dust had stirred over the flat land obscuring the dark line of the horizon, though it was not yet the sandstorm weather of spring. There was a vague promise of rain in the broken clouds that slipped down the sky, revealing glimpses of the high new moon. He stepped to the side of the road onto the gravelly shoulder when he heard the car coming down the road behind him and saw the oil-shiny road brighten ahead in the lights. He felt no pleasure when he heard the car slowing, for he had a whole night to kill and he had figured that the walk to town and back would take care of a good part of it. He didn't feel like speaking pleasantly and appreciatively to anyone for a lift.

When the car stopped beside him he turned and said curtly, "Thanks, I'm just taking a little walk."

"You need exercise?" said the voice from the car. "After a day in Bruner's gang, you still need exercise?"

He hesitated for a moment, looking into the dark car. Then he opened the door and got in.

Lee Montgomery didn't start up right away, and there was laughter in her voice.

"Going to Pinky's?"

"I don't know. I may do that."

"Well, if you're going to Pinky's you should save your strength for dancing."

"Or something."

"I understand Pinky's has a new girl."

"I'm not really going to Pinky's. I'm going to town—same old reason—just to be going."

"What a strange coincidence," she said, putting the car in gear and starting up. "That's exactly why I'm going. And when you're going to Coker City just to be going, you haven't got a heck of a lot to do. My husband is conferring in Odessa with somebody about something to do with a new field-accounting system."

Jim McNeely grunted lightly and watched the road ahead.

"I have had trouble generating enthusiasm over a new field-accounting system," she said. "Have you?"

He shrugged noncommittally. "I guess they need it."

After a moment she said, "You don't sound as if you had an opinion one way or the other about anything tonight. Well, anyway, it's an interesting night. Look at the rain drops on the windshield. When I first came out here I would turn on the windshield wiper at the first few spatters of rain. Now I know better. I'm desert-wise. It only makes a big smear of mud so that you can't see anything. You have to wait till it's really coming down. Wisdom comes with experience."

"Mm," said Jim McNeely curtly. The proximity of this fresh, clean, fragrant, desirable, inaccessible woman so full of fresh talk somehow deepened the depression of his spirits.

When she headed the car into the boardwalk by the drugstore, he started to get out.

"*Say,*" she said. The bright mischievous sound in her voice stopped his hand on the door handle. "I've been wanting to ask you something. What do *you* want?"

She looked straight at him, her dark eyes sparkling with almost laughing boldness. "I've been thinking about what you asked me. I've been thinking that's a very queer and presumptuous thing to ask anybody, unless you're prepared to tell them what *you* want."

Jim McNeely looked around at her curiously in the light from the drugstore and the flicker of a smile came and smoothed out the bitter lines around his eyes and mouth.

"I guess that's fair. Well, I'll have to think about it. Right now, what I want is razor blades. Again. You can always use some more razor blades."

"Razor blades. Men are slaves to razor blades."

"Women aren't?"

"Women, too. Only more so."

"Did you ever wonder why people cut the hair off themselves in some places and not in others?"

"I've wondered why we have hair at all."

"Well, some hair is pretty."

"Hair"—she shrugged—"is hair. We're creatures of convention."

"You sound like Dent Paxton."

"Oh, I like Dent. He's in Odessa learning about accounting procedures, too, isn't he? Well—here we are at the place that sells razor blades and enables us to face the world properly shaven."

They got out and went in and he held open the door for her. Then they wandered around the store, idly looking at the corn plasters and hot-water bottles and cheap toiletries in the show cases, not exactly together, but coming back together, very casually, every little bit, looking at the same things and exchanging small joking remarks, like a pair of children window-shopping. They stood for a while at the magazine rack leafing through the current issues. She bought a movie magazine and he selected a Blue Book. He started to ask her to have a Coke at the soda fountain then thought, hopefully, of something better, and when she didn't go to the soda fountain he began to think, or hope, that maybe she had the same idea.

A couple of times, out of curiosity, he cast his glance down at her bare, slender brown legs. Slick, smooth-shaven, almost shining. Beautiful legs. Firm, strong, and wonderfully shaped.

Soon he found himself having a pleasant time, wandering around, killing the dull hour in this drugstore. It was almost as if he were with this girl, yet not really with her. Presently when she said, "Oh dear, look!" and pointed through the windows to the dark street where rain was driving down now in sudden violence and they were marooned in the store alone, except for the old man behind the fountain who owned the place, Jim McNeely experienced a very pleasant feeling.

"Looks like we're trapped," he said.

"We'd drown before we could get to the car. And I left the window open on my side."

"I put mine up."

"Men are so practical and far-sighted. I hate them. The seat on my side will be soaked."

"Khakis are absorbent. I'll drive you back and soak up the rain. That's one way I can pay for my taxi fare."

"Who said chivalry was dead? It's a deal."

When the downpour slackened for a moment they went out the door and ran through the thinning rain to the car. Jim McNeely got under the wheel and she ran around to the other side. Then he backed out and started down the rain-mirrored street, feeling the wetness soaking into his clothes. After the turn onto the Camp road he drove slowly, then almost timidly he said what he had been thinking about.

"A cold beer would sure taste good to me."

She laughed. "You've been reading my mind."

He angled the car across the road toward the dark shack with the single red light bulb over the door.

Lee Montgomery opened her purse and took out a dollar bill. "Tonight it's on me. I insist."

Getting out of the car, Jim McNeely said, "A beer paid for by a lady wouldn't taste good."

In a moment he returned with four cans of beer, two in each hand. "What—? Well!" she said, verging uncertainly between surprised indignation and laughter. "What is this going to be? An orgy?"

Pressing two cans upon her and getting in and starting up the car, he said, "Before, when I went home, I wished I had another beer. One just makes me kind of restless. Two will make you sleep good."

"Sleep! I'm sleeping my life away already!"

A moderate rain had started again and by the time they reached camp the slanting white streaks in the darkness poured heavily down into the headlights.

She said, "Drive to the bunkhouse porch so you won't get wet."

He said, "I've got another beer to drink and I'd rather get wet than drink it alone. I can pull into the garage. It might hail before morning."

For a moment she thought about this. Then she said. "Well. All right. I guess you might as well."

He headed the car up the drive into the narrow single car shed and turned out the headlights. The sudden dark closing in around them was utterly black and so close that they both were surprised and left without speech for moments.

Then in a low funny voice, almost a whisper, he said, "Man, ain't it dark! I can't see the hole in the can."

In the same low, almost whisper she said, "You'll have to use Braille."

"Mm!" he muttered. "Wouldn't it be tough to be blind?"

"I don't know. Maybe," she said, still almost whispering. "But there'd be a lot of ugliness you wouldn't have to look at."

"Yeah, I guess so. At least if I were a blind man I wouldn't have one problem."

"And what is that?"

"I would never have seen you."

"Oh?" she said.

153

"I mean that."

"Oh, that's so silly." Her voice was still subdued, but she was not angry. "Why should that be a problem to you?"

"You're a problem to any man that has eyes."

"That *is* silly, Jim. I just happen to be the only young woman in Camp. You ought to get out and circulate more. There are lots of young women in the world."

"I've seen plenty of them. They're not problems to me."

"Oh, Jim. You're such a—you boys, men, have such an unnatural life, living out here alone, with nothing but Pinky's and those awful places in Odessa. Haven't you got a girl somewhere? Haven't you ever been in love?"

He pondered this a while, sipping his beer. "Once I thought I was. Seems like I always pick on the wrong people."

Gently and with interest she questioned him, and he told her about Mazie, and something about his early years in Winfield, about his mother, and Mazie's family, and what had happened to him and Mazie. She drew it out of him and listened respectfully and with what he somehow felt was real sympathy and interest. She said finally, "That was very hard for you. Life is very hard. But sometimes it's best that way. This might turn out for the best. I mean, that you didn't get married then. You might still marry her, and I'm sure—at least I have a feeling—that you'll be better prepared now and have a better chance of making it work, than if you'd run away and married her then."

"Maybe so, but I doubt it. Because that's over and done with now. I've almost forgotten her. She doesn't bother me any more. Only—"

"Only?"

"Only *you* bother me. That's the story of my life. Now *you* fill up my whole head, and body—any time, whenever I try to think about anything."

She answered him, quietly, with sudden tenderness. "Jim. You mustn't talk or think like that. You're just a lonely young man. And I just happen to be here, in sight. You'll meet some great girl one of these days. You've got your whole life ahead of you. You'll meet her."

He had finished one beer and it lay empty on the floor board under his feet. He placed the other, half consumed, on the top of the dash next to the windshield.

He turned toward her in the darkness and said, "That's not so. I won't ever meet anybody I want but you—"

Feeling for her, naturally, without violence or awkwardness, he found her arms with his hands, and he kissed her. Then, when he drew away the fraction of an inch he said, "I'm really gone about you."

In the palpitant darkness, in the moments outside of time that followed, he kissed her again, gently at first then with rising fierceness, and the shocked compassion with which she received his first kiss reeled into a mindless passion, at once submissive and responsive, as their lips clung together. His free hand fumbling at her waist groped its way upward until it touched then closed upon the swollen tenderness of her breast. He cut off her small gasp with his lips and drew her tight against his deep chest. Then, without design, in a pandemonium of desire, his hand was on the firm silky flesh of her knees, then between her thighs sliding lightly inward, upward. When the smoothness stopped in a corner of hot, humid, hirsute, tactile springiness, the passion rising in his throat almost choked him and it was as if an electric shock had shot through them both.

She tore her mouth from his with a fierce wailing sob and fought his hands from her body, straining rigidly from him in a paroxysm of grief and anguish. "*No!* Oh, God, *no!* Don't do that! Get away from me! Please!"

But the pent-up passion of months and years was upon Jim McNeely and he closed his arms about her shoulders, crushing her into him as he tried to kiss her again and again.

"Lee," he breathed, "I'm really gone about you. I need you, Lee! I need you so bad."

With surprising strength she broke his grip and caught his shirt at the throat in her two fists and held him away from her, trembling and sobbing, near hysteria. "Don't! Stop it, Jim! Leave me alone! I'm not a tramp! Don't make me a tramp! Don't make me bad!"

"I wouldn't make you bad. I love you, Lee."

"Then for God's sake, stop! Let me alone!"

Against her tigerish, steel resistance his fever drained out of him. He slowly relaxed and let his arms draw away from her. He sank back against the seat, a sickening feeling surging into him, through him. He had done a terrible thing. And he had been rejected, once again. And he had made a fool of himself, and had shattered something which he realized in a moment of agony that he valued—the image of himself in this Lee Montgomery's eyes, the image of himself as somebody decent, somebody good. He had revealed himself as just another ape, another hot-blooded goat, and a sap besides, who would try to mount any woman that treated him halfway decent, and gave him half a chance.

She sat bent over in misery, her fists against her forehead, shaking, crying, pathetically as if her heart would break. He sank deeper and deeper into a bottomless depression, black as the air around them.

"I'm sorry," he said in a dry voice, barely finding the ability to utter words. "I don't know what made me do it."

After a time her sobbing came slowly under control. She pushed back her hair and wiped her wet eyes with the heels of her hands. Then she straightened herself and smoothed her dress out with her hands.

"Somebody ought to shoot me," he said bleakly.

She took a deep breath and tried her voice. It was still fluttery. "It was my fault." She paused and took and expelled another slow breath to calm herself. "You haven't got a chance out here—it's like somebody who's been in prison. You're a male, after all. You just lost control. I shouldn't have let it happen."

"That's not what happened, Lee. I've seen plenty of women since I've been out here. It's you. I wasn't lying—what I said—I'm not a kid. I know what I say and I know what I want. But I know, too, that I was hoping too high."

For moments she said nothing, pressing her fingertips against her lips and eyes, drying the tears that kept flooding her eyes. The racing of her heart had slowly diminished and she was nearly in control of herself. Her voice was almost calm, but its timbre was liquid and soft. "Jim—you mustn't think—you mustn't punish yourself about this, because I know you're a good person. You can tell about people, instinctively. I'm not angry with you—because I know it was my fault. And—I don't know how to say it—you're a very attractive man. You mustn't think that I don't feel—that, well, if I were a single girl—but I'm not, so—"

"You don't love the man you're married to," said Jim McNeely, suddenly dogged and bitter. "I've got instincts, too."

She waited awhile before she answered. Then she said quietly, "When you're married to someone—while you're married to someone—you owe certain things to him, and to yourself. Loyalty is one of them—if you're any good at all. While you claim the status of a married person, and accept the loyalty and support of the one who keeps you, and gives you loyalty, as long as you keep on accepting, you owe something that you can't escape, even though no one would ever know about what you did. That is, if you want to be able to live with yourself. If you want to be able to *stand* yourself. Maybe that's Victorian, but it's the way I was taught to believe. It hasn't got anything to do with you, Jim." She picked an empty beer can from the seat and set it gently above the dashboard and added very quietly, "I guess I could say, it's in spite of you."

Jim McNeely felt for the door handle in the darkness and pulled it. The metallic mechanism clicked as the door cracked open.

"All I can say," he said with utter humility, "is I wish I hadn't done it." He pushed open the door and started to get out. "And—I'm sorry."

Quickly, lightly, she touched his shirt and found his face with her hand. She wanted to kiss him, quickly, once more for good-bye and good luck and God bless you, but she stopped herself. It wouldn't help, and she only held her fingertips for a moment against his lean, faintly rough cheek.

"You're a good man, Jim McNeely. Don't let this, or anything, or anybody, ever make you think you're not."

When he had gone, swallowed up in the darkness, and his footsteps had faded in the silent blackness, she still sat in the car a long while, and then she clamped her fists to her temples and let out a plaintive, sobbing wail that was almost a shriek. "Oh, God! I'm so unhappy!"

Jim McNeely sat late with Dent Paxton, who had returned late from his day's indoctrination in Odessa. He sat slumped in Dent's old canvas chair, talking more than he had in a long time, looking nervously, moodily off into a dark corner, as if he had just taken a staggering blow out of the darkness and was momentarily expecting another. He turned in his fingers the water tumbler which Dent kept pouring whiskey into.

"You trying to get me crocked?"

"I would dearly love to get you crocked," said Dent with light enthusiasm. "You've been mighty aloof lately. I thought maybe you were mad at me."

"I been feeling rough."

"Are you sick? See a doctor."

"I'm not sick."

"A malaise of the mind, then."

"A what?"

"Most everybody suffers from it to some extent, sooner or later. It's a recognized mental ailment, referred to in medical textbooks as the 'red ass.' It's when you're just generally dissatisfied, discouraged, disappointed, and disillusioned with yourself and the world in general."

"You sound like you've had it."

"I have a mild chronic case all the time. It generally gets worse at night. I take a little of this medicine which you have so cavalierly described as rot-gut. It keeps it in check." He raised his glass. "Have another little treatment."

Jim McNeely grunted and let him pour his glass half full.

After a while Jim McNeely said, abruptly, "What's your slant on love?"

"Love?" said Dent, his eyebrows peaking in mock consternation. "Love?"

"That's what I said. I guess you wouldn't know anything about it? The boys say you're queer as a three-dollar bill."

"The *boys* say a lot of stupid things," said Dent with sudden waspish anger.

"You never go near girls."

"I haven't noticed you've been much of a Romeo yourself, old buddy. Not since you got your whang scorched a couple of years back."

"Anyway, whether you go for girls or not, everybody must have *some* love in 'em. What is it? I'm a sonofabitch if I understand it."

Dent circled the room and looked at the ceiling and swirled the drink in his glass. "I take it you have been smitten by the bug, old buddy. You shook up about that new babe at Pinky's? Well, you have come to *the* authority on the subject. And not a moment too soon."

"Piss on you and your authority. I'm serious. Why does a man feel bad if love is so goddamn glorious the way everybody lets on it is?"

"All right. You want to be serious? Let's talk serious," said Dent avidly, getting on the bed, kicking off his shoes, and drawing his feet up under him. "Every time I try to talk serious, you get mad and cuss me out and go storming off saying I'm a damn half-baked philosopher. Let's *talk* about love."

"Talk. I'm listening."

"All right. First we've got to see eye to eye on the subject of discussion."

"Go ahead."

"Love, *real* love, is not pussy."

"Oh, that's deep as hell. I know that."

"Well, maybe you do and maybe you don't. Ort says love is when you still want to kiss somebody after you've been in the sack with 'em. There may be something in that, but he's talking about romantic love, or passion between men and women. And don't think that's not important. It's why and how the race continues. I mean that's the main reason we're here. Not because our fathers were so damned impressed with the nobility of our mothers' character."

"How many times you been in love?" said Jim McNeely scornfully.

"All right, I can tell time without knowing how to make a watch. Anyway, what I'm getting at is that love is a lot bigger than that. Love is what makes you do things for somebody when there's not anything in it for you, personally. Nothing."

Jim McNeely grunted, disparagingly. "And who does *that*? Who really does that?"

"Everybody, to some extent. It's a matter of degree. Most people, not very much. But it's a thing present in everybody. Men rush into burning houses at the certain risk of being burned, to save people they never saw before. Why do they do it? Do they want to be heroes? I don't think so. Love is when you go against your animal instinct, that is, your natural inclination to think only about yourself. It's a fundamental ability present in every man to forget himself and think and feel and care only about somebody else."

"It sounds silly as hell. But keep talking."

"I don't know much else to say about it. Love is the most misunderstood thing in the world. It's what we all need more of. Hell, I'm no damn oracle, but I think it's the key to everything. For everybody. Why, I don't know. But I know that when I feel it I feel right. Then I turn animal again, fighting and scratching and living it up, for myself only. Thinking about *my* problems and *my* pleasures. And I end up being miserable and mean."

"If it's that simple," said Jim McNeely, feeling the anger grow in him, "why don't you go around being loveydovey and acting like a happy idiot instead of the jerk you are? Why don't I?"

"Just because we don't know how to do it," said Dent Paxton, separating the words for emphasis. "If I knew how, don't think I wouldn't. When I feel love, it's like a cool breeze blowing on me on a hot day, and I like everybody and I like myself, and I feel good. When I don't, I hate everybody, including myself."

"You hate me, Dentie boy?" Jim McNeely was beginning to feel the bourbon sinking deep into his crevices.

"No," said Dent, studying him. "I don't ever hate you, Jim."

"Well," said Jim McNeely, getting up and draining his glass. "I thank you for nothing. Your philosophy chaps my ass. You haven't helped me a bit."

"I can't really help you," said Dent meekly. "Everybody's got to fight his way out of this mess by himself. All we can do for one another is cheer from the sidelines."

16

THE NORTHER CAME UP BLUE RIGHT AFTER DINNER and by two o'clock it was whipping across the plain in unleashed fury, charged with sleet and rain flurries and stinging sand, punishing everything in its sweeping path. Visibility closed in around the men to a small enclosure of tortured, twisting mesquites which struck like taut snakes, stinging their thorns into shoulders and thighs within reach. The rest of the world was swallowed in the gray driving storm which swirled down across the land, and sucked the warmth out of a man as it went.

The pipe-liners braced themselves against the wild wind that tore at their clothing and blistered against their cheeks and eyes and turned their ears into a numb, excruciating hurting. The wind drilled the cold into them as they bucked against the tongs and pitted their muscles against the dead weight of pig-iron. The wind was an evil, tricky thing, almost alive. It doubled the weight of pipe, ceasing abruptly, flinging men off balance so that they floundered for their feet, and the next moment striking again as if with a huge fist.

Jim McNeely braced his back against the wind and fought the pipe before him to maintain the precarious balance between the two forces. He had to keep his teeth set together to keep going this day, for he was sick in his mind and in his body. After taking down almost a bottle of Dent's whiskey he had awakened with his belly raw and heaving with nausea and his head a single dizzy, pounding ache. His agony was not relieved by the comforting knowledge that this was merely a wholesome, whacking hangover which the strong young body would throw off in a few hours, for it was compounded and worsened by a deeper sickness of spirit. In the cold light of morning the remembrance of his encounter with Lee Montgomery, of his crude, high-schoolish pass at her in her garage, all but destroyed him. How could anyone do a thing like that, and having done it, having bungled it so disastrously, and having slunk away so abjectly, still think he could ever do anything right, much less wedge his way into the big hard world and subdue a piece of it for himself? She had not even been angry. She had merely shown pity for him, because she was bigger and better than he was, and this knowledge made her all the more lovely in his thoughts, and her inaccessibility all the more excruciating.

For breakfast he had enjoyed the taste of his own vomit. He had heaved at the white toilet bowl until his whiskey-blistered stomach was empty and grabbing. The morning had been an endless torture. Each time he caught the pounding jar of the pipe through his frame a shower of hot sparks had been shaken loose in his head. He did not report sick, for it was a part of the simple code of this world that a man, a real hand, never laid out sick because of a hangover. To keep his head from spinning and his gorge in place he concentrated his gaze on the face of the jack-man before him, a gaunt profile of dull, painful hopelessness etched against a moving tableau of miserable men working along the pipe, lifeless, color-less, runny-nosed, wind-beat human beings, who were only dumbly aware of their misery and incapable of fighting their way out of it. Over and over the thought came: every day that passes I'm getting closer to them. Every day I'm getting to be more like them, one *of* them.

It had been three months since Pluto had left, and the faint possibility, which Jim McNeely had scoffed at but still had hopefully thought about in secret, that Pluto really might, somehow, spring him out of this trap, had slowly died away. He told himself bitterly that he didn't want any of that kind of help, anyway. The hell with them all. He'd make it, and he'd do it all by himself.

Yet how many times during this abysmal morning had he slipped off his glove and felt under his jumper with his cold bare fingers for the flat outline of the savings-bank book, pocketed in his shirt? The feel of that thin flatness against his chest had been an opiate to his misery and the generating source of renewed hope these long and weary months, now run into years. He rubbed it hard this morning to start its old magic working, but it refused to come. This morning there weighed down upon him, like a heavy atmosphere, a conviction that there were mysterious and omnipotent powers that decided which men should progress, which men should go "on up" and live in the green fields, and which should not. He had fought back against the encroachment of this conviction at times in the past, and the little bank book had always done the trick, but in each added year that he had set his guts against the pig-iron his confidence had grown a little less certain. The odds had loomed perceptibly larger with each returning solstice and the tunnel of daylight into the future, which had once seemed so clear, was now obscured.

During the break for lunch, when the rest of the crew sought the shelter of a shallow arroyo and tried to nurse a little warmth out of a blowing fire while they ate their bologna sandwiches, Jim McNeely went off by himself. Farther up the arroyo he lay on his side on the frozen earth in the bottom of the shallow rut that had been washed into the flat plain by long forgotten cloudbursts. The cold of the ground soaked into his bones but his head felt hot and swollen and the bulges at the base of his skull throbbed painfully. He had unwrapped his bologna and bread and thrown it away for the coyotes, and he preferred the cold to looking at the drawn, hope-empty faces of the men shivering around the fire, and to enduring the distant scowl of Cap Bruner from his vantage point in the cab of the truck, where he ate his lunch alone, out of the cold and the bite of the wind.

Jim McNeely lay down with his cheek on the meat of his forearm. His other hand slid automatically under his jumper, his fingers gripping and poking at the savings-bank book, almost angrily, argumentatively, as if cross-examining the poor wafer about its long pretended significance. It had been his priceless carnet, his passport to escape. When it was filled to the magic number, he would be a free man. The magic number had been three thousand dollars. These supernatural ciphers had been entered and passed, months ago, and nothing had changed. He had anticipated that sum with the same avid eagerness with which an adolescent anticipates his twenty-first birthday, as the date of sudden arrival at manhood with all its power and prestige and privilege. Yet he had arrived at that crucial point with the same chill of awakening that the young man knows when twenty-one quietly arrives one day and finds him not perceptibly wiser, stronger or more commanding than when he was twenty-and-a-half. Jim McNeely now knew that four thousand dollars was not certain passage money to where he wanted to go. And he now had no confidence that five thousand or six, or even seven would be, either. He began to fear that he was losing his nerve. If his guts turned watery on him, he was lost. He lay with his eyes shut, half-dozing, angrily kneading and flexing the little book in his fingers, until he broke its back.

Cap Bruner's voice returned him harshly to reality, as if a hot iron had been run between his thighs.

"Git up from there, you gold-brickin' sonofabitch."

Jim McNeely blinked the fog out of his eyes and brain. The fingers of his mind scratched at the sound, trying to steady himself in the time and the place. Cap Bruner stood above him on the cut-bank of the arroyo, bulking huge and heavy in his thick wool mackinaw. Raising himself quickly to a sitting position, Jim McNeely stared up blankly at the big man.

"You been askin' to git yo' ass run off," said Cap Bruner exultantly. "Think you're a little too smart to be layin' pipe any more." Bruner had caught his man in the fault he had been waiting for. He had a reason now and he meant to nail him down. "Well, I been onto you a long time. You're just a gold brickin' sonofabitch."

Rising slowly to his feet, Jim McNeely brushed the gray dirt from his side and pondered his situation. At last Cap Bruner had pointedly and directly cursed him. There could be no mistaking it this time. That was an old rationalization of which he was ashamed: for four years Cap had fouled the atmosphere he breathed by cursing all around him. But Jim McNeely had always passed it off as not being the straight, unequivocal insult which a man with any pride in his bones could not shrug off or ignore. Any pusher was entitled to do some general cursing. But Jim McNeely had always assured himself that if Cap ever hurled the curse straight at him, the unmistakable insult, using the words which the code defined as unacceptable, as death-fighting words, it would be his signal and his unavoidable duty to cast off all the restraints and inhibitions and rise in whatever strength of manhood he could summon and try to beat hell out of Cap Bruner, whatever the consequence.

The realization, the undodgeable knowledge that the moment had now come, circled in his head like a fluttering bird as he stood there, still half-dizzy, feeling the weakness of his knees. It was a kind of academic recital of an ancient order of battle. It brought no fire into his limbs. He glanced up at the big man, who, aware also that the deadly words had been shot, added contemptuous emphasis to his challenge by kicking dirt from the bank onto the man below him. Jim McNeely tried to reason the thing out, clearly, and find the passion that was supposed to come. Now was the appointed time. He must either claim his manhood, or lay it at Cap Bruner's feet.

The length and intensity of the silence between them had begun to have its effect upon Cap Bruner. He said, "A sorry devil that'll sneak off an' go to sleep on my job don't work for me long. If you aim to make another pay day you better git yo' ass back on the job, an' I mean *fast!*"

It could have been the hangover or the weakness from lack of breakfast or lunch, or the devitalizing remembrance of his shameful clash with Lee Montgomery, or all of those things together. And it was, without doubt, struck through with a cold, physical fear of the looming man above him, whose great strength was a legend in the oil fields, and who, in addition, was girded with the armor and eminence of authority. Whatever it may have been, Jim McNeely at this moment could not lay his hands on that ultimate resource, the raw, irrational manhood, to meet the challenge.

With an almost detached realization of his defeat wheeling through his brain, like a nightmare in slow motion, he walked down the ditch toward the gang. As he went past the men, waiting nervously with their tools, Cotton said to him in a low voice, "I woulda waked you up, but I didn't know where you was."

Jim McNeely did not hear him. He could not hear anything but the slow pounding of his heart, tolling out his defeat.

As the afternoon wore on, the violence of the freezing norther slackened and settled to a dark, blowing rain. Jim McNeely told himself mournfully that he had waited too long. All of his guts, his lust for battle, had been fired and burnt out in the long forgotten playground struggles to defend his honor when the curse of "Nigger Jim" had been laid upon him, in the miles of pipe, now buried and rusting in the earth, that he had helped to lay in the ignominy of Cap Bruner's gang, in the blows that people called Mazie and Pluto and Lee had rained upon his pride and his self-respect and hope.

He felt, too, the deep pall that settled over the men in the gang. Jim McNeely, their pride and their champion, had failed them. He had not reacted, even slightly, to the long awaited challenge. The rain streaking down the wind soaked into his jumper and spread coldly across his back. The men sensed his defeat. They sensed it in the new, malevolent, almost wildly triumphant horning of Cap Bruner's voice as he strode up and down the ditch, having forsaken the refuge of the truck in his victory, after all these months of frustration, of grappling with the silent, maddening challenge which this half-smart kid had hung around his ears. Oh, this smart-ass McNeely was like a biggety nigger or a young mule that you finally had to knock down and teach some sense to. Except he hadn't even taken any knocking down. When he had finally put it on him, he had folded. Just like a paper sack full of hot air.

In the driving rain Cotton looked like a rat terrier that had fallen in a river and crawled out on a bank to freeze. Ort was shrunken in his stiff, wet clothes and upon his face was the look of early death. The wet-black iron pipe crawled on into the teeth of the dying winter storm, and the men, having run out of the fuel of hope, operated on the old adrenaline of fear. Their energy came from the raw necessity to survive, and from the adrenaline of fear.

Late in the afternoon they topped a shallow rise and emerged from the brush into a clearing, a shallow pan of earth in the edge of which lay a newly completed oil well with the derrick and draw-works, still and deserted, above it, and the steam boilers alongside, now cold, and the test tanks and doghouse and pipe-racks still clustered around it, deserted on the fresh-scraped ground. When the gang had made its way to within thirty yards of the derrick the men laid down their tools and took up picks and shovels to dig the ditch into which they would lay the remaining joints, slanting down to the level of the well-head in the cellar beneath the rig floor.

Now completely dominant, riding hard, driving home his victory, Cap Bruner ordered Jim McNeely peremptorily out of the gang and sent him off to perform a task which was customarily assigned to a junior hand, since it was one of the dirtiest and most distasteful jobs in the field, and required no skill or experience whatever.

"You, *Mister* McNeely. Git the drain plate off a' that test tank an' clean the bullshit outa the bottom of it. Maybe *that'll* wake you up." Without a word Jim McNeely stowed his mahoney wrench in the tool box and took down a crescent wrench and a shovel and a pair of rubber boots from the truck and went coldly, automatically, to the task. Ort Cooley watched him, unbelieving, shaking his head and muttering over and over to himself, "God!"

Jim McNeely made a shallow V-shaped ditch in the top soil leading from the hatch at the base of the steel test tank, cutting it with the sharp shovel into the slush pit at the base of the derrick. Then with the crescent wrench he began to remove the nuts bolting the drain hatch cover to the tank. When the plate was freed, a thick, stinking slush which lay a foot deep in the bottom of the tank gushed out of the opening into the shallow ditch and started to flow slowly toward the pit. In the well reports this unwanted substance was noted as B.S., for basic sediment, the dregs of an oil well's flow.

When he had done this, Jim McNeely put on the rubber boots and climbed the steel ladder outside the tank to the small round hatch on top. Then he inserted himself into the opening and descended the slimy inner ladder into the murky interior. In his sorry condition of spirit and body the foul air arising out of the black, gummy putrescence brought up with the oil made him gag and retch dryly. When he had landed on the tank bottom he shuffled through the shin-deep muck to the hatch opening. There he drew in his shovel, then set automatically to shoveling the B.S. toward the opening and the ditch outside.

As he worked he felt a dogged, perverse satisfaction in his ignominy. He began to hum and then to sing in a whiskey-hoarse voice the juke-box tune—

"Corrine, Corrina, whereja stay las' night?"

The words reverberated in the huge cylinder and rattled dully in his head. He sang louder, as if trying to drown out his thoughts, but he could not. He had been served no worse than he was due. And things would get worse now. He had been kidding himself. He wasn't the man he thought he was. Two choices were open to him: tuck his tail between his legs and run, or unlock his knees and get down and kiss Cap Bruner's ass and become his man. It didn't make much difference which way it went. If it wasn't Cap Bruner it would be somebody else, on the next job. This was the order of life when you couldn't lay hands on the guts to be your own man. This was the manner in which those born to toil must proceed. In four years of sweating and saving he had become afraid—afraid of failure. He had pitched his chili, and he felt the last illusion of his boyhood slipping from his grasp.

"Oh, sweet Corrina, whereja stay las' night?"

In a moment he realized that it was the shovel that was slipping, not any illusion. He watched the handle slide through his hands and splash in the cold muck. He seemed unable to stop it. He could only curse it, and when he stooped to retrieve it, trying to strip the handle clean of oil through his fingers, the wooden shaft seemed to wave, as though it were made of rubber. Then he felt himself swaying, going down, slowly, as if in a dream, and he found himself sitting in the cold, putrid ooze, floundering to get up, in slow motion. Then, simultaneously with the realization that he was going to pass out, came the impersonal, almost academic realization that gas was hissing slowly into the tank from the inlet pipe, high in the cylindrical wall. A valve somewhere was leaking, and the poisonous vapors from the pressure-charged well were seeping down into the tank.

Instinctively he leaned and kicked himself toward the hatch opening, toward the clean air, though it seemed almost a mile away, and he felt as if he were floating and trying to swim through black, foamy clouds that gave no traction ...

After what seemed hours the fresh, cold wind stung life back into his lungs and his brain. He sat in a heap against the outside wall of the tank. He had no recollection of getting there. His hair, face, clothing were smeared and dripping with B.S. His plight struck him, somehow, as hilariously funny. He drew in deep breaths of air and laughed and settled comfortably against the tank, thinking that nothing could give him so much pleasure as to sleep a little, just now. A kind of singing clearness washed through his brain, sluicing away in a flood of brilliance and clarity all of the distortions of life, and in this moment he felt free. Absolutely free. He went to sleep, chuckling.

It was Cap's foot that awakened him, a contemptuous, kicking toe, shoving against his thigh, pushing him over, and Cap's voice cursing him, reiterating, making explicit the same manhood-destroying epithet that he had thrown in his face after dinner. And now it was done in the presence and hearing of the gang, frozen on their shovels in plain sight through the undergirts, on the other side of the derrick.

"You sorry, gold-brickin' sonofabitch!"

Jim McNeely wiped a greasy bare hand across his face. Unaccountably his impulse was to laugh. He struggled to his feet and had to hold his voice in to keep from laughing in Cap's face as he found himself uttering the old schoolground retort to mortal challenge.

"And you're another, Cap," he said.

With the momentum of rising dizziness he fell straight into the big barrel of Cap's body and half turned him, then he drew away and clumsily drove the heel of his left palm into the side of the big man's face. The awkward soggy blow pushed Cap's head back, whacking it against the tank with a hollow boom sound, knocking Cap's stockman's hat into the river of B.S.

Reacting with the shock and violence of fury, Cap uncoiled the great bulk of his body in a lashing backhand blow that caught Jim McNeely under the jaw and hurled him heavily to the ground.

It was a punishing but not a stunning blow, and it had a cleansing effect. Jim McNeely, on hands and knees, stared at the ground, spitting mud and oil from his mouth. It was as if the blow had knocked loose a wall of scar tissue, allowing a poisonous pocket of pus, the pus of defeat trapped in his brain, to escape, drain out of him. He was freed. Free to fight and win, or get the hell beat out of him. Which it would be didn't now seem important. He was unshackled. That only was important.

One rubber boot had come half off in his fall. As he rolled to a sitting position he kicked it away and pulled the other loose and slowly got to his stocking feet, feeling drawn, pristine, empty, hungry for battle. Cap stood a mammoth figure above him, breathing wordless challenge through his nostrils.

The blow struck Jim McNeely on the ear like a wide-swung sledge. It hurled him around, but he kept his feet like a cart-wheeling acrobat. With his ear ringing and burning like fire he came in at the big man from an angle. Cap shifted his stance and his balance. Then Jim McNeely, moving with the concentrated, flowing speed of a good-sized cat, drove his back, shoulder and arm behind an oil-streaked fist into Cap's belly. It went deep and hit with a muffled thud against the man's backbone. Cap's mouth erupted in an open-throated roar of rage and pain. It was the trumpeting of a bull-elephant, smacked with fatal lead in its vitals.

Thrown, strapped into a half crouch, Cap still advanced. With the same trumpeting of rage he swung a wild blow that glanced off Jim McNeely's head and ended in a looping, strangling death lock around the younger man's neck. But for the lubricant quality of the B.S. this would have been the end of the fight, and, perhaps, of Jim McNeely. But with an explosive effort that half-tore the ears from his head, Jim McNeely pulled his head from the breath-stopping stranglehold and faced Cap once again.

He rocked slightly on his stocking feet, flexed his knees and then drove a short-traveled right hand squarely into Cap's face. His fist felt the solid crunch of breaking teeth. It jarred him all the way back to his shoulder. With a shriek of rage which itself would unnerve a faint heart, Cap launched himself upon his adversary, both fists swinging wildly like great wooden blocks on hawsers. Jim McNeely ducked the swinging arms. It was really too easy. He was in full command now and he knew that he could take him. Glancing upward at the huge, swaying target, he brought up a short left, and then a straight right that cracked like two rifle shots against the big man's jaw. There is no sound in the world like the sound of a man's bare fist striking another man in the face. It is the sound of the beast. Pin-point hemorrhages popped out all over Cap Bruner's brain. He stood paralyzed, pawing, floundering, but still on his feet. A careful, deliberate left whose destination was the back wall of the great skull crashed between his eyes and rocked his head back and shook his whole frame down to his ankles. Still he kept his feet. His eyes, now glazed and stupid, stared sightlessly. His apelike arms hung helplessly in front of him.

Jim McNeely stepped back and shaped his right fist, his eyes focused on the cheekbone above the slackening jaw. For a second he crouched poised, tensed, full of fury. Then, slowly, he relaxed and straightened. He wiped his dripping nose with the back of his muddy, greasy sleeve and opened his fists, and wiped them on his thighs. The desire to kill went out of him a little with each gasping breath. He backed away a couple of steps, still watching the foundering hulk, then, breathing hard, he walked away from Cap Bruner, whose pulpy lips and blind staring eyes as he stood there unable to fight back yet unable to fall told Jim McNeely that it was over, and that he had won.

He felt no elation, and he felt no hatred for the massive, almost inanimate form hanging there, swaying, almost as if on a clothesline behind him. He felt only free, and a kind of clean, clear, penetrating sadness, knowing that he was alone, and cut loose from all men, and swimming on his own through the endless crystalline air. He walked past the roustabouts of the gang and did not even notice that, knee deep in their ditch, they were screaming and beating themselves like frenzied, terrified children.

It was dark and the men sat straight on the beds in two rows, talking soberly in low voices as if they were holding a wake. Most of them had put on dress shirts and pants and their hair was wet-combed, though this was only Tuesday. It was a kind of mark of respect. They were watching Jim McNeely as he dressed and packed his old suitcase. Every few minutes one of them went to the door and peered down toward the office where lights were burning and a number of cars were parked, which was also unusual at this hour. Now and then a car would depart rapidly and a new one would drive up. There was serious concern flickering over the nerve network of this brachiate arm of the great Bison Oil Company, for a mutiny had been committed, authority had been challenged. It was very serious. Though Cap Bruner was not loved or admired by anyone, he represented Management, the command echelon, the control of the Company.

"That there's the deppity sheriff just rolled up," Ort said from the door. "I know it. I know that ol' sumbitch too well."

"Hell, he can't do nothin', 'less Cap swears out a warrant," said Otho.

"You reckon he will?"

"Hell, no. Least I don't think he's *that* dumb. After Buster an' them gittin' gassed, all Jim got to do is say he was gassed an' Cap kicked him an' cussed him when he was dozin' there half passed-out. Wouldn't no court jury give him nothin'."

"I'd *swear* he was gassed," said Cotton belligerently.

"Gassed's ass!" said Tyson. "What do you know 'bout whether he was gassed?"

"Well, he said he was, an' I'd swear to it. I'd take a paralyzed oath to it on a forty-foot stack a' Bibles!"

"Man, that Cap was the one looked like *he* was gassed when ol' Jim hung that first one in his breadbasket."

"Oh, that was the one. The rest was decoration. Wa'nt no fight after that."

"If ol' Jim'd hit him one more time, we'd a had some sheriffs out here, sho' nuff. Man, did you see him cock that last right, then uncock it an' jes' walk away."

"He'd a' tore his fuckin' head off."

"They say the doctor was up at Cap's right 'fore dark. I reckon he's got the belly-ache."

"Hell, his ol' gut is so tough he ain't hurt bad. What he mainly needs is a tooth dentist." Ort laughed softly and held up a piece of yellowed bicuspid. "I picked this up on the ground. Think I'm gonna have her gold-mounted fer a watchfob, like a' elk's tooth."

Jim McNeely shut his suitcase and set it down on the floor. He was dressed in shirt and tie and the suit he had worn when he arrived in Dead Lake, now two sizes small across the shoulders and chest. His expression was calm and serious, and the dark red abrasion on the corner of his forehead and the swelling that almost closed his left eye gave his dark face a look of solemn, wistful sadness. He spoke to Ort. "There's dirty khakis and safety shoes and gloves on the porch. You can have 'em if you want. If nobody wants 'em, burn 'em up."

Ort stood up and swallowed, as if about to give a testimonial in church. "I'll take 'em, an' thank ye for 'em."

Cotton giggled. "Guess that'll make you the new stabber."

"Shut up, kid," said Ort, disapprovingly. He worked his mouth and made a serious face, for he was spokesman for the group and about to pose the question that was in the front of all their minds. "Ah, yuh, where you be headin', stabber? Whatcha figger to do now?"

Jim McNeely took from the closet his old, now rusty blue overcoat with the peaked lapels and padded shoulders, long ago redeemed by mail from the pawnshop in Winfield, and pulled it on. It fit him like a younger brother's might have, gapping open in front and holding his shoulders back in an unnatural brace.

"I got two or three things in mind. Nothing definite yet. I'll drop you a line. I'll be seeing you boys. Don't worry about that."

"Well, ah, now, Jim, ah, we thought we'd like to walk up to the gate with you—"

"Oh, the hell with that."

"Naw, now. We'd like to."

"Ort, I appreciate it. But, man, I'm poison now. You got to live here. You got to get along with Cap and everybody. It wouldn't do you any good."

Cotton got to his feet. "I don't give a *shit* about that! I'll be proud to walk out with you. I don't give a—"

Jim McNeely swung his arm and clapped his palm with a smack into Cotton's hand and gave him a handshake that moved the youth all over. A big grin was on his face and his voice was full of pleasure and affection. "Cotton, you tough little horny-toad, you take care of that kid. He'll make a driller one of these days. Now you boys sit still. It'll be better for me if I just slip out without a delegation. I'll be seeing you. I'll buy you all a beer down at the Tascosa one of these Saturday nights."

He walked around the room and shook hands solemnly with each man in turn, and every one said something in a low, strained voice that all added up to "Good luck, I'm glad t'knowed yuh."

When he pushed through the screen door, suitcase in hand and the door sprang closed behind him, no one spoke for a while, then Ort Cooley in a choked voice said what was in the mind of every man present.

"There went a good son-of-a-bitch."

At the end of the porch Jim McNeely stopped and felt perplexed, troubled disappointment. Dent's room was dark. He looked down toward the lighted office. He wasn't going down there, for sure, but he wanted to see Dent. He could write him, but somehow that wouldn't be right. He stood for several moments, eyes drawn, thinking what to do. He could leave him a note, but that didn't appeal to him either. He never had been able to write worth a damn. But he didn't want to hang around, either. The big fever of the afternoon was still upon him and he wanted to ride it out into the unknown world, while it lasted, and he knew the timing, the sense, would go all haywire if he hesitated and stumbled around with sentimental farewells. He kicked the porch post lightly in irritation and started to step down to the ground when he heard the light crunch of footsteps off in the darkness. Straining his eyes, he saw the spare form of Denton Paxton materializing out of the night.

Dent hopped up on the porch, his eyes glittering, liquidly reflecting light from down the porch. Brightly, but with the brittle stiffness of a sensitive soul knowing he was about to be rebuffed and rejected, he said, "As I live and breathe if it isn't Gene Tunney! And all saddled up. Going somewhere, I take it?"

"Knock it off, pardner. I'm glad you showed up. I'm on my way."

"Well, friend, you really stirred up a hornet's nest. They've been trying to decide whether to prosecute you or just fire you."

"They're too late to fire me. I've already quit."

"Don't go," Dent said, suddenly, stubbornly, almost pleading. "I think you can beat this. I think you can run *Cap's* ass off, before it's over."

"Hell, I don't want to do anything to Cap. I don't want his job, or do him any dirt, either. Even if I could beat it, I'd be bad medicine in this outfit. I'm overdue to leave, anyway. You know that, buddy."

"Yeah," Dent sighed. "I know it. You want to go to Mexico? I'll go with you."

"Hell, I haven't lost anything in Mexico."

"All right, New York. LA. You name it."

"Buddy, we're on different tracks. You know that, too."

"You sure you're on the right one?"

"How the hell do I know whether I am? But I got to go my own way."

"Yes. I guess so. Let me hear from you, then."

"I'll let you hear."

"I'm getting sick of this place."

"I'll let you hear."

"I'm getting goddamn sick of this place."

"OK, buddy. I'll let you hear. Pretty soon."

"Listen. I'll borrow a pick-up and drive you to Odessa."

"Nah. I hitch-hiked in. That's the way I'll go out."

"Whatever you say, buddy."

"OK."

"Take it easy," said Dent Paxton. "But take it."

"OK, buddy. I'm gonna take it."

"You can."

"OK, buddy."

"OK."

In the cold night with the wind soughing across his face, he walked up the road and left Dead Lake Camp. The storm front had blown past and the high stars were specks of fire in a black velvet sky. When he passed the Montgomery house he slowed and his eyes tried to see through the gauzy curtains of the windows for one last glimpse of the desirable, the enigmatic, the unattainable. A kind of washed-out, high-keyed suspension propelled him, moved his limbs, kept the spring in his backbone, and he pushed away the encroaching temptation to anticipate the lost feeling that he would flounder in tomorrow, and the sad, wrenching pangs of the last chance he would ever have to see someone he could visualize behind the opaque squares of light of the house windows and the last chance to tell her squarely, to her face, that she had meant something important to him.

Crossing the cattle-guard at the gate, hearing it clong hollowly under his feet, he turned down the road away from Coker City, toward State 385 that led to Odessa. It was a bad night for rides and he thought he might have to walk all the way to the state highway before he got picked up.

He found himself unwilling to level, eye to eye, with the realization that he was leaving Camp for the last time, that he was, now, truly, on his own, with no plans and no prospects, with no real competence or knowledge except in the basic, narrowly limited skills of oil-field gang-work. With all its ugliness and desolation Dead Lake had been his home. It had been security, a place to go, a place where he belonged. He had no other. The world was a wide, cold, friendless expanse, and no one would miss him if the ground opened up at his next footfall and swallowed him and he was never heard of again. No one depended on him, in any way. He was a loose puff of thistledown blowing fitfully down the wind.

His hopes rose when he saw the reflected lights of the car coming up behind, flickering along the fence wires, as the darkness ahead lightened and he heard the growing sound of the motor. His hopes rose because he realized now how tired he was and how weak he was in his stomach and legs. He really wanted a ride, a ride to some place where he could find food and a bed to sleep in and to gather up his strength for the opening of a whole new life, tomorrow.

As the car approached and slowed he stopped and stood off to the side and waited. He felt a keen wave of gratitude for the—camaraderie, spirit of kinship in hard circumstances, whatever you wanted to call it—that made people stop and pick you up in the oil fields, when they could just as well whizz by and give you nothing but the smell of their swirling exhaust.

"Many, thanks," he said, peering into the dark car when it had stopped and he had opened the door. Then he said, "Good God Almighty."

Lee Montgomery said, "Put your suitcase in the back seat."

He stood frozen, staring, trying to make her out, not really believing it was she.

"Put your suitcase in the back seat and get in," she said again. "It's cold."

Reacting like a mechanical man, he opened the back door and slid his old leather gladstone into the floor. Then he got in the front and closed the door and she started up. Her voice was clear and solemn and a little tired, as if she, too, had had a trying day.

"I heard all about it. It was all over camp by sundown. I saw you go by."

A long ribbon of the road skimmed under them before he could speak. He said, "I guess you know I'm leaving for good. I'm sure glad to get a lift." He glanced over his shoulder and saw another suitcase on the back seat. "Where are you going?"

She didn't take her eyes off the road, or change the even tone of her voice.

"Wherever you are," she said. "If you'll let me."

PART
II

17

IN SEPTEMBER 1930 A WIRY LITTLE MAN WITH A heavy nose and sleeve garters and a dream found his big oil field that he had spent most of his life searching for. His name was Columbus Marion Joiner and his well was on the Daisy Bradford farm in Rusk County, Texas, in an area that most major company geologists had condemned as unpromising for oil production. It was the third well that Dad Joiner had attempted on the Bradford place. The first two had been junked and abandoned due to bad luck and old worn-out equipment, and it took Dad years of dogged shoestringing, drilling until the money ran out, then shutting down while he went about the country selling shares in his leases to get money to drill some more, before he finally got the hole down to the Woodbine sand at 3,700 feet, which was his objective. When he finally made it, he merely discovered the biggest oil field in the USA.

Within a couple of years there were thousands of wells flowing from this great East Texas Field which produced from a buried sandy shoreline that stretched for fifty-five miles north and south and from three to nine miles east and west. Wells were even drilled on town lots in the hamlets that lay in the field's fairway, and overnight these hamlets became raging boomtowns choked with adventurers of every shape and hue drawn from all quarters of the land by the smell of oil and money. Show people, come down to Kilgore from Dallas to entertain the grimy throngs, had to step over flowing rivulets of oil in going from hotel to theater. East Texas was the biggest, richest, wildest, gaudiest oil bonanza of all.

Dad Joiner didn't make much money out of his discovery, and once he had made the strike it seemed, almost, as if he didn't care. But, without intending it, he did a lot more than find a gigantic oil field. He set wheels and forces in motion that fundamentally changed the character of the oil business.

Jim McNeely married Lee Thomas Montgomery three months to the day after he left Dead Lake. In the interim, after her flight from the gross, self-centered husband she had never loved, Lee went home to her father's house in McCamey, Texas, and, in due course, obtained a divorce from Clyde Montgomery. She hired a lawyer in Odessa who filed a routine divorce action alleging mental cruelty.

Clyde Montgomery, with shocked and outraged pride, responded by filing a countersuit charging her with desertion and with adultery, naming a violent, disreputable, discharged ex-Bison roustabout called James McNeely as the other guilty party. Jim McNeely, who had landed in Odessa and was by then having dickering talks with Ben Sullivan and exploring other possibilities, sent word to Clyde that he wanted to meet with him face to face and straighten the matter out, and that any time and place that suited Clyde would be all right with him, so long as it was immediately.

In a couple of days Clyde sent word back through his lawyer that he didn't have time to waste on such sordid affairs. But at the same time he withdrew his countersuit and said he would not contest Lee's divorce. Then he told it around that he felt that it was good riddance of bad rubbish and that he was letting *her* get the divorce out of courtesy though she didn't deserve it, and that he felt damned lucky to have found out about her before they had any children. He soothed his injured feelings with the incensed sympathy he received from the Bison elite who lived in the little box houses at the Dead Lake Camp and stuck together like a bunch of company sheep.

During this time Jim McNeely made regular trips to McCamey to see Lee. He had several long talks with her father, whose first name was also Lee. They sat after dark in the backyard of the older man's comfortable house, under a big willow tree. Lee Thomas told him many things about his daughter, Lee Montgomery, that were pleasant to the father in the remembering and sounded good in the listening to Jim McNeely, who felt strangely happy to find himself in love with a young, beautiful married woman whom he hardly knew, and to be talking with her father on terms that were not only not dangerous but downright friendly.

Lee Thomas Montgomery had been christened Lee Thomas, after her father. This, Jim McNeely learned, was because she had been born when her parents were past forty and because Lee's mother, knowing there would be no more children and that her husband had his heart set on a son, thought the next best thing was to name the child after him.

"Good thing my name wasn't Roscoe," Lee Thomas said. "But hell, Lee was more fun than any boy would have been. She *liked* to go fishing and hunting with me. Not too many boys really like to go rambling around with their old man. I put 'Helen Lee' on her birth certificate so she could have a girl's name if she wanted it, but before she got out of grade school she dropped the Helen. Said it was tacky. Took her about a year to break me of calling her by the two names."

Lee Thomas had had a slight stroke the winter before, and he walked rather poorly with a cane, and the muscles on one side of his face sagged, pulling down one eye and the corner of his mouth, and his speech was a little marbled. Jim McNeely liked Lee Thomas and thought he must have been a fine-looking man when he was younger. He would almost have to have been to be Lee's father.

"I never thought too well about Lee marrying Clyde," the gray-haired man said thoughtfully, swirling the last of a toddy in his good hand, sitting back in his canvas chair in the darkness under the tree. "But you can't live other people's lives for them. After they get grown about all you can do is hope for the best. And then help pick up the pieces if they stump their toe."

He was silent awhile, then he said, "This one seems a lot more likely to me than the first one. I don't like divorce. I really don't. But if you've made a bad mistake I figure it's better to rub it out and start over than try to live with it all your life. I don't know a thing in this world about you, Jim, I mean not very much. But I can see the difference in Lee. She's real worked up and ready to go out and fight wildcats barehanded, and that's the way it ought to be with a young woman. It wasn't like that before." He paused again and drained his glass. "I'm not well-to-do by any stroke of the imagination. But I've got a little property and I still take a little out of the mud-business I started here, just enough to run me, though the two boys I've turned the franchise to have a right to take me out for a few thousand any time they want to. They tell me keeping my name in the business helps them, but I know they're just doing it to give me something to do and some place to go to get out of the house. Anyway, Lee's sold on you, and if she is, I am, too. And so if you need any help getting started, why I'll do whatever I can, money or otherwise. I figure that whatever I've got, why it'll do Lee more good now when she needs it than later on down the line when the Lord decides I've been around too long. It might not mean anything to her then."

That was the offer, set before him without strings, and Jim McNeely felt called upon to speak. He was touched. Nobody had offered him money without strings ever before in his life.

"Mister Thomas, I appreciate your—your trust in me—and that Lee's not making a mistake. I don't know what to say. I love Lee and I want to marry her. But I don't need anybody to help me. Well, maybe I do—I guess everybody needs help. Anyway, I don't want any. I'll make it, or I won't, on my own. I've got a little money. I think I'll make it."

The old man set his empty glass down on the ground and laughed. "Looks like little old Lee's finally gone and lucked out and got herself a man. I don't know where you all think you're headed, but it ought to be an interesting ride. Wish I could be around to see how it comes out."

"Aw you'll be around a long time, Mister Thomas."

"Yeah," said the old man dubiously. "Maybe so. Anyway, if I can help you, holler."

"I will," said Jim McNeely. "I appreciate it." And he did.

18

IT WAS NEARLY MIDNIGHT. JIM MCNEELY SAT AT THE battered desk in the office of the Sullivan Well Servicing Company in Odessa, Texas, knuckling his brow under the naked globe which hung on a fly-specked wire from the ceiling. He had sat a long while filling pages of a tablet with figures, then tearing them off, wadding them up, and throwing them irritably at the waste basket in the corner of the room. He still wore a white shirt with dark blue tie from the funeral. His coat hanging on a wall hook still had the wilted pallbearer's bud pinned to the lapel. The small office was sparsely furnished with the old desk, three dirty yellow-oak chairs, a filing cabinet, an ancient hand-crank adding machine, and a still more ancient Oliver typewriter. A calendar of an oil-field supply company, depicting a full-ripe girl wearing only a tin safety hat, hung on the back of the door.

In several hours of figuring he had engaged in a bitter running argument with himself over what he should do about Mrs. Sullivan. He did have some choice. She didn't have to buy his interest in the business if she didn't want to. She probably didn't have the money anyway. But he didn't have to buy her out, either, and certainly not at the same figure that he had, gradually, over three years, acquired his interest from Ben. The equipment was old when he had started with Ben, and Ben had put in a hellacious "going concern" factor when he set the price. This seemed all right at the time because Jim McNeely was out of a job, and didn't know anything about anything except oil-field pipe-lining. But he knew that he could now duplicate the equipment, brand new, for what he would have to pay Mrs. Sullivan for her half on the old basis.

The best deal for him would be to sell out to her for what he had paid Ben Sullivan. The next best thing would be to buy her out on the basis of the best offer they could get for the whole works from somebody else. The figures on the wadded sheets in the waste basket had made that crystal clear. Figures! If you knew how to "put the pencil to it" as the fellow said, you were OK.

All right, so maybe she wouldn't agree to either of those alternatives. He could always force the business to be put on the block and sold. If he did, it wouldn't bring more than the old worn-out equipment was worth. The "going concern" value would be worth nothing without Ben or him either in the business to run it. He could get somebody to bid the stuff in for next to nothing at the sheriff's sale, and then turn it to him at the same price. That way he could accomplish his purpose of hanging on to the business and keeping it going at a decent figure.

He got up from the desk and walked around the room, scrubbing one hand over his burning eyes and whiskery jaw. He had no legal obligation to Mrs. Sullivan, sweet old gray-haired motherly woman that she was, nice as she had been to him, like her and feel sorry for her though he did. He didn't owe her a thing. Sure, Ben had taken him in when he needed a place to light, Ben had taught him all he could. But when Ben decided to start letting him buy a half interest, he had put such a fancy price on it that it had taken all his savings and everything he had made during the past three years to pay him off. And there hadn't been any doubt that Ben needed somebody to *take* in.

Ben knew he was in trouble with his lungs and during the last year that he lived he hadn't been to the office or the field a single time, and for the last five months he had been so low, just fighting for breath, that Jim McNeely hadn't even been able to talk to him, even at home, about anything, and had had to carry the whole load all by himself, which he wouldn't have minded if he had known what the hell he was doing half the time.

Yes, much as Jim McNeely had liked Ben Sullivan and much as he was grateful to him, he felt he had discharged his obligation. And he had a long, long way to go. Hadn't really even started. He suddenly stopped pacing the floor and smacked his fist into his palm as if to settle once and for all the fair and reasonable conclusion he had reached. He was under no legal or moral obligation to Mrs. Sullivan, and, goddammit, he had his own life to think about. Mrs. Sullivan would get along all right. She had a married daughter living in Louisiana. It was her job to worry about the old lady, not his.

He had begun to pace around the office again, without meaning to. Suddenly he stopped pacing again and stood in the middle of the floor under the light, tired and upset. He scratched the back of his head with his hard nails. Then he threw the last wadded paper at the waste basket and said, "Low-life sonsofbitches," at no one in particular.

Muttering to himself, he threw his coat over his shoulder, snapped out the light, and stalked out into the night air. He was a plain damn fool because he knew he was going to tell Mrs. Sullivan he would go whichever way she wanted about the business. It didn't make a damn bit of sense but he didn't know what else to do because he didn't know how else he could explain it all to Lee.

Sweet, motherly, gray-haired Mrs. Sullivan was no fool and she chose, just as Jim McNeely knew that she would, to sell her half interest to him at the price he had paid Ben for the first half.

When they sat down in the lawyer's office to draw up the papers she, not having lived forty years with shrewd old Ben Sullivan for nothing, gently suggested a monthly payment on the balance owing, which Jim McNeely figured he could just barely meet if he worked eighteen hours a day seven days a week and gave up breakfast and chewing gum and picture shows, and picked up an odd job relief roughnecking now and then in his spare time, and was lucky as hell. When they parted, Mrs. Sullivan kissed him on the cheek and blessed him, and he walked out onto the hot summer streets of Odessa. His face prickled with heat and anger and he cursed himself and wondered where he had been hiding when the Lord passed out the brains.

Sundown shadows had moved in from the west and a dry breeze had begun to soften the white hardness of the dusty streets of the town as he turned the pick-up in the driveway beside the small frame house that was his home. He felt weary and deeply discouraged. Then the kitchen door flew open and Lee stood there, arms wide, beaming expectantly, a big spoon in one hand, the hem of her apron caught in the other.

"Jim! You did it!"

"Hello, sugar," he said dully, bending to kiss her as he entered the tiny kitchen. She fended him off strongly.

"Oh, no!" she said. "Don't give me that sugar business. Did you do it? *Tell* me something!"

"All right, I'll tell you something. That old lady got to me and we are the sole owners of the sorriest, oldest, wore-outest collection of junk in West Texas, and you are married to the biggest goddamn chump east of the Rockies."

Lee McNeely gave a happy cry and threw her arms around his neck and hugged him and kissed him full on his sad unresponsive mouth. "You wonderful man!" she cried. "This is the next to best day of my life!" And she meant it and he knew it and couldn't help but feel some better.

Late at night in bed they talked, lying without cover next to the window to get the small puffs of night breeze that found their way into the slowly cooling house, she with her dark head cradled on his bare outstretched arm.

"I made a bad deal, Lee."

"You made a good deal."

"How can you say that?" he flared. "I paid too damn much. I didn't owe her anything."

"You made a good deal because you did a good thing. You did right by her. Ben helped us. You did right by his widow. You can't go wrong doing right. It'll work out."

"Baloney!"

"It will work out, sweetheart. I know it will. It won't be easy. But I'll help you. And it's going to be fun because it's going to be our business. All ours."

"Yeah. It's gonna be fun like owning a poor farm. I don't even know how we're gonna eat."

She was silent for a moment during which she turned her head and nibbled the smooth skin on the inside of his muscular upper arm.

"Jim."

"Yeah, baby."

"Don't worry about feeding us. You just concentrate on paying off Mrs. Sullivan. I-I've taken a teaching job. School starts two weeks from tomorrow. We'll eat."

"What!" He pulled his arm roughly from under her head. They were both sitting up suddenly in bed.

"Lee—!" he said in sudden, rising fury.

"Jim McNeely, you listen to me!"

"You know what I said!"

They started talking, both at once, sharply, loudly, neither listening, then Jim McNeely started angrily to get out of bed. Lee caught him around the neck and she was strong, and he tried to get away and they wrestled furiously for violent seconds, he trying to escape in his anger without using all his strength and hurting her, she knowing that if he did escape she would lose something, irrevocably, a vital point, a position in his life that she could not, perhaps, regain once he had stalked off, swollen in anger. And she sensed deeply that it could affect the whole direction of their lives together. In the wild grappling melee they rolled off the bed. He fell to the floor on his back and she fell heavily on top of him, her flimsy gown twisted up around her waist. Grunting and wheezing tightly, he tried to rise, but she covered his body with hers with desperate strength like a wrestler. Then she clamped a kiss on his mouth and held him down and kissed him hard again and again.

"Jim McNeely, I love you—I'm going to help you, dammit!"

He turned his head aside. "You know what I said, goddammit! How I feel!"

"I know, my hardheaded darling," she whispered, grasping his thick hair in her fingers and twisting his head back roughly so that she spoke right into his face. "I know what you said. I do know how you feel. I know you don't want me to work, and I know that you can take care of me, and you have, real good, and I love you. But this is something extra, for us—for just a little while. While you get over a big hump—for us! So let me help! Let me feel important, too! Please, Jim, you've got to let me help!" She kissed him again with a warm melting kiss that had tears in it and he could taste the saltiness of her tears. And the wonderful unsolicited surge of passion began to rise in him and melted the adamantine corners of his pride and the anger in his mind, and his arms went around her, almost involuntarily, and he ran his hand down the strong narrow valley of her back to where the gown ended and over her flexed, round, bare buttocks, and the elemental surge rose stronger and his arms drew tighter and he returned her kisses. She sighed strongly into his nostrils and knew she had won. Scarcely interrupting the kiss, she stripped the flimsy gown above her head with her free hand and prepared to celebrate the victory by offering herself a willing, submissive sacrifice to his love, to do with as he would. And in this heated, mindless moment there on the hard floor it seemed that both were victors and vanquished. And there, with all her heart and mind and body concentrated, she healed and annealed the passing wound to his pride.

19

FROM THE FIRST DAY THEIR MARRIAGE WAS ALMOST incredibly right and satisfying to both of them. Neither held any childish illusions about what marriage was supposed to be. Both had been through bitter times and had grown up fast of necessity, and each was under good rein, emotionally, to himself. Yet each day each experienced, almost as if by surprise, a new rush of pleasure in the sudden sensing that he was married to and belonged to and was owned by, that wonderful, vital, tantalizingly interesting human being across the room, across the tiny dinette table, next on the seat of the old pick-up truck, and that they each and together had all of an endless, exciting lifetime of unlimited possibilities out in front of them.

No small part of this was the constant state of subdued physical excitement which they created in each other. Both felt an unspoken pride that they had not partaken of the full pleasures of love together until they were legally man and wife, and it was not merely the embarrassed counseling of Lee's lawyer that caused them to observe this propriety during the pendency of Lee's divorce action. The ultimate consummation, though not without gayety and excitement, was neither embarrassed nor carried out in the usual frantic high-strung exhaustion of honeymooners. It was deliberate, premeditated, and good, exceeding all expectations of either.

There was an awareness about Lee Thomas McNeely, a controlled eager awareness in sex matters, and a natural skill, that enabled her to follow, to move instinctively, intuitively into any situation like a good dance partner, never demanding more than was offered, never trying to lead, yet never failing to respond fully to the exact degree of the depth and intensity of passion which this man brought to her. Jim McNeely did not *know* how lucky he was in this, but he sensed it, and when, spent and mindless, his breathing slowly returning to normal, he would look into the twinkling eyes and the thick dark tousled head of hair and feel her quick kiss against his lips and hear her say, "You wonderful man!" he began to experience an awakening sense that the mastery of life, the good things of life, was actually within his reach and his power. He had survived some bitter trials in his twenty-seven years, by luck and by the skin of his teeth. Now he began to feel for the first time that he could master life and direct his destiny by his own volition.

And so when he brought his love to this beautiful, twinkling woman-wife, it became almost an act of faith. And he never went away unfulfilled, unsatisfied, though for forty-eight hours after each encounter, drained of the seed of love, he was invariably mean as hell and difficult to live with, though he never realized why. Lee understood why, again perhaps intuitively. She smiled to herself, knowing that her man-lover would, in due course, come to her again, an eager, docile supplicant.

Lee Thomas McNeely understood more than this, with an awareness that went beyond her young vigorous intelligence. She knew—and when she thought of it, a trouble-mark accented the smoothness between her dark brows—that this pent-up man she had married kept a part of himself reserved from her—a personal devil coiled in his innards that drove him with spurs hard set in his liver.

She had never challenged this devil, and she avoided talking of basic drives or ultimate goals or anything of the kind because she had learned very early that conversation on this scale made Jim McNeely irritable and unhappy. They talked only of tomorrow, of the next practical problem in their path, as if they were both headed hell-bent for the same objective. Slowly, however, through loving and living with this man, she came to divine something of the nature of the devil.

In this way she came to know, instinctively, that babies and the normal building of a family and the accumulation of the responsibilities that go with birthing and bringing up and educating and launching a new generation into the world were not in Jim McNeely's plans, at least not for the present. A few times he had referred to "having some kids" later on. Now and then he even called Lee "Mamma," jokingly, which pleased her. But that was down the line when he had got a few things out of the way. Meanwhile she sensed strongly that an accidental pregnancy would be a bitter blow to him, and though she sometimes dreamed of the black haired, button-eyed baby that could be hers by him, she nevertheless became an expert at the art of contraception and after the first few anxious months Jim McNeely dismissed the worry from his mind, secure in the knowledge that Lee would take care of things until he gave her the word.

And so they lived and loved and enjoyed life and each other to the utmost and worked and struggled with their payments to Ben Sullivan and later to his widow in those first years in the dusty little West Texas oil-field town. Their days were full of busy-ness and anticipation and they did not mind the heat or the cold or the sand that sifted under their doors and windowsills when the wind blew, summer and winter.

Lee went to church nearly every Sunday because she felt the need to go to church, and also because Jim McNeely was away working on Sunday mornings more often than not. She went most frequently to the Christian Science Church in Odessa, because her mother had been a Christian Scientist and that was the only church she had ever had any formal connection with. She never joined the church because when she felt the need of an aspirin or a little medicine, she took it. This troubled her sometimes. There was a lot to Christian Science that appealed to her deep inner springs, but Mary Baker Eddy was an uncompromising prophetess, and Lee couldn't go all the way with her. Yet she felt a need to worship, to seek, to express gratitude, regularly, in some more formal way than just looking out the kitchen window and silently thanking God for her blessings. She was a lot like her father in this. They had talked a good deal about religion.

"Everybody needs a framework for worship, sissy," old Lee Thomas had said. "That's why we have religion. At least that's my thinking. Most people just inherit their religion, and it seems to satisfy them. But some people have a hard time finding one that really sustains them. I guess I'm one of those. You ought to either find a religion you can live with, even if it isn't a hundred percent, and stick with it, or else you ought to keep looking until you find one you can stick with. A steady, honest searching is a kind of religion, itself.

"Your mamma found hers. She might be alive now if she had gone to a doctor, instead of dying when she was fifty-eight. I don't know. But she had a joy about her religion and I couldn't bring myself to make her go against it. Her faith never wavered. She told me she had just not worked hard enough to purify her thoughts and get her demonstration and healing, like it was her fault and not her religion's, and she didn't seem to mind the pain. She passed away optimistically, courageously, almost with a glow. I've seen people who have been kept patched up by the doctors and have lived, stricken with fear, until they were eighty or ninety, and then went in stark terror when they finally went. I honestly don't know which is best. But I kind of envy Mamma."

And so Lee kept up a constant search. She went to many different churches without finding what she was looking for, and sometimes she thought almost grimly that she was going to have to invent a religion of her own in order to get to heaven.

Once or twice when Jim McNeely was at home on Sunday morning she had proposed, rather timidly, that they attend together the services of the Presbyterian church, which had been his mother's church. He passed off the suggestion with a laugh and a pat on the fanny and said he would go except he was afraid the steeple would fall off when he walked in the front door.

Still the pattern into which their life together was slowly flowing, dimly seen at first then with increasing clarity, troubled her. Once, in bed in the silent dark on the edge of sleep she said, seriously, thinking far out away from the immediacy of this day's problems and tomorrow's: "Jim . . . what are you aiming at? With your life. And mine. Isn't that our real religion? What do we really want to do with them?" Jim McNeely yawned broadly, but it was not a relaxed yawn. He reached across the bed and felt for her and patted her bust then her cheek in the darkness and said, "Anything you say, sugar. But I'm bushed. Let's catch a little shut-eye."

He rolled over and settled into sleep. It was time to shut off this conversation. But he was secretly glad that Lee went to church and worried about all that kind of thing.

20

THE WELL-SERVICING BUSINESS UNDER JIM McNeely's sole ownership and management made modest progress. There was work to be had in the growing oil province, and Jim McNeely was gaining a reputation for competence and fast action. He bid jobs down to the bone in order to get the contracts necessary to keep his crews working, and he didn't make much profit on any job. But he managed to keep his old equipment patched up and operating and he kept up the payments on his note to Mrs. Sullivan.

A big part of his well-servicing work was rod-and-tubing jobs, pulling the sucker rods in a pumping well that had quit pumping because the rods had parted or the tubing had sanded up or clogged up with paraffin, fixing what was wrong, then running the tubing and rods back in the well and getting the well back on production again. He used his two old truck-mounted pulling units in this work. His work-over rig was used on more extensive jobs which became necessary when a well started making water and a casing liner had to be run and cemented and perforated in the top part of the pay sand in an effort to shut off the encroaching water, or when one producing formation played out and there was another pay up the hole behind the pipe that needed to be brought in. This rig was really a light drilling rig with a jackknife mast instead of a derrick and could be broken into components and moved on trucks and rigged up again on a new location in a short time.

With these three units working around the clock over a six- or seven-county area, Jim McNeely spent most of his days and nights roaring about in the old pick-up truck over the highways and lease roads that fanned out of Odessa over the dusty Permian Basin, carrying a spare part for a broken-down engine here, a new set of swab-rubbers there, working under floodlights with a driller, or when the trouble was critical, a hired mechanic, until he was streaked and soaked with grease and sweat, sleeping on the hard seat of the pick-up almost as often as he did in his own bed.

On Saturday afternoons, unless there was a dire emergency on a job somewhere, he would come in from the field and pick Lee up and go to the little office and try to catch up on the paperwork. Gradually Lee took on this responsibility as a regular part of her wifely duties, without saying anything about doing so, and in time she was keeping the books for the company, and Jim McNeely was depending on her to do it because he had his plate full trying to run the work in the field and keep the old equipment functioning. Afterward on Saturday nights he always tried to take her out to have a couple of beers and eat someplace like the Ace of Clubs, or maybe see a picture show, because this was about the only social life they had. But sometimes it was so late and they were so tired when they finished at the office they would just eat a hamburger at a drive-in and go home.

This one Saturday night, which could have been almost any one during that time, Lee pushed back from the desk and stuck the yellow pencil in her tousled hair and said, "Well, we lucked out again, pardner. I figure you worked about eighty-nine hours this week. All bills, note payments, interest and taxes are paid, and you made a clear profit of one dollar and thirty-one cents."

Across at the other old desk Jim McNeely threw down his pencil and shoved back the papers which he had been glaring at, trying to straighten out the Social Security deductions on the payroll.

"Now ain't that one hell of a kummy-shaw!" he said, with disgust.

"It's wonderful!" said Lee. "Everybody's eating. All the crews are working, and before you know it we'll be paid out."

"And the damned equipment will end up a worn-out, useless pile of junk at exactly the same time!"

"But, *baby*, you've got a business going. You're getting a reputation. Two suppliers are ready to stake you to new equipment anytime you want it. Sure, Mrs. Sullivan ought to be paid off before we take on new obligations, but that won't be long, and when we've got good tools that don't have to be patched up every five minutes and with new business coming in every month and the payments on the new equipment spread over three or four years, man, we'll be the going—Jesse's of the well-servicing business in West Texas—and start putting money in the bank!"

Jim McNeely had been scowling at her under lowered brows as she talked. When she finished this buoyant, enthusiastic look into the future, he got up and crossed the room and caught her smooth chin in one hand and lifted it firmly so that she looked right at him.

"Sweetheart," he said, gazing down as though she were a child, "you are a born ribbon clerk. You got to start thinking bigger. Well-servicing is peanuts."

"It's a good business. It's a good living. It's honest, and doctoring sick oil wells is important," she said defensively. "I'm proud to be doing it."

"Balls," said Jim McNeely in a voice that had a bite of anger in it. "Well-servicing is chickenfeed. It's only a sideshow. Get to thinking about the main tent. That's where I'm headed."

"Balls, yourself," replied Lee tartly, "I'm ready for the main tent any time you are."

21

INDEPENDENT OIL MEN WERE FROM THE BEGINNING
a highly unregimentable breed of human beings, to the point of
acting downright churlish when anybody tried to tell them what to
do. What really made them roar was for any scent of government regulation of their business to come on the wind.

Before East Texas the oil business had always been a wide-open, hell-
bent scramble to see who could get the most wells drilled the fastest in
a new field, to cash in on the flush production and the available markets.
But nobody had ever stuck a bit into an oil pool like this monster of East
Texas before. The torrential flood of oil that began to gush out of literally thousands of wells that were drilled in the ensuing months after the
Number 3 Daisy Bradford came in, soon overwhelmed, then drowned the
market for oil, everywhere, and drove the price down to ten cents a barrel.
Economic chaos impended. A whole industry was threatened with ruin.

The governor of Texas declared martial law in the field and sent the
National Guard to close in the wells. The legislature passed a law empow-
ering the State Railroad Commission to limit or "prorate" production
from the wells in the field to something approximating market demand.
Such governmental tampering with the venerable economic law of supply
and demand was naturally repugnant to oil men in general, but as their ox
was getting the horn pretty bad in East Texas and as the curtailment of
production had the effect of boosting the price back up close to a dollar a
barrel, most of them, reluctantly, went along with it.

For a time there was a good deal of "hot oil" running through hidden
valve by-passes and secret flow-lines in the field and there was a

considerable law-suiting back and forth between the Commission and a few die-hard producers who maintained that proration was unconstitutional as hell (which brought about some re-tailoring of legislation), but in the end the forces of regulation prevailed and the near chaotic situation was slowly brought under control. Statewide proration of oil production evolved in a few years into a workable way of life for the oil-producing business in Texas, and then in other states.

The oil business was never the same after that. Though a philosopher might view what had happened as just another step in the necessary ordering of men's affairs as they became more complex, so people wouldn't kick dirt in one another's chili, the idea of regulation in general was a natural abomination to oil men. However, when the kinks were ironed out of proration and everybody was fairly prosperous under it, they rationalized that it wasn't really so bad because it was, after all, *state* regulation. *Federal* regulation, now that would be the Devil's own doing. The smart boys in Washington had tried to muscle into the act during the East Texas crisis and had been successfully thwarted, but they were still lurking in the wings.

The thing that raised the short hairs of oil men was the specter of nationalization of the industry. The US of A was one of the few countries on the globe in which the government didn't own and license and regulate the production of all subsurface minerals including oil and gas. Federal control of production, they feared, would be the first step in that unthinkable direction.

It was time to push out, and Jim McNeely knew it. He had been putting off the day on which he knew he must confront himself, resolutely, and say, "Now, move!" Because he didn't know just where or how he would take his first big step. It wasn't easy, when you got right to the jump-off place, to plunge into a real oil deal of your own. Yet the devil in Jim McNeely's innards was beginning to set its spurs painfully. He knew he was way behind on his self-imposed timetable.

He had lain awake countless nights thinking about possibilities. The trouble was they all needed money. Which he didn't have. And there was risk in all of them, even if he could go in hock somewhere and raise the capital. Mrs. Sullivan would be paid off in another four or five months, but he was sure he couldn't raise even a couple of thousand dollars on that loose-traveling junk pile he worked with. Two supply companies had indicated a willingness to stake him to a brand-new outfit because they knew he could operate it profitably and they would eventually get paid. But that would marry him to the well-servicing business permanently and that was not for him.

One idea had kept coming back to him, only to be kicked out of the way half a dozen times. Too many others had tried this one and failed. But about the seventh time the spur in his liver was hurting him so and making him so restless and irritable that he was ready to try anything. He made his decision sitting at the counter of a cafe in Odessa one hot, glaring midsummer afternoon. He had just finished his third cup of coffee, alone, whipsawing himself into a state of tension with caffeine. Pushing aside the empty cup and saucer with a stiff forefinger, he muttered aloud, "All right, buddy, you think you're about half tough. Let's see you take a run at this."

He threw a dime on the counter and got up and walked out, glowering, into the bright, hot sunlight.

As he started around the side of his pick-up, parked head-in, he saw the tall, bony wraith leaning back against the front fender, arms folded like a propped up scarecrow. Jim McNeely's face flooded with recognition and all other thoughts were broomed from his mind.

"Ort Cooley! You old goat!" he cried. "How the hotel are you?"

The two men gripped hands in a wrestling handshake full of unfeigned pleasure. Ort was haggard. He looked like a refugee from a camp for alcoholic tuberculars.

"How're things at Dead Lake?" said Jim McNeely, a frown of concern flickering over his face as he saw the hollow-eyed haggardness of his old friend.

"Aw, I quit them sorry bastards las' March. Ort to done it long ago."

"Whatcba been doin'?"

"Aw, I been pickin' my spots. Takin' a job here and there. I ain't been too anxious to rush into anything permanent."

With a sidelong look Jim McNeely said, "You been eatin' regular, I guess."

"Reg'lar as a rooster goes barefooted," said Ort firmly, swallowing his Adam's apple, which reemerged like an elbow rising in his throat.

Jim McNeely cast his eyes down and studied the ground a moment, frowning, thinking fast how to do this gently without hurting. "Well, ah,

I don't reckon you'd be interested in taking on with me." He glanced up. "We're not the Bison Oil Company but we're staying busy. Lots of jobs going. Keep a lot of stuff stacked around in the field between jobs, and I've been losing some of it to thieves. Lost a damn pump last week. Been thinking about taking on a watchman. That is, if I could find the right man. You know, somebody dependable and responsible."

"Aw, I ain't sayin' I'm *agin* a steady job," said Ort quickly, swallowing again, his face brightening under the sallow leather. "If it was to help you out. Now, I did kinda halfway promise a feller out at Penwell, but I mean, what the hell, well—" He latched up the offer fast before it could get away. "Why, *hell yes!* I'm ready to start tonight if you are."

And thus Ort Cooley joined the fold and was put on the straining payroll as chief (and only) watchman, a post well suited to his decaying physical capabilities.

That same afternoon Jim McNeely made his first real move into the oil-producing business, the move he had been thinking about for a long time and rejecting as too improbable of success to be worth the try. His meeting with Ort firmed his resolve to take a run at it because he felt that Ort's appearance on the scene was a good omen. He took Ort with him for luck.

They drove long miles up into Jarrett County to the Coker Ranch to see old man Coker and try to talk him out of an oil and gas lease on the forty-acre quarter-section upon which the so-called town of Coker City lay scattered. The forty acres now had wells on three sides of it and was almost certain to produce oil. There was room for just one well in the townsite under the spacing rule which the Railroad Commission had decreed for the Dead Lake field.

"Yeah, but now, Jimmy boy," said Ort, frowning, pulling at the loose skin of his face, "you know I ain't one to say you can't do anything you set yer mind to once you set it, but maybe you ort to think about this here one some more. I mean that man done '*nounced* in the Scharbauer Hotel lobby that he's gonna *shoot* the next lease-brokin' sonofabitch that comes out to his place tryin' to lease that townsite. Right betwixt the eyes."

"Well, Ort, don't you see? That makes it all right," said Jim McNeely lightheartedly. "Quite a few say I'm a sonofabitch, but I never once been accused of being a lease-broker."

"What the hell difference do that make if he *thinks* you're one. You're gittin' *at* the same thing. That ol' man's crazy as a bessy-bug, Jim. He's 'witched on the oil business. Livin' out there all by hisself on that no-count sandy ranch. He says the oil men done ruint the country fer the ranchers. Lot they had to ruin! Oh, he's crazy fer fair and maybe he's not 'sponsible. But that ain't gonna help you none when them bullets go zingin' by."

"Ort, I believe you got your chili up, pardner. I better let you out right here so you won't get mixed up in this." He was teasing Ort, but he braked the pick-up as if to stop.

"I ain't got no goddang chili up!" cried Ort belligerently, offended. "I'll kiss yer ass in Sanger Brothers' winder if I won't walk right up to that ol' man and say, 'Coker, you ol' sonofabitch, you better—'"

"Oh, no you won't," Jim McNeely cut him off firmly. "You won't say a thing. You'll set right still in this truck and keep your mouth shut. If you hear any shooting, you just blare ass out of there and get the sheriff."

They drove many miles over a twisting, dusty one-track ranch road through flat mesquite country, passing numerous crudely lettered signs nailed on posts that told them to go back. POSTED—KEEP OUT, POSTED—NO HUNTING, TRESPASSERS PROSECUTED, they said. All were signed with a rough, painted scrawl, A. COKER. When the pair arrived at the Coker Ranch headquarters, a collection of low, gray-weathered barns and sheds and pens spread around a barren one-story house, Jim McNeely stopped the pick-up at the wire gap leading to the clearing and cut off the motor.

"Ort to brought my ol' double-barrel twelve-gauge shotgun is what I ort to done," said Ort ruefully. "I sold the sonofabitch an' give the money to a faithless, cross-eyed woman."

"Never mind, pardner," said Jim McNeely, peering ahead through the dusty windshield. "Just grab ahold of your left one and maybe we'll make out."

"I already got it," said Ort forcefully. "An' I'm a-squeezin'."

As he walked slowly across the hard-packed ground toward the house Jim McNeely scanned the layout cautiously and wondered what he was going to do and say. A lone horse stood in the lot before the low barn, half asleep, switching at flies with its tail. Jim McNeely passed the corner of the lot and had gone ten paces beyond when a querulous voice from his rear jerked him to a halt.

"Do?" said the voice.

Startled, Jim McNeely flinched then caught himself and turned with careful casualness. A smallish man in dirty clothes and a sweated-out

Stetson leaned against the rail fence of the horse lot, gazing at him. The man could have been on either side of sixty. He had the face of a half-demented chipmunk with small eyes deeply sunk in and too close together. He hadn't shaved in days. The cracks running down from the corners of his mouth were filled with tobacco juice. A lever-action Winchester was leaned against the fence in close reach behind him.

"Mister Coker?" said Jim McNeely. He walked slowly toward him.

"Eah?"

When the younger man approached within three paces of him the man said sharply, "That'll do."

Jim McNeely stopped. "Mister Coker. My name's McNeely."

The old man looked deliberately up and down the frame of the slender, lean-muscled visitor wearing brown sport shirt, city pants, and brown and white shoes, obviously not a ranching man, being hatless and clean-shaven as well. The rancher eyed him narrowly, suspiciously, then said, "Eah?"

Jim McNeely hooked his elbow carefully over the fence rail at the bidden distance and faced the man.

"Heard you all had a rain out here last week, Mister Coker."

"Eah?"

"Guess you could always use a little more, though. But the grass don't look too bad, what there is of it."

"Eah?" The old man twisted his head, his eyes pinched-looking.

"I passed a heifer about two miles back on the road. Looked like she had worms in her bag. Don't know if it was one of yours or not." The old man narrowed his eyes further, puckered his lips, and spat a large brown-golden stream of tobacco juice which arced through the dry air and struck the dust a bare inch away from Jim McNeely's shoes. Jim McNeely flinched slightly and looked down, unbelieving. It was the old tobacco chewer's insult. Spit close enough to a man's feet without hitting them, so that the dust and splash spattered the shoes. A silence followed, during which Jim glanced down thoughtfully at his desecrated footwear.

"What d'ye want?" Mr. Coker's voice was a snarling whine. "That road don't lead nowheres but here."

"I don't want anything," said Jim McNeely quietly, flicking his eyes past the small figure to the Winchester and wondering how fast a little old man like that could move.

Mr. A. Coker worked up his mouth and let loose another arcing stream of tobacco juice, this time right at the edge of Jim McNeely's right shoe.

The impact spattered dust and brown liquid clear across the white buck instep. It was a snarling challenge, too close and direct to be accidental, calculated to unnerve a faint heart.

Jim McNeely glanced down again at his foot then looked back at the rancher. "I said I don't want anything, Mister Coker. Not a thing, that is, that you don't want to give me."

"Then git off my place."

For a full minute Jim McNeely held his position leaning against the fence, looking steadily into the small unfathomable eyes. Another bolt darted suddenly from the filthy mouth and this time hit right in the welt of his shoe, laying a larrup of brown liquid across the white leather and even splashing up on the white rayon socks with the red and gold clocks in them.

"I heard it said in Midland," said Jim McNeely steadily, holding his anger in check, "that you'd shoot the next man that came out here to lease your Coker City piece. Well, I'm not a lease broker and I don't aim to get shot. I'll tell you that for sure." He groped for his next words, playing it by ear and not hearing a tune. Another shot from the old man struck home between his feet, speckling the white of both shoes.

"Then what in the compounded hell do ye want of me?" said A. Coker, beginning in spite of himself to feel a little admiration for the gall of this young fool who stood so steadfast against the insults squirted at his feet, in the face of the thirty-caliber authority in easy reach behind him.

"I told you, I don't want a damn thing." said Jim McNeely flatly. "Unless you can spare a little of that Beechnut you're chewing."

"Eah?" Mr. A. Coker gave a startled grunt. Creases puckered the dry skin around the small agate eyes. He had been prepared for violence but this fool had challenged his hospitality. He hesitated. Then he pulled a mashed paper packet from his hip pocket and after a second thrust it across the open space between them. Jim McNeely took it, dug out a double fingerful of soggy tobacco, crammed it into his mouth, then handed the packet back. He chewed the tobacco around rapidly, settled it in his jaw and said, looking straight at his man, "Some folks are saying you're a damn fool, Mister Coker."

The little old man drew back in sudden tension, as if he had been slapped. His small face hardened into a venomous smirk. Jim McNeely held his breath and watched the Winchester. "But I don't agree with 'em," he said quickly, "because I know better. But that's what they say."

"Eah?" said the man. His voice had tightened dangerously.

"Eah," said Jim McNeely, mouthing his tobacco. The fat was in the fire and he knew that any sign of weakness now would bring disaster. He chewed up a juicy mouthful and spit it loosely, inexpertly, toward the man's weathered boots. He intended to hit close, but not, as happened, squarely on the scuffed toe of the man's right foot. Mr. Coker jerked his foot back in an instinctive movement of surprise and rage. Then he caught himself and loosed a responsive bolt that traveled in a flat arc and landed squarely at the point of the younger man's left shoe and riccocheted wetly up on the vamp.

"Eah?" he said again, viciously.

Without moving a muscle or looking down Jim McNeely said, "They're saying you're a fool for not leasing that Coker City townsite because there's oil under it and the oil companies have got wells on three sides of you and they're sucking it out from under you, your oil, every day. Worth a dollar sixty-five a barrel. And in time they'll suck it all out and drain you dry, and you won't get a dime because, or so they say, you're so stupid and hardheaded you'd rather let them rob you than drill a well and get what's rightfully yours. Of course I know better or I wouldn't be here." Jim McNeely's mouth was overflowing with the loose unnatural weed-juice. He spurted it boldly at the man's feet, missing the mark and lacing it well upon the frayed cuff of his faded levis.

Mr. Coker straightened and his small eyes flew open and he looked down with amazed disbelief.

"Sh-it to what they say!" he snarled, halfway between shock and rage. He ground his jaws rapidly and emitted a curving stream that hit the ground right beside Jim McNeely's shoe and spattered up on his trouser cuff.

"What I say," Jim McNeely said holding firm and working his cud, "is that nobody's offered you a fair deal yet. They've been trying to steal your lease for an eighth royalty. Peanuts! I don't blame you. If you left it to the thieving lease brokers and oil companies the landowner wouldn't get anything. I'm just a well-service contractor myself. Just a plain working man. And I think you deserve to have a partner who can get your oil out—what's rightly yours, before they suck it all out from under you. That way you'd damn well show people that you knew what you were doing by waiting and not leasing to any company or lease hound for any measly eighth royalty." He had no inkling that he was getting through to this man but he knew he had to play out the hand and he charged ahead to the finish. "Then there'd be some people know who was stupid and who wasn't, and it wouldn't be old man Coker!" The juice was running out of the comers of his mouth and down his chin. He squirted wildly in the direction of the boots but his aim was worse than ever. The brown saliva struck squarely on the fly of the old man's dirty levis and dripped rapidly down his pants legs into the dirt.

A. Coker drew back in a braced fury and for a second Jim McNeely was sure he was going for the Winchester and was prepared to make a diving tackle for him. Then suddenly the old man exploded in a shriek of inhuman laughter. His mouth opened in a gaping hole studded with broken stumps of teeth and a repulsive cherry-red tongue all covered with chewed-up tobacco. He shrieked and choked and spewed out tobacco, beating himself on the ribs with his little clawlike hands. When he caught enough breath to speak he cried, "You the wuss goddamn t'baccer chewer ever I seed in my goddamn life! Who the hell ever told you you could chew t'baccer?" Then he grabbed the fence in a renewed spasm of uncontrollable laughter.

Jim McNeely wiped his palm across his chin, then wiped his hand clean against the soft weathered wood of the fence railing. He grinned, knowing he had won something, though he wasn't sure what. "I never claimed to any expert at chewin' tobacco or anything else, Mister Coker. I'm just a pore boy tryin' to get along."

That is how Jim McNeely obtained the lease on the Coker City townsite, or at least an interest in it. Before sundown, sitting on the bare boards of A. Coker's front porch in his stained socks, he made his deal. No cash money would change hands. He would drill the well with his rig—he referred to his rickety old jackknife work-over contraption as his "big rig," wondering to himself whether it would hold together to drill the 4,000-foot hole that it had not been designed to drill even when it was new. He would pay himself back his actual drilling costs out of the proceeds of the first oil produced, then he and Mr. Coker would own the well and share in the production fifty-fifty. It was not an especially good deal for Jim McNeely, considering the risks involved, but it was not a bad one either if he could handle it. In any case it was the very best he figured he could make with this little old half-demented man. Most important, if it worked, it would put him in the oil business as an *oil man*, an independent producer, and this he felt was the important thing. It would open doors and deals to him that he could not otherwise get close to. It would "get his feet wet" in the oil business.

Lee was jubilant when he told her and threw her arms around his neck and kissed him hard and repeatedly and said she was so proud of him that she could almost take up chewing herself. The next night, which happened to be his birthday, they went out to the Ace of Clubs and had some drinks and a steak, and Lee had wrapped up a birthday present in frilly pink wrapping, and when he opened it, it was a fresh fifteen-cent package of Beechnut chewing tobacco.

Jim McNeely laughed and felt good this night, though an apprehension about what he had taken on kept prickling at his neck. But he loved this dark, exciting schoolteacher wife that he had married. And her absolute confidence that he could figure out some way to make the thing work made him feel, after a couple of drinks, that he damn well could and would make it work.

22

"I DON'T KNOW IF THAT OLD RIG WILL HOLD together. That's the first problem. It's never drilled a hole that deep before."

"Oh, it will, it will!" said Lee positively. "I'll give it a Christian Science treatment. It will make it."

"That's not the big knot, though, sweetheart. The drilling is gonna take a month. Nobody's paying for this hole but me. Where the money's coming from to meet the second week's payroll is something else."

"Can't you borrow on the lease? It's just bound to produce."

"You don't know bankers. They've got to see oil in the tanks before they'll turn loose of a dime. I can probably get the pipe and well-head equipment from a supply company on the credit once the well is down and they see it's gonna produce. But that don't help with the drilling. Drilling crews got to eat, same as you and me."

"It seems a pity. You know you're going to make a well—or almost know it. If the crews could wait for their paychecks for a couple of months—"

"Hell, sugar, those boys are living right next to the bone same as I am. They got groceries to buy and rent to pay and car payments to meet. I'll bet there's not one of 'em got fifty dollars in the bank."

They sat in the tiny dinette of their small house over empty supper dishes. Jim McNeely leaned on his folded arms on the table drawing circles in his plate with his fork, thinking and talking his thoughts as they rolled out of his head.

"Everybody's got a *little* credit. Nearly everybody can stall the landlord for a month. And anybody could get by on beans and cornbread for that long if they had to. We *could* lay in a couple of hundred-pound sacks of pinto beans and corn meal and keep 'em in the warehouse. Anybody who got really hard up could just take what they needed."

Lee's quick mind grasped the shape and purpose of the forming thought and she began to tug at it enthusiastically before it had fully emerged.

"Well, of course they could! Then they wouldn't need any money for groceries! We could get a big sack of white onions, too. I know a dozen different ways to fix beans. I'll conduct a bean-cooking school for the wives!"

"Yeah," said Jim McNeely tapping at the plate with the fork. "But why would anybody want to go along on that basis? Hell, the well could be dry."

"But it won't be dry, will it?"

"I don't think it will, but no well's a cinch til it's in the tanks. They might never get paid. There ought to be some odds laid on to make it worthwhile for 'em to take the gamble."

"Odds? Like what? A bonus?"

"Something like." He carefully laid the fork down across the plate as the thought hardened. "Like double wages out of oil, maybe, if, as and when produced—"

"Jim!" Lee cried.

"I never heard of it being done. But these boys are all crapshooters—"

"Jim McNeely, it's a great idea!" Lee cried. She reached her bare brown arms across the table and squeezed his frowning face between her strong fingers. "It'll work! I know it will! You're a genius! A natural-born genius!"

Jim McNeely caught her wrists and pulled her hands down, grinning. "I'm not a genius. You just married a poor boy that's tryin' to invent a substitute for money. It may not work."

But it did, and that is exactly how the McNeely Oil Company Number 1 Coker was drilled. On beans, faith, and thirty days' credit for the drilling mud and fuel and incidentals. And a promise of two-for-one out of oil for the drilling crews' wages.

It was perhaps a minor miracle that the spindly work-over rig held together in drilling beyond its capabilities to a depth below 4,000 feet. Lee gave the operation a Christian Science treatment every day, as best she knew how, and had a practitioner helping her and even thought about paying the practitioner two-for-one out of oil, as well, though that wasn't necessary.

The drilling went ahead, slowly and cautiously, because a fishing job would have been fatal. After they passed the thousand-foot depth Jim McNeely seldom left the location, which was on vacant ground west of the main street of Coker City, as near to the field as Railroad Commission spacing regulations would allow. He slept in the pick-up or in the rig's doghouse when he slept at all, which wasn't much. He usually walked over to the Club Cafe for coffee and a doughnut about daylight, skipped lunch, and Lee fixed him a big supper, based on beans, and brought it out to him every night from Odessa and sat in the doghouse grading papers while he ate.

There was a lot of talk about the well because old man Coker's tract had been the subject of conversation among the local oil fraternity for a long time and there were going to be some red faces, especially in the Bison organization, if some unknown independent picked off this small but juicy plum, because everybody had said it couldn't be done. And so Jim McNeely had as many people hoping that disaster would overtake him as he had well-wishers. Lee discussed this with her practitioner and did special protective work against "mental malpractice."

One of the well-wishers who also happened to be a Bison man was Jim McNeely's old friend, the geologist Berry Wakely. Berry came by to see him several times when he was in the area and looked at the cuttings and the driller's logs and was glad to give his opinion, gratis, that the well was running about flat with the field and ought to do all right. He discussed with his friend and former fellow-employee how the well should be completed.

The geologist said, "When you hit the top of the San Andres I'd come out and run in a core barrel and core about twenty-five feet. If the core looks good, then I'd take a drill-stem test and if that's OK, too, why run your pipe and tubing and you're in business."

"Hell, I'm afraid to core with this wobbly old sonofabitch. Goddamnit, I mean, this sweet wonderful rig! Lee says if I want the old rattletrap to act right I better quit cussin' it. Anyway a core-head and a core-barrel cost money that I haven't got"

"In that case I'd just drill about twenty feet into the formation and drill-stem test her. If she spits, why, set pipe and complete."

"That's kind of what I was thinking." He cut his eyes innocently at Berry Wakely. "But reckon how I'm gonna know when I'm twenty feet in?"

"My boy," said Berry Wakely sagely, "that's what geologists are for. You get sick, you don't call a blacksmith."

"Well now, Berry, you don't chance to know an ol' broke-down geologist that might just happen to be milling around these parts about day after tomorrow afternoon that might like to help out an old oil-patch buddy by picking the top of the San Andres formation for him, do you? Out of friendship and, say, about two hundred and fifty bucks out of oil?"

Wakely's face wrinkled in a wry smile. He looked at his friend in the greasy, sweated-out khaki shirt. "I used to know a green kid that I tried to talk into going back to school, to smarten up. Mother of Christ! Why go through all that drudgery when you can con somebody into doing the job for you?" He gave Jim McNeely a meaningful smirk. "If I run across some old broken-down geologist who isn't tied up day after tomorrow afternoon, I'll send him around."

And so Berry Wakely was there forty-eight hours later with his microscope, and he picked the top of the San Andres for him early in the afternoon and they drilled twenty feet more and Jim McNeely, on the rig floor and beginning to look a little haggard and anxious, having missed his morning shave as well as breakfast and lunch, drew his finger across his throat and shouted over the roar of the engine to the driller, "Shut her down!" The driller closed the throttle and set his brake and Jim McNeely said, "Snake that pipe out of the hole real easy, driller, and let's test this sonofa—let's test this sweet little hole in the ground!"

It was a few minutes before dark when they got back on bottom with the testing tool. All day the sky had been overcast and gloomy, without rain. Now just at sunset the sun broke below the edge of the clouds in the west and lighted up the vast plain with a yellow brilliance, as if a great floodlight had been turned on in an enormous circus tent.

"Sunshine," said Lee to the little group standing before the doghouse. "A good omen."

"'The weary sun hath made a golden set,'" quoth Dent, who had come over from Dead Lake Camp. "'And, by the bright track of his fiery car, gives signal of a goodly day tomorrow . . .'"

"I bound ye," said Ort, with amazement. "He's talkin' in tongues again."

"That's Shakespeare, my ungainly friend," replied Dent.

"Who the hell do *he* work for?" said Ort contemptuously.

Yet everyone felt a little relieved, as though the sunlight breaking through might truly be a good omen. The tension had built unnoticed to a high pitch in the last hour and they were all a little jittery.

"Sandwich, anyone?" called Dent brightly from Lee's car. He had brought a picnic basket with small sandwiches, a bottle of iced martinis, and small paper cups.

"Chicken and watercress!" Lee exclaimed, biting into the finger sandwich. "Dent! *Water*cress! Where on earth did you get it?"

"Flew it in for the occasion, my dear," said Dent casually. "Goddang clover, looks to me like," said Ort spitting and picking the green stuff out of a sandwich and popping the remainder in his mouth. "Think we was a bunch a' goddang cows."

Jim McNeely was on the derrick floor working with the crew. They had been straining and sweating in a huddle, changing teeth in the slips which had begun to fail at this critical point. They stood back blowing and looking at one another for a moment, then Jim McNeely nodded, and the floor men set the slips, the driller eased up on his brake and let the pipe down. The slips held. Another joint was screwed on and the drill-stem was lowered to bottom. Then one of the roughnecks snapped the floating tongs on the pipe and leaned into the handle, steadily, carefully turning.

"She ought to be open."

"Cut the engine, driller," said Jim McNeely. "If we've got anything, we don't want a fire." He went rapidly down from the derrick floor, his feet ringing on the steel steps, the others trailing behind him. He walked out to the mud pit over which a pipe from the well-head extended, open ended. Lee, Dent, and Ort hurried out from the doghouse, feeling the tension of the moment. Everyone was quiet. With the engine stopped it was very still in the late evening air.

"Been open three minutes now," said Jim McNeely, looking at his wrist watch.

One of the roughnecks knelt by the flowpipe and held a bare hand over its open end. "Good blow," he said, sweeping his hand up to his nose. "Of air. No. Hold on." He kept sweeping and sniffing. "Comin' gas. Beginning to stink. Pickin' up, too."

In a moment the air flow from the pipe became a soft, audible soughing and moments later the aqueous transparent plume of hydrocarbon gas became faintly visible in the failing sunlight. "Real gas," said the roughneck, the excitement plain in his voice.

The soughing became a whisper and then a soft, throaty roar that began to cough, as if gasping for breath.

"Five minutes," said Jim McNeely.

The hollow coughing became louder and more persistent. Then here she came, first a little trickle of drilling mud, kicking and spitting in dirty spurts, then a belching of mud, gas and oil and gravel, and then all at once a violent bursting forth from the pipe as from an awakened giant erupting in a pent-up antediluvian orgasm. A solid four-inch column of green-black oil shot powerfully from the pipe twenty feet across the slush pit, flowering at the end and splashing in a wave of golden green bubbles over the gray mud of the pit that sloshed up against the far earthen firewall.

The roar from the pipe was now deafening, drowning out all yells that rose from the collected throats of those lined up at the edge of the pit. Lee clapped her hands and hugged everybody in reach. Dent waltzed around snapping his fingers and went into a giddy Charleston, alternating with the Black Bottom, singing unheard, "Money, mon-ey, money, money, mon-ey!" Ort walked around rapidly in circles, hitting everybody in the chest with the back of his hand, shouting, "Bound ye! *Bound* ye!" Before it was over, unable to express his joy any other way he ran and grabbed up Dent's bottle of martinis and began swigging out of it, striding around holding the bottle aloft by the neck, roaring, "Bound ye! Didn't I tell ye? *Bound* ye!"

Jim McNeely alone seemed unmoved, standing stolidly head bent, peering at the magnificent column of oil glinting in the last rays of the sun, his arms folded across his chest. Lee finally came back to him and embraced him and kissed him on the face and yelled in his ear, "You wonderful man!"

Without moving his gaze he put one arm around her shoulders and drew her close.

"We're in the oil business now, sugar," he said against her ear. "This—is only the beginning."

Lee clung close to him. Though his words were inaudible, she felt their meaning and as she did the thrill leaked out of her and a chill came over her, a sudden chill from nowhere, and she tightened her arm around his waist and pressed her cheek against his shirt, as if battening down hatches and closing bulkheads for a storm gathering on the horizon at sea.

He seemed to sense her fear for he grinned down at her and pulled her closer.

"Don't worry, sugar," he said.

For the time being everything was in hock to the hilt, and this baby would be a long time paying off. At this moment he was glad he was married to a schoolteacher, so they could eat something besides beans.

23

I T WAS NOT LONG AFTER THIS GREAT DAY THAT DENT
Paxton joined forces with the McNeely enterprises, which then
consisted of half an oil well and a small oil-field servicing operation,
the equipment for which was now literally held together with baling wire.
This reuniting of the two friends, though perhaps inevitable, had not been
consciously planned by either.

They ran into each other on the main street of Odessa on a Saturday
in the fall when Dent was in town on his monthly trip to replenish his
whiskey supply. A sandstorm was blowing and visibility in the dulled
afternoon light was no more than a block. Sand snakes ran and twisted
fitfully along the sidewalks.

"Let's get the hell out of this dirt and drink a beer," said Jim McNeely,
holding onto his doeskin Borsalino. He had started wearing the hat almost
immediately when the Coker City well came in. It appropriately marked
his new status as "oil man." "I'm dyin' to hear the news of Cap and all my
other good friends at Dead Lake."

"Cap still loves you," said Dent, returning the smirk. He nodded toward
a beer joint across the street and headed for it.

When they were settled in a booth and Dent had opened a pint of
bourbon and was mixing himself a drink and Jim McNeely was pulling
on a cold bottle of Jax, Dent said, "Well, here we are, old buddy. How's the
world been treating you and all that jazz? How's Lee?"

"Fine. Fine. Lee's at the office gettin' out billings. She's the fastest two-
finger typewriter operator in the West. I got to get over there and help

her. I was on my way when I saw you. Just got in from Penwell. We're plenty busy."

"That Lee's a fine citizen," said Dent. "I'll never understand what she saw in you." With a quizzical cat's expression he studied the face of his friend and thought of the changes that had come over it since that day, these years ago now, when a distracted, ill-at-ease youth named Jim McNeely had walked into his office at Dead Lake. It was a man's face now, handsome, virile, confident, with just an occasional cast of boyishness showing through the deepening lines around the eyes—the faint residue of the half-belligerent, half-uncertain cockiness that he remembered so well.

"She's just a good judge of character," said Jim McNeely.

"Ol' Clyde Montgomery got married again," said Dent. "Got him a real sow this time. She thinks he's a pistol."

Jim McNeely nodded. "Give 'em my regards."

"I'd like to see Lee," Dent said.

"She'd like to see you, too. Maybe we'll go out and eat somewhere. There's nothing cooking at the house. She's been working on the books all day. Every Saturday and most of Sunday she does. It's about to get away from her. It's that blamed oil well. Seems like it takes a barrel of paper to produce a barrel of oil—all the reports and forms to fill out and the bookkeeping, on top of everything else. I've just about decided—" He stopped and squinted at Dent Paxton closely in scowling silence. He rubbed his palms together slowly and the silence became so long that Dent looked up and said, "You were saying—?"

"Hey, sweetheart, bring me another Jax. Denton, old buddy, you know, it smells to me like there's going to be a war."

"Perish the thought."

"This country's not gonna let England go under. One way or another we're bound to get into it."

"Perish the *thought* of the thought."

"Things are liable to get real rough, but one thing is sure. They got to have oil. I been holding off going into debt for new equipment because well-servicing is not where the money is. But I've about decided maybe I better do it. I think I'm gonna take on a new drilling rig—one that can drill to 6,000 feet and do heavy work-overs. That and a brand new truck-mounted pulling unit for rod and tubing jobs. While the getting is good."

"That'd make you a mighty essential defense worker, wouldn't it, old buddy," said Dent with a fey smile. "Make it real hard for any draft board to send you greetings. Me, I'm pure, pristine cannonfodder. Candor compels me to admit that I could be replaced by an eighty-year-old woman."

"Probably strengthen the company, at that," said Jim McNeely. "Set the Army back five years, though, if they drafted you."

He pulled on the fresh beer and squinted his eyes, working out his thoughts. "What I'm thinking is I'm to the point where I got to have somebody to take over the paper work—to get Lee out of the bind I've put her in. I'll figure out some way to keep the feller I take on out of the draft. Send him to the field now and then, call him a production foreman or something. With a little oil smeared on him and a tin hat on his head he'd look essential as hell, too." He paused a moment, then said, "Whaddya say, buddy?"

"I pledge allegiance," said Dent with fine sarcasm, but pleased nonetheless, "to Jim McNeely and the nefarious aims for which he stands."

"Anybody that goes with me is gonna make out." There was a long pause. A change seemed to come over his face as Dent watched him. When he resumed, the bantering tone was gone. His voice sounded strange, almost stilted. Dent felt as though his friend wasn't even talking to him any more, but was reciting by rote some incantation learned in childhood. "There's an oil field somewhere that's got my name on it. A big one. Just lying there like a lonesome woman, waiting for me. Well, I'll find it. I'll keep looking until I do. But I'll find it. You can count on that."

Dent caught himself before he spoke the words, but he thought them: "And when you do, that'll get you a free pass into heaven where you'll live happily ever afterwards with all the other millionaires that rode their mother-lovin' camels in through the eye of the needle." He controlled the impulse because he saw that Jim McNeely was deadly serious. There was a subdued excitement in his friend's voice and Dent loved this young man like, well, like a brother, and he felt it would be ghastly to ruin this moment with a joke. He said, "Yes, I really believe you will find it, Jim."

"Well, are you gonna help me? You want me to beg you?"

"Beg, hell, I've just been wondering if you'd ever ask me."

"I don't know what I can pay you."

"Who cares?"

"It's kind of chancy."

"I'm a chancy fellow."

"OK, buddy," Jim McNeely stuck out his hand. "Put her there."

"Oh, for cryin' out loud!" Dent gave a high-pitched embarrassed giggle. He slapped aside the proffered hand. "Don't make a B picture out of it! Let's go see Lee."

24

JIM MCNEELY GRADUALLY FOCUSED THE
concentration of his life on one central conviction and aim: somewhere a giant oil field lay buried, waiting for him to find it. This
as yet undisclosed reservoir belonged to him as surely as if it had been
willed to him by his father. Slowly everything else became subordinate
to the single goal of finding it and making it his own, and, unconsciously,
he began to judge people, occurrences, and opportunities as valuable or a
waste of time according to their usefulness in the achievement of this goal.

Sometimes in rare reflective moments he felt that everything done by
or to him in his life had been necessary preparation for the fulfillment of
this ambition, and he cursed and shuddered at the risks he had had to run,
the disaster and destruction to which he had had to expose himself in its
pursuit. How close he had come to killing Buster Drum! How near Cap
Bruner had come to grinding him out of existence as a man! What an
agonizing miracle of luck and timing it had been that had enabled him to
make his deal with old man Coker and then drill and complete the Coker
City well. He was filled with dark resentment at the fate which put him
to these trials and wondered in anger how many more lay in store for him.
Defiantly he muttered to the air, "Go ahead, Lady Luck, you bitch, do
your worst. I'll meet you head on!"

He still thought of Mazie Wales sometimes, vaguely, and without purpose. Her remembered image brought a lingering residual pain, not the
violent pressing agony of passion that he had once felt, but the dim, dull
aching that comes from a chronic deep-buried infection.

He had never seen Mazie again. This was not strange, for he had not returned to Winfield once since that unhappy Christmas. He had, in fact, gone to considerable lengths to avoid going there when well-servicing business had made it almost imperative that he do so. He had definite ideas about when and how he would return to that city of his birth and youth, Winfield, blazing jewel of the prairie on her sluggish, septic river.

He had had news of Mazie only twice, once when he had seen her picture in the home-town paper, taken as she sailed from New York with a group of college girls on "her European tour." Later he had winced at the sudden sight of her likeness on the Sunday society page, among her bowered, petal-fresh peers, when she made her debut at the Tuileries Ball. He told himself that it was all a bunch of low-life snobbery and nonsense, but he felt again rejected and left out of the good life, and the old anger deepened.

Lee's knowledge of Mazie Wales consisted only of the few bare brush-strokes that Jim McNeely supplied before they were married, though, womanlike, her imagination filled in many uncomplimentary details. She looked at the newspaper picture and screwed up her lips and one eye and thought Mazie Wales didn't look so hot and wondered how she would really stack up against her in all departments. Then she shrugged lightly and flipped her short thick hair with her fingers and saucily thought, "She's got her picture in the paper, but I've got the man."

It came as a hard shock to Jim McNeely one Sunday morning as he lay late in bed stretched out in his shorts leafing through the Winfield paper when he saw Mazie suddenly smiling out at him, taking up the entire front page of the society section. She stood radiant and resplendent in her wedding gown with a lace and satin train fanned out in a magnificent swirl at her feet. The caption read, "Mrs. Clayton Bedford LeMayne III, the former Miss Mazie Marie Wales, who was married in one of the outstanding social events of the season on Friday evening at First Presby-terian Church. The couple will be at home at Fort Sill, Oklahoma, where Lt. LeMayne is stationed."

"*Pluto! Mazie and Pluto!*" shouted Jim McNeely, springing from the bed. He crashed the paper to the floor and let out a violent string of cursing. "Goddamn low-life bastardly no-account sonsofbitches!" He kept shouting, wildly pacing the floor in a livid rage until Lee came to the door from the kitchen. She held an egg turner in one hand, her eyes wide, half-angry, half-alarmed.

"What—in the world? What is it?"

Jim McNeely glared at her under dark brooding brows. He ran his fingers through his scalp. "Nothing important! The goddamn Dodgers got shut out yesterday. I lost a fin to that smart-ass Shag McQueen."

"Oh?" she said, her tone showing her displeasure at the profane outburst. "I thought maybe you were doing your Sunday school lesson."

Later in the morning after he had gone and she was straightening up the bedroom she smoothed out the crushed newspaper and saw the picture and sat on the bed studying it a long while. Then she shrugged lightly and sighed and understood that it wasn't the Dodgers.

25

THE WAR WAS OVER. THE WAR YEARS HAD FAIRLY raced by, for Jim McNeely was in the business of keeping the oil patch patched up to fill the pipelines with crude—without which the machinery of twentieth-century wars would grind to a clanking halt. This was not easy, because most of the steel that normally flowed into oil country tubular goods and equipment was diverted into Sherman tanks and Liberty ships and Momsen mats.

The restless surge of youth to go where the excitement was siphoned many young men out of the fields, and the draft took many more who were of a less bellicose nature. Old men came out of retirement to go back on the job and two men did the work that three had done before.

Ort was transferred from his watchman's job to running a pulling machine, for even the thieves, it seemed, had gone to see the war. Ort performed well and dependably. Even Dent was set to driving a heavy truck and filling in as relief on light oil-field jobs, though only after frantic and shocked protestings, in the beginning, that he would sooner bare his breast to shot and shell than don a working man's gloves. Whatever Dent did, however, he did well, with intelligence, alacrity, and a fastidious dexterity that enabled him to work all day around an oil well without getting any grease on him.

Lee quit her teaching job and took over the office work. The war was a wonderful time for her, a beautiful, satisfying, exciting time. She grieved for the people whose husbands and sons were taken away from them, but the courage and the killing were too far away, too impersonal, for her to feel or understand. The war was a good time for her because she felt needed and important, and because, in the world's state of suspension and uncertainty, the many-clawed devil-in-the-gizzard driving this lean, dark Jim McNeely that she loved seemed to have gone away, and with it the part of him that was reserved from her and which she, only vaguely understanding, feared. It was a space of living today to the maximum intensity, of loving as though love would be taken away tomorrow, of putting one foot in front of the other and thinking no farther into the future than the next step because the horizons all around the compass were clouded in swirling smoke, laced with flame. These were intense and wonderful years.

Jim McNeely knew he was doing as well as could be expected under the circumstances and was satisfied, for he knew that if he wasn't here he would be somewhere else doing something very much less pleasant, probably a great deal less important to the war effort, and undoubtedly a lot more dangerous. The thought that he was not sharing the dangers of war with his contemporaries in the armed forces caused him a pang or two. But he took consolation in the fact that while he had not volunteered, neither had he asked for a deferment. The draft board had classified him as an essential worker and any time they wanted him to take off his safety hat and put on a helmet, they knew where they could find him.

This feeling was reinforced when someone returning from the Pacific Theater told him of seeing Pluto LeMayne in Hawaii, where Pluto had maneuvered himself into a job as aide-de-camp to some rear-echelon general. Given his genius for avoiding the hard things of life, it was even money that Pluto would fight out the war right there, mixing excellent martinis for his general, supervising a splendid mess that catered to gold braid and visiting VIPs, and, in his off time, entertaining nurses in a beach-front apartment which he and another officer maintained and repaired to for rehabilitation when administrative fatigue set in.

The only news Jim McNeely had of Mazie during the war was contained in a squib in the Winfield paper that told of her being in France with the Red Cross. The state of emotional flux and uncertainty that gripped men generally during the war years when normal peacetime drives shifted into an abeyant neutral was such that this intelligence affected him neither one way or the other.

The money, meanwhile, came in steadily, almost unnoticed, and began to mount up. Mrs. Sullivan was paid off in full, and the new tools were paid off in late 1945. The Coker City well ran a small but steady stream into the bank account every month. When his financial situation improved Jim

McNeely bought a larger house, an old roomy brick bungalow of 1925 vintage which had belonged to a rancher who moved East to live with a daughter when his wife died. The house had some trees and a windmill in the back and was just two blocks off the main street. Jim McNeely reasoned it would be a good investment for the future. It would also be cooler in summer and warmer in winter than the crackerbox he and Lee had been living in. More than this, there was a new element involved—status, public image. He was becoming a factor to be reckoned with in the business community of Odessa. He conducted a profitable business, maintained a respectable payroll, and ran a substantial amount of money through the banks. People began to ask him to contribute to the Community Chest and considered him for committees of the Chamber of Commerce.

Lee, who was presented with the deed-cum-mortgage to the "new" house as a surprise birthday present, was pleased, though she had been perfectly happy in the old one and the new was twice as much trouble for her to look after.

Her awareness of her importance as bookkeeper and office manager kept her constantly reminded that a baby was out of the question. Even if there had not been this practical necessity she could not forget the wild, violent profanity of the Sunday morning of the newspaper that carried Mazie's bridal picture, at which time she had renewed her vow, perhaps out of pride, that there would be no baby until Jim McNeely asked for it. She still felt, with vague, growing discomfort, that she had been the aggressor. She had been, after all, a married woman and he had been going away and she had pursued him. In effect she had asked him to marry her. Not the other way around, the way it should have been. She could never quite forget this.

26

JIM McNEELY WAS IN HIS OFFICE FIGURING A BID on a drilling job when a young man with a limp came in to see him. The fellow had come out to the office on foot, which branded him as nobody right off. His suit, though clean and neatly pressed, was an old-style double-breasted model which obviously had been cut down from a suit bought for somebody else a long time ago. He was slight and wiry and had a fresh-washed country look about him that Jim McNeely liked, despite the fact that his ears stuck out and his shirt collar was too big. He walked across the office and said his name was Jeff Dofflemyer.

"Howdy, Jeff. How you come on? Sit down," said Jim McNeely, shaking hands without getting up from the desk. He figured he was about to be hit up for a job and he thought he just might take this one on. There was an openness and lack of anxiety in the light blue-green eyes that made him think the fellow would be a dependable hand. Jeff Dofflemyer sat down. One knee bent normally, but the other leg stuck out in front of him, only half bent, the heel resting on the floor.

"What's on your mind, pardner?"

"I'm looking for a job, Mister McNeely. I heard you had a young company that was growing, and I thought you might be able to use me."

Jim McNeely grunted noncommittally, but felt pleased. "Don't know as there's anything right now. What kind of work are you looking for?"

"I'm a lawyer, Mister McNeely," said the young man, "I thought maybe your company had got to where you could save some money having your own attorney."

"Lawyer!" said Jim McNeely sitting back, almost laughing. He looked closer, at the slender, country-looking youth. "You a lawyer?"

"Yes, sir." Jeff Dofflemyer took an old wallet from his hip pocket and drew out and handed across the desk a fresh, pale green card that certified to the fact that Thomas Jefferson Dofflemyer was a member in good standing of the State Bar of Texas.

"Well I'll be doggone!"

"You probably want to know about my experience," Jeff Dofflemyer said. "The truth is I haven't had any as a lawyer. Except law school, of course. But it wouldn't take much salary to hire me."

Jim McNeely, though impressed by the straightforward manner of this white-skinned, freckle-faced youth, told him reluctantly that he didn't have enough lawyer work to justify taking one on full time. Judge Sanders down in town did what little legal work he had, and the old man surely wasn't getting rich out of his business. He suggested, however, that he might be able to use a fellow accustomed to working around farm machinery on one of the well-servicing units.

"I thank you, Mister McNeely. I was raised around farm machinery but I've set out to be a lawyer now and I reckon I'll keep trying. As far as just a job I already got one, over at the Sinclair station, working nights. Gives me a chance to look around in the daytime for something in my line. Come by and fill up with me, any time after six. And thanks again." He got up and put out his hand.

"You don't have to rush off," said Jim McNeely. "Stick around a few minutes and I'll run you back to town." He felt a warm, almost patronizing interest in the young man, though there was little difference in their ages. On the way to town Jim McNeely learned, by a little probing, that Jeff had got the limp from a Jap .25-caliber bullet through the knee joint on Guadalcanal. When they found they couldn't patch him up to fight again they let him out, and with the aid of the GI Bill he had gone to Abilene Christian College and then to law school at the University of Texas. He had had a real struggle, getting through law school and his grades were not too good. There was no demand among the big-city law firms for a fellow who came off a small farm and graduated near the foot of his class. He didn't have the money to set up in practice for himself so he had come out to Odessa because he had heard that the Permian Basin was a growing area with lots of oil activity and maybe people out here wouldn't be so particular.

Jim McNeely told him he would keep his eyes open for any possibilities, and that he would surely come by the Sinclair station and fill up with him, in any case. There was something about Jeff Dofflemyer that he liked.

Not long after this a broker brought Jim McNeely a deal involving a section of land, 640 acres, on the northeast flank of the Sheets Pool in Crane County. The Sheets Pool was one of the most prolific fields in the Basin and was almost wholly owned by Consul Petroleum. The section had never been drilled, for two reasons: it was unattractive geologically, being in a trough below the oil level of the Sheets Pool anticline, as the Consul geologists projected the beds on their subsurface maps, and the title was so involved in a family lawsuit between two sets of heir-claimants that nobody had taken a serious interest in the land, even for speculative purposes. Still, the tract was a square mile of undrilled land next to a good oil field, and the broker, following the maxim "to find oil get close to oil," had taken leases from all of the heirs that he could locate on the side he thought had the strongest case in the suit, agreeing to pay them ten dollars an acre for their respective interests, subject to title check. He hadn't paid off on the leases, of course, but had put them into the local bank on a thirty-day time draft while he tried to peddle the deal. He had about a week left before he would have to come up with the cash or let the leases go back to the heirs. Jim McNeely knew that the broker had shopped this deal to every big operator in the area before he brought it to him. When the fellow told him he wanted a thousand dollars cash and a one-thirty-second override for the works, his first impulse was to tell him to take the lousy deal and shove it. But something made him hesitate. He told the broker to leave the map and the papers with him and he'd sleep on it overnight.

He sat studying the map on his desk a long time, thinking. That afternoon he drove down into Crane County. As he rolled through the flat, unlovely mesquite country that suddenly mounded up into Saharan dunes, with the hot sandy wind whipping in the car window he thought angrily how hard it was for a poor bastard to get anywhere in this business, and how risky it was. Every deal was "go for broke." If you were lucky, you were a genius. If you missed you were just another sap, and there were ninety-nine saps for every genius.

In late afternoon he drove through the magnificent Sheets Field, a six-mile forest of oil wells two miles wide. Many of the wells still had the high steel derricks standing over them. Most of the wells were still natural-flow wells, and only those around the fringes of the field were on the pump. The untold wealth in barrels and dollars that this buried hump in the earth's substrata would give up before it ran dry was enough to make a sultan cry.

He drove through the field until he saw a pumper rattling down the road in a dilapidated pick-up. Flagging the man down, pretending he was lost, he engaged him in conversation. Jim McNeely knew how to talk to working stiffs because he had been one, and before they parted he had learned, with growing interest, that the wells on the northeast edge of the field were "pretty sorry" compared to the wells in the fairway. They cut some water but they still made their allowable just as regular as sun-up came, and the percentage of water wasn't increasing.

"It don't seem right but the water seems like it's tailin' off, like," said the pumper, glad to have somebody to talk to. "Fact is, I can't see how come the bosses don't drill that last row of locations on the northeast side of the lease. Over round Breckenridge where I come from they'd think them edge wells was real bitch kitties."

All the next day Jim McNeely stayed in the office waiting for the broker to come to see him, because he knew it would be bad psychology to call him. The fellow finally came out about midafternoon. Jim McNeely searched around the desk under invoices and equipment catalogues before he finally found the man's lease papers, as if he hadn't given them more than a passing thought.

"Naw, I guess not, pardner," he said. "It's pretty thin. Bad title and off structure. You'll find somebody, though, I bet. Somebody with some Confederate money to spend."

By the time the broker left he was glad to have Jim McNeely's check for $350, strictly salvage money he considered it, and no override, and Jim McNeely had an assignment of some leases of dubious worth that weren't yet paid for. But he also had an idea.

That night he went by the Sinclair station and filled up with Jeff Dofflemyer and asked Jeff to stop out and see him tomorrow, because he might have something that just might possibly interest him in the lawyer line.

When Jeff showed up early next morning, scrubbed to the hide, Jim McNeely said, "What are you making where you're working, Jeff?"

"Twenty-seven-fifty a week, Mister McNeely."

"You rather be making twenty-seven-fifty as a grease monkey or a lawyer?"

"I'm a lawyer, Mister McNeely."

"You call me Jim, and you got yourself a new job, as of now. As head lawyer of McNeely Oil Company. Twenty-seven-fifty a week. I've bought a lease with a bad title and seven days to pay off on it or let it go back. I got no law books or nothing to help you. You figure out how to make a good lease out of it and maybe you'll get a raise—" He grinned. "If you don't, you're fired!"

Jim McNeely did not see the young lawyer for three days after this. Then late in the afternoon of the third day Jeff showed up at the office again. He sat down, lips compressed, as if awaiting a signal to speak. "All right, pardner," said Jim McNeely. "Got her all worked out?"

"No," said Jeff Dofflemyer. "I haven't. But I've worn out my welcome at every law office in town, using their law books. I reckon I'll have to give up on it. There's no way you can be sure who really owns that section short of a final judgment in this pending law suit. That's a long time off. There's a will in the chain of title that has to be interpreted and it could go either way. There are no Texas cases on the point. The suit is now in the Court of Civil Appeals on appeal from a judgment in the trial court. Before you can know for certain who the true owners are might take a year or even longer."

"Well, that's that," said Jim McNeely raising his eyebrows in disappointment. "Anyway I know you did your best, buddy, and we had a go at it."

"I'm sorry. But I wouldn't be honest with you if I told you one set of heirs had good title and the other didn't. I honestly don't know. The only way to get a good title would be to take a lease from all the people on both sides."

"Well, why don't we do that?"

"Gosh, that wouldn't solve the legal question. That'd just be choking it with money."

"What's wrong with that?"

"Well, not anything, I guess, if you've got the money."

"Look, buddy, I haven't got *any* money. Not even for one side. But tell me this. If we did take a lease from both sets of heirs and drilled us an oil well, what would we do with the landowners' royalty money?"

"Why—I never read a case on it but I'd say you would just pay the royalty money into the court and tell the court to give it to the rightful owners—whoever finally comes out on top in the suit. Nobody could complain about that."

"Well, then let's do it. Get going. I just changed your title to landman. Go get me a lease from that second set of heirs. They all live right around here. We haven't got a hell of a lot of time, so get crackin', buddy!"

Jeff Dofflemyer exploded with laughter. "Gol-ly, Mister McNeely— Jim—this is crazy! You'll have to pay double lease bonuses. Twenty dollars an acre instead of ten."

Jim McNeely poked a pencil across the desk at the young lawyer. "Jefferson, I told you I'm not going to pay anybody anything. I'm going to turn these leases to somebody else. *They're* gonna put up the money. If I can't find that somebody in the time we've got left I'll just let the leases go back. Nobody can fault us on that because the title, right now, is clouded as hell. Agreed?"

In the following two days Jeff Dofflemyer, operating in his new role of landman, signed the other set of heirs to ten-dollars-per acre leases, except for one old eccentric who held out for fifteen and was passed by because his fractional interest was negligible.

Early on the morning after the new set of leases had been drafted into the bank Jim McNeely drove the twenty miles of highway to Midland through the flat ranch country in the cool, sparkling hour after the sun was up and presented himself at Consul Petroleum's office and asked to see the general manager. The Consul office opened an hour before other companies because the general manager couldn't sleep after daylight and didn't see why anyone else should. Jim McNeely had acquired this minor but helpful bit of intelligence in a telephone visit the night before with his field foreman who had formerly worked for Consul.

"Mister Naylor is in committee," said the Consul receptionist, sizing him up with a canny eye. "Did you have an appointment?"

"Didn't have a chance to make an appointment. But I need to see him right away."

"About a trade? Perhaps a drilling deal?" said the receptionist warily. She was an old hand at protecting the boss from lease brokers and promoters.

"It is. A real important one, for Consul."

"They're all important," said the receptionist, squaring off for the old sparring match that she had been through so many times. "I suggest you see Mister Holcomb, our landman. He's in committee, too, but he'll be out in half an hour or so. He handles trades, not Mister Naylor. Mister Naylor is the *general* manager."

"Look, sugar," said Jim McNeely pleasantly but firmly, "I haven't got time to talk to Mister Holcomb. The deal will spoil by the time it gets to Mister Naylor through channels."

"Well, I'm sorry, sir. All drilling deals and farmout submittals have to originate in the Land Department."

Jim McNeely smiled at the woman, who was not pretty and no longer young. "Honey, do this for me. Write it down for the general manager. Say that Jim McNeely, president of the McNeely Oil Company, is out here to see him. Apologize for buttin' into the committee meeting. Then tell him I'm about to move a rig on the Turpin section offsetting your Sheets lease. I intend to be making hole by Monday unless somebody stops me. That'll kind of shake him, or make him laugh, I don't know which. Tell him I need to talk to him this morning, and I can't come back because I have flat run out of time."

The receptionist looked at him with annoyance and exasperation. It was too early in the day to have to grapple with one of these *dynamic* feather-merchants.

"Go ahead," he said, smiling right into her eyes. "He can't do anything but tell me to go away."

"He can do a lot more than that to *me*," said the receptionist crossly. She bit her lips and was on the point of telling this insistent young man to go peddle his lease some other place. But there was something formidable and at the same time boyishly charming about him, in his brown sport shirt open at the throat, his sun-brown face and clear eyes, obviously flirting with her, his dark, slightly wavy hair with the perfect widow's peak—

She hesitated, then almost angrily made some rapid strokes in her shorthand book and with a sharp look at him went off through a door, talking to herself. Jim McNeely sat down on the imitation-leather couch and began to leaf through a copy of the *Oil and Gas Journal* on the table.

Moments later the receptionist returned, flushed, "I should have known better than to do that! I have been thoroughly reamed out, and it isn't even eight o'clock! Thanks to you, mister."

The disappointment that flashed in Jim McNeely's face was quickly smiled away. "Sorry, honey. Anyway, you tried. When I bring this well in, you remind His Majesty that I gave him his chance," he stood up, tossed the magazine on the table and started to leave.

"No, wait!" said the receptionist, almost frantically. "For God's sakes don't go now! He's going to see you, Lord help you! Gad, what a foul mood he's in! I don't know why I don't just follow orders."

A broad grin spread over Jim McNeely's face. He beamed at the receptionist. "That's par for the course. You get reamed out for using your head. Which way to the slaughter pen?" As he walked past he gave her a wink. "If you ever get tired of working for these clowns, come to see me."

When he entered the general manager's office a big, corpulent man with iron-gray hair and a look of high-tension wrath on his face was striding into the room through another door leading from a conference room.

Jim McNeely stuck out his hand and started to speak but the general manager brushed past him, ignoring the proffered handshake. Behind his desk angled across the corner of the office like a magistrate's bench the man planted himself and said, "Now what in the hell is this crap about the Turpin section? And what in the hell has that got to do with Consul Oil Company? I've got an oil business to run here and I get so goddamn fed up with people that think they're too important to talk to our landman. Just who are you anyway? I never heard of the—whatever the hell kind of oil company you're supposed to be president of!"

Jim McNeely fought down the flutters of anger that stirred in his stomach. Instantly he decided that the only way to play this gentleman— a powerful thick-set man in his late forties, obviously accustomed to overpowering people by the sheer force of position, size, and supreme self-confidence—was to give it back to him just as hard and cool as he put it out hot and heavy.

He stood in front of the desk without answering, looking at the man. The silence lasted for many seconds, long enough to show that he was not unduly impressed. Finally he said, "Mister Naylor, would you like to hear what I have to say, or do you want me to leave?" He waited another spell watching the general manager's face redden. Then he went on. "I'm not talking to your landman because I haven't got time for your organization to chew on my deal and write memos up and down through channels until it goes out of style. I figured it was important enough to Consul to take up a few minutes of the general manager's valuable time, but if it's not, well that's that." Still looking at the man he waited another moment, then shrugged and started to leave.

"Jesus H. Christ!" the big man exploded. "You got me out of the goddamn meeting, didn't you? Start talking! I'll tell you damn quick whether it's important to Consul!"

Jim McNeely stopped, a hard smile playing across his eyes. "That's fair enough. My name is Jim McNeely. I run a well-servicing business over in Odessa—haven't had any work from Consul, I'm sorry to say. I also own a little production. We've signed up leases on the Turpin section offsetting you."

"Oh, for God's sake!" said the big man contemptuously. "The title to that section is so screwed up you couldn't drill it in a hundred years. Our legal department knows all about it. Anyway, the section is off structure. Way off. I don't know why you people don't give up. Hope springs eternal in a goddamn lease broker's breast. I never saw anything to equal it!"

Gazing at the man, flat-lidded and unawed, Jim McNeely said, "You've got several things slightly wrong, mister. I'm not a lease broker, and I am going to drill a well on that section, directly offsetting your lease. By this time Monday I'll be turning to the right and making hole. You say the title is bad. It is. But I've got leases from the people on both sides of the squabble, except the owner of a small interest who's a hold-out for too much money. That doubles the lease bonus, but when you're looking at oil land what the hell's twenty dollars an acre?"

He continued easily but purposefully and confidently, "Is your head geologist gonna stick his neck out and say that section won't produce oil? Not if I know geologists. Anyway, if he will, I'm gonna prove him right or wrong right quick. Your company has been sitting here looking at that unleased land right next to you for a long time. It seemed like to me that somebody would feel pretty silly if some little feller came in and leased the section that was too tough for a big outfit like Consul to handle, and then drilled it and made a good well. You better take another look at your edge wells, Mister Naylor. They're holding up real good. I'd feel pretty bad if I was general manager of Consul and somebody came in and took something like that right out from under my nose. I'd think maybe my bosses would wonder what I'd been doing all this time." He gave Mr. Naylor a bland, penetrating look.

"Oh, you would, would you?" said Mr. Naylor with withering sarcasm.

"And just what qualifies you to do all this heavy thinking for me? You know what I'd bet? I'd bet money you couldn't dig a good-sized post hole on that lease, much less an oil well."

Jim McNeely returned the man's contemptuous gaze with steady eyes. He had forgotten that he did not have the bonus money to say nothing of the working capital to drill this semi-wildcat, for the heat of combat was upon him and he played his hand through to the finish without a backward glance.

"I can drill it. I'm just a small independent, but I can drill it, and I thought you might want a piece of the deal so you won't look like such a sap if I make a well. You might do a little quick checking with your high-powered lawyers and geologists while I'm eating my breakfast over at the hotel. That'll take me about one hour. When I leave there I'll be long gone because I'm going back to Odessa and pay off those leases and start my rig moving in on that section, and once I start I'll not be looking for any partners, and the deal won't be available."

The general manager leaned back in his chair and canted his head and squinted at the younger man who talked so big and confident. "You know what I think, Mister McNeely? I think you're full of Grade-A bullshit."

With an effort Jim McNeely controlled the anger that rose up in his gullet. He wanted something from this man and it wasn't the satisfaction of knocking him on his ass.

"You can think anything you like," he said, "but you just raised the price twenty-five percent." He started to leave, then stopped and leveled his eyes at the man. "Before you write this off I advise you to ask around about Jim McNeely. Ever hear of Coker City? You're talking to the man that leased and drilled that townsite when nobody else could. I'll drill the Turpin section, too. And when I'm setting out there pumping oil and draining your lease I'll tell anybody that's interested that I did my damnedest to turn the deal to you and you were so damned smart you wouldn't have any part of it."

He ate his breakfast in the coffee shop, chewing slowly, wondering just how badly he had overplayed his hand. And what he would tell Lee. He had been impertinent, downright disrespectful, to the general manager of an important division of a major oil company, an older man in a high position. But he told himself that if he, Jim McNeely, was going to be a big man and take his place among big men, he had to talk up like a big man. Age didn't have anything to do with being a big man. When you were old enough to shave you had a choice of two ways to go. You could either assert, demand, and claim your right to be a man, an equal among important men, or you could accept the role of the follower, listener, head-nodder, order-taker, and that is what you would be all your life. He didn't think all of this specifically. He felt it.

But where was he to go from here? Maybe it didn't matter that he hadn't been able to pull off this particular deal. Except for a few hundred bucks he wouldn't be any worse off than when he started out with it, would he? Yes. Yes, he would. He had run a bluff that hadn't worked. In this business, if you got caught bluffing too often you acquired a reputation as a hot-air merchant. That wouldn't help his cause. He knew that by selling his equity in the Coker City well and by hocking everything else that wasn't already mortgaged to the hilt, by stalling off suppliers and maybe pulling the Coker City rinky-do on wages again, he probably could drill this well. And, he thought with a sigh, he could probably get the ten or twelve thousand dollars to pay the lease bonuses from Lee's dad, something he had never resorted to. But if the Turpin well was dry, or a noncommercial dribbler—and when he faced the facts he knew that chances were good that is what it would be—he would be wiped out. Way in the hole. Probably have to go back to working for somebody on a salary. It just didn't add up. There was no leverage in the deal that way. It was one roll of the dice—all or nothing—go for broke. The prospect was deadening. It pulled the curtain down on the future and the open, wide-ranging field that he had to break into and ramble in if he was to get where he was headed. This choice that fate set before him angered the deepest nerves in his chest.

This old anger made him feel suddenly tired and defeated, though it was not yet ten o'clock in the morning. He pushed back his plate and in deep audible tones said, "Well, shit-house!" He was reaching in his pocket for a dime for a tip when the man came up behind him.

"You Jim McNeely?"

Jim McNeely looked up and said, "Yep."

A sallow, paunchy, cagy-looking man in a soiled Panama pulled out a chair and without shaking hands sat down. "I'm Birge Holcomb. Landman for Consul. I got orders to cool you off and find out what in hell you've got up your sleeve. If it's legitimate I'll try to trade with you—provided it can be done on a reasonable basis."

Jim McNeely put the dime tip back in his pocket and replaced it with a half dollar. A big smile crossed his face and he felt suddenly light and young and rested again.

"I trade real easy, Birge. And I'm a reasonable man. How about a cup of java?"

27

S TARTING WITH THE CERTIFIED AXIOMATIC PREMISE
that some people are born to be poor and some rich, an old
bunkhouse philosopher once reasoned to the conclusion that if
cast-iron radiators were made the legal medium of exchange and one of
these was bestowed upon every man alive, it wouldn't be long before a few
citizens would have their backyards stacked high with radiators and the
radiatorless multitudes would be looking over the fences with envy and
wonder.

Not many years after the Civil War, when petroleum was just beginning to make an impact on the nation's economy, a young businessman
out in Cleveland who had been trained as a bookkeeper began to deal in
this new greasy substance that nobody then really knew much about. His
name was John D. Rockefeller and he had this radiator—accumulating
genius in a very high degree. He had, as well, a vision of the future of oil
that few besides himself perceived. At first he didn't concern himself with
finding oil or with its production, but concentrated on refining, trans-
porting, and marketing the stuff. In a few short years he had very nearly
captured control of it with an interlocking maze of enterprises which
became the powerful Standard Oil Company.

This company, in the minds of the independents, at least, soon grew
into an omniverous monster which threatened to swallow up or squeeze
the life out of everybody else in the business.

In those days of brass-knuckle business morality there was no Antitrust
Division in Washington to run crying to, but there were enough tough
little independents getting swallowed or squeezed that their howls came

to be heard in the halls of Congress. Out of the melee new mores of business conduct emerged: competition in the market place was vital to the public weal, ergo big enterprises should not devour or strangle little enterprises that were struggling to survive.

After years of litigation, the growth of the great Standard Oil empire was halted and Standard Oil was, by court decree, broken up into a number of component pieces which set about growing into an equal number of great new empires. By the twenties some of these and a few other integrated oil concentrations had developed into the dozen or more major oil companies which were to dominate the hydrocarbon energy business in the world thenceforward.

As he drove toward home from Crane through the whiskered sand dunes, now purple-shadowed on the east, Jim McNeely realized that he was driving too fast and that he was tired. He had been up and out since before daylight. This, it seemed, had been the tempo of his life these past months now running into years. It was not the good old physical exhaustion but a tension tiredness of nerves. It seemed now that he never had time to sit at the wheel relaxed and cruise home at fifty miles per hour enjoying the desolate landscape and his thoughts. It was the kind of tiredness that put a hard, humorless, irritable edge on his words and he realized that he had been less than pleasant to be around for a long time. He had been cross, even sullen, with Lee, and it suddenly came to him that she was tension-whipped, too. Nerve-worn almost threadbare. But she didn't show it by snapping back at him. She just retreated into a tight silence. He didn't like that. It would be better if she would flare at him, the way he did at her, too often.

He also realized, once he started thinking about it, that they hadn't had a break, not a single real vacation, since they had been married. It had been a hard, sustained drive all the way, much of it under critical tension and uncertainty, all too serious, with too few laughs. Not nearly enough laughs. Partly it was the war. Nobody was entitled to relax or take time out during the war. But mainly, he knew, the trouble lay within himself, in his impatience, his fear that time was passing too fast and progress coming too slow.

Then suddenly one day he had seen the shadows under Lee's eyes. They had been there a long time unnoticed by him, half-circle smudges that told of stress and unspoken, ill-defined fears kept inside her too long.

It didn't really make good sense. Things were rolling very well now. True, he owed more money than he ever had before, but his net worth, on paper, was beginning to look quite respectable. His present program was sound and his prospects were good. The trouble, he nodded to himself again, was not serious, just nerves, due to tension and to being tired. Nevertheless, the situation forced him to admit that it was now necessary to take a break, to shake the cramp out of nerves and muscles and hitch up britches-before plunging into the next big phase of his life, which plunge he knew he was bound to take, had to take, in the early future. And which he also knew would be a dive into dark, unknown, and dangerous waters. For this, he and Lee and everybody ought to be in top form.

The deal with Consul on the section offsetting the Sheets Field had turned out incredibly well, better than he had dared to hope in his most fanciful scheming about it. On that critical day when the Consul landman had overtaken him in the coffee shop, he had succeeded, after hours of hard trading, in turning the two sets of conflicting leases to Consul for enough cash to pay for the leases, plus a retained one-sixteenth override and Consul's promise to drill a well immediately and worry later about who the rightful owners were. To cap the deal, and this is what took most of the hours of dickering, Consul agreed to employ the McNeely rig at the going rate to drill the first well, and if this resulted in a commercial producer, to keep the rig continuously at work on the lease, drilling one well after another until Consul elected to stop drilling further wells, at which time the undrilled acreage in the section would revert to McNeely Oil Company, free of cost.

The override meant that out of every sixteen barrels of oil which Consul produced from the lease, one barrel was Jim McNeely's, gratis. The drilling agreement meant that if any considerable part of the lease was productive, Jim McNeely would make a tidy profit from the drilling operations. Consul certainly wouldn't stop drilling and turn any land back to him so long as there was even a fair prospect of completing more oil wells.

"You're easy to trade with, all right," said Birge Holcomb, worn down and wilted in a sour sweat toward the end of the day. "Long as I give you every goddamn thing you ask for, you're a real sweetheart!"

Sweating out the drilling of the first well was another time of hair-raising suspense, because if the well was dry this effort was all for nothing. But the well came in handsomely—not a spectacular producer, flowing like the Coker City Number 1, but a good solid pumper that cut a little water but made a lot of oil out of a thick pay sand. This meant that substantial reserves were there in the ground, and that is what Consul was looking for. The next well, farther into the lease, potentialed even better than the first one and was flat with it geologically, making it almost a certainty that there would be at least four more good locations to drill, as well as others that looked very promising.

At this point Jim McNeely cast caution aside and bought a big new drilling rig, a beautiful National job painted bright blue with powerful twin Waukeshaw diesels. He went in debt over a hundred and fifty thousand dollars for it. But there was plenty of work for the older, smaller rig elsewhere, and with any luck a big dent could be made in the pay-out of the new rig before the drilling on the Sheets Field lease played out. Getting into the contract-drilling business in a big way wasn't a part of his long range planning, but the little rig wasn't really adequate for the tough digging in the Sheets Pool, to which the new lease was now definitely an extension. Besides, the prestige value of being able to say "my rigs," in the plural, and the ability to drill as deep as anybody in his right mind wanted to drill in West Texas, would open doors that a 6,000-foot-workover-rig operator could not enter.

When he bought the new rig Jim McNeely had gone out and raided Stanolind for a top-flight drilling foreman, whom he lured into his organization by the simple expedient of offering him a twenty percent salary increase and the promise of an opportunity to buy into any good royalty deals that came along. Jeff Dofflemyer was looking every day more like a top hand himself and was perfectly capable of making the decisions that would come up at the office. There really was no excuse for not taking this vacation. And though he had no real enthusiasm for it, he knew he needed it and knew he owed it to Lee, many times over, and long past due.

As his car whistled into the shacky southern fringes of Odessa, the idea firmed in his mind and bloomed into a sudden inspiration that made him laugh aloud. When he braked to a gravel-flying stop in the Company parking lot before the low asbestos-shingled office building he was still chuckling to himself.

Pushing through the front door, sighing in the pleasant evaporatively cooled air, he went through the small reception room and down the hallway and barged into a cubicle where Lee McNeely was grimly attacking a typewriter with two fingers. She still spent a good part of each day helping Dent Paxton with purchasing, personnel, accounting, and general worrying. She saw that there was work to do which Dent couldn't handle alone and she came down and did it. When Jim McNeely entered the room she was finishing up an invoice, a yellow pencil stuck in the dark wing of hair over her ear. He stopped, scowled, then rapped sharply on the desk with his knuckle. Lee jumped with fright and gave him a vexed look.

"All right," he said in a hard voice. "That'll be all. You can draw your time. You're fired."

Lee stared at him in momentary amazement, then fell back in her chair as if the elastic had suddenly been pulled out of her. She laughed with a giggle that was giddy with exhaustion but full of warmth and pleasure.

"Yes, my lovely brute?" she said, taking his hand and stroking her cheek against it, looking up at him. "What did you say?"

"I said you're fired," he said sternly, pulling his hand away. "Canned."

"Really? You're trading me in on a new girl!"

"I'm trading you in on a full-time wife. I'm sick to my stomach of hamburger joints. From now on you stay home and cook—period, unquote. And something else. I'm gonna run down to Mexico for a few days. Don't reckon you'd care to join me."

"Mexico!" She stared at him. Then she sat upright. "Mexico?" She jumped up with a cry and threw her arms around his neck. "You darling! You're *serious!*"

"Now wait a minute. I'm just talking about Monterrey. It's not hardly Paris, France, so don't get excited. Just a little vacation."

"What a beautiful word! I've forgotten how to spell it! Let's see, it begins with a V. V-a—?"

"All right. Save the comedy. You haven't heard it all. I'm full of ideas tonight." He grinned at her like a mean boy who had just thought up a dandy trick to pull on another boy. "Why don't we take old Dent with us—provided—listen to this—" He could hardly contain his laughter, "*Provided* he gets a *girl* to go with him. You know, two couples. No stags allowed, if you can call him that."

Lee pondered this a second, then frowned. "I—don't know, Jim. Dent needs a vacation. But let's be practical. I don't know about the girl. I'm certain he'd rather go with just you and me."

"The hell with that," Jim McNeely said, pleased with himself. "He'll get a female date or he won't go—period."

238

"Jim, that's kind of cruel. He won't have any fun."

"How do you know he won't have any fun? How does *he* know he won't have any fun? He'll never know what it's like till he tries it. Who knows, he might take to it!"

"Oh, you're terrible!"

And thus the great vacation to Monterrey was conceived and set in motion. To Jim McNeely's amazement, Dent did not voice the slightest objection to the requirement that he invite a female companion but got right about making plans.

"Wait a minute," said Jim McNeely. "Where you gonna find any girl that will go with you?"

Dent shrugged this off lightly. "I have several friends that might like to go."

"You and who else?"

"You want to select somebody for me?" Dent said sharply.

"Nooo. But just be damn sure she's female."

"Oh, you are a funny man."

Once the departure day was set planning went ahead with happy abandon. They would leave in the early afternoon driving in the Company's big black Buick sedan, the last prewar model made which had belonged to a rancher's widow and which Jim McNeely had bought, he said, because he needed a car with some class for driving visiting big-shots to the oil fields. This car also happened to be a later year of the identical model that the Dr. Wales family had always driven. Jim McNeely liked the luxurious feel of the deep upholstery and the smooth power of the big engine under his foot. But it was something more than that that made him buy it, though he never admitted this, even to himself.

They planned to spend the first night in San Antonio. The next day they would drive the three-hundred miles on to Monterrey. There they would stay—Jim McNeely shrugged—as long as they were having a good time and their money lasted. A new lighthearted almost carnival atmosphere filled the McNeely offices in the following days and Jim McNeely fell into the spirit along with the others. This was another hiatus in his life, another plateau, necessary, therapeutic, and he meant to take full advantage of it.

When pressed on the subject of his "date" for the holiday Dent replied casually that he had asked a girl named Rossie Faye Doggett, whom he had known for quite a while, to accompany him. She worked as a dental technician in Big Spring, he said, but would return to her home in Odessa on her own vacation, in time to make the trip.

At home that night Jim McNeely considered this with a scowl and to Lee he said, "God! Rossie Faye Doggett! With a name like that I'll bet she's a stunner!"

"Don't look at me," said Lee. "It's your stupendous idea. I don't know the girl. But she must be the original virgin. I've been on the phone off and on all day talking to her mother. I think Mrs. Doggett is having us investigated. She wanted references, can you imagine? And she asked for a complete itinerary, to the minute. I told her something. She wanted to know exactly how our rooms would be situated in relation to each other's, ours, Rossie Faye's, Dent's. I assured her that Dent was a very proper gentleman—"

"You could say that again."

"And that I personally would chaperone them."

"Don't worry. That babe couldn't be safer in a convent."

"Oh, you know so much!"

On the day of departure Jim McNeely made an early run to the field, then drove by the office to deliver last-minute instructions to Jeff Dofflemyer. Then he hurried home, had a quick sandwich with Lee, loaded his suitcase and hers into the car, locked the house, and drove over to Dent's apartment, feeling suddenly glum and unhappy. Now that the day was here he knew he should not be leaving, taking time off, at all. There was too much at stake and time in his life was too valuable. There was too far to go. Moreover, though he would not have mentioned it for the world, his big joke of forcing Dent to bring along a girl had turned very sour on him. It meant that for the next ten days or two weeks they would be living at close quarters with a total stranger, probably an arty, oddball female at that. She could spoil the whole deal. He had really outsmarted himself and he was quite angry with Dent for not putting up more of an argument about it.

"Where does this dog Doggett live?" he said in a surly voice when Dent had climbed into the back seat with his bulging Val-pac.

"Now, Jim," Lee said sternly. "You're going to be nice to this girl, or I'm not going. Let's have that understood. It was your idea, and we all went along with it. So now you behave and we'll all have a good time. Otherwise we'll all be miserable, including yourself."

At Dent's directions they drove across town and into the driveway of a small, white frame house on a sandy side street. Dent went to the door, knocked, and went in. Lee got out of the car with Jim McNeely and prodded him into opening the trunk to receive Rossie Faye's luggage.

In a moment Dent came out of the house struggling through the door with two large suitcases which he pressed upon Jim McNeely, who began trying to fit them into the already crowded luggage compartment.

"Where in the hell does she think we're going? Around the goddamn world?" he said.

"Shush!" said Lee, trying to help him.

"This is Mrs. Doggett, Mr. and Mrs. McNeely," said Dent.

Jim McNeely glanced over his shoulder and nodded and murmured at the large square-jawed, gray-haired woman who was walking down the steps, drying her hands on an apron.

"Pleased to meet you," she said. "Well, so you folks are goin' to Mexico? I sure hope you're a good driver, Mister McNeely. I never have let my girl go off on any such floomadiddle as this before."

"Oh, he's a real good driver, Mrs. Doggett. We'll take good care of Rossie Faye," said Lee. "Try turning it sideways, sweetheart. There, that's it."

"It *won't go*," fumed Jim McNeely, growing angrier by the second as he struggled with the heavy bags.

At this moment Rossie Faye emerged from the house and was hastily introduced, and with everybody now hovering and shoving around to help him Jim McNeely caught only enough of a glimpse of her that his heart sank and he said, "Ooh Christ!" under his breath. Rossie Faye was one of those big rawboned girls whom nature had intended to be a man but who, through the whim of some sadistic fate, was destined to wear skirts. She was almost as tall as Jim McNeely. Her legs were atrocious and her face, what he could see of it under the coy little blue net veil, was horse-jawed like her mother's and badly painted. She actually wore her hair in long ringlets of curls. Now everyone was crowded around him trying to help force the two bags into the trunk so the top would go down, and somebody in the crowd—Jim McNeely groaned inwardly again—somebody smelled like a saloon. It would be his luck that this hag that Dent had chosen for his companion on this, the gala vacation of all vacations, was not only a monumental dog but a booze-hound as well, and it slowly dawned on him that he was going to be the butt of the joke after all, and that this was Dent's way of getting even with him.

Finally in a fury he threw out his arms and shoved everyone back. He was sweating and livid.

"Folks, this goddamn suitcase is not going to go in! If she's got to take it, put it in the back seat. Get in the car! It'll be nine o'clock before we get to San Antonio!"

"Jim, please," said Lee.

"Hope he don't drive as temperous as he talks," sniffed Mrs. Doggett.

"Oh, he's just had a hard life," said Dent, with genuine sounding indignation. "He *needs* this vacation. Come on, kids. Let's go."

They drove out of town and the big black car nosed down Highway 385 toward Rankin and Ozona and Sonora and San Antone, its powerful engine surging to its work under Jim McNeely's angry foot. Lee and Dent Paxton kept up a nervous chatter as if trying to force this group into a holiday mood.

Jim McNeely was grimly silent, and Rossie Faye said not a word except for little giggling chirrups and grunts, and Jim McNeely knew now, definitely, that the booze smell originated with her. The prospect of the trip that was to have been such a joyful holiday and had only now begun was suddenly almost unbearable to him. He knew he had seen this Rossie Faye somewhere before. His memory pawed back over long-forgotten nights in the Tascosa and other honkytonks, trying to place her. Dental technician in a pig's eye! He knew this Rossie Faye from someplace.

The conversation thinned as the highway unwound like a black tape ahead, and everyone settled down for the long drive. Then, in a second of utter quiet, Rossie Faye emitted a long, rolling, rattling belch that riffled the little veil covering her face. There was a stunned second in the car when no one said anything. Jim McNeely lifted his foot from the accelerator and sat frozen over the wheel, his mouth slightly open, his eyes slowly narrowing to steel points as realization dawned. Then he jammed the brake pedal clear to the floor and the heavy limousine squealed and swerved to the shoulder, leaving tire marks behind, fish-tailing through the gravel to a lurching stop.

Throwing himself around in the seat in a violence of fury he clawed out a hand and tore the piquant hat and veil from Rossie Faye's head.

"Ort Cooley! You low-life sonofabitch!"

In the pandemonium that followed, bloodshed was averted only because

Lee was strong of arm and despite hysterics clung to Jim McNeely's neck so that his wild slashing blows with his free fist glanced off the head and shoulders of Ort Cooley without connecting solidly. Ort, now dewigged and exposed, slid off the seat and lay wedged helplessly roaring in the floor. Dent, drawn up in the corner of the back seat, shrieked like a bird that somebody was tickling to death.

Choking and hollering with laughter, Ort cried, "Bound ye! *Bound* ye! I even shaved my goddang laigs!"

28

From afar Monterrey glints like an antique jewel set in Carlotta's crown. Nearer at hand it is a hodgepodge of old and new, of pungent odors and automobile exhaust fumes, of *turistas* and *gente decente*, of the clangor of industrialism, and of the gentleness of art. It works a slow, unexplainable magic.

The four visitors from West Texas drifted through hazy flowing days and nights of light, shadow, and mirth. Nights that did not end but continued through sleepy laughter and the cloudy taste of *ron anejo* and the coarse grain of *mariachi* music into new days, without formality or breakfast or plan. It was as if this space of their lives was isolated in time, without prologue or sequel. The four came and went, slept and ate mindless of clock or convention. They embarked upon no proper tours. They merely wandered up and down the narrow streets, in and out of hotels, shops, bars. They had not planned it so. In their receptive states of mind and body they merely surrendered to the holiday, and it took charge and had its way with them.

At irregular intervals they returned to Gran Hotel Ancira, fount of old luxury dispensing cheap money at the cashier's desk. Saddle Mountain mauve and green looked down upon them as they sallied forth in the dusty purple dusk.

"This here Mexkin money makes a feller feel rich as a goddang doctor," cried Ort, cramming a handful of paper and silver in his pocket at a bar and listing off down the street in search of another.

"Wait up, you drunken West Texas hick!" said Dent. "Now we got to go buy somethin'!" Lee had early established a single rule of discipline for the group: one bar, then one shop. Never two bars in a row. This gratified her female instinct to shop for useless treasures and served the more practical purpose of keeping the party reasonably on its feet. In the process the four acquired armloads of flamboyant Mexican *chucherias*: hand-blown glass birds, tin picture frames, straw men on straw horses, fat tissue-paper *piñatas*, enormous *charro* hats, much of which gorgeous junk was broken or left forgotten in later bars or on park benches before it reached the temporary haven of the hotel suite.

This ugly but somehow romantic town in the dry mountains of northern Mexico worked its sly Mexican magic on the taut nerves and tendons of Jim McNeely. He became, in spite of himself, like a schoolboy on vacation. He slowly relaxed and the pain of the spur in his liver was dulled and then forgotten as the *ron añejo* and the laughter and the happiness and warmth of people that he loved had their effect upon him.

Only once did he resume command and tighten the reins. Lee had wandered out of a bar into a *tienda* next door when the old, hard urge flamed in Ort Cooley.

"God-a-mighty!" Ort cried lurching to his feet, almost upsetting the table where the three men sat sampling an aromatic concoction founded on ancient rum. "*Look* at the *tits* on that there little pepper-belly! Boys, I'll take up with you back at the hotel." He started after the girl like a gaunt beagle on a scent.

Reaching out an arm, Jim McNeely caught a handful of Ort's shirt and soft belly skin and hauled him around to a halt. Suddenly very serious, he said, "Ort, this is Lee's vacation. Don't screw it up. You go to goatin' around here like you do at home and these Mexican bulls'll throw you so far back in the jail they'll have to feed you with a bean-shooter. I swear to God I won't get you out. You can just stay here till you rot."

Dent nodded. "Family outing, ol' pod. Mexican womanhood will suffer. But for good cause. Stick with the troop."

And so, amazingly, Ort behaved himself during the entire stay and caused no crises or international incidents. It was a great effort of self-restraint, made only because he had great respect and admiration and affection for Lee McNeely.

After a time the clock hands seemed to turn around in opposite directions and lost their meaning and the four tourists from Odessa napped at noon, drank tequila for breakfast, and laughed at the moon through tattered banana fronds that ringed the patio of Posada Carapan. With relish they drew in the sweet, pungent flavors of Mexico; baby kid sizzling brown and candied over mesquite coals in little off-street restaurants, aromatic, lemony-iced drinks in early morning in the curio shops along the square, the piquant, old-world smell of aromatic soap in the high vaulted baths of the hotel, the intriguing, musty smell of Mexican cigarette smoke . . .

To Lee these days took their place among those rare interludes of happiness in life seldom experienced outside of dreams. This was one of those accidental times, when all of the lights came to the surface and life was good, shining by day, sparkling with a thousand stars by night, and endless. The past and the future did not exist. It was one of those rare ineluctable spaces between time when the vibrant present was experienced with an almost unbearable clarity, tasted and savored without purpose except the joy of being young and alive and aware of it.

Here for this moment she was in full and complete possession of the Jim McNeely that she loved. And there were these two wonderful, ridiculous friends to provide the laughter.

"The first time I married, I married for love," said Ort in the night time as they sat around a table in the courtyard of the Posada sipping iced drinks. "Now there *wuz* a purty woman. That short-legged gal could peep th'oo a keyhole with bo'f eyes at the same time. I ort to knowed better than think I could handle her. What she had was jus' too strong for any one man. Run off with a pencil-sharpener salesman. Nex' time I'll marry for wealth, I bound ye." He took a deep swallow and wiped his mouth with his hand. "Had me a well-to-do widder woman picked out last year. Owned nine quilts an' a sewin' machine. But she got a better offer. *She* thought. Hey, Pedro, bring some more o' that there rum-jolly."

"Not for me," said Lee, giggling. "I'm rum-jolly already."

"Now, Lee, I want to tell you about this ol' boy you're married to," Ort went on, sitting forward and digging a horny thumb into the ribs of Jim McNeely, who was half reclining in his chair, long legs stretched out before him, completely relaxed, happy-minded, half drunk, and feeling no compulsion to talk or command or do other than breathe the cool night air and feel of Lee's firm brown arm and the good muscle in it now and then.

"This ol' boy," said Ort, "can do any dang thing he sets his mind to. I *know*. Y' might say I raised him from a pup in the oil patch. I 'member when he first come to Dead Lake. Like it was this mornin'. He weren't much fer smart, but he were hell for try. Him an' me, man, we had some times! Aye, stabber?" He gave a high-pitched cackle, "You ort to seed him when he tuck in after ol' Cap. I mean, he fair went bear-sack! Lissen—"

Jim McNeely grunted. He, too, was happy. The holiday was a success. He had quickly forgiven them all, Lee, Dent, and Ort, for the Rossie Faye conspiracy, contrived with an old schoolteaching colleague of Lee's who played the part of Rossie Faye's mother. Before they reached San Antonio he had switched off the old deviling current that impelled him forward and his mind had let down on this good, restful plateau, where cares and plans and deadlines were, for the moment, forgotten.

In the night he made love to his beautiful wife, to the music of the shrill cornet and deep guitars of the *mariachi* down in the square, and it was good and he knew a space of happiness and of peace.

They arose from their bed and walked naked hand in hand to the high windows and looked down over the little square, now silent and shadowed in early morning darkness. The smooth tiles were cold under their bare feet.

Lee closed her eyes and breathed in the dry sweet air. She turned to her husband and locked her arms around his back, pressing herself against him, looking up at him, putting her cheek against his smooth chest.

"Oh, oh—it's all been so wonderful," she sighed.

Pressing his lips against her hair with unaccustomed tenderness, he said, "Aw, it's just a little vacation. Put off too long."

She looked up. "I don't mean that. I mean everything with you. All the way. Since the first time I saw you."

There was a long silence. He settled back against the edge of the window, holding her against him. Old rum still rang in his head. His thoughts formed themselves like pictures coming slowly into focus as he stared over her head into the palpitant darkness.

"I never should have let you tie up with me," he murmured.

"Jim, don't say that!" She tightened her arms around him. "I wouldn't trade places with anybody in the world!"

"No, baby. What I've got to do—it's no good for any woman. It's too tough."

"It's not too tough for me. It isn't tough at all. Because, you see—we don't really *have* to do *anything*." She drew back and placed her palms on his bare chest and looked up at him with shining eyes. "Don't you see that, Jim? Don't you feel that, here? It's so clear to me here away from everything. All we really have to do is love and live, and be happy. Our problems aren't really problems. They're just things to keep us occupied. In gear with life. When we realize that everything is so clear and simple."

For a long time he didn't answer her and when he did it was in a voice that she did not know. A voice of the part of him that was denied to her.

In a low tone he said, "A man is gonna do what he's gonna do, Lee. That may not make sense to you. It may not even make sense to me. But a man can't change the way he is. You either take him that way, or you go on down the road."

The arms around her were then strange and had no warmth. The night air became suddenly chilled and he felt the gooseflesh rise and spread on her hips under his fingers.

The next morning it was all over. Jim McNeely awoke with a pounding hangover and the old thorn was back in his side. The lotus had lost its sweetness and its pain-dimming power. He dressed without shaving and stalked across the *sala* to the adjoining bedroom where Ort and Dent were respectively loudly snoring and slumbering quietly in their beds.

"Get up, you brush-apes!" he called in a harsh, cotton-mouthed voice. "Saddle up! We're going home." He slapped his palm sharply against the sole of Ort's enormous bare foot.

"Well, dog my cats," croaked Ort in a whiskey voice that sounded as if it came from a cave. "I ain't hardly went to bed good yet."

"Get up! Wake up, Dent. We got a long way to go."

"My God," groaned Dent in a fog, cracking his eyes. "Why so early? Odessa's not all that far."

"We got a lot farther to go than Odessa," said Jim McNeely. "And time's a-wasting."

And so the restless march was on again.

29

T HE ADVENT OF THE MAJOR OIL COMPANY WAS
undoubtedly a necessity of the times, because the refineries, the
long pipelines, the oceangoing tankers, and the costly exploration and drilling efforts necessary to find oil and pump it up from the
depths of the earth and convert it into useable products and sell it and
run it into the gas tanks and crankcases of any man's tin lizzie required
tremendous concentrations of capital. Bigness was essential for this, and
if it was to be done in the free-enterprise way, big incorporated stock
companies, widely owned by widows and post-office clerks and druggists
and chiropractors, as well as by the radiator men, were a natural answer.
No master mind designed the system. It simply grew.

And with the growth of the oil companies and other incorporated
enterprises in other lines of endeavor all across the land there emerged
another new breed, the Corporation Man. The highest expression of this
breed was the Manager, the captain of twentieth-century industry. He was
generally a radiator acquisitor par excellence, now playing his life's game
according to the more confining sophisticated rules of a semi-regulated
economy that was highly organized, tremendously complex, and fiercely
competitive. He was an able, hard-minded, ambitious man who started
out in the accounting department, or as a junior engineer or geologist or
title clerk and rose through the massed ranks of employees by his own
drive and desire to the top, or very near to it.

This new breed produced one peculiar, overbred offshoot variety with
rather alarming characteristics. Those of this strain were capable of so
completely identifying themselves with the corporate vehicle on which

they proposed to rise in life that they developed a new criterion of ethical conduct—that which resulted in improving the corporate balance sheet and profit-and-loss statement was *per se* good—as well as a new credo which said that whatever was good for Amalgamated Hide & Fur was good for mankind in general.

Unfortunately, some of this ilk reached the top levels, along with those who, while working hard to promote their employers' interests, were still able to see a bigger picture and a longer view, and who, gifted with a basic humanity and wisdom unbeguiled by the belief that growing bigger and pushing up the price of the company's stock on the Big Board constituted the *summum bonum*, were capable of saying no, even though saying yes would result in personal corporate success and a quicker, easier profit. But this business statesmanship was often put to a heavy test, especially when stock options were involved, for corporation executives were, after all, human beings, too.

The old oil-patch philosopher found in the unnatural stance and attitudes of the overbred type of Corporation Man something disturbingly reminiscent of the pure-blood grand champion bull, whose creative powers are too valuable to waste in the natural, willy-nilly way of bulls with cows. This splendid creature is trained to mount a rack for reproductive purposes. When a comely heifer is paraded back and forth before the rack, and at the moment when his mating urge reaches fever pitch, insensitive men more interested in calf-crop profits than in the integrity of bovine romance clap a contrivance upon his bullish particulars, causing him precipitately to release his grand champion seed. This is thereupon collected and carefully preserved to be later measured out and artificially, unromantically inseminated into a score of high-caste bovine females who would never know conjugal bliss or have the vaguest notion of how they became mothers.

It is said that bulls thus trained and conditioned, when turned into a pasture full of young, attractive females, will ignore the heifers and run lowing and panting for the rack.

The old philosopher could not foresee what the final outcome for our blue-ribbon rack-conditioned type of Corporation Man would be, but he speculated about a day when a single grand champion Manager would have electrodes implanted in his brain lobes and, titillated to cerebral orgasm pitch by stock options waved back and forth in front of his nose, would magnificently inseminate a whole battery of preprogrammed electronic computers and thus more efficiently perform the work which otherwise would require the efforts of a hundred merely human corporation executives.

Lee's father once told her about the oil business and luck.

"There's an element of luck in all business, baby, but in the oil business luck is the queen of destiny. You say this boy you're fixin' to marry is set on bein' an oil man, that he has dreams of a big oil field somewhere with his name on it, waitin' for him to find it. They all do. That's kind of a lifelong disease. It drives some crazy, some crooked, breaks the hearts of the strong and unlucky, and rewards a few lucky ones with wealth and power beyond their deserving."

"But, Daddy," said Lee, sitting forward in a canvas chair by the hammock where her father lay in the cool of evening, puffing his pipe. "*You're* not like that."

"I'm not an oil man, baby. I'm not infected. I work in the oil business, *for* oil men, but I am not an oil man. I'm just an ordinary businessman rendering services to the breed. Can't say why I never was bitten by the bug. But I wasn't. I'm like an armorer to one of the knights of old. They get the glory, but they also get the lance through the gizzard.

"That's not to say that it's all blind luck. Being smart improves your chances. Working hard helps your percentages. But finally it's luck that tells the tale. Good men, strong men, smart, talented, persistent, hard-working men fail and fall, because their luck is bad. No amount of all those good qualities will help if you drill where there's not any oil, and never was any.

"On the other side, there's some sorry characters I know that are not even half smart and are considerably more than half crooked that have made it big. Just because they were dog-lucky. Now I don't mean to give oil men a black eye. By and large they're good and bad and in between just like everybody else. But in the main bein' an oil men is engagin' in a form of legalized gamblin', with luck the main decider. I just hope that this boy of yours, if he's set on bein' an oil man, has got a real good rabbit's foot workin' for him."

After the war, after the Sheets Pool success, and after the Monterrey interlude, the number of deals that came to Jim McNeely doubled, then quadrupled. They were mostly bad deals, but some had merit and Jeff Dofflemyer soon learned to screen out the thin ones and the impossible ones and present the ones with a little meat on them to Jim McNeely. When he had a rig that wasn't working Jim McNeely was a prime prospect for any reasonable drilling deal that would allow him to take a piece of it, a percentage of the working interest or an override as his profit, drilling the hole for just enough cash to pay fuel and labor bills. He drilled a number of dry wells doing this and had nothing to show for it but the experience, but some of them hit and began to pay off. The immediate cash income wasn't great because of proration, but he began to accumulate a growing interest in oil reserves in the ground—an eighth override in a producing forty acres here, a quarter working interest in a checkerboard spread of forties in a half-section there. There were no bonanzas and this was not what he was looking for but it made his financial statement, on paper, begin to look fairly decent.

And so Jim McNeely and his little organization prospered by any reasonable standard and though he had not come upon the mother lode he was waiting for, he twice thought he had. Twice he bought into deals, taking a major interest in each and going far beyond merely investing his drilling profit in them. To make the second of these he had borrowed heavily, encumbering the income from his scattered producing interests for several years into the future. Both were wildcat drilling blocks, one in Terry County and one in Martin County. Both had real merit: good regional and subsurface geology and positive geophysical anomalies or "shot-highs" on which to drill. Both had maddening shows of oil but in neither was there a commercial accumulation, and both wells were eventually plugged, D. & A.—dry and abandoned.

These were two rolls of the dice which came up respectively snake-eyes and boxcars. They hurt. Yet the wounds were not fatal. The rigs and the servicing equipment stayed busy. Everybody was eating and in time the profits and the small but steady oil-run checks would pay off the banks, and there would still be oil left in the ground to replace the lost fat. The right deal would come along. It would come. He had to be patient. The percentages would help him. So many dry holes, then there would come— Golconda, his Kettleman Hills, his East Texas, his Spindletop that he was waiting for.

One day, out of the blue, a broker walked in with a deal in Scurry County. A solid block of three and a half sections a little way north of the dusty cattle town of Snyder. The broker had no geology, no geophysics, nothing but a lot of hot air and high hopes and cheap leases: six dollars an acre to the land owners and a well obligation, plus fifty cents an acre commission and a one-thirty-second of seven-eighths override for the broker.

Jim McNeely pondered the deal for several days, because the broker hadn't short-fused him, and the deal had almost certainly been shopped to the majors already. Still it was a lot of land without a hole on it.

"What do you think, Jeff?" Jim McNeely said.

Jeff pulled off his metal-rimmed spectacles and looked up at his employer. "I'm not a geologist, Jim. But since you asked me, I'd say Scurry County is not oily country. It's clear out of the basin as you look at it on the map, still, like you say, it's a lot of land without a hole on it. It's cheap and it *is* in West Texas. How do you feel about it?"

Glumly remembering his recent failures in Martin and Terry Counties, Jim McNeely said, "You're sure right it's not oily country. There's no shooting dope and there's a dry hole a mile to the south. All I got to go on is hunch. But I've got a helluva hunch to take it."

"You're the boss man," said Jeff. "I don't know anything about hunches, either, but I'm with you whichever way you go."

The hunch remained strong upon him, though it was against his better judgment. It made him edgy and restless. In the afternoon he got in his car without saying anything about where he was going and drove east to Midland, then to Big Spring, then to Colorado City. Then he cut north to Snyder through the flat, drouthy ranch country. When he reached that spare, dusty town he parked on the courthouse square and studied his county land map a while. Then he drove out of town bumping across the railroad tracks and headed north-northwest on a dirt road, his tires throwing up a choking dust trail, until he reached a point he figured would be about in the center of the lease block that was the subject of his quandary and his indecision.

He stopped the car on the side of the road and got out and looked around. A cold north wind had begun to sweep down across the vast open land. The late sun was hid behind a high overcast. Its diffused light reached the earth weakly and without warmth. Jim McNeely could not say why he had come all the way out here. It was silly, kind of asinine, in fact. You couldn't see anything. He had really come out here to see if he could *feel* something. To see if he could get some strong, positive conviction, on the ground, to firm up his hunch.

He crossed the road and let himself through a wire gap and walked into the pasture on a road that was nothing more than two ruts that led toward a windmill in the distance. An old white-face cow with a good-sized calf at her side threw up her head as he approached, then the two broke and ran away from him, tails high.

After a while he turned off the rutted trail and walked a little distance out into the dry grassy pasture. There he stopped and turned, looking all around him. This is about where he would set the rig.

His gaze swept around the far horizons that circled the point in space on which he stood. He raised his eyes to the wind-streaked clouds and breathed deeply of the big cold wind. Was there anything to Santa Rita, Saint of the Impossible, patroness of Frank Pickrell and Dad Joiner and all the others? He was alone and nobody could see him as he intoned his prayer. *Good Saint Rita. Give me a sign! Is this the place?* He felt suddenly very foolish and sheepish and started to leave.

But then a feeling did come! It came to Jim McNeely strongly, up through the ground into his legs and through the trunk of his body into his throat and head and tingled in his scalp. Unconsciously he put his arms out wide, wide, his fingers outstretched, taut, curving downward, as if to feel and embrace and caress the—what was it!—the shape of a great buried hog-back structure, gently sloping away in all directions. He *could feel it!* And the irrational feeling became a thrilling turmoil in his chest that constricted the muscles in his throat and choked him like an unbearable emotion. The thing—it was there! He felt it as clearly and surely as if it had been spelled out in words in his head. Then he knew that this was his oil field, and that he was going to drill it!

He didn't stay long after that, turning, breathing the cold, immense wind, but started walking rapidly, almost running back down the road toward the car. And as he went he was filled with a growing excitement that made him laugh, because it was so ridiculous. Yet, by God, it was there! He had felt it!

When he was nearly to the gate his eye caught something on the ground, half-buried in the hard mud of a long-ago rain in the rutted trail. He stopped and dug it out, then he laughed aloud, incredulous, exuberant. The thing he had found was half of a horseshoe, worn thin and broken in two at the toe, and the horseshoe nails, bent and rusted, were still in it. With a whoop he hurled the rusty metal into the air. This was the sign! Thank you, Saint Rita! Thank you! Much obliged! He caught the spinning horseshoe out of the air and ran the rest of the way to the car, hand-vaulting the wire gap on the way. Backing the car around in a tight circle he roared down the road toward the town and home beyond, his whole body ringing with inspiration and discovery and good omen!

It is twenty-two miles from Snyder to Colorado City and fifty-eight on to Big Springs and another thirty-eight to Midland, and then twenty on in to Odessa. It was too far. The cold, windy night had settled dustily on the land and its chill searched for him and reached him as he fought the wheel of the car, wincing at the glaring oncoming headlights. By the time he passed Colorado City the thrill had drained out of him and cold rationality was sinking back into his bones.

He was almost certain that Humble had looked at this deal and turned it down, and he was fairly sure that Gulf had, too. Those big companies had all the scientific know-how that money could buy. So was he smarter than they were? Just because he had gone out on the ground and held out his arms and felt the structure? Great geophysics that was! Wouldn't *that* get a laugh in the Scharbauer lobby! The mystical certainty he had felt back there in the pasture had begun to fade.

As he drove through Big Spring he coldly calculated what this well would cost him. A dry hole wouldn't mean a gnat's ass to Humble or Gulf. Even so they had passed the deal up. But another deep dry hole would come close to sinking Jim McNeely. Oh, he could probably drill it. But it would be Coker City all over again. He was already in hock to his nostrils, thanks to the two dry wildcats he had just drilled. But by straining and lying and begging and grunting and sweating and lying awake nights and mortgaging his whole life for four, maybe five years into the future, he probably *could* do it.

When he drove out of Midland and headed down the last straight stretch toward home the wind had picked up and tumbleweeds hopped across the road in the headlights like acrobatic hedgehogs. He felt a kind of loneliness and he only wanted to get home to Lee and the good meal and comfortable bed that would be waiting for him. He was tired and the old fear was upon him, the fear of being broke again. It was fatal to the dream a real oil man must keep ever burning in his mind. He felt for the broken piece of iron on the seat beside him and held it up to the light through the windshield.

"Jesus Christ!" he said under his breath. He saw something he had not seen before. It was a straight-sided shoe, not curved as a horseshoe ought to be. "It's a goddamn mule shoe!" And that it was. He rolled down the window and hurled it angrily into the dark whistling windrush.

Home again he ate his supper glumly, in silence. Before he went to bed Lee kissed him lightly but with a look of care on the corner of his mouth. She said, "Is everything all right, sweetheart?"

"Yeah," he said. "I found a mule shoe today and damn near made a jackass out of myself on account of it."

And so Scurry County was passed up. Less than two years later there were flowing Pennsylvanian Reef oil wells all over the lease block, and when the great Scurry County Field was finally defined the three and a half sections that had been offered to Jim McNeely, almost as a gift, lay right in the heart of it. There in wide-spaced orderly rows of high-pressure Christmas trees, glinting silver in the sun like a well-tended orchard of iron, were fifty-six of the finest oil wells ever drilled in America. These could have been Jim McNeely's.

The knowledge nearly crippled him. Though his instinct had told him "go" he had made a logical, reasoned judgment of caution. It had cost him—lost him—easily ten million dollars. Finding an oil-bearing structure like this great, anciently buried coral reef in the earth's crust was like discovering a new Everest. There were only a rare and wonderful few of these to be found. Now there was one less and, who knew, maybe it was the last one. Was this his oil field that fate had offered to him only to have him pass it by in a moment of timidity? The thought had a deep, petrifying, almost maddening effect upon him when it came, which was often. And even when he was not thinking about it, it hung in his rib cage waiting to be thought of again, like a recurring malignant pain. And Lee McNeely knew this, and knew not how to console him.

It deepened his despondency to learn that the two oil men he most envied and against whom he measured his own success, Big Jim Wilfong and Boyd Hallam, had, as usual, by acting quickly and astutely, ended up with fine holdings in the Scurry Field. Oh, the rich got richer and the lucky got luckier, and the poor snake-bit bastards like Jim McNeely got what the little boy shot at.

30

FOR YEARS OIL MEN AND OIL COMPANIES HAVE HAD their bitter interfamily differences over the importation of crude oil into the United States, depending on whether they are foreign producers or not. But to see them solidify and back their rumps together and stick their horns out like a herd of brother buffaloes set upon by a pack of ravening wolves, just say something derogatory about their depletion allowance. That is a thing they don't like to joke about, any more than they joke about motherhood, the Stars and Stripes or miscegenation. Any talk of eliminating or even reducing the twenty-seven and a half percent statutory depletion allowance strikes very close to the pocketbook nerve.

The oil-producing business is an extractive industry and oil and gas are classified, for good and sufficient reasons no doubt, as minerals. It is now a well-established principle of tax law that the owner of a mineral deposit should in fairness, since the minerals are irreplaceable, consider a part of his income from mining operations as a return of capital without paying income tax on it as he must on ordinary income. If this principle seems fairly reasonable to people who don't own any oil or gas, it is perhaps understandable that it is as hallowed as the First Commandment to those who do.

In 1926, after several years of legislative sparring, the Congress hit upon twenty-seven and a half percent as the percentage of gross income from an oil or gas property which a producer could keep, off the top, without income tax, to replace his capital which was being depleted. This figure was arrived at by the scientific process of adding the thirty percent which the Senate favored to the twenty-five percent the House thought reasonable, and then dividing by two. The percentage depletion law has been on the books ever since and the ravening wolves from the non-oil-producing but heavy oil-consuming states have been snarling and snapping at it, calling it a tax-dodging loophole, ever since.

The practical reason and justification for the depletion allowance, fairness and logic aside, was that it gave oil men an incentive to risk their money in the legalized gambling of wildcatting, with odds of at least ten to one against them. Such odds are not attractive unless when you hit you get to keep an important part of your income out of the hands of the tax collector. The theory worked out very well. The law accomplished its purpose. The wildcatters drilled and the oil the country needed to grow on and fight its wars with was found.

Unfortunately for oil men some of their number who hit, hit very big, and some of these, far from being economic statesmen, were big-spending show-offs or feather-heads that made the front page, and the many more who rolled (drilled) and crapped out didn't even get a small notice on page 10. This made the oil man a favorite whipping boy for the politicians from the non-oil states, since politicians thrive on prosperous whipping boys in somebody else's constituency. Consequently the old twenty-seven and a half percent depletion allowance has been a perennial target in Congress right down the line.

Strangely enough, in these latter days when wildcat drilling has drastically fallen off, the hue and cry against the oil man's depletion allowance has increased instead of diminished. Some of its defenders with fairly acceptable logic argue that since the odds against the oil hunter have now gone way up the depletion allowance should also be increased, so as to provide the greater incentive needed to keep the search going.

Pondering the problem, the old oil-field philosopher concluded that the oil man had about as much chance of getting an increase in his depletion allowance as he would have of getting an Eskimo Pie in hell. He further prognosticated that if the successful oil men, and especially the oil companies, didn't fall off their bankrolls and get some more wildcat well starts going into the record books to justify and fortify the existing depletion allowance, regardless of the worsening success ratio and the increasing cost of wildcatting, the old twenty-seven and a half percent would not be long for this world, fairness and logic to the contrary never you mind.

"The best thing you can give your children," said Dent, "is *nothing*. Or next to nothing. Most everybody will admit this in principle, still nobody will pass up the chance to leave their grubby kids a million bucks apiece and in the process turn 'em into a bunch of worthless slobs. They don't do this because they love the little bastards. If they really loved 'em they'd leave 'em poor so they'd have some incentive to work hard and amount to something. But leaving the loot to your own flesh and blood is the next best thing to taking it with you, which is what most people would really like to do, if they could."

Jeff Dofflemyer tossed his pencil on his desk and sat back with a groaning sigh. Dent had walked into his office in the middle of the afternoon, had sat down, put his feet on the desk and proceeded to embark on a philosophical foray into this subject which chanced to be on his mind, and Jeff's train of thought, which had been pursuing an intricate chain of title through the pages of the bulky abstract, was derailed and shattered.

"There are exceptions," Dent continued, putting his fingertips lightly together and gazing at the ceiling, unmindful of his interruption. "Now and then a rich boy with a mission will come along. One scorched with a saintly desire to succor the poor heatherns and start up hospitals in Haiti or the Congo, and so on. But these are rarities. A slightly larger number of the 'inheritors' feel challenged to show that they can do as well as the old man, and with the head start their money gives 'em they sometimes succeed and become second-generation tycoons, usually insufferable in their assumption that inherited wealth and its consequent authority are the equivalent of wisdom and human merit, but these are fairly rare, too. Most of the inheritors coast through life sitting on their fat asses, not using or developing the talents they were born with, neither creating or adding anything, not a blessed thing, to the asset side of the human race's balance sheet. This is bad for society, and especially bad for the individual scions who are crippled with their inherited wealth and condemned to the existence of white slugs. It all points inescapably to the necessity of passing a law that no citizen can inherit more than five thousand dollars."

Jeff Dofflemyer looked over his glasses at his colleague and shook his head. "Boy, you are really wild-eyed today. You can talk up a storm on any side of any given question, but you know what? You wouldn't even make a good Communist. You know why? Because you don't really believe a damn thing you've said. The trouble is you don't believe *against* what you said, either. Do you really, honestly believe in *anything?*"

Dent held up his right hand and intoned solemnly, "I believe in Jim McNeely."

"Aw, knock it off," said Jeff. "I asked you a serious question."

"I'm serious."

"Well, hell, I believe in Jim, too. I wouldn't be working for him if I didn't. I'm talking about principles."

"Principles, platitudes, mere words," Dent answered positively. "They confuse me. I believe in a man. That's something I can see and understand and come to grips with. Our boy has got a thing. He's doing a thing. He's making something out of nothing. I'm not saying that what he's doing is noble or nobly motivated. But it's vital and creative and vivid. It's raw and hell-bent and unafraid and alive. And so it's good. It's the natural unfolding of the vital, natural man. It's something he's got to do, like the pictures Van Gogh had to paint. I can't paint pictures but I know an artist when I see one and I can believe in him, and clean his pallet for him. Some of us are pallet cleaners. My God, Jeff, what got you started on all this philosophical jazz, anyway?"

"Ah, you're a real comedian. Beat it boy, I'm busy."

Later in the afternoon Dent strolled back into Jeff's office and seated himself again.

"Speaking of crazy talk, what do you think of our leader's newest caper?"

"What do you mean?"

"I mean this great new idea of lining up some Eastern tax money for his drilling deals, and moving the office to Winfield."

"When's he due back, anyway? I got a requirement on this title I need to talk to him about."

"He's due back Saturday, but don't bet on it." Dent made a grimace of distaste. "That Charley-blue-blood Dupre is a party boy. They're liable to wind up in Vegas after they finish their business in New York. That Dupre is no damn good."

"Oh, Charley's all right," said Jeff. "Anyway, he's gonna be useful. He knows big money. Socially. Related to some of it. Two or three operators out here have made out pretty well with Eastern money working for 'em. If Jim can line him up some 'mullets' in the ninety percent bracket, hell, there's no reason why it won't work for him, too."

"I don't know. He's been acting kind of nutty since he passed up Scurry County."

"So how would you feel if you had passed up a thing like that? The wonder to me is he hasn't sure 'nough jumped his trolley." Jeff shrugged. "This new 'mullet' idea may be just what he needs."

"I just don't trust that Charley Dupre," said Dent waspishly.

"Oh, don't worry about him. He's just an old Ivy League boy on the make. Thinks he sees a chance to parlay Jim and some of his rich friends into a soft buck for himself. Jim can handle him. The thing I don't like is this move to Winfield. The cement's not hardly dry on this new office building. It's fine. Just what we needed. So now we got to move to the big city and take a whole blooming floor in the Citizen's Bank Building. It don't add up, Dent. We can't afford it, for one small thing. And then that big damn house he's gone and bought in there. He can't afford that, either. At least not the way I read it. He's changed his whole concept, his whole way of life. The worst part of it to me is him buying the house and having it redecorated without telling Lee a damn thing about any of it."

"It's a surprise."

"Hell of a surprise," Jeff said angrily. "A woman wants to pick out her own house. Anyway, how does he know she wants to move to Winfield? I don't think she'll like it. Especially since he's going so far in debt to do it."

Dent shrugged. "*Me no sabe.* Scurry County kind of changed the way he looks at things. He figures he's got to play it different now. Got to get in there with the big boys and quit acting so conservative if he's gonna roll for the blue chips."

"Has he ever seen the damned house?"

"He hasn't been back to Winfield since he came out to Dead Lake. But he knows it. From long time ago. Anyhow, *I've* seen it. Where do you think I've been? You didn't even miss me. I've been up to my ass in interior decorators. It's the old Streetman house in Glen View Park. Pure Warren G. Harding Tudor. Sixteen turrets and five acres of front yard. Twenty thousand dollars' worth of brand-new air conditioning. Tell me any woman wouldn't like that. When he's ready, he'll take her there. That'll be going back in style. Grand homecoming of the native son who made good and all like that."

Jeff heaved a disgusted sigh. "If I was the native son, I'd clean up a few debts first."

"Boy, you got to get over this potato-patch idea about debt," said Dent Paxton disparagingly. "You can't make it any more without going in debt. If you've got resources that bankers will lend money on, you don't have to worry about how much you owe. So long as you can still borrow money you're solvent. Jim's got the oil reserves in the ground. They're in bits and pieces and hocked to the hilt, maybe, but as long as that pipeline keeps pumping he'll keep paying off and get in shape to borrow some more. And he'll keep looking. One day the old blind hog's liable to find a big acorn."

31

THE LITTLE HAIR-CRACKS WHICH THE STRESSES of life start in the foundations of any marriage, if not soon filled and annealed with the cement of love, begin to spread and join up with other cracks and fill with corrosive fluid and widen in a webbing network which begins to weaken and erode the whole structure. Lee McNeely had instinctively sensed this and had accepted and discharged the responsibilities of marriage-maintenance-engineer with remarkable success in the early years of their life together. But it was not so easy any longer. Not since Scurry County. Scurry seemed to be the traumatic beginning of many undefinable, almost imperceptible changes in the whole complex of their marriage. It was as if she could not get close enough to her husband in certain vital areas of his mind and heart to do her healing, restorative work. And she wondered sometimes if perhaps she had changed, and was changing, too, with time, becoming more brittle, less flexible, more sensitive, less loving, and less willing to take the blame for any roughening of their relationship, less willing to accept the role of the one at fault, the one misguided, uninformed, unreasonable, and so the one who recanted like a sweet simpleton and begged her lord's forgiveness with kisses and tears when anything went wrong, regardless of where the fault really lay. This she recognized to be the good wife's proper role. But this was not as easy to do as it once had been.

She picked him up at the airport in the late afternoon. As he came down the aluminum stairway in the line of deplaning passengers, gripping the brim of his Borsalino, the hot dry wind blowing his tie, she felt a sudden shock to see how he had aged. Not in the eight days he had been away in New York, but in the twelve years since that evening when she had first picked up a lean, elegant young roustabout walking down an oiled road into Coker City. Living with him she had not noticed the little brush-strokes that each day of passing years had laid upon him. It was like living with a child who one day is an infant and one day is grown, with no perceptible change in between.

In some way the week's absence had enabled her suddenly to see her husband for the first time in the depth and breadth of his maturity. He was thicker of body. The strong, graceful slenderness was gone from his neck. There were lines of fatigue and strain raying from his eyes, and these were not all from the eight hard days and nights of business and drinking and lost sleep in the great City of Tension. She even noted for the first time the sprinkling of silver in the thick brushed-back hair over his temples. It was a handsome touch, but it shocked her. A fleeting thought that the same artist of time had no doubt been at work upon her, as well, crossed her mind and she involuntarily drew her hand across her flat stomach and down her thigh and restrained an impulse to take out her compact for a reassuring glance at the blackness of her hair and the firmness of the flesh under her chin.

Jim McNeely smiled and put the arm holding the light brief case around her shoulders and drew her in and kissed her.

"How's my girl?"

"Happy, now," she said.

At home the amazed realization of the working of time was still upon her. As he took off his coat and tie and unbuttoned his collar and mixed himself a drink while she placed the already-cooked roast to heat in the oven, she cast appraising little glances at him. He was truly a magnificent and desirable man. All boyishness was gone now. The slight puffiness and tiredness around the eyes added to rather than detracted from his physical desirability. The same was true, even, for the fullness now apparent at his belt line. He was a man, full grown, powerful, beginning to show the first ravages of time and trouble, but a herd bull in the height of his powers. A flutter of tenderness and desire crossed below her heart.

Later she came into the living room and stood above him with the fresh drink he had called for. She smiled down at him as he lay stretched out on the sofa. As she set his drink on the coffee table he pulled her down to him and kissed her.

"Did you miss me?"

"I always miss you."

He kissed her again, hard, running his fingers down the strong valley of her back to her hips, and the desire that rose in them simultaneously was so sudden that they both laughed.

"Supper's in the oven," she said. "I could turn it off."

"Man's got to eat, too," he said. "We've got all night"

"And the rest of our lives. Tell me about New York."

"It's a lousy place. Oh, I did what I went to do. Been acting like a big-shot oil man, working all day and staying up half the night carousing around with a bunch of blue bloods. Rich ones."

"I'll bet there were lots of cool, chic New York girls hanging around."

He shrugged. "Some. Out on Long Island. They think I'm pretty hot stuff. Rough-cut, self-made oil man from Texas. Every time I looked at one of them I thought how much better-looking you were."

"I'll bet."

"No fooling." He made a kidding face at her. "Oh, I was nice to them. Even flirted a little with the important ones. Y'see, these people are gonna be my 'mullets.' They've got big money. Old money. Some of it's got moss on it. They don't know what to do with their income. Uncle gets most of it. I'm gonna put 'em in the oil business so they can keep a little. Thanks to Charley Dupre."

Lee thought of the sandy-haired young man with the close-set ears and blue blazer and striped tie and white rumpled trousers and white buck shoes and involuntarily made a face as if she had just tasted a fresh-cut lemon.

"Now, don't make a face. Charley's all right," said Jim McNeely.

"All I know about Charley Dupre," she said, "is that he thinks three drinks at the country club entitles him to feel your fanny and ask you to go riding in his Mercedes runabout."

"Charley's related to big money," said Jim McNeely seriously. "He went to school with some real rich jokers at Princeton. He's down here on the make, but what the hell. Everybody's got to make it, one way or another. He puts these rich dogs in touch with a feller like me and takes a three or four percent override on the deal for himself. At the same time he's learning the oil business. One of these days he'll start making his own deals. Right now he's working for me."

Lee sat up and was now very serious and very pragmatic. "What exactly is your position in relation to these people?"

"I'm a smart, successful oil operator who knows the business from A to Izzard. Anyway, that's what Charley says to his rich friends. So I work up the drilling deals. They'll put up all the money. If the wells are dry, it'll only cost them ten cents on the dollar because they're in the top bracket. If we hit, I'm in for a fourth interest. It's a good deal for top-bracket people. Incidentally, that's where we're headed, sugar doll. The small, exclusive club at the very top."

Lee looked askance at him and said, "If it's all the same I'd rather not join. I like it fine being one of the poor, merely prosperous."

"Oh, come on. We're gonna sack up this oil business, sweetheart. I can make deals for these people. A percentage are bound to hit. I'll get in shape, then when the right deal comes along, I'll knock that one off for just you and me."

"Like Scurry County?"

A cloud spread across Jim McNeely's eyes. "Yes, like Scurry County! There's other Scurrys to be found. One of 'em belongs to Jim McNeely. I'll find it."

"Jim, suppose you'd taken that Scurry deal, instead of passing it up. We'd be real sloppy rich now, wouldn't we? Well just what would we have that we haven't already got? Really? A new descriptive title—'millionaires'?"

A flush of anger grew in Jim McNeely and came out in his words and separated the closeness between them. "In case I never told you," he said, "I am a millionaire. Add up the value of my oil in the ground and the rigs and the new office building and this house you live in and my BVDs and your teddy bears and subtract what I owe, there's a million dollars left! Not bad for an old Winfield boy that never went to college." He shook the ice in his empty glass, and when he spoke again the intimacy and warmth and closeness that had been there before was gone from his voice. "I guess I need another drink."

Lee McNeely was nobody's fool in business matters or otherwise. She knew that if you put an optimum value on your assets it made a pretty picture. She also knew that if you went out and tried to sell those assets it was very unlikely you could find a buyer just then who would pay you even a half of the value you placed on your accumulations of property, be it oil in the ground, machinery, BVDs, or whatever. But if Jim McNeely wanted to call himself a millionaire, that was all right with her.

But what if he *wasn't* a millionaire? What if he was only *half* a millionaire? What was so magic about a million? The new label worried her. Well, there was magic about it, and she knew it: until you reached that first major level, when your net worth clicked over to the seventh digit and kept on climbing, you were still fooling around in the minor leagues, especially in the oil business. It was a thing of the mind, but she knew it was very real and important to Jim McNeely. When you passed a million, you became some*body*.

Later in the evening a devil nudged her to return to the old touchy subject.

"Suppose we had taken the Scurry deal, Jim? We'd be big rich now. Suppose we were. What would be any better than the way we have it?"

A defiant look came over Jim McNeely's face and an edge of belligerence came into his voice. He said, "Sugar, when you get that rich it just keeps coming in by force of habit. You can't hardly keep from making more money. That's what would be better!"

"Jim!" cried Lee McNeely. "*More money!* What are we going to do with more money?" She stood in the center of the room legs planted. She threw out her arms in exasperation. "What are *we* going to do with *ourselves?* That's what I'm saying. I don't care what we do as long as we're together. But I don't have a good feeling about this new thing. I mean, about you and me, us. Maybe it's silly, but I just don't understand it. If I only had some feeling about a certain goal or something that we were working for, together. Something genuine and worth working for, then maybe I wouldn't feel this way. I'm scared. Here we've got almost everything anybody could want. Where do we stop wanting? Where? When? Will we be satisfied when we really get to be millionaires?" She was swept into the edges of anger without meaning to be. She suddenly wondered, with annoyance, if she was about to start menstruating.

Jim McNeely got up angrily from the couch and shook his drink at her, spilling it on the carpet.

"I told you I *am* a millionaire, goddammit to hell!"

"You don't have to cuss."

"Well, I am!"

"And I don't wear teddy bears!"

She had gone to bed alone, unloved and angry, and had at last fallen into a fitful slumber. When he crawled in beside her a long time later and nuzzled against her neck there was a strong odor of whiskey on his breath and a burr of whiskey in his voice.

"Sweetheart."

She stirred and half shrugged away from him.

"Sweetheart, I'm sorry. There's something I forgot to tell you. We're moving to Winfield."

She shrugged her shoulders again.

"Surprised?"

"No. I knew we were going sometime. I just didn't know when."

"Next week."

She lifted her head and patted the pillow hard and nestled her head into it. "I'm with you, sweetheart," she said. "Where you lead me I will follow."

32

I N T H E O I L - P R O D U C I N G B U S I N E S S *GAS* H A D A L W A Y S
been more of a problem than a prize. If a wildcatter drilling way out
in the middle of nowhere stumbled into a big blowing gas reservoir
with no oil he was commiserated with rather than congratulated. It was
like drilling a dry hole except that it wasn't a dry hole. What could you do
with the gas? You couldn't truck it to the railroad and ship it in tank cars
to market the way you could oil. And a thousand mile pipeline to pipe the
airy stuff to the big population centers astronomically, financially out of
the question. So the wildcatter usually either plugged the well or shut it in
and capped it under a shut-in gas-well provision in his lease that allowed
him to hold the mineral rights by making a small annual cash payment to
the landowner until he could find a market. Many oil men held on to gas
deposits this way because they knew that gas would burn and heat homes
and run factories and someday, somehow, it would almost certainly be
worth something.

That time came for a lot of far-out, lonesome gas soon after World
War II. A great deal of it had been found unintentionally here, there
and yonder by wildcatters looking for oil, and it wasn't long until the
sharp-pencil boys figured out that there was enough available to make
the tremendous cost of long transmission lines from the Southwest to
the population centers in the East an investment that would pay out and
show a reasonable profit. The conversion to gas transmission of a big-inch
oil line built to the East Coast when U-boats started sinking our coastal
tankers gave a big shove to the interstate gas business.

Then, almost overnight, gas became as desirable as oil and sometimes more so. There was a hungry market for natural gas in the cold country, and wildcatters began actually looking for it.

This new development became a somewhat mixed blessing for oil men, because they began supplying gas to millions of people who came to depend on gas's BTUs to cook with and keep warm with and so the gas-producing business, at least in the minds of some people on the consuming end, began to take on the character of a public utility. They began to think it should be subject to the same controls and rules of public convenience and necessity as the electric power business. In 1954 (in the technical language of the trade) it really hit the fan when the Supreme Court handed down a decision that in effect said just that. The gas producers cried in anguish that this was a rank piece of judicial legislation. Nonetheless oil men thereafter had to get approval of a federal government agency before they could sell their gas that was going across state lines to market and if the bureaucrats thought the price was too high (and they always thought so, to hear the oil men tell it) no permit was granted. The trouble was there were hundreds and thousands of gas producers of all sizes and conditions, and the Federal Power Commission, through no fault of its own, virtually choked down with paper trying to administer an impossible situation. Nobody in the business knew for sure where he stood or how it would all end up, except it was pretty clear to the producers that they were going to come out on the short end of the stick.

Observing it all, the old oil-patch philosopher noted that while people down in the producing states thought things were going to hell in a hand-basket, most folks up in Minnesota and Rhode Island who didn't produce any gas but only bought it for their cookstoves and water heaters and boilers seemed to thing this Federal regulation was not so bad. This led the old philosopher, after considering the fungible nature of the human species, to conclude that if the Minnesotans and Rhode Islanders were suddenly transplanted to Texas and Louisiana and vice versa, reactions to the whole situation would most likely be exactly reversed. Which led the old philosopher to the further conclusion that ordinary people's power of reason and logic is centered in their left-hand hip pockets.

The speaker clicked on and the bright young voice of the stewardess announced that the plane was coming in for a landing at the Winfield airport. Adding the usual chipper reminder of possible imminent disaster, she admonished the passengers to fasten seat belts and extinguish all cigarettes.

"So that we will not hurtle through the cabin showering sparks and set fire to the wreckage when we crash," was Lee McNeely's quavering thought. She hated flying. Instinctively she felt for the hand of her husband. But it was not so much fear of the landing that made her do this. It was as much her apprehension about the place of landing—Winfield, Texas, their new home. It had been sixteen years since Jim McNeely had left here. This returning was an event of unknown import, a significant way-mark in his life, hence in hers and theirs. Things would never be the same again. That much was certain. What was not clear was *how* different and in what degree. In this lay the real anxiety and the fluttery fear.

The airliner's wheels screeched and streaked black on the landing surface. The craft bounced into the air, hovered, then calmed, settled, and reversed props furiously, pressing all passengers forward against their belts. Slowing, it revved its motors as if with relief and satisfaction, then turned off the runway toward the landing ramp. The passengers began to feel about for belongings, preparing for debarkation, happy in the knowledge that they were down and would never have to fly again if they didn't choose to.

As they came down the stairway into the warm dry wind that swept across the field on this sunny afternoon Lee clutched at her handbag and tried to set her small hat slightly less askew on her head. Her mind was racing with many emotions and thoughts.

"Mister McNeely?" A tanned man in a rumpled white shirt and blowing tie approached them from an angle as they streamed with the other passengers toward the terminal.

"That's me."

"Joe Klein. Southwest 'Copter Service. You folks have a good flight in?"

"A little bumpy at the end, otherwise OK."

"If you'll come this way the chopper is over here. Give me your baggage checks. I'll turn 'em over to this boy." He motioned to the porter following behind him. "The limousine will take your stuff in."

"Dear me," said Lee. She had prepared herself for surprises but not this. She wanted to show herself pleased and excited, and at the same time not act like a West Texas bumpkin. But this was totally confusing.

"Don't panic, sugar." Jim McNeely grinned at her, gripping her arm and steering her out of the line of people. "It's just a little special service for VIPs."

They followed the man in the white shirt toward a machine which looked like a giant undernourished dragonfly perched on the concrete ramp by the terminal building.

"We're gonna take a little ride in a helicopter," said Jim McNeely. "I want you to see this place from all angles."

"Oh, dear," said Lee again as the helicopter pilot helped her up into the cockpit under the Plexiglass bubble. Mounting behind her, Jim McNeely shoved and positioned her into the padded seat and helped her strap across her middle another hateful safety belt almost identical to the one from which she had just escaped.

When the pilot had taken his seat and adjusted the headphones on his ears and started the motor he nodded and held up a thumb to Jim McNeely. Then Lee, feeling very small and insignificant between them, heard and felt a great fluttering roar overhead and all around, then a sharp unrealistic lifting, and suddenly they were above and sliding across the sprawling airport with people and cars receding below like big and little bugs in no earthly way related to this fantastic new world in which she found herself.

"Dear me," she said again, touching her throat.

"There it is, sugar pie," said Jim McNeely presently, opening his upturned hand as if offering to her all that lay ahead. "The metropolis of Winfield, Texas. Scene of my birth and youth. An overgrown country town full of jerks!"

"If you feel that way, why are we moving here?" said Lee, leaning toward him and shouting to make herself heard.

"I'm kidding. Every place has its share. Winfield has some on-the-ball people, too." He winked. "Or will when we get there. Pilot, you know this town?"

"I live here."

"OK, let's give the little lady the three-dollar tour. First I want you to circle the Citizen's Bank Building. That's it there, Lee, the tallest one. Go down a little, pardner, just swing around to the left. Count down two windows from the top, baby. There. That's the new headquarters of the McNeely Oil Company. Whole blooming floor. See that corner office there with the wide windows? That's where your sugar daddy's gonna put his feet on a desk and make like a big oil man." There was excitement in his voice, and in spite of her state of shock Lee was glad to hear it.

"Jim, when did this—happen? When did you come to Winfield? You were supposed to be in New York!"

"I haven't been here yet. Old Dent worked it all out. OK, pardner, now take us to 4641 Antelope Street."

"That beats me," said the pilot. "I only lived here twenty-five years."

"I'll show you. It's on the south side. Can you find Bryan Drive?"

"Yeah. I can find that."

"OK, take out, and come down, man. You're too high." He scanned the geometric pattern of the suburbs stretching out below.

"Now you're talking. There she is. Take a hard right down Bryan. Go right down to it and slow down. Just like a parade. Take a look, sugar. There is where the rich folks used to live. I've been thrown out of some of the best houses on this street. Looks a little seedy now. They're not spending much on water. Most of the rich folks have moved out on the west side. Slow down, pilot. There! That big yellow brick! The former home of Waldo B. Wales, MD, and family."

"Oh," said Lee, craning. "Oh. Mazie's house."

"The old doc died about five years ago. Mrs. Wales sold out and moved into an apartment. OK, pilot, go to the end of the street and kind of veer south across the tracks and you'll see two little streets branching off the road that crosses the bottoms. The second one is Antelope. A little more to the left. There it is. There's a little old frame house halfway down the— slow up, dammit! Wait a minute. Swing around. No, that's got to be the street. Hell, it's gone!"

"What's gone?" said Lee.

"My house is gone! Where that flat building is. It's a goddamn warehouse or something."

"It's a box factory," said the pilot. "I know that place. My cousin works there."

"They tore it down."

Lee felt for his hand and gripped it. "I'm sorry."

He was silent for a moment, then he gave an incredulous laugh. "They tore the hot little sonofabitch down. Well, that takes care of that." He sat back and seemed to relax. "OK, driver, you know where we're going to land."

"Yep. I been there."

"Well, the tour's over. Let's go."

273

The pilot touched the throttle and took the craft up and they spun diagonally across the suburbs to the west, across the winding, crawling river and the streaming traffic arteries that channeled life in and out of the heart of this middle-sized city.

"That's the coliseum where they have the rodeos," said Jim McNeely. "That green area up ahead this side of the bend in the river, that's the Glen View Country Club. Any given day you can find some of the saltiest old reprobates in Winfield hoofing it around those fairways. Only they ride now, they tell me. I used to caddy there some." He was silent a moment studying the terrain below, intently.

"There," he said. "There it is. You know what to do, pilot."

"Circle a couple of times, hover, then go down when you tell me."

"Looky yonder, Lee. You see that house?"

"*That* one. It looks like a young castle."

"Take a good look."

"It has beautiful trees, and whoever lives there *doesn't* mind paying water bills."

"It's got its own well."

"And a swimming pool. And my goodness, look at the people! They're having a party, a garden party!"

"They're having a party for you, sweetheart." Jim McNeely cut his eyes at her as she leaned forward peering earthward as the craft hovered, beating the air with its great rotor.

"They're not having a party for me because I don't know them, and I wasn't invited," said Lee, going along with the joke but beginning to have a sinking, slightly sick feeling that wasn't from the helicopter ride. "They're having a housewarming party for you, sweetheart. Because that's your house. That young castle is your home from now on. And since you're the queen of it, here's the key to the front door." He held a shiny, fresh-cut key on a dark blue ribbon in front of her eyes. She looked at it cross-eyed and took it in her trembling hand.

"Jim—"

"Don't talk, sweetheart. Just relax and enjoy it. Take us down, pilot. I can use a drink."

Lee Thomas Montgomery McNeely was never able to remember the rest of this day and night in anything approaching clear focus. It was a confused nightmare of hilarity, hurt feelings, embarrassment, anger, shame, ridiculousness, and excitement . . . people streaming across the wide lawn like an attacking wave in gay summery dresses, pink linens and rust colored jackets and yellow trousers, drinks in hand, all cheering and laughing with a sound of well-bred insincerity as if enjoying a tremendous joke among themselves . . . people gripping her hands as she tried to push her tousled hair out of her eyes, people shouting introductions to meaningless faces with meaningless names . . . Dent standing around grinning like a cat as they all milled and moved toward the large Tudor manor house and she saying to Dent between her teeth and meaning it that he was a traitorous bastard she had thought was her friend . . . and the feeling of anguish at remembering that she had purposely decided to wear an old tacky dress to travel in.

It was a fantastic kaleidoscope-viewing with an idiot turning the tube. She could not remember the sequence of the scenes. The parade across the terrace with the combo playing wild, jumping Dixieland music . . . dark waiters in white jackets coming and going from the bar set up by the pool . . . the entry through leaded French doors into the huge vaulted Tudor living room, the great hall hung with heraldic banners and breast plates and stag horns . . . everyone talking and laughing and looking at her with eyes that seemed to gouge grooves into her chilled flesh . . . the older women who were at her elbows and never stopped talking to her, one of them it turned out a newspaper columnist, who led her on a conducted tour of "her house" . . . the long black-and-white checkered hallways, the pantries, the chintz-hung sun room, the dining room with ornate unfriendly furniture, and the great table laden with exotic food, the pearl-carpeted stairway curving upward to the second story, the doorways, the baths, and the grilled registers every five steps that breathed cold air upon her already goose-pimpled flesh . . . the pervading smell of strangeness, of somebody-else-ness.

"Tat-*taa*!" Someone made the sound of a trumpet as she was ushered into the master bedroom. The quailing first sight of the great triple bed with draped satin valance above, and a little leggy chick in a tight skirt sitting on the bed bouncing up and down and querping, "Oh, boy! It's like a trampoline! You could really do tricks on this baby!" And the appalling crash of laughter that followed.

In all of the turmoil and confusion she reached and looked repeatedly, frantically for her husband, then for Dent, then anybody she knew, but they were not there and the laughter came in paroxysmal bursts as she wandered or was pushed with the stream of people around the house, and drinks were put into and taken out of her hand and the noise level rose and fell and rose again and it was dark outside and then suddenly she found herself alone. She listed as if on a steep slope through open doors and found herself in a room she felt must be the library since it had old books in shelves to the ceiling. She sank into a deep brocaded couch and fell back exhausted and put her limp hand to her forehead. In a moment, before she had caught her breath well, she heard two male voices drift into the room out of the streaming hallway.

"Here, have one of mine." A match flared.

"Thanks."

"God, what a clam-bake. I came for laughs, but it's really kind of embarrassing."

"I came because Charley Dupre threatened to make me chairman of our prep school fund raising committee down here if I didn't."

"I'll bet old lady Streetman would spin in her mausoleum if she could see the sharecroppers that have moved into her house."

"That wife of his, though. That's a real nice little piece, that is."

"There you go, Herbie. Always thinking about something to eat."

Jim McNeely moved through the rooms shaking hands trying to relate familiar names of his youth to faces of middle-aged people who resembled only faintly some acquaintance or enemy of his childhood. He rather enjoyed the curious, appraising stares that he felt on all sides. After a few minutes he became entangled in multiple greetings, and Lee was swept away as he was propelled in a succession of introductions and renewals of old "friendships" through a disorganized tour of the house conducted by Dent. They moved in a herd from room to room and from bar to bar, of which latter there were three doing land-office business.

"They're all here," said Charley Dupre coming up at his side, winking. "I got 'em out."

"Good boy, Charley."

"It was easy. Some got out of sick beds. Nobody wanted to miss the show. They'd be left out of conversation for days. Oh, Jim, I want you to know Ted Wanamaker here. I caught Ted in Jamaica and he flew in here on his way back to New York. Ted and his associates in Bakke &

Company are looking for some good oil deals to put some of their cruddy money in. I've told him he'll have to wait in line, but if he's a good boy and behaves himself we might let him have a small piece of a deal sometime."

"Howdy, Ted. Don't let old Charley fast-talk you. He thinks the oil business is a gut-cinch. It's not. Nine out of ten wildcats are still dry."

"I'm aware of that," said Ted Wanamaker, a tanned, shrewd-looking man casually dressed in expensive silk jacket and slacks. "We're just looking for someone we think can beat the percentages a bit."

"Our batting average hasn't been too bad," said Jim McNeely. "But you never know. You can always hit a slump."

"And you can just as well hit a hot streak," said Charley. "Hey, looky, there's Dave Pendleton. He was looking for you, Ted. Hey, Dave!"

"Well, what do you think?" said Dent when the others had moved away. "About what?"

"About the damned house? You think you can struggle along in this little ol' Tudor bungalow?"

"It looks like a damn museum."

"You picked it out, buddy. I just redecorated it."

"You spent too damn much money. I can tell that from here."

"I can assure you I did. Did you want me to furnish it out of a Monkey Ward catalogue? The gentle folk are impressed. Repulsed maybe, but impressed. That's what you wanted, isn't it?" said Dent, smiling, pleased with himself.

"You did a good job, Dentie buddy. Where's the downstairs crapper?"

"There are three. One in gold. One in rose. One in pickled oak. Which would you prefer?"

"The closest one."

"Jim McNeely!"

"Well, hello, Mrs. Wales." He ran into her in the hallway as he exited from the gold powder room, and, aware that he had insufficiently dried his hands on the tiny, monogrammed towel, hastily rubbed his palm against his shirt front before he shook hands with her.

"Jim McNeely!" she said again, obviously and sincerely moved by the sight of him. "You do look wonderful!" The music from the combo on the terrace just off the hallway doors made it necessary for her to raise her voice in order to be heard.

"You're looking mighty sharp yourself," he said, rather amazed at the erosion that takes place in some women between the ages of forty-five and sixty. The pink firmness was now a powdered sagging frailty and the braids of hair twined around her head had the brittle look of spun glass rather than the golden taffy he remembered.

"I'm so glad you invited me to your house-warming. I wouldn't have missed it."

"I'm real glad you could come."

"I'm just sorry Dr. Wales couldn't have lived to see this. He would be very proud of you."

"I'm sorry, too. Can I get you a fresh drink? I need one myself."

"Yes, I believe I will. And I want to talk to you."

Jim McNeely caught a passing waiter and sent him off for new drinks then walked with Madelon Wales into the sun porch where they found an eddy of relative quiet and sat down together on an antique iron divan.

"It's a lovely house, Jim. I remember so many gay parties here when I was a girl. And now it's your house. I met your wife. My, she's lovely! So simple and straightforward, and good looking! Remember what I told you?"

He laughed. "I remember more than I want."

"Now, Jim. The past is a long time gone. You have done so magnificently well. I've been keeping up with you. You really have made an outstanding success. I like to think that Dr. Wales and I were partly responsible for giving you the right push that got you started."

Jim McNeely was beginning to feel his drinks. He gave a loud laugh of delight. "It was a pretty good shove, all right."

"Jim, you're not bitter, are you? Bitterness could take the pleasure out of your wonderful success."

He reached over and patted her hand reassuringly and gave her a smile that had warmth and pleasure and friendliness in it. "I'm not bitter, Mrs. Wales. Why should I be bitter? How's Mazie? Is she gonna be here? I haven't seen her."

"Ye-s, I think she'll be here. She certainly planned to be here."

"It sure is nice she and old Pluto got together. I mean Clayton. We called him Pluto. You know he and I were buddies together a while in the oil fields."

"Yes, I know."

"I know you're happy that Mazie married such a fine boy from a good family and all. The LeMaynes are fine people. Pluto—Clayton made quite a name for himself in the short time he was out in the fields."

"Jim—" Madelon Wales frowned and looked at him, touching one hand that shook ever so slightly to the corner of her brow, trying to discern whether he spoke from sarcasm or ignorance. "I don't know how much you know. It hasn't been all sunshine for Mazie."

Jim McNeely frowned back with concern, as if he did not know that Pluto LeMayne had lived up to his early promise and turned out to be an incredibly sloppy and impossible alcoholic who, after the war, had drunk himself out of a good job with Bison Oil, then had drunk himself out of a face-saving partnership with his uncle in an almost fool-proof independent producing operation in which all he was required to do was stay out of trouble. And as if he did not know, either, that Pluto was now "officing" daily in the men's tavern at the country club, drinking and playing gin-rummy with anybody who would take his IOUs, which weren't any good. It took all of his trust fund income to pay his bar bill, and Madelon Wales refused to do more for him than pay the household upkeep for him and Mazie and supply Mazie with reasonable pocket money.

"I'm sorry to hear that," he said seriously. "I figured you all had it made. Pluto comes from such good stock."

"Yes, his uncle was Dr. Wales's dearest friend. But it hasn't been all sunshine, Jim. I do hope Mazie gets here. She is dying to see you."

Ted Neighbors had been designated as the best possible man to capture the NcNeely business for the Citizen's Bank. He didn't agree with this assignment at all, but he was only the executive vice president, and John Winterman, the president, and Elias Ponde, the board chairman and chief executive officer, were firm in their opinions, mainly because they didn't want to tackle the job themselves, and they surely coveted the McNeely account.

"Goddammit, we weren't back-scratching buddies or anything. I knew him, sure. But sometimes it's a lot better if strangers make the approach. He probably still thinks of me as a snotty-nosed kid. I think John would be a lot better. I'm just the executive VP. It'd flatter him a hell of a lot more if the president hit him up."

"John wasn't invited to the house-warming, Ted," said Elias sagely. "You were. Now go on out there and nail him. Our good competitors across the street will be hot after him. Let's get in the first lick. You're the boy that can do it."

And so Ted Neighbors wasn't as overjoyed as his jovial smile suggested when he caught Jim McNeely coming away from the bar in the wide hallway momentarily unattached.

"Well, Jim, old boy!" he cried with hollow heartiness. "It's been donkey's years and by golly they've sure treated you right! How in the world are you anyway, as if I need to ask?"

"Hello, Ted. Well. You haven't changed a hell of a lot," said Jim McNeely, shaking hands.

"Call me Buzzy, Kid. I still go by that. At least a few old middle-aged drunks around here that you and I know still call me that."

"That's right. Buzzy. And let's see, what was it you used to call me?"

Ted Neighbors's face clouded. "You? I can't remember that we called you anything but Jim. It's been a hell of a long time."

"Yes, it was something—what was it? Don't you remember?"

"Golly, I don't. But say, speaking of the old bunch, I'm playing golf with Arthur Daley Saturday. We haven't got a foursome yet. How about joining us? But maybe you're a pro and couldn't stand us short-knockers. We're all about fifteen or sixteen handicap but we have a hell of a lot of fun."

"Yeah, old Art. What was it you guys used to call me? Don't you remember?"

"Oh, gosh, what the hell! It's been too long, and my memory's terrible. Say, Jimbo, while I think of it and before you're jumped on by our competition, whom I shall call 'Brand X,' I'd like to get my oar in for Citizen's National. We try to reach out a little farther to give progressive people the kind of service they are entitled to. You've made quite a name for yourself. I'd sure be proud to have you banking with us. And I'm thinking about more than taking care of your spare cash for you. We've got a hell of a fine oil loan department and more than that we're always on the look-out for young, vigorous blood for our Board of Directors. We've got several old boys about ready to turn in their suits. Of course I don't have the final say on anything like that but you're the kind of successful, go-ahead home-town product that we need on our board, Jimbo."

"Goddammit, I *know* it wasn't Jimbo," said Jim McNeely, playing the man like a hooked and struggling trout. "It was something more like Nig or Nigger-something. I always figured it was because we were poor and lived in a house over by nigger town. I flew over it today. They tore it down."

"Oh, hell, man. I don't know what you're talking about," said Ted Neighbors, unhappily. "What about the golf? We could have the girls meet us afterwards for drinks and lunch. I want Marge to meet Mrs. McNeely. And by the way, if nobody has signed you up yet Marge wants you all to be our guests at the Tuileries Ball next month. Debutante deal, you know. New folks in town can go as guests only one time, and we'd like you to be ours. It's kind of a silly snobbish deal but the gals attach a lot of importance to it. Hard as hell to get into. Your wife will surely be going in as a member on her own soon. No doubt about that. Marge says she's heard what a lovely person she is. In fact, when it comes to putting her name up for membership—"

"Surely seems like it was Nigger something you guys used to call me. Don't you really remember?"

"Oh, *hell*, man," cried Ted Neighbors, distraught. "How can I remember that far back?"

Jim McNeely's face broke into a broad grin. "Well, what the hell! It doesn't make a lot of difference anyway, does it?" He put his arm around the unhappy man's shoulders. "Let's have a drink, Buzzy. For old time's sake."

With an audible groan of relief Ted Neighbors gave him a most grateful banker's smile and said, "You bet! Make mine a double! And say, what about the golf game Saturday?"

Walking toward the bar with him, arm still around his shoulders, Jim McNeely said, "Hell, man, what do I know about golf? I couldn't hit a bull in the ass with a mashie-niblick!"

Lee wandered out of the library and into the large crowded living room in a kind of daze.

"Hello, lady," said a familiar voice at her elbow. She turned and looked with pleasure and relief into the plain, good face of Jeff Dofflemyer.

"Y'know," he said, "You can make a roomful of ugly people average out fairly beautiful just by walking into it."

"Jeff!" she laughed. "What a devilish thing to say! But how nice! Where did you learn to talk like that?"

"It just came to me," said Jeff, smiling smugly, "And I said it."

Jim McNeely was talking with a group of men in the cool, dark air of the garden on the edge of the sound of the combo which floated, muted, across the surface of the pool. Green and orange lights from giant paper fish swaying overhead made shimmering streaks on the water. He heard his name called from somewhere on the terrace, then again, closer, urgently. He looked and frowned, then, smiling, excused himself from the group and went to meet Madelon Wales, who was literally towing her daughter, Mazie, by the hand behind her.

"Jim! Here she is! This bad girl finally arrived! I knew you two old school-mates would want to see each other. Well, Jim, here she is! Has she changed? For the better?"

"Mother! You sound as if you're exhibiting a registered heifer. God, it's good to see you, Jim."

"Hello," said Jim McNeely, taking her two hands. He felt a strange prickling at the nape of his neck. He looked her slowly up and down. "Little old Mazie Wales turned out to be a big physical blonde."

"What?" said Madelon Wales.

"Thanks, pal," said Mazie. "You didn't turn out so bad yourself."

"I was telling Jim," said Madelon Wales, almost gobbling with excitement, "That Dr. Wales would have been so proud. He would have taken real satisfaction in thinking that we had some part in launching Jim's career."

"I know I ought to be grateful, Mrs. Wales," said Jim McNeely, winking at Mazie. "Like a cat that somebody threw in a pond when it was a kitten so it could learn how to swim. I learned."

Mazie threw back her shimmering blonde head and gave a rocketing peal of laughter. "You picked up a nasty sense of humor in the process," she said.

"Oh, now Jim," said Madelon Wales, her blanched expression quickly overcome with warmth and *joie de vivre* and the two martinis she had swallowed. "Human beings are fallible, and life is a gay, never-ending whirl. A gay mad—" Her voice fell. "Oh, hello, Clayton."

"Where the hell did everybody disappear to?" said the thick-bodied young man stalking up.

"Pluto! You old bull-shooter!" said Jim McNeely, grasping his old friend's hand and moving into a warm-back-slapping embrace, like a South American *abrazo*.

"Stabber!" cried Pluto, his voice choking, nearly overcome with emotion.

"Stabber! Gahd damn, *Stabber!* It's so goo—! Mazie, this *man!* I mean this man and me—! I mean, Jim—Jesus! We had it! Mazie, this guy and I had some—! We got to go somewhere and sit down and talk, Stabber!" Pluto LeMayne was drunk but deeply moved. Jim McNeely saw at once the change in him. His state was a kind of firm, settled drunkenness. He was not the vital, revved-up youth that Jim McNeely had put on a sleeper one night in the long ago. His face was now puffy and mottled red and gray, and any sparkle of humor and humanity that had once been present there had been boiled into a kind of doughy nobody-ness.

"How come you didn't send for me, Pluto?" said Jim McNeely reproach-fully, his dark brows furrowed as if with great concern. "I waited a hell of a long time."

"Aw-w man, we got to talk!" said Pluto, clinging to his hand. "I've had hell. Bad luck all the way. We got to go somewhere an' talk."

Madelon Wales had begun to look sick. She said in a give-up voice, "I'll leave you children to it. I came with Susie Ponelli and she's been wig-wagging to go for half an hour."

"Good-bye, Mrs. Wales. Sure am glad you could come," said Jim McNeely as she departed, a harrowed look on her face. He turned back to Pluto and Mazie. "Now, how about us men and women havin' a drink."

"I'm for it!" said Mazie slapping her hands together. "Clayton doesn't drink, but I'm *ready!*"

"The hell I don't," said Pluto.

Lee McNeely had hardly seen her husband since they arrived, and she had not sought him out. She was certain he would ask her how she liked her little vine covered cottage or something like that and she didn't know what she would say or what kind of look she would be able to keep on her face, or whether she would be able to hide the hurt and anger and confusion that welled up in her eyes like recurring waves of heat and sickness as she walked about, a semi-dazed stranger in the big rooms and corridors of "her house."

Charley Dupre came up behind her and slipped his hand around her waist with an intimacy neither warranted nor welcome. He gave a low wolfish growl in her ear. Lee disengaged herself and looked at him with distaste.

"I'll bet you growl like that at all the girls," she said. She knew that

Charley Dupre was in the picture now and so she made an effort to keep from showing her utter dislike for him.

"That's my passionate Saturday night growl, kitten. Just for you."

Charley joked but his light blue eyes looked into hers with the unabashed, naked frankness of a well-bred satyr and it was clear that he had only one thought in mind. His pointed chin and slick, acne-scarred face and close-lying blonde hair gave him a peeled, sensuous look that made Lee uncomfortable.

"What do you think of the local stuffed-shirtdom?" he said in close, conspiratorial tones. "Ain't they a bunch of jerks?"

"No, they're not a bunch of jerks. They're nice people who were kind enough to come to our house-warming. They didn't have to, you know."

"They're jerks and they've got egg on their faces. All of 'em. They came to inspect you and pick you to pieces. Don't let 'em get away with it, kitten. Hate 'em. Cut their guts out every chance you get. That way they'll come to respect you and, eventually, accept you."

"You really are an odd-ball, Charley Dupre."

"Odd but honest. And passionate. Let's run away to Acapulco and make crazy love on the beach." He slid his arm about her waist again, laughingly, but with the same penetrating, cloven-hoofed seriousness underneath. Lee knew she could not keep on play-acting and being nice to him another minute. She peeled his fingers from her hip-bone and freed herself and stepped into the door of the powder room next to the small elevator.

"I'll be ready to go in five minutes," she said with a sweet acid smile. "Right after I throw up."

Jim McNeely steered Mazie into the panelled library and sank down heavily into the deep sofa. He patted the cushion beside him for her to sit.

"My dogs are barking," he said. "Damn! Look at the books! Come over and borrow some. I'll fix you up with a library card."

"I can't read," Mazie said, looking at him brightly. "Don't you remember?" She sat sideways on the sofa next to him, her arm resting on the back. She had, indeed, turned out to be a "big, physical blonde," and a very attractive one, he thought, as he approved the changes of fifteen years. The pouting baby look was gone from her face, and her hair was a burnished gold. The fifteen years had added sophistication and frank, full-blooming sensuousness to her face and figure. She was at ease and she had her mother's confidence and poise, as if from unshakable inner knowledge that in spite of all she was of and with the right people in this place and time.

"Well, Jim," she said after a pause, "this is wonderful. You look simply great."

"You don't look so bad, yourself. Old Pluto must've been treating you right."

"That's another story," she said. "But you're the star of this party. Let's talk about you."

"What do you think of the 'casa'?"

"It's atrocious. It always was, but it's what you need for now. I should have sent a potted plant or something for the house-warming. But I have another little present for you. I've been saving it a long time." She opened the small purse in her lap and drew out a smaller box wrapped in faded red tissue paper and tied with a green ribbon and bow that had been iron flat from long years of storage under things in a drawer. A little Christmas tag with a holly wreath was tied to the package with a gold string. In a girlish hand the card said, 'To Jim from Mazie with Love.' She placed it on his palm and said, "Your Christmas present. Fifteen years late. It just means congratulations and welcome back to the old home town."

Jim McNeely looked at the package, turning it in his fingers. "Golly. Sticker says, 'Don't open til Xmas.'"

"It's all right. Open it. That Xmas is ancient history."

He slipped off the ribbon and unwrapped the dry paper and opened the box, then lifted off a powdery bat of cotton. Underneath lay a pair of square, gold plated, now tarnished cuff links of a style no longer in vogue. Picking one up between thumb and middle finger he read the old English letters 'J M' engraved on its face and chuckled warmly to himself but didn't say anything.

She said, "Isn't that tender and girlish. I just wanted you to know my heart was in the right place then even if I didn't show it. The head sometimes gets in the way of the heart."

He said, "If I remember rightly I gave your Christmas present to a whore at the Ajax Hotel."

Mazie's response was a shriek of delight. "How touching! What a relief to know that you didn't go completely unconsoled! God, the worrying I did about you!"

285

He put the cuff link back in the box and slipped the box in his coat pocket. "I kept up with you pretty well in the papers."

"While you were busy making forty million dollars?"

"Just a couple, so far."

"Jim." She looked at him with wide, serious eyes. "That's the best Christmas present I could ever have. Knowing that you've made it. Wonderfully well. I'm real proud to know you. I can't tell you how happy I am for you. And I know you have a wonderful wife. I got just a glimpse of her and she looks like a great gal. I want to get to know her and do everything I can to make her like our old home town."

"You might as well start right now," he said, rocking tiredly to his feet. "Here she comes."

Lee McNeely entered the room looking travel-worn and unhappy and angry. She was closely pursued by Charley Dupre, by now well oiled with Scotch mist, his arms outstretched as if in flight as he did a silly titchy-toe dance right behind her.

"Shoot this cuckoo and I'll cook him," she said crossly. "He says this is the mating-dance of the Long Island bull-bat."

Seeing Jim McNeely, Charley Dupre went into a sharp banking turn and circled out of the room, making loud squawking noises like a frustrated cockatoo.

"Sweetie," said Jim McNeely. "This is a special old friend I want you to meet, Mazie LeMayne."

"Hello, Mazie," said Lee casually, knowing well who Mazie was but determined not to give any hint of recognition or attach any importance to the introduction. "Jim, sweetheart, I'm beat. I'd like to go to bed, but there are two gentlemen who seem to have settled down to an all night drinking party in what I presume is our bedroom. Do you think I'd bother them if I put on my pjs and slipped quietly into bed?"

"You poor dear," said Mazie. "What a day you must have had! Jim, why don't you take a stick and drive us all out! Stop the music and close the bars. I'll lead the way. Lee, I'll call you soon. I want to get to know you under less hectic circumstances." She took Jim McNeely's hand and pressed it firmly. "Good show, old man. You really have it made."

33

WHEN THE OIL BUSINESS REALLY SHIFTED BACK into gear after VJ-Day, the wildcatters, big and little, corporate and individual, began to punch down holes across the land in ever increasing numbers—11,756 wildcats were drilled in 1951 alone, mostly dry. But they found a lot of oil in those years, big accumulations like Scurry County and the Williston Basin in the Dakotas, and hundreds of little puddles. There was still romance in the oil game because it was still possible for some half-smart country boy with a lot of luck and guts to stumble into a million dollars. And there was plenty of backing for wildcatters then because the revered and maligned statutory depletion allowance and a generous number of allowable producing days gave investors enough of an incentive to gamble on the long-shot of wildcat drilling.

At the same time the majors were hunting for oil overseas in many parts of the world. A few of them struck it fabulously rich around the dry and desolate fringes of the Persian Gulf. In the small, all but unknown sheikdom of Kuwait a single field (actually discovered just before the war) revealed itself, as development drilling resumed, to contain more reserves of crude oil than all of the known fields in the continental United States, and once drilled, it cost but a few cents a barrel to produce.

This Middle East and other cheap foreign oil began to knock at the gates of America, the greatest oil market in the world, and domestic per-well production was gradually reduced by the state regulatory bodies as the foreign oil came in, and the price per barrel began to drift downward. Those that had foreign oil said it was in the interest of national defense to let the foreign oil come in, so we could save back our own domestic oil to use in time of international crisis. Those that didn't have any foreign oil said it was in the interest of national defense to keep it out so we could maintain a profitable, hence healthy and vigorous, domestic industry that would be able to develop and deliver the oil needed when war clouds made the foreign oil unavailable. This was all confusing to the old oil country philosopher, but it did kind of give him a tug to see so much patriotic concern on both sides over national defense.

"Boatman, you dumb shit!" said the man with the cigar clamped in his jaw as he shuffled the cards. "I hope your gin rummy is better than your goddamn lousy golf was today. I got six hundred and fifty bucks to get back from these crooked bastards."

"Why, you clumsy horse's-ass," replied Boatman angrily, stirring his Beefeaters-on-rocks then sucking his finger, "if I hadn't pulled you out on those last two holes, this McNeely joker woulda ended up *owning* that little old two-bit flour mill your daddy left you!"

This gentle badinage took place in the men's tavern of the Glen View Country Club, whose wide windows looked out over the green velvet 18th green and the rolling tree-lined fairways beyond. It was five o'clock, and the room was well filled by now with golfers in from the course at the end of the afternoon. They sat grouped at tables where gin rummy and bridge and drinks and the rehashing of golf rounds occupied their full attention.

The first speaker, Joss Lattimer, owner of the Lattimer Grain & Milling Company, was partnered with Gene Boatman, an affluent oil producer, in double gin rummy, as they had been partners in golf against Jim McNeely and Ted Neighbors, the banker. The first two, in their mid-thirties, were second and third generation Mandarins respectively who had succeeded to the wealth, power, and basic toughness of their forebears and lacked only the desire and drive which had enabled those elders to carve out of nothing the fortunes which the younger men were content to guard and enjoy without adding to creatively. These were peers of the highest stratum of local society. With his usual questionable degree of accuracy Dent Paxton broadbrushed it thus: if you had had your money for two generations you became automatically one of the "fine old families" of Winfield. If you lost the money, you lost the rating in one.

The hands were dealt across the table corners and the adversaries began to draw and discard cards and sip the drinks which sat upon the small tables at their elbows.

"This goddamn McNeely ought to be outlawed as a pro," grumbled Joss, chomping his cigar as he played, still stinging from his defeat on the fairways. "If he's a seven handicap I'm a goddamn thirty! Two birdies on the front nine and one on the back."

Jim McNeely smiled contentedly and played his cards.

"Quit belly-aching, Joss," said Ted Neighbors. "He turns in his score cards same as you do. The handicaps are figured on a computer. You're just erratic."

"What was his handicap when he started out here? Nineteen?" said Boatman. "In ten months he's down to a seven."

"And he's won twenty-thousand dollars from me in the process, god-damit!" said Lattimer. "He's a damn two or a three if I ever saw one."

"Some people are natural athletes," said Ted Neighbors, "and some people will swing like a wash-woman all their lives. Jim just happens to be one of the naturals."

"Aw, you make me sick at my stomach," said Joss Lattimer. "You already got his goddamn bank account. Quit brown-nosin' him! A damn banker will do anything for a deposit!"

"Fellers, it's just beginner's luck," said Jim McNeely, smiling. "I'm just getting the hang of this game. Up until I came back to Winfield I hadn't had a golf club in my hands since I was a kid, when I used to caddy out here."

"I knew it!" cried Joss. "Another goddamn ex-caddy! They'll sandbag you every time!"

"We-ll," said Jim McNeely, studying his cards seriously, "I reckon I'll go down for four." He laid his hand down. "You gonna undercut me, Joss, old buddy?"

"God damn!" Joss said, throwing his cards violently onto the table. "The son-of-a-bitch has *got* to be a crook! He goes down on the third card and here I am with forty fucking points in my hand!"

The other players at the table and a couple of onlookers hollered and cackled with glee. Everyone enjoyed seeing Joss Lattimer burn when he lost because he was reputed to be the tightest man in town. It was said he still had the first dollar his daddy ever gave him.

"Whoever let a fucking ex-caddy in this goddamn club, anyway?

Boatman, you simple son-of-a-bitch, what're you laughing at? This is costing you money, too!"

Everybody laughed some more and nobody took Joss Lattimer seriously. He did hate to lose but this was all the more funny because he sat on a sprawling grain empire that produced more income than he could count by himself, and nobody felt sorry for him. Jim McNeely winked at Ted Neighbors and smiled contentedly.

"I'm just a poor boy that's worked hard and scratched his way up in the world so I could associate with you high-toned bastards. But you know what? If I shut my eyes and just listened to you talk, I'd swear to God I was back in the bunkhouse."

And so it was that in a few short months Jim McNeely had moved into the top layer of Winfield society, and if not exactly accepted as one of their number, he was nevertheless admitted provisionally to the company of the elect as a tough, formidable competitor and a *comer* who could not be ignored.

With the big eastern money behind him now and know-how in the oil business under his belt, Jim McNeely felt he was at last on his way. His new, expanded organization was brain-centered in fifteenth-floor offices in the Citizen's Bank Building. From there he began an almost furious campaign of wildcat drilling. He could move in a hurry, and he didn't have to go through channels to a head office somewhere to get decisions, and so the better deals began to gravitate his way. Brokers knew he had money to spend and would buy anything that had geological merit provided the terms were reasonable, especially if there was a little "romance" in the deal—that is, at least an outside chance to hit something big. At times he had six wildcats going, two with rigs of his own and four with contract rigs in widely scattered parts of the oil country from Mississippi to Wyoming to New Mexico. He was giving his eastern mullets a lot of action for their money, and sometimes when a deal looked especially promising he exercised the option he had reserved in his arrangement with the mullets, to carry an extra quarter interest for himself at his own cost.

To keep up with the widely scattered operations he bought a reconditioned Lockheed Lodestar and put a pilot and co-pilot-mechanic on the company payroll, to the distress of Lee, who did not like airplanes, and of Jeff Dofflemyer, who didn't mind flying when necessary but was appalled at the added expense. Dent was delighted. It was he in fact who planted the seedling idea and fertilized it to fruition. He loved to fly and he personally supervised the redecoration of the plane in Chinese blue with the easy chairs and gin rummy table, divan, picture windows and a fully stocked bar and galley for preparing cocktails and exotic hors d'oeuvres in flight. Dent was seldom left behind when Three-Two-Tango (the plane's official call-letters) headed down the runway.

Jim McNeely was absent from Winfield as much as he was at home. Lee at first was always invited to go along when the trip was to be an overnight one. But after a while she realized that she was a non-productive drag on the fast moving operation and thereafter stayed at home and tried to find something to do with herself.

"I'll open with two spades," said Mazie LeMayne, closing her bridge hand like a fan and setting it down precisely on the table where she riffled it in her manicured fingers. The foursome of well-groomed women was one of a number of like foursomes scattered about the Chinese Garden, a handsome room done in red lacquer, silk screens, and figurines of ancient Cathay in the club house of the Glen View Country Club.

"Hag!" said the angular woman with the expensive platinum-mink coif at her left. She spoke in a deep resonant voice almost like a man's. "Talk about luck! Rich, good-looking, and sexy, too! I pass!"

"Bid 'em up, kid," said Mazie, winking at Lee McNeely, her partner.

"Oh, dear," said Lee, sighing at the insignificant cards in her hand but remembering that an opening two bid by her partner was an imperious command to bid something, anything. But what!

"Maid," the deep-voiced lady called to a passing Negress in black uniform with tiny white apron and head-piece. "Fetch me another Bloody Mary, please. Everybody else ready?"

"Mm," said Lee, pondering her cards. "No, not for me, thank you."

"Just three then," said the lady. "And hurry. I'm getting desperate. I haven't held an ace since I sat down."

"Two—diamonds," said Lee finally.

"You have to bid three, sweetie," said Mazie.

"I'm sorry. I know that. Three diamonds," said Lee.

"Pass," said the lady on Lee's left. "And remind me to tell you—this will slay you—I just thought of it when I saw that prissy waitress—what

Emily Service said to Brad and what she *did* to him, while he was *asleep*—when she heard what went on with the colored showgirl during the boys' latest golf junket to Las Vegas!"

"Tell!" thundered the platinum-mink lady. "My God! Now!"

"Spill it," said Mazie avidly. "Tell all."

"Play the hand," said the lady with the information. "This little morsel is worth your undivided attention. Mazie has cards, obviously. I will relate the hair-raising details while my darling partner deals the next hand."

The bidding went on. Mazie bid three hearts and Lee, remembering vaguely that she had to keep things going until game was bid, said four spades. Their opponents having passed supinely, Mazie bid four no-trump then Lee, suddenly tired of trying to remember rules of a game which she despised and feeling confused and unhappy said, "I pass."

"Aay-ee!" cried Mazie with annoyance, throwing up her hands. "You can't pass! I'm asking for your aces, dear!"

"Never mind," said the lady with the man's voice. "She's a big girl and this is for a cent a point. She passed. Play your four no-trump, sweetie."

"I'm sorry," said Lee. She shook her head. "I'll never learn this game." She spread down her cards. "See, I do have the ace of clubs by itself."

"Aay-ee!" wailed Mazie again.

"Oh, don't break my heart," said deep-voice. "You'll make four no-trump in a walk."

"But I have a little slam in spades!" cried Mazie. "It's a lay-down!"

"I'm very sorry," said Lee, disgusted with herself and so generally miserable that she hardly listened, after the hand had been played, to the shocking things that somebody named Emily had said to her husband, Brad, and what she had done to him with brown Dye-an-Shine while he was asleep, in reprisal for his alleged misconduct in Las Vegas.

Lee's first year in Winfield was the most trying period of her life to date. When Jim McNeely was at home he seldom came into the house without bringing someone with him. Lee wrote her father that her principal household duties consisted of running an open bar and restaurant from 5 p.m. on. Sensing her dislike of this, Jim McNeely told her, half defensively, half apologetically that it was necessary if he was going to get on top of the local situation and stay there. Competition for good oil deals was fierce and there was a lot of politicking to do.

After the first few months she learned to stay out of her own kitchen. Mondrella, her cook, was a high-caste professional who could handle any menu for any number of guests on any notice, and nothing disturbed her but interference and advice from the lady of the house. She drew more pay than Lee had made as a school teacher, as did Richard, the tall, thin-nosed colored butler and houseman who also chauffered Lee when she would allow it. The gardening was contracted to a pair of Mexican brothers who came in a truck and worked and went away without speaking to her, having learned what the place required from the previous owners. It was almost as if she were living in a resort hotel that was not really her home but a place to which someone before her had already imparted a character which was too old and set to be changed by her.

The fact was, she soon found, that there was really nothing for her to do at all but live and be waited upon. This was rather pleasant at first but took on uncomfortable undertones as the time passed. She felt so utterly unnecessary, so completely useless. Jim McNeely told her, "Don't fret about being a lady of leisure, sweetheart. What you've got to do now is a lot more important than frying my bacon and eggs."

And so she tried to find enthusiasm to throw herself into the role of the gay, sparkling, witty, and charming hostess to the strange groups of people that streamed in and out of the house. Half the time the bar was not closed down before eleven and their whiskey bill, she knew, must be astronomical. Jim McNeely, largely through Charley Dupre, tied in almost from the beginning with the young very rich crowd who gravitated together more on the basis of their common affluence and freedom from confining jobs and responsibilities than because they liked each other or had other interests in common. It was a glib, cynical, and sophisticated set whose members in general took little seriously except the business of being rich and staying that way.

The days of their lives in Winfield were filled with golf, gin rummy, bridge, and cocktail hours, and they seemed to rush from one to the other as if in mortal fear of blank spaces of time in between with nothing to occupy them but their own thoughts. There were regularly one or two tables of cards going in the late afternoon in the bar or sun room of Lee's towered and turreted home. People came and people left, occasionally total strangers among them. She could not gear her mind or heart to enter into the spirit of the apparently carefree life which everyone seemed to enjoy almost with hilarity.

A number of women attempted to take her under their wings for one reason or another, Mazie LeMayne among them. Lee tried to be interested and to show her appreciation for the luncheons-cum-style-shows, the bridge afternoons, the interminable pre-dinner cocktail hours when the "boys" separated themselves into tight groups around the bar or card tables and the "girls," left to themselves, yammered and laughed raucously about their servants, their children, and the intimate personal affairs of those not present. But she could not join up, partly because she felt a small-town girl's sense of inferiority in the big city and partly because the vapidity of the life appalled her. Try though she did she could not make herself into an eager neophyte anxious to be initiated into the narrow, exclusive, meaningless society.

Sensing her discontent, Dent Paxton, in his whimsical philosopher's way, tried to comfort her. "Don't take this circus too seriously, little buddy. You will find that there are very few people in this jolly new milieu of ours who live lives of any real significance. Those few, unfortunately, don't seem to have any particular time for the likes of thee and me. A larger number of our new friends give token service to one or another of the local Klaverns of charity or culture, but more for the sake of appearance than out of real concern for the poor starving heathens. Most of our new playmates dedicate their lives wholeheartedly to pleasuring themselves, reserving a minimal time to carefully rearing their atrocious brats in their own flawed images. But it is really very simple to fit in. You have only to stay up late, drink deep of the laughing waters, and burn your incense at sunset to the God of Fun. Do that, or *appear* to do it, and you'll get along fine."

"Ugh!" said Lee.

Pluto and Mazie and Charley Dupre seemed to be in her house every time she looked up. Jim McNeely included the LeMaynes in nearly everything he did. He justified this, rather lamely, on the grounds that Pluto was his old "oil field buddy-buddy." But Lee could not believe that one as vital as Jim McNeely could really be interested in such a sloppy alcoholic sponge as Pluto had become. It annoyed her tremendously to come home from shopping in the late afternoon and find her husband and Mazie playing gin rummy in the solarium, laughing and talking about their misspent youth, with Pluto sitting on a stool at the bar goggle-eyed.

During this time there was something else that occupied a large part of her mind. Though painful, it sometimes seemed almost a welcome distraction. Her father had suffered another stroke and lay half paralyzed in his home in McCamey. She begged and stormed at him to let her move him to Winfield to her home, or to a hospital or rest home, where she could properly see after him, but he firmly refused.

"Sissy, don't force me into that," he said in his halting, half mumbled speech. "Outside of seeing you, all I have to look forward to is dying in peace in this old house, in this old bed where Mamma died. I'm taking a hell of a time doing it, but I don't mind dying, this way. I'd be unhappy and scared to death in some strange bed somewhere. You don't have to come out to see me so often. Isidro takes good care of me. Just call me up on the phone every few days and tell me how you are."

Nonetheless, Lee made the long drive to McCamey every other Monday and returned on Wednesday. At first Jim McNeely insisted on sending her out and back in the plane but she preferred to stay on the ground even though it was a hard six hour drive each way. She hated that airplane. Not so much because she disliked flying, which she did, but because the craft symbolized her new way of life which she had come to despise.

Jim McNeely called her from the office one morning before ten o'clock.

"Hey, sweetheart, pack your party pants right quick and let's go to New York."

"Jim! You and *me*? I mean—wonderful!" Lee cried.

She was almost breathless with excitement. She had no burning desire to see New York though she had never been there. But to go somewhere, anywhere, alone with her husband—! Shades of Monterrey! "*When*, sweetheart? What should I take? How long will we stay? What's the deal?"

"Oh, hell, just take a toothbrush. We'll buy you a whole new outfit when we get there. Have the boy drive you out to the airport. Be there for an eleven o'clock take-off. We'll be in New York in time for a late supper. I got to go up and sweet-talk my mullets and get some more money. Charley Dupre will have to go along for this. And Dent, of course, and Jeff, because we'll have to draw some new contracts. Oh yeah, and I told old Pluto I'd give him a ride next time I went to the Big City so I asked him to come along and bring Mazie if he wanted too. We'll have a bash!"

Lee's face fell and the joy went out of her. She was silent a moment. "Jim, do you really think I should go? I mean, if it's business you'll be so busy."

"Now look, sugar foot, I'll take care of the business. But this is a party, too. For you and me and everybody. Just get packed like I tell you and be there. On time." He hung up, and she knew that he was disappointed and slightly angry at her cool reception of the grand idea.

34

EIGHT MEN SAT AROUND A POLISHED MAHOGANY table in the conference room of Thorp and Saye, Attorneys and Counselors at Law, in a high tower overlooking the financial district of lower Manhattan. Jim McNeely sat on one side of the table flanked by Jeff Dofflemyer, Charley Dupre, and Dent Paxton. On the other side sat Mr. Arthur Fell, a graying senior member of the firm which represented the next three gentlemen whose names were Messrs. Canby, Warfield, and Delano, the first two middle-aged men and the third in his late twenties, all obviously men of breeding, polish, and substance. The table was covered with a disarray of county land maps, geological contour maps, sheafs of paper with typed columns of production figures, cost figures, and reserves estimates.

"Gentlemen, that's about the story to date," said Jim McNeely, leaning back and scratching his widow's peak with his pencil. "It's not world-shaking but it's not too bad, either. We've drilled nine prospects together. Six were dry. One's a non-commercial stinker. Two produced. Along with the two keepers we've completed a third producer offsetting one of them—on the Terry County block. The engineer's and geologist's reports show without any doubt that you've got reserves in that block alone that will pay out your overall investment and double your money in the long haul. The well in Reagan County is just so-so. It'll get back drilling costs in time but I wouldn't recommend drilling any more holes there for the time being. We'll watch what the well does and probably farm out some of our acreage in the block to another operator, retaining an override. What we need to think about now is looking for something better."

"How long will that Reagan County well take to pay out?" said young Delano.

"Oh, about three and a half years at current production rates," said Jim McNeely.

"Well, my stars, a three and a half year pay-out sounds pretty good to me," said the young man, showing how sharp he was. "Why don't we drill the lease ourselves? Where else can we invest money and get it back in that time?"

Jim McNeely shook his head and smiled warmly. "This feller won't let me get away with a thing. Dent, make a note of that. Don't ever try to rinky-doo Mr. Delano." His face took on an earnest sincere expression. "Seriously, it's a good question, and here's my answer. That well is producing from a very thin pay section. It doesn't look like the reserves are there. The well's cutting water and the history of other wells in the same general area is that if you get water the water is gonna increase. I could be wrong, but I don't make any money unless you people make money and my nose tells me let's don't plant any more dough in this block right now. Let's let somebody else try it on a farm-out basis. We'll still have acreage left if they do better. Let's spend our time and money looking for something with a little more juice in it."

This pleased the two older mullets and they nodded at one another and one of them, Mr. Warfield, obviously favorably impressed, said, "I'll buy that. After all we don't know anything about the oil business. We're investing in a man who does."

Nodding his appreciation of the compliment, Jim McNeely said, "To date I can assure you gentlemen that you own oil in the ground in Terry County, as proven by these engineering and geological reports, that will pay back your investment with a good profit. Now we're out of money and out of business. The question is, do we go on or do we quit? On the next go-round we may be snake-bit and drill a hundred percent string of dry holes, or," he shrugged and smiled a sudden boyish, disarming smile, "we may just stumble onto another East Texas, who knows? I don't."

"Or another Scurry County," said Dent.

Jim McNeely flashed a glance full of sudden hate at Dent Paxton and went on, "We've got five new drilling deals to show you and another that we might get, though it's not certain yet. These are all deals I can and will drill on my own or with other partners if you folks aren't interested. They've all got merit. The first one here," he took a folded contour map out of a large envelope, opened it, and smoothed it out on the table, "is in Schleicher County. It's a little east of the real oily country, but it's got good seismic on it, major company shooting. I know that because the fellow that brought it to me is a geophysicist that used to be with Consul. He quit 'em and went independent. Consul hasn't leased the prospect because the ranch it's on has been tied up in an estate. This ex-doodle-bugger is getting ready to marry the daughter of the lawyer that represents the estate. That's how he got the lease, no offense intended to the legal profession," he said, winking at the solemn lawyer. "That's just the way these things come about."

The group around the table leaned forward with interest and approval and gazed down at the map with the lined whirls which said that some trained interpreter of electronically recorded dynamite shock waves who happened, also, to be unfaithful to his former employer, thought that there were at this place subterranean geologic conditions conducive to the entrapment of commercial quantities of petroliferous hydrocarbons. Titillated by the near-larcenous flavor of the deal, the mullets individually concluded that this was a reasonable opportunity to make a further investment.

It was one of those chill, windy days of early autumn in New York. The air was like wine touched with a smoky cast of automobile exhaust and a sea smell. Lee found the surging, impersonal canyoned city with its professional, aloof, well-groomed people exciting. Forbidding but fascinating, in fact, all but overwhelming. Mazie flipped about the city with an almost contemptuous familiarity, taking her in tow as they raced from Bergdorf-Goodman's to the Museum of Modern Art to '21' to Sak's Fifth Avenue, Mazie calling sales people and head waiters by first names and taking real pains to make Lee see the best of everything. By the end of the second day in Mazie's care, Lee had almost begun to like her, though it was more a feeling of dependence and gratitude than trust.

At five o'clock on the second day they arrived package laden back at the huge corner suite at the Pierre where Jim McNeely, under Charley Dupre's tutelage, had set up his command post. They found a cocktail party going full-out. Loud talk laced with laughter greeted them as they entered. The principal mullets were there along with a number of good-looking, well-dressed women of assorted ages who Lee presumed were the female mullets, though she never was able to sort them out. People came and went and Lee found herself talking to a pleasant, attractive older man. They stood at the window looking out across the Park as the murky shadows of dusk moved across from the Hudson. After they had chatted long enough for the beginnings of identity to register the urbane gentleman pressed her hand and said, "My dear, it's suddenly clear to me that I'm at the wrong party. I must be down the hall. I'll just slip out quietly. You're very charming. Good luck. Good-bye." Lee was delighted and told Mazie, who told everybody in loud hilarious tones and everybody began to tease Lee about luring strange men in off the streets.

Drinks flowed and canapes and shrimp were passed and nibbled and more people came and went and a reasonable dinner hour came and passed. Lee, who had been enjoying herself immensely, nursing two drinks for three hours, finally had a third and then began to lose the aura of glamor and excitement as fatigue, both physical and emotional, and the beginnings of boredom set in. It was the same old trouble she had at home in Winfield. Everybody had drunk as much as anybody ought to, had talked up a Kansas storm about nothing that mattered, and now it was time to eat, or go to the theater, or to the opera, or to a dog fight, or bed! Anything! But they kept on. Drinking and talking louder and less coherently and more meaninglessly every half-hour that passed.

Mazie seemed to gain strength and glitter as the evening wore on. She could hold her liquor and a lot of it and she laughed a loud, slapping man's laugh at the men's off-color jokes and the men drew her from one group to another because she was a good-looking and appreciative audience. They gathered her in and put arms around her shoulders as someone uncorked another corker. Then the little group erupted like a big fat balloon exploding from accumulated gas with an obscene flubbery aftermath, with Mazie's gay outlandish shrieks of laughter leading the chorus. Lee enjoyed a joke, even an off-color one if it wasn't too dirty and was really funny, but most jokes were appalling to her and she didn't laugh if they were only dirty and not funny and after the first try or two the little groups ceased to gather her in. She felt a kind of angry envy and admiration at Mazie's knack of laughing at anything and of responding to a really dirty story with unbridled shrieks of merriment. It was a real asset.

Jim McNeely had shed his coat and loosened his tie which set him apart and was in character with his role of rough, uninhibited Texas oil man. He was successively engaged in long, close conversations at one side of the room or in an adjoining bedroom with one after another of the important mullets, nailing down and clinching the commitments made by each over the conference table in the afternoon.

"You folks ought to come down and see where your money's going," he said to Mr. Warfield. "We can't stage any spectaculars for you because we don't know when we're going to drill into something important and we can't wait when we do. Rig time costs too much. But I'll call you up when we're getting down to where we're looking for the pay and you can come down and see what happens. If she's dry, you at least can see what all that money goes for. However it turns out, when it's finished we'll take off on a hunt and that I can guarantee. You'll have quail or deer meat or both for your freezer, whether we get any oil or not. The company has a hunting lease that's well stocked with game."

"My dear," said Mr. Warfield to a slender, silver gray woman in an expensive sheath who came up just then. "Jim has invited us to Texas to slay a hundred-thousand-dollar deer. Shall we go?"

"By all means," said Mrs. Warfield. "But to El Morocco, not Texas. We're an hour late now. Sandy will be squiffed and Doris will be livid. Mr. McNeely, it was very nice. I'm so glad you are going to make us rich. Your wife is charming. So vivacious. What utterly gorgeous blonde hair."

"My dear, that's not—"

"Good you could come, Mrs. Warfield. Make old Bob here come down and see what we're doing with you-all's money. You come, too. We'll cook up a hunt and a square dance. Something special, just for you."

"Good-bye, Mr. McNeely. Do come, Robert." She called to someone across the room, "Alex, dear, hold the elevator. We're coming."

Mr. Warfield winked as he was towed away. "Just send me a little oil in a bottle, old boy."

The party settled itself down, as usual, to the hard core drinkers, and those who could not escape from them. Lee had taken off her shoes and had sunk down exhausted into the couch, putting her feet up. She was whipped, having made an unsatisfying evening meal out of too-rich hors d'oeuvres, it now being after 10:30 p.m. She wondered with dread whether their midnight dinner would be steaks sent up to the suite or an alcoholic taxiing across town to one or the other of two small restaurants which Charley Dupre and Mazie were loudly arguing about.

Dent drifted in from somewhere, pleasantly tight, smiling quietly. He sat down on the couch and put Lee's feet in his lap and began to rub them.

"You angel," she sighed. "They're numb." It was strange that she did not mind Dent's touching her. Yet Charley Dupre's touch made her flesh crawl. "Where's Jeff?" She had missed the only other face in the party that made her comfortable.

"That German farmer is gonna eat his supper at seven o'clock if it hare-lips the governor," said Dent. "He took off to eat and go to the UN. They've got a night session going tonight. The asinine Russians are acting up again."

"Imagine," said Lee with a wry smile. "Here we are in *New York. We* could be going to the UN. Or a play. Or just walking around looking at the tall buildings. And so here we sit in a blinding hotel room, lapping up the booze. We might as well be at home lapping it up."

"You don't get the idea," said Dent. "If you know you're in New York gettin' loaded, that makes it better."

"Oh, I'm glad you told me. Nobody explained it to me before."

"Hey, Lee, sweetheart!" Jim McNeely raised up from a group sitting and kneeling in a circle on the floor across the room and waved for her to come over. She slipped into her shoes and forced a look of expectancy on her face and went over and kneeled down by her husband putting her hand on his strong shoulder.

"What are you cats doing, shooting craps?" she said. "I shoot a buck."

The young mullet, Roger Delano, was seated on the floor intently drawing out a crude map on the back of a large sheet of hotel stationery resting on a telephone directory. His young wife, a slender sunbrowned girl with dark hair lapping across her eyes, leaned over his shoulder arguing with him about some point on the map.

"Mombasa is more here, lamb. It's southeast of Nairobi. Not there."

Mazie and Charley Dupre and Pluto were the others in the circle, all attentive to the map maker except Pluto, who sat cross-legged in a stupor, like a young puffy-faced Buddha with a glass in his hand.

"We're givin' birth to a big-game hunt," said Jim McNeely. "You want to go shoot an elephant?" He was well on his way to being tight. His voice had taken on the burr that Lee had come to hate, and in his wrinkled shirt sleeves he showed the weight he had taken on around the waist and neck. A cringe went through her stomach.

"I couldn't possibly eat an elephant," she said with distaste. "If I can't eat 'em, I don't shoot 'em. What else have you got?"

"Aw, for cryin' out loud!" said Jim McNeely, not amused, turning back to the map maker and tapping the map with his middle finger. "Rog and Hazel here have been to this place where you can hunt fourteen different kinds of animals, from elephants down to dik-diks. Well, I mean to do me some of that. This big-game hunting won't last much longer. Not more'n a couple a'years. The natives are gonna kill 'em all off. Right Rog?"

"Right, old boy. African independence. Very bad for hunting. One of my ambitions during my lifetime is to kill at least one of every species that exists. I have well over a hundred now."

Incensed, Lee said, "When you get around to homo sapiens let me know, will you, so I can hide."

"My wife is a comedian," said Jim McNeely. "Listen, just as soon as we finish this next string of wildcats we're gonna take off on a safari. Rog and Hazel are ready. Right, Rog?"

"Absolutely correct."

"Well, count me in," said Lee. "I'll guard the camp and take pictures of you great white hunters sitting on top of your dead elephants."

"We'll make up the party right here," said Jim McNeely, ignoring her and not trying to hide his annoyance. "All of us. The Delanos and Pluto and Mazie and Charley, and the McNeelys if one of us don't turn chicken-hearted."

Under her breath, Lee said, "Oh, God."

"Whee!" cried Mazie.

"There you are," said Jim McNeely. "Mazie's not afraid to shoot an elephant, are you, honey?"

"Can I really kill an elephant?" cried Mazie in a delighted little girl's voice. "Little old Mazie kill a great big enormous elephant with a trunk and tusks and everything?"

"Honey, I'll fix it so you can kill the biggest damn elephant in Africa, and then I'll have his foot mounted for an umbrella-stand and paint his toe-nails gold!"

Mazie clapped her hands together with delight. "How divine! Imagine! Getting to kill an elephant!"

"God," said Lee.

"Whee," said Pluto thickly, weaving in his Buddha posture and raising his glass. "Me Jane, you Tarzan."

"Dent, c'mere!" said Jim McNeely sharply, giving orders, the man in charge now buttoning up a deal, the forceful man of action who made decisions and carried them out. "Rog, you and Hazel know Dent Paxton, my vice president in charge of everything up to twenty-five dollars."

As Dent came sauntering over swirling his glass in his slender fingers, Jim McNeely said patronizingly, "A very highly uneducated feller. But he's got a way of impressing reservation clerks and head waiters. Denton, line up one safari. Two-four-six-eight people. And you better come along to mix the drinks. McNeely Oil Company will pick up the tab—we're gonna be scouting out some oil prospects in north Kenya. Set it up for two weeks after the date we ought to finish the last well in the next string. Keep it flexible in case we run into some fishing jobs. Just take care of it. Rog will give you details."

"Yes, B'wana," said Dent, putting his palms together and bowing.

"C-crazy!" shrieked Mazie rocking ecstatically on her hips and leaning forward and pressing Jim McNeely's face between her palms.

"Oh, God," said Lee McNeely again under her breath, raising her eyes to the ceiling.

35

IN THE LATE FIFTIES AND EARLY SIXTIES THE
international oil companies encountered a grievous problem that
elicited little sympathy or concern from anybody but themselves,
though it might well have, since it involved a major part of the world's
reserves of hydrocarbon energy.

The undeveloped countries—which some years before had encouraged
or at least permitted the oil seekers to come into their wild domains and
spend millions trying to find oil, on the basis of a fifty-fifty split if the
foreigners were successful, later, in the few places where major discoveries resulted—promptly and without batting a lash said fifty-fifty was all
right before the foreigners found oil but now that they had struck it rich
the split would be sixty-forty or seventy-five-twenty-five, or better, in the
local's favor, and what was all this childish talk about sanctity of contract?

If the locals had been able to drink the oil or otherwise use it or pos-
sessed the ability to market it, which they didn't, few doubted they would
have taken it all away, for the greater glory of Allah or some other equally
plausible reason, without a quiver of conscience. The old oil-patch philosopher with grease in his knuckles found this not too surprising since
he had long since arrived at the conclusion that nations are really just
extensions of the people who make them up and that the average camel
driver or rig builder or car salesman or any other member of the human
club you cared to mention, white, black, or sallow—when the chips were
down and cash money was involved, all too often exhibited the morals and
ethics of the Poland-China hog.

Home once again in Winfield, Lee sat before her mirror pinning up the ends of her hair, getting ready to slip quietly into the bed in which her husband was already deeply sleeping—a sleep of exhaustion from the trip and too many nights of late, hard drinking. As she stared without approval at her reflected image she realized that she was losing control of her home, had jeopardized her position as wife-in-charge of the domestic establishment. She realized also that she was losing control of herself, of Lee Thomas Montgomery McNeely, an individual human being given by some higher power into the care and keeping of her own hands for a certain time, to make and do with decently in accordance with certain vague ancient standards of conduct, modified by the hard exigencies of living in the modern present here and now.

The concern and heartache about her poor stroke-crippled father weighed heavily on top of her unhappiness about herself and she knew that she must leave early in the morning, rested or not, to drive to McCamey, for tomorrow was Monday, the day of her regular visit. She would stay Tuesday, a long day of trying to be cheerful and of trying to keep him from being uncomfortable when talk ran out and she had done all of the little things that one can possibly do for a sick person. The end of Tuesday always came as a relief to both of them and the early Wednesday departure for the drive back to Winfield was a time of forced casualness with both hiding the realization that this might be the last time they would ever see each other.

She woke on Monday morning before Jim McNeely was awake, quietly packed her overnight bag, and slipped out of the house, leaving him a note that she had gone to McCamey and would be back Wednesday in the afternoon.

On the long drive, during which she fought sleep that came as an analgesic for discouragement and emotional distress, she stopped several times for coffee even when she did not need gasoline. Speeding across the dusty flat land with the dusty purple mesa country beginning to show up in the distance, she found herself sympathizing with herself in her sad plight and she forced herself, with the old honesty, to admit that she didn't really know exactly what her sad plight was. She was confused and disturbed. She knew she had acted very poorly on the New York trip. The whole past year, in fact. She had been unassertive of her rights and prerogatives as wife to order things, at least part way, the way she wanted them. Yet, she had the old lingering feeling of insecurity, of having been the aggressor in this marriage from the beginning and before. That feeling had been in her mind's background all the way. He hadn't sought her out. She had sought him. She had pursued him and caught him and trapped him when he had been going his lone way, seeking out his own star. She was, in effect, excess baggage who had attached herself to his life. So his goals and his means to them did not please her? So why hadn't she left him alone? This had always put her at a psychological disadvantage with herself when she had felt it was time to assert her position, her prerogative as wife, co-head of the family. And so it had kept her from entering in whole-heartedly into the scheme of his new way of life.

In McCamey she found her father visibly weaker. As he lay there soft, shrunken, and colorless it truly seemed, as he himself had said jokingly, that he clung to life only because he couldn't seem to get the hang of dying. She had so much to talk to him about this time. She had to talk to someone. She had reached a point of intense unhappiness with herself and her situation that required some change, some action, and she did not know what to do or how to do it. But she could not unburden her troubles onto this poor old, worn-out, dying man whom she loved, and whose loss she was already beginning to anticipate and inwardly mourn.

They talked a while in low kidding tones as they always did and the news and the meaningless pleasantries soon ran out. Then Lee Thomas, perhaps with a father's perception sharpened to clairvoyance by his nearness to his earthly end, felt her unhappiness and with a wan hand waved away her protests that he should not talk so much or tire himself or concern his mind with her problems and came to the point.

"Save myself for what, sissy? I haven't got anything to worry about but you. I want to make my time worth something. Anyway, I'm bored. So spill it. What's gone wrong?"

She groaned and sighed a struggling sigh and ran her fingers through her hair, then she quit resisting and sat close to his bed holding his soft limp hand in hers and let open the flood gates. She cried copiously for a few minutes and then she began to talk it out. It wasn't that anything had gone wrong in particular. On the contrary, to all appearances she should be the happiest and most grateful person alive. She had so much, so many things that most women would give their last chance at heaven to have. Oh, there was this old flame that was always around and that annoyed her, but she wasn't really afraid of that. She was sure that Jim McNeely loved her, and a lot of what he did was paying himself back for a lot of hurts and rejections he had suffered when he was young, and incidentally he was enjoying the hell out of it. It was just the *feel* of the thing. She didn't know where they were going, or what they were working for, and she couldn't see anything good or valid at the end of the road they were traveling.

Lee Thomas put up his hand. "Now let's stop right there, sissy. You're too damn general for me. What do you mean the *feel* of the thing? Your husband loves you. He's good to you. You're living pretty well, at least you're not wondering where your next bowl of chili is coming from. Let's analyze what this *feel* is."

"Oh, I don't know, daddy. I guess it's silly, and I'm acting very immature. But it all seems so pointless. It's such an empty life we're living. And these people that we're with all the time—they're so futile! When Jim and I were scrambling and struggling we seemed to have a purpose. I don't remember now what it was, but I didn't have time then to worry about it. Now I feel so utterly useless and unnecessary."

Lee Thomas said, "Most women your age are so dang busy keeping their children out of trouble and trying to feed 'em and give 'em piano lessons on the money available that they haven't got time to worry about where they're *going*."

Lee brushed a dark strand of hair away from her face. "That's part of it. Children. I feel like a steer. Strictly non-productive. And I'll soon be past my prime for the market as dressed beef."

"Well, damn it, have a baby!" The old man seemed to gain strength as he talked and a spark came in his eyes.

"Never!" said Lee positively. "Not until he asks me. That was a part of the deal. I mean, we never talked about it, but it was understood."

"Horse-feathers! Have an *accident!* After all these years you're entitled to it. Listen, sweetheart, you've got to quit apologizing for being his wife. Take hold! Take charge!" He folded his hands across his thin chest and looked at the ceiling. "Everybody has a job to do, and nobody knows for sure what it is. Don't worry about these things. Everybody's circumstances are different. Don't try to reform Jim McNeely, or make him into what you think is 'worthwhile.' Hell, you didn't marry a prophet. You just married a man with a set of problems and a set of qualities and abilities to work them out with. You don't do it for him. But you can help him."

He turned his gaze on her and poked a finger right between her eyes.

"You can help him by taking care of what kind of a person Lee Thomas McNeely is. You see that you're on the right track. Don't try to reform or guide him, or all those rich folks you live with either. Let the Lord take care of them. They don't mean to be anything that's not good. They're like kids turned loose in a candy store. They're bound to eat too much candy. They may get a little fat and flabby, but there's good bone and sinew underneath. And good heart, too. In most, anyway. When the hard times come they'll come through about as good as you and me. Because they're really not much different from you and me. Their circumstances are different, but they're just people. And they're your people now."

He dozed a while, then awoke in late afternoon, and she took the soup and vegetables from Isidro and fed him, and he resumed talking as if he had only paused a breath since his last sentence.

"The Lord put you down on this earth in a place and a time and a set of circumstances, to do your best with what you've got to do with. Now you can't do your best if you go around low-rating all these folks, and showing it. Live with 'em, keep flexible, roll with the punch, but stay in there and mix it up with 'em. Learn how to play this gin-rummy you talk about they waste so much time at. Take up golf. You could belt a golf ball a mile. You don't have to go cuckoo about it. That's just the price of admission to the circus. You got to like these people. Love 'em. That's the ticket. *Love* 'em! That's not to say you approve of everything they do, but approving's not your problem, sweetheart. All you can do to help the situation is to make yourself the very best person you can. Then maybe they'll want to be like you. Remember that and you'll be OK."

He dozed again, and Lee was already feeling better. A surge of warmth and a thousand thoughts created a pleasant turmoil in her chest. Oh, dearest, wonderful daddy. This was what she wanted, this is what she needed. He was suddenly awake again, poking a finger at her.

"You go on that elephant hunt, and I mean you take charge of it. You don't have to shoot an elephant if you don't want to. But don't show you think it's a bunch of silly nonsense if your husband wants to. This hunting business is something pretty deep in a man and you're not going to change it, or him, by preaching about it. You have to whittle away at people without carving 'em so deep it hurts. You just take care that Lee is a good girl, and stick by your husband. Just remember, your main problem is *you*."

It was now toward the end of the day and the square of fall sunlight had moved across the floor and up onto the east wall of the bedroom. Lee Thomas said, "You're feeling better already. I can tell. Now you jump in that bus of yours and get for home. Don't waste any more time on me. You've got a whole new start to make. The sooner the quicker. Get going. I'm fine. I'm going to get up from here next week, anyhow. Now get going. You'll bother me fussing around here all night."

Lee protested that she had planned to stay until her usual departure time tomorrow, but he wouldn't hear to it. "Horse-feathers! Scoot! The time to start something new is right now!"

She felt a kind of relief and elation and resolve and a lifting inner surge that she had not felt in a long, long time. Everything was suddenly clean and bright and new. She did not argue but hurriedly repacked her overnight bag.

Bending over her father she kissed him tenderly and said, "You're a wonderful man, my daddy."

"That's OK about that," he said, "But you do what I tell you. And leave off that dad-gum diaphragm do-majig, or whatever it is that keeps the babies away."

She pressed her cheek against his and said, "I love you, daddy."

His voice was almost inaudible when he said as she left the room, "I love you, too, sissy."

The night drive back to Winfield was a three-hundred-mile exhilaration. All fatigue and discouragement and depression had evaporated, and she felt sustained and light as if invisible hands held her up and propelled her forward. She could not get home fast enough to make a whole new start. She would be a new and different Lee, the best wife a man ever had. The best woman a man ever wed. And it was so clear to her now that she was the only one whose aims and ideals and moral fibre she had to worry about. She would love them all. She would even love Charley Dupre, and knock him sky-winding, lovingly, every time he laid a hand on her back-side. Several times she caught herself laughing out loud. Her elation and happiness were so irrepressible and contagious that when a constable of a small town speed-trap stopped her with every intention of giving her a ticket he only waved her on with a smiled warning to slow down and be careful.

The mood of exuberance and love was still strong upon her as she wheeled her car, after midnight, up the winding drive of the Tudor castle that was her home. She felt a sudden affection for its ugly turreted facade. She would cease to be a stranger in this house. She would make it shine and sparkle with light and warmth and love.

Stopping under the porte-cochere she found her door key and let herself into the service entrance and went into the darkened kitchen and snapped on the lights. "This is my kitchen," she said to herself. She hardly knew where anything was kept. She would find out, and she would do some cooking now. She had missed that. Mondrella and Richard would have to make room for her and do things her way. If they couldn't adjust to the new order she would advise them, lovingly, to make a change, and would give them the best references.

She was thirsty and hungry from the long drive. Taking a silver thermos pitcher from the counter she filled it with ice water from the electric water cooler and found an apple in the vegetable crisper and a handful of crackers, and biting the apple in her teeth and with her hands and arms laden she went out of the kitchen into the hallway, nudging out the light with her elbow as she went. She fairly tingled with excitement. This was the return of the new Lee. If Jim McNeely was asleep, well he would just have to wake up. She had to tell him. What? Something, anything, just that she loved him, that she loved this house, which she hadn't really appreciated before. That she was going to make it shine and sing as a home-base and background for whatever he desired to do in this world, however he pleased to do it, because she was his friend, his No. 1 Girl Friday and his life-love, and he was hers. She might even let that long longed for baby begin tonight!

As she went down the hallway she saw that the tall doors leading into the library were slightly open and a light had been left on inside. There was no sound in the house but the faint breathing of the air conditioning. She wedged her way through the doors and entered the book-lined room to turn off the light. Turning out lights was good policy. She remembered hearing that John D. Rockefeller went around at night switching off lights to save money. "Me and John D.," she thought happily.

Someone had been in the library since the servants had left, for there were two highball glasses on the table, beyond which the long couch stood. She started toward the table to snap off the single lamp that burned softly upon it, then her face clouded with puzzlement at the scattering of clothing, partly visible on the carpet at the end of the couch.

311

As she came to the table to turn out the lamp her approaching angle of vision gave her eyes and ears, without warning, a sudden shattering disclosure of the deep lap of the divan, and of the two people upon it. She stood, struck dumb, paralyzed, unbelieving—her tongue curled backward, convulsively, and clove to the roof of her mouth. The ceiling opened, the heavens opened, and the hammer of Thor came down and bashed her brains into her jaw bones. Her sundered gaze, frozen down and over the back of the couch beheld first a man, then a woman, naked, heaving and writhing, totally engrossed in the demented elemental act of making what only Shakespeare could call the beast with two backs. In the seconds required to identify the man as her husband and the other half of the beast as the blonde wife of Pluto LeMayne, the image was burned through her eyes into her brain, for all time and eternity.

How long she stood thus transfixed she did not later know, nor did it matter, for her world as a woman and a wife came there to an abrupt end. The rest was mere reflex action. The apple dropped from her mouth. With numb hands she removed the silver stopper from the thermos and flung it dumbly aside. Then she extended her shaking arm and poured a thick, sparkling stream of ice water upon the back and cloven seat of preoccupied male passion.

At the impact of the freezing water the male back arched with thunderstruck shock. A sound that was more a stricken "squack" than a cry arose from its owner who disengaged and fell wildly to the floor, looking up with the eyes of a stunned idiot.

Lee McNeely held the vessel relentlessly in her strong outstretched arm and emptied its shattering iciness into the exposed female harbor of man's passion, and the female half of the two-backed beast screamed and screeched and looked wildly upward in frenzy and tried to faint but could not, and kept on screaming until the thermos jug was empty. Then Lee Thomas McNeely released it and let it fall upon the flailing form of Mazie LeMayne, now all drawn-up knees and shins, so that it bounced and fell and rolled across the floor.

In a shaking voice that was like a terrible sound grated up from hell, Lee McNeely said, "That's the only way to separate dogs!"

Then she turned and stalked blindly out of the room and out of the house and out of the life of Jim McNeely.

36

A S THE FIFTIES ROLLED BY AND ADDITIONAL thousands of wildcat wells were drilled at home, the hunting became deeper and more difficult and more expensive. Each new wildcat that was completed, successful or dry, left one less place to drill. Geology and geophysics became more sophisticated, but even so these earth sciences could not find subterranean structures that didn't exist, and though nearly everybody conceded that there was a lot of undiscovered oil in non-structural stratigraphic traps, the drill was really the only effective way to find these, and it cost too much to find it this way, just punching holes down in the dark. It was simply a matter of economics.

And so the independent wildcatter knew that his day was drawing to a close. It is easy for a man to know when he runs out of money and can't get any more backing. It took the majors a little longer to see the light because they had big bank-rolls, and the geologists were on different floors from the accountants, but gradually the boys with the sharp pencils and the slide-rules began to believe what their figures said: that it was costing them more to find a new barrel of oil in the USA than they could sell it for. They didn't quit drilling, but they slowed way down because they weren't in business to throw money away. They began to buy up production that the independents had already discovered, finding they could buy it in the ground from somebody else cheaper than they could discover it for themselves, and they also intensified their search overseas in the vast untested areas of the world.

The foreign oil search was a big company game. It took blue chips to play it, and there were only a few independents like the Hunts and the John Mecoms and the Perry Basses who could get up the ante in that league. At home some of the majors began to look into the difficult problem of extracting the tremendous reserves trapped in oil shales and tar sands which up until now had been considered uneconomic sources of hydrocarbon energy.

Meanwhile oil was being consumed at an ever increasing rate. And every barrel produced left one less barrel in the ground. The immediate economic problem in the world oil picture was a temporary oversupply resulting in restricted domestic production and a depressed market price, resulting in turn in reduced exploration and drilling. But to anyone who could look beyond his nose it was clear that before too long, twenty-five or fifty or sixty years hence, when every Bantu and Kurdish jellybean would be racing around in a six-cylinder sports coupe, the situation would be exactly reversed. You can't keep going indefinitely to the cupboard for sugar without putting any back. In time we were going to run out of oil.

Lee never returned to the big house after that fateful night but had sent a friend to gather up her belongings. She filed a simple petition for divorce before the week was out, alleging the least scandalous of the statutory grounds: mental cruelty. Jim McNeely was beside himself, gyrating in the hellish fury of a man caught red-handed, dead wrong, guilty as sin, who was constitutionally unable to get down on his knees, admit his wrong-doing and human frailty, and beg abjectly for forgiveness.

Forgetting his own *flagrante delicto*, he railed at Lee (to Dent) for many things, for returning home unexpectedly, for spying on him, and especially for moving out of the house. If she was set on getting a divorce, *he* should have been the one to move out. It made him look like a heel and horse's ass for *her* to move out. In fact he did move to the Winfield Club for two weeks during which he drove Dent, over Dent's frantic protests, repeatedly to see Lee in the efficiency apartment she had taken, to try to get her to move back into the house. Such a controversy developed over this side issue that the central cause of the disaster was all but forgotten by Jim McNeely. Lee steadfastly, and with still-stunned grimness, refused to budge. She also refused to see her husband.

"Whatever each of you owned when you got married was the separate property of each of you," said Jeff Dofflemyer precisely. "If you can follow it through and identify it, land, chattels or even money, it is still your separate property. Everything you have made or accumulated during coverture, except that acquired by gift, devise, or descent—"

"Coverture? What the hell is coverture?" Jim McNeely had had two double Bloody Marys for breakfast and his tone was rough.

"Marriage. During your marriage whatever estate you built up is community property in this State, and each of you owns an undivided one-half interest in it, whether it be land, oil in the ground, or money."

"What about the debts?"

"The community property is burdened with the community debts. In other words, whatever your net worth is, not counting your separate property, Lee owns half of it, and upon divorce she's entitled to her half. That's the law in Texas."

"Yeah? I guess she figures she's entitled to half a million dollars. She'll say I said I was worth a million. Well, I may be worth a million, but you try to go out and find somebody that'll give a million for it. That's a little different." He talked with growing belligerence. "If she's so damn set on getting this divorce she'll have to come off of that figure. I couldn't raise half a million with a crow-bar. You go and see her, Jeff, and find out what in the hell she's got in mind."

"Not me, Jim," said Jeff Dofflemyer in a quiet voice leaning forward and looking down at the yellow pencils on his desk blotter.

"What do you mean by that?"

"No, I can't do it."

"I don't get you. You're my lawyer, aren't you?"

Jeff Dofflemyer drew a slow breath and sat back and put his hands on the desk and looked up at Jim McNeely. "No, I don't guess I am, Jim. Not any longer."

"Oh? Is that right? Well, when did this happen?"

"About five minutes ago."

"Well, I'll be a son-of-a-bitch," said Jim McNeely. "When things get a little rough my old country-boy lawyer takes out on me."

"That's not it, Jim."

"This is the kid I took out of the filling-station and made into a high powered attorney. Well, I guess it won't put me out of business."

"You can pick up the phone and have any one of the top lawyers in

315

town over here in five minutes. You won't suffer from lack of legal representation, Jim."

Jim McNeely ground his teeth together. "The thing that scorches my ass is having my old pal, the boy I picked out by hand, to turn tail and run out on me when I need him."

Jeff Dofflemyer shook his head. "Jim, I'm sorry. You've treated me mighty good. I've tried to give the best I could in return. It's hard to explain. Things have changed—and so gradually I can't say when it began. I haven't been happy here for a long while. You're not the same man I started out working for."

"Is that a fact?" said Jim McNeely. "I ought to whip your ass is what I ought to do, if you weren't so little and so goddamn pure!"

Jeff Dofflemyer looked at him in silence for several seconds. His face was colorless. "That might be a bigger job than you think, Jim." He shook his head slowly, then he said, "I'm sorry for you. I wish there was some way I could help you, but I don't know how."

Dent said, "I don't want to do it, Jim. Let your lawyer do it."

Jim McNeely reached over and grabbed Dent's arm, slender as a girl's, and twisted it up behind his back, half in jest but hard enough to hurt. "Don't *you* start buggin' out on me, buddy boy."

"I'll do it," said Dent meekly. He flushed slightly, really pleased by the physical contact. He rubbed his arm. "You son-of-a-bitch." He went out, dreading the interview with Lee McNeely which lay ahead of him.

"He wants to talk to you, Lee," said Dent. "He'd like you to come to the office."

"What is there to talk about?"

"Damned if I know, property settlement and all. I'm bugged about the whole thing. Maybe it wouldn't hurt to talk to him."

"It would hurt. No, I don't want to talk to him."

"But what'll I tell him?"

"Nothing, as far as I'm concerned." She sat cool and quiet and pale, as if she had been a long time physically ill. "I'll be here until the divorce is granted, then I'm going back to West Texas."

Dent made a face as if he were about to cry. He shook his head and pounded his forehead with his palm. "Lee, this fractures me! I don't know what to *do!* It's crazy! I'm going crazy!"

"Dent, please, don't let it bother you. Don't feel badly. I understand. Stick by your boy. You had him before I did. He needs you."

It was late in the afternoon when Dent returned and the strain of the interview showed in his thin face. Jim McNeely was waiting for him in his office hunched over his desk.

"It was a lousy thing you made me do," Dent said, flopping down in a chair and looking at his old friend with a strange, curious gaze. It was obvious that he had been upset by his interview with Lee.

"She won't see me."

"That's right."

"Well, how in the hell—! We got things that have got to be talked about! Property settlement. She's entitled to what's hers under the law, but I can't raise the kind of money she's thinking about!"

"You have no problem, old pod," said Dent eyeing him with a flat gaze. "You know what she wants from you?"

"I have no idea!"

Dent pursed his lips and made a big round zero with his fingers. "What's that?"

"*Nada.* Nothing."

"What in hell are you talking about?"

Unfolding his slender hands like the petals of a sad, languid flower, Dent continued gazing strongly at the heavy man who scowled at him across the desk. "You have no problem. She doesn't want any money from you at all. Not half a million. Not two hundred and fifty thousand. Nothing. Nothing but a divorce. As far as she is concerned you no longer exist. She wants nothing connected with you."

"Oh, now *wait* a minute," said Jim McNeely, incensed. "She hasn't got any call to act so high and mighty. She's got a legal right to what's hers. She can't get away with that!"

"Jim, you know what she told me? And I'm sure she wasn't telling me this so I'd spill it to you. She said she didn't need anything because she could work, and even if she couldn't, her daddy had plenty to take care of her. She said you'd need all the money you had and then some."

"Oh, now wasn't that sweet! Well you just go back to her and tell her she'll damn well take what she's entitled to. What's she trying to do? Make me out a rat-fink? Well, she can't do it! I don't need her money! I'll have an evaluation made! No, let *her* have an evaluation made. By any legitimate goddamn petroleum engineering firm in the business, and I don't mean Winkelman. Whatever they say I'm worth she'll damn sure take half of it!" Jim McNeely's face had colored a dark red. "You go back and lay that on the line, right now!"

Dent whistled silently over the tops of his pyramided fingers for a moment, then he said, "Why don't *you* go, Jim?"

"Why don't *I*?" Jim McNeely scowled darkly at him. "I sent word I wanted to meet with her. What the hell else can I do?"

"In the spot you're in, buddy, you don't send emissaries. Unless, of course, you want this divorce. I guess you do, at that."

A change came over Jim McNeely's face. He rubbed the heel of his hand into his brow, and for a moment Dent thought, almost, that he was going to break down and act like an ordinary human being.

Jim McNeely's voice, when he spoke again, was low, almost inaudible. "I don't want this divorce."

Dent's reply was pragmatic, surgical. "Then there's only one hope, old friend, and that is to go to her yourself. And when you do you'll have to unlock your knees, and get down on 'em. Hard as that may seem, it's your only chance."

Jim McNeely said nothing but sat staring dourly into the carpet across the room until Dent finally got up and said, "Well, let's fix a drink, shall we? I wonder how our livers would look if we took 'em out and hung 'em up on sharp sticks. I'll bet mine would look a sight worse than yours."

The next day Ort Cooley showed up in the Winfield office in his dress pants and white shirt and brown satin tie looking like a man who had come to a funeral. He had heard about the trouble, and there wasn't anything for him to do but come in, because these were his people. He talked to Dent a long time, doggedly, unhappily.

"I don't know what's the matter with ol' Jim, dang it. I jes' don't feel right workin' for him any more. He's different." He heaved a weary sigh. "I dunno. I'm low in my mind. I got a feelin' the whole shit-eree's gettin' ready to blow sky-high."

Dent didn't say anything. He understood what Ort meant.

"Naw, I dunno," Ort shook his head. "I might git me a' oil field job out in Salty Arabia. They're lookin' fer people to go out there now. It's way the hell an' gone acrost the big water, 'bout to China."

Dent said, "Aw, Ort, you better stay where you are. You wouldn't like those A-rab women. They wear veils and you never see their faces."

"I dunno," Ort said. "Like the feller says, you put a sack over their head an' one woman is much like another."

Before he went back to West Texas Ort went in to see Jim McNeely.

Sitting behind his desk silent and sullen as a suspicious frog, Jim McNeely eyed his old oil field crony and said, "Well? Did you go to see Lee?"

"I did," said Ort.

"I figured you would. What did you tell her?"

"I told her I was sorry."

"What did she say?"

"She didn't say nothin'," Ort said. "She jus' bursted out cryin'."

For a long time he stood outside the long, low row of apartment buildings. His hands were thrust deep into his raincoat pockets. The light mist falling in the dusk dampened his bare head and his face, unnoticed. He walked slowly to the end of the block and returned several times under dark, wet branches of leafless trees, struggling with his indecision.

It was full dark when he finally turned abruptly up the walk and entered the apartment unit. He found Lee's card in the row of brass mailboxes, then went up the stairs to the second floor. At her door he hesitated, turned away once as if in sudden revulsion, then caught himself and with a grim visage turned back and knocked on the door.

Inside Lee McNeely was sitting at the dinette table, trying to start a letter to her father. When she heard the knock it was as if she knew, instinctively, who it was. She let out a deep painful breath and pressed her hands to the sides of her face. Her first impulse was not to answer, but when the knock came again she went to the door and without opening said, "Who is it?"

"It's—me."

She caught her throat to control her voice. "What do you want?"

"I want to talk to you."

"What is there to talk about?"

A long silence, then: "Lee, I didn't mean to do you any dirt. It just happened." He said it doggedly, argumentatively.

She restrained the impulse to scream and cry out at him. "A man is going to do what he's going to do. Is that the way you justify everything?"

"Lee, open the door."

She stood tensed, trembling all over, her fingers clamped into her eyes as if to blot out the image of the man on the other side of the panel.

Then Jim McNeely did something he had never done in his life before. He sank down slowly to his knees, his arms upraised and his hands flat against the blank door. With his forehead pressed against the unyielding wood his voice was low and muffled, almost bovine.

"I'm asking you, Lee. Open the door."

Leaning against the other surface of the panel, her fists tight against her lips to suppress the wild sound that rose in her throat, Lee McNeely shook her head, then in an agony of hurting and resentment and uncontrollable female anguish she screamed, "Go away! Leave me alone! I never want to see you again!"

The flood-gates were opened and she let herself go in a paroxysm of wailing and sobbing. For how long she continued this she did not later know, but when the pent-up rush was spent she stood there crying softly, broken-heartedly, her wet cheek rubbing against the thickness of the wood that separated her from her husband.

"Oh—! Jim—! I didn't mean it. God knows I should, but I don't!" In a moment she straightened herself, took a Kleenex from her sweater pocket, and wiped her red swollen eyes and blew her nose. Then she shook out her tousled hair, drew and expelled a deep breath, and prepared to face him.

She turned the lock, hesitated a fraction of a moment to compose her face, then opened the door. But there was no one there. Jim McNeely had gone, and she never knew that he had been down on his knees begging forgiveness. No one would ever know, for whom would he ever tell that he had got down on his knees and had been rebuffed in his life once again.

And so the affairs of Jim McNeely and those that he had drawn around him as he painfully and laboriously clawed his way up the thorny hill of his life unfolded without beauty or peace or understanding.

His divorce from Lee was marked only by a "Lee McNeely vs. James McNeely, Divorce granted" line in the fine print of the legal notices in the paper. A similar infinitesimal legend marked the final wreckage of the marriage of Mazie and Pluto LeMayne two months later.

Cut loose from any semblance of discipline or respectability, Pluto spent his days in the tavern at the country club, drinking. The waiters totted up his drinks like the score in a pitch game, often reaching a total of thirty before the day's play was over and some charitable soul carried the inflated, watery carcass that once had been a man to its night's resting place. Pluto died four months after Jim McNeely and Mazie were married, and his passing was memorialized by a two hundred dollar floral piece from the McNeely Oil Company.

Old Lee Thomas went into a steady decline after his big effort with his beloved "sissy," daughter, prize of his life. He never knew about her trouble. After the brief divorce hearing in court at which Jim McNeely did not appear, having duly signed the necessary waivers, Lee went to McCamey and sat by her father's side for eleven days, during most of which he was semi-comatose, until he died. After she had buried him and attended to the necessary immediate details of paying bills and closing the house, she went home with a cousin, one of her few near relatives, who had married a sheep rancher and lived in a pleasant flag-stone house with their children on a ranch a few miles west of San Saba in the upper hill country of central Texas. She spent much of the hard following days with Tom Huston, her rancher cousin-in-law, a taciturn, understanding man of sixty, riding with him in his rattly pick-up over the dusty ranch roads as he tended to his sheep business and tried in his rough way to keep her mind occupied and help her ride out her trouble.

The family drove into San Saba in the evening sometimes with the Hustons' two teenage boys in the back of the pick-up to get ice cream, and once or twice they stopped to visit with the school superintendent and his wife, who were their friends. That is how Lee got started thinking about the idea of teaching again and ended up teaching seventh grade math and social studies in the San Saba Junior High.

37

MONUMENTAL PERPLEXITY BUILT SLOWLY, agonizingly in Dent Paxton until he felt that his head had grown to the size of the balloon-domed men from Mars pictured in the cartoons. He vaguely understood the mental and emotional storms that swirled in this woman which made her coldly, and beyond ability to turn back, divorce from her life the man she had loved as much as life itself. The great blow to her pride, the deep and cruel wound to her sense of trust, the utter destruction of the framework of her life in which she felt warm and secure—these were the sorry profits of infidelity which Jim McNeely had collected and paid her with. They left her walking alone, a stranger in an unconcerned world. Dent vaguely understood this, for he was one of those sad, interesting people made of female stuff and poured at birth into the form of a man.

He was perplexed because he had accepted as fit and sufficient for his brief burning on this planet the role of satellite to Jim McNeely. They also serve and are worthy, and entitled to feel satisfaction who, incapable themselves of doing, can nonetheless advance the fortunes and accomplishments of the doers-born. Every man had a purpose. Dent had found his, or thought he had found it, until now. And it was now too late for him to change, to turn, to find another purpose, and so, like the proverbial "staff man" who has lost sight of the objective, he redoubled his efforts.

There was much to do, and as Jim McNeely began to drink more and do more he began to depend more on Dent to do and to think for him, to fill in, automatically, all the blanks required to be filled in, in the mechanical process of living and merely getting along.

Besides being the major domo of Jim McNeely's business life, Dent arranged everything about his wedding to Mazie and the safari honeymoon which followed. He planned, then carried out almost single-handedly this ridiculous African affair and saw that Jim McNeely, who stayed drunk almost the entire trip, was sobered sufficiently on a few occasions to go out and slay a respectable number and variety of beasts so that he would not feel ashamed when he returned and was asked what he had bagged.

Dent had always been a devout worshipper of the Wine God, but he was a disciplined worshipper and it perplexed him further to see that some devotees, Pluto, for horrible example, and now the much stronger Jim McNeely, did not remotely understand and could not control or handle the worship rite. And how destructive their ineptness and lack of discipline became!

One day barely two months after her divorce Lee McNeely came out of a store in San Saba and ran straight into Jeff Dofflemyer.

"Jeff! How glad I am to see you!"

"Not half as glad as I am to see you."

"What in the world are you doing in San Saba?"

"I came to pay you a call."

She held his hands warmly and looked into his plain frank face, puzzled but delighted.

"You did? I mean—I know you're not with Jim any longer. Is there some left-over business?"

"No, I just came to see you, Lee. No business at all."

It was late in the afternoon and they drove in Lee's car to a cafe on the edge of town. They sat long over coffee cups and talked avidly and with real pleasure about what each had been doing, getting up-to-date on each other, but never mentioning, even once, Jim McNeely or the old times. Then they ate steaks and afterwards they drove back to the square where Jeff had left his car. It was a clear moonless night. A few lighted business establishments gave a perky cheeriness to this small ranching town square with its old stone courthouse.

"Oh, Jeff! It's been so wonderful to see you! You're like vitamins. Thank you for coming."

Jeff Dofflemyer sat back and pressed his hands against the steering wheel.

"Lee, I'm a plain-spoken small-town German boy and I don't know how to go about things like this rightly. Please excuse my Teutonic approach. I came down here to tell you that I love you. I always have loved you. Almost as long as I've known you. I would like for you to think about marrying me. Not now. But sometime. I know you need time to get over things and get squared away. But that's what's been on my mind and heart, and that's what I came down here to say. I wanted to come sooner, but I figured I ought to wait this long. I hope I haven't offended you by coming too soon."

"Oh, Jeff."

"Don't let it upset you, Lee. I had to tell you. There's no rush. I'm getting started pretty well with a small law firm. If you don't like Winfield, I'll go someplace else. Just tell me that you'll let me come back to see you sometime, before too long, and we can talk some more about it. No commitments. I just had to open the subject and let you know how I feel. I want to spend the rest of my life loving you and taking care of you."

Lee began to sob. She took a small handkerchief from her purse and held it to her mouth until she stopped sobbing, then she dried her eyes with it and drew deep, silent breaths.

When she felt she could talk she said, "Jeff, I feel—I—I'm an old worn-out gal. Inside. All used up. I've had my run, you might say. I don't think I could ever get 'up' again to give any man what he ought to have from a wife. I'd die if I hurt you. Dear, sweet Jeff. I can't. You mustn't waste any time, or hopes, on me."

Jeff Dofflemyer reached for her hand and squeezed it. "It's OK, Lee. I understand. I feel like a heel upsetting you like this. I won't ever change how I feel, and I won't ever give up hope. I'll be there, if you need me, or change your mind. And I'll be back sometime, whether you like it or not."

"Jeff, please, don't say that. *Make* your life. Find somebody. I'm no good for anybody. Don't make me feel I've messed up somebody else's life."

"OK, Lee. I'll do whatever you say. Don't you give it another thought, because I will do what you say, and everything will work out all right for everybody."

38

I T WAS JIM MCNEELY'S FORTY-SECOND BIRTHDAY AND
he and his wife, Mazie, happened to be in New York, staying in the
suite they now kept year-round at the Carlton House. They were
planning to celebrate the day by having dinner with several friends at Le
Pavillon and going on for a bit of dancing afterwards.

Jim McNeely had been drinking steadily since four o'clock. It was now
seven. He sat in his dinner jacket in the living room talking with Dent.
Dent, trim and spruce as ever, paced precisely up and down the deep
carpeted room as they waited for Mazie to appear. He cast an occasional
disapproving glance at Jim McNeely, who sat in a heavy man's stance on
a small chair, legs wide spread, a drink gripped in his beefy hand. Dent
clucked disapprovingly to himself. In his forty-second year Jim McNeely
loaded up too quickly, too early in the day and became assertive, over-
bearing and sometimes pugnacious before the evening's sport was well
begun. This offended Dent Paxton, who believed that people were within
their rights who wished to drink themselves into oblivion nightly, provided
they did it in a gentlemanly manner, reasonably observing the proprieties
so as not to interfere with other people's pleasure in the process.

"You didn't wish me happy birthday," said Jim McNeely. "It's been my
birthday all day and you haven't said happy returns, kiss my ass, go to hell
or nothing."

"Happy birthday," said Dent.

"What is happy?" said Jim McNeely. "That's a stupid word. It doesn't
mean anything. You measure by success. You've either made it or you
haven't."

"Successful birthday, then," said Dent.

"It is that. I thank you for the spontaneous, unsolicited good wishes. A man that owes nearly three-million dollars and is only forty-two years old has got to be successful. When you owe that much money, your creditors are gonna see that you make out."

"I wouldn't ride that theory too hard," said Dent. "Your old friendly mullets are looking a little fishy-eyed to me. Some of'em know sixth grade arithmetic. At the rate their runs are coming in it's beginning to dawn on them that they may get their investment back in 1998, if the wells hold up that long."

"Oh, what the hell!" Jim McNeely waved a brown-spotted hand. "Who could forecast that the damn Railroad Commission was going to cut the producing days in half? My mullets got no right to beef. They stepped up and laid their money on the line the same as I did. So we haven't hit another East Texas. Hell, they've got reserves in the ground to show for their investment. They'll get their lousy money back in time. They're spending ten cent dollars anyway, so what the hell?"

"Jim, I've got a little news for you. I have reason to believe that some of the good old mullets are beginning to have some doubts about the reserves, too. A pal of mine tipped me off that the Warfield Estate is having DeGolyer and MacNaughton make an independent appraisal of the reserves attributable to their interest. It's liable to come out a little different from the so-called certified Winkelman reports you've been sending 'em."

"So it does?" said Jim McNeely angrily. "So what? Winkelman's a damn good independent petroleum engineer. He's as good as anybody DeGolyer and MacNaughton have got!"

"He's about as independent as I am," said Dent wryly, "Seeing that 90 percent of his income comes from you. In very handsome fees, I might add. He's the only petroleum engineer I know that drives two Cadillacs. Anyway, I'm just dropping a hint of a little line squall brewing. Among other things your investors are complaining about your overhead charges. Two airplanes and all the travel and entertainment expense are going down a little hard."

"The hell with 'em. If they wanted a shoe-string operator they shouldn't have tied up with me. These mullets remind me of the damn bankers. They all have hot flashes. You got to service 'em. Stroke 'em a little now and then. Give 'em a lot of talk and some money along. They'll be all right."

"Speaking of bankers, what about Dingler? Is he going to put on that new loan for you?" Carl Dingler was the vice president and petroleum engineer in charge of the oil department of Northeastern Bank & Trust Company, New York City, which institution was now carrying the bulk of Jim McNeely's personal oil loans, secured by his personal interest. Jim McNeely had become very close to Dingler over the past several years through Charley Dupre, and had consolidated most of his indebtedness with Dingler's bank, somewhat to the Winfield bank's relief. Dingler had been a classmate of Chick Winkelman in engineering school and he accepted Winkelman's reserves reports and projections without question. He loaned Jim McNeely accordingly. Through this friendship, Jim McNeely had included Dingler, personally, in several drilling deals on a carried basis, which is to say that Dingler put up no cash. A couple of the deals hadn't panned out and Jim McNeely had picked these up for his own account. A couple of others had hit and would pay Dingler off handsomely.

"Well of course he's gonna put the new loan on," said Jim McNeely. "The reserves are there. Any damn pessimistic engineer can predict a production decline that will make it look like I'll be out of business tomorrow. Winkelman just happens to be an optimist. And hell, oil properties *always* do better than you think they will. With secondary and terciary production—water-flood and fire-flood and new recovery methods that haven't even been invented yet, everything is gonna pan out. Demand is increasing, production days have got to go up. What the hell are you so nervous about?"

Dent stood frowning. He brushed the back of his slender hand across his brow. "I don't know. I'm not a conservative but sometimes I wish you'd draw in your horns for a while and let some of these things pay out before you get in any deeper."

"Oh, for Christ's sake, you're getting neurotic. Let me do the worrying. One of these days we're gonna hit, buddy. That sweet spot. It's got to come. Then all this stuff will look like chicken feed. You just be my happy boy."

"Listen, amigo," said Dent, facing him squarely. "You're talking to old Dent, not one of your mullets. *You* know that *I* know that the old sweet-spot days are over. It ain't that easy any more. The odds against us go up all the time."

"Oh, quit it," said Jim McNeely with disdain. "I think you better put in for early retirement."

"OK," said Dent. Suddenly he was laughing, almost sparkling again. "I've quit. Whither thou goest, buddy. But I wish you'd take off a little of that lard." He poked his finger at Jim McNeely's middle. "You make me feel like I'm just one heartbeat away from being unemployed."

Jim McNeely laughed happily. He opened his dinner jacket and slapped his ample girth with both hands. "Aaah, Dentie, I had too much fun putting it on. Don't worry, I got a heart made out of bull rhinoceros hide. That's not the way they'll count me out."

"Then, happy birthday, my captain, and many more to come."

Jim McNeely put down his glass. A solemn look came over his face. "Dent—Lee—you know, Lee's birthday is day after tomorrow. She always had her birthday right after mine, remember? Send some flowers, from the Company. And get somebody to see if she needs anything."

"Already taken care of. Two dozen roses from the McNeely Oil Company will be sent as usual. Tomorrow one of the boys from the law firm will drive out to San Saba and duly call on her and duly receive the same old answer—namely that she doesn't need a thing, thank you very much."

"OK. OK!" Jim McNeely puffed his cheeks out and started to say something else, then Mazie opened the bedroom door and entered the living room. Both Jim McNeely and Dent gave appreciative whistles.

"Wow!" said her husband. "What a dish!" She was indeed a lovely sight in a gold lame sheath, low cut and fitted to display her handsome bosom and curving torso and statuesque hips to best advantage. A matching jacket trailed from her hand. Her pale golden hair was swept up from her neck and arranged in a swirling coiffure that had taxed the creative energies of a Mr. Peter for fully four hours.

"Baby," said Jim McNeely admiringly, "I'm halfway afraid to take you out on the street. Le's just stay home and play mamma and pappa."

Pleased, Mazie whirled, holding out her arms. "A girl's got to dress up for pappa's birthday. You really like?"

"I like."

"And ooh, Dent, look!" She ran a long-nailed finger under and around a delicate but elegant necklace of diamonds and rubies. "Isn't it lovely to be married to a man who gives *me* a present on *his* birthday?"

"Aw, I just thought it was time she had a new set of beads," said Jim McNeely, winking at Dent.

"I was going to say something about that," said Dent testily. "Jim, will you please for Christ's sake quit charging stuff like that to the hotel room!

328

Can't you remember a damn thing?" He turned to Mazie. "It gives the IRS bloodhounds the panting quivers, even though the company charges it back to his personal account. You heard about the static we had over the Coupe de Ville on the hotel bill in New Orleans."

"Aw, what the hell," said Jim McNeely. "The plane was grounded. We needed a car to drive home in."

"You needed a Cadillac like you needed this necklace. Oh how that senator what's-his-name from Minnesota would love to get ahold of that! 'Texas oil man charges limousine and diamond necklace to hotel room.' Good-bye depletion allowance! Write a check, goddamit!"

"Dentie, I didn't have a check in my pocket." Jim McNeely smiled, enjoying Dent's annoyance. He got to his feet. "I want a drink."

Mazie glided over to him and pecked a kiss lightly on his mouth. She took his glass away from him. "You can have oodles of drinks at *Le Pavillon*. Mustn't be late for your own birthday party. Some jolly friends are waiting. *En evant*! Dent?" She held out two bare and lovely arms to the men and they left for the party.

39

JIM McNEELY'S YEARS OF MARRIAGE TO MAZIE Marie Wales LeMayne McNeely were never boring. He sometimes even wished for a little marital boredom, or just some time to sit and get his breath. Mazie did everything she did as if she had just time to race through it and catch a plane leaving for a distant place and occasion of tremendous importance. Jim McNeely was grateful for this at first. It kept his mind from lapsing into reflective thought, and this was necessary for his sanity for a long time after Lee left him. Then, as he lived his way deeper into his forties and his weight and his intake of liquor steadily increased, he began to experience recurring periods of longing for a little stillness, a space of doing nothing but resting and getting over the feeling of mental and physical exhaustion and the breathlessness that had become chronic.

He began to dread the act of love with Mazie. He would sit propped up in bed in his silk pajamas, leering at her with half-closed eyes as she undressed her big white, dimpled, full-blossomed body, wishing he could just go to sleep, but knowing what was expected of him as surely as if he had received an engraved invitation. Yet she was so patently erotic, built like a big vulgar Venus, that he was always sufficiently inflamed to make the effort.

Making love to Mazie was a strange, almost impersonal act. Making love with Lee had been so different, something drifted into as naturally as going to sleep or waking up, a vital, integral part of life itself. With Lee he had always been utterly engrossed, absorbed. He would look at her with a mindless, child-like fascination, and she endured his scrutiny with smiling, knowing, womanly patience and love. But with Mazie, even as he was driving to a climax, it was as if he were standing aside observing himself as he struggled to reach the top of a high hill, or at times as if, almost viciously, he were slugging someone, to pay somebody back. Mazie was demanding, and his satisfactory performance was the necessary proof of her security as wife. And sometimes he had too many drinks in him to perform.

"Sorry sugar, ol' rascal's gone to sleep. Can't wake him up. Too much booze."

"That's the story of my life."

"Give you a rain check."

"Oh, you're all heart."

Mazie occupied her spare time and boundless energies the first year of their marriage, and a great deal of Jim McNeely's money, in completely remodeling and redecorating the old Streetman Tudor mansion into a modern French villa.

With the aid of a decorator from New York she turned the interior into a House & Garden feature in dusty pinks, baroque gilded mirrors and furniture, marble floors, gold filigree ceilings, and abstract paintings and sculpture pieces. The house's turrets came down and were replaced by a dusty pink facade with mansard roof. In the riverpebbled garden there were important abstract bronzes by Lipchitz, which addled and pleased Jim McNeely because they were beyond his comprehension and because they angered some of his neighbors who didn't "understand" them either, though he was slightly staggered when he learned what they cost.

Dent Paxton ran into Jeff Dofflemyer on the street now and then. They waved, or stopped and chatted briefly, but seldom had much to say to one another. Then one day as Dent was going to lunch in a particularly foul mood he came upon Jeff just leaving his office building. Jeff had only that morning finished a long and taxing court trial and had it in mind to treat himself to a solitary barbecue sandwich and a relaxing hour of browsing in the Public Library, and so they greeted each other as if they were brothers who lived on opposite sides of the planet.

Dent proposed lunch in the Slave Room at the Winfield Club and Jeff accepted readily. Jeff was in such a good humor that he even took an unaccustomed noon-time martini and Dent had two and they fell to talking, bringing each other up-to-the-present. They remained over their coffee cups past the noon hour.

"It's not so much the deep dry holes," said Dent, grateful to have someone to listen who knew and understood what he was talking about. "And I do mean we've been snake-bit—but it's the damn cut in allowable days. Producing days have done down, down, down. The Railroad Commission is choking us to death. Our production income is way down. The mullets' income is way down. They're disenchanted. Those rosy engineering reports Jim had been feeding them for years have lost their charm. The New York money-bags have started putting the pencil to it and found out that, even with depletion, it's gonna take 'em far too long to get their money back. Reserves in the ground be damned! They've just flat snapped the purse shut. We've got a hell of an overhead. Jim won't let anybody go. We've got a rig that hasn't worked in a month. His own debt on his personal production is beginning to eat his lunch. You know how he always joked about 'servicing' his debt-give 'em a lot of talk and a little money. It's not funny anymore.

"He's two months behind on his loan payments to the Northeastern Bank & Trust. Remember old Dingler? He's got ulcers on his ulcers. Some sorry bastard tipped off the bank's management that Dingler has made a pot-full out of oil investments that Jim put him in. The bank has laid it on the line to Dingler—get the loan current, and keep it that way or call it. Dingler talks to Jim on the phone every day. He's trying to get him to sell his production and clear his debt. Dingler says this is a good time to sell. The majors are knocking each other down to buy production from the independents now. Paying hellacious prices.

"Anyway, Dingler's suggestion went over like a lead balloon. Made Jim mad as hell. And you know why, Jeff? We've been living on the engineering reports of that no-good-bought-and-paid-for Winkelman. Jim knows that if he sold out now on the basis of any legitimate engineer's report, even at a top price, he wouldn't have enough left over after paying off the bank to buy a gun to shoot himself with."

"How does he think he's gonna hold out?"

"You know what he's holding out for? Oh, he says we'll get an increase in producing days next year, and the price of oil has got to go up. But he doesn't really believe that. No, what Jim is banking on, *still*, is that big strike he's gonna make. That big old juicy oil field lyin' out there somewhere that's got his name on it."

"Well, I hope he finds it," Jeff said, taking his napkin out of his lap and folding it neatly and placing it on the snowy tablecloth.

"He better hurry," said Dent grimly. "His chances are running out."

"How's he doing on his drinking?"

"Just fine," said Dent. "By that I mean the only way he could take on any more booze would be if they gave it to him intravenously."

Jeff shrugged his sandy eyebrows. "How's he getting along with Mazie?"

"Oh, everything is hotsy-totsy. She runs the world's only continuous cocktail party at 'Chateau Rose.' That's what she calls the house now. It's a very stimulating life they lead. Golf or bridge afternoons, gin rummy and poker on alternate evenings, hilarious football weekends, flying parties to the race tracks in season, Las Vegas, Acapulco, duck hunts on the coast, home for the Tuileries Ball and the ensuing silly season, New York on odd weeks when things get dull at home. It's like Mazie would go nuts if she had to spend a day or an hour without something to keep her mind off the fact that she's an ordinary constipated citizen like the rest of us, with the same problem of getting old and dying and trying to get to heaven facing her. Jim is burning up fast but Mazie—that big blonde is made of tough material. Not that she's a bad person. I don't think she is, really. She's just what she is. Just Mazie. And unfortunately, at the moment, we're all tied to her tail."

40

JIM MCNEELY KNEW THAT BERRY WAKELY WAS NOW
stationed in Bison's Winfield Division office. His old geologist
friend from the Dead Lake days had missed the boat somewhere
during the years since then. He hadn't wanted to be an executive particularly—though he could have used the extra money—and he wasn't cut
out to be one. He was a scientist at heart and probably would have been
happier as a teacher than as a working geologist. But he had kept slugging away year after year with Bison, being transferred from one district
to another, getting a few raises, carrying on. Now that oil exploration had
become a rather sick business and geologists were a dime a dozen he felt
lucky that he still had a job. At the same time he felt bitter and defeated.
Jim McNeely sensed this from one or two brief conversations he had had
with the geologist when he had bumped into him on the street.

That is why, when the grimness of his own situation began to intensify,
Jim McNeely resurrected an old idea that had lain dormant in the back
of his mind for a long time. He called Wakely and invited him to lunch
at the club.

The geologist had aged poorly. His face was thin and sallow and
unhappy and he had lost all but a few grizzled strands of hair from the
top of his head. He was glad to have the couple of martinis and loosen up
and talk, for he had always liked and admired Jim McNeely and he had a
lot on his chest that needed airing.

Jim McNeely listened and encouraged his old friend to talk, saying he
had thought of him many times through the years and had meant to call
him for lunch or a golf game or a bird hunt, but hell, life was so damn

complicated and busy that you never got to do any of the things you wanted to.

The geologist told him, ruefully, that he was just hanging on for a pension, and that that was a hell of a ways off. But he had gone too far with Bison to get out now. It took money to go out on your own if you had a family, and he hadn't saved a dime in twenty-five years with the company. Besides, the oil business had gone to hell and it was too tough to put deals together any more. He shook his head, "I should have got out when you did, Jim. I couldn't be any worse off. But when you got a family you keep hanging on for that regular pay check. And hell, Bison used to be a good outfit compared to what it is now. These days it's run by a bunch of cold-eyed bastards that think 'morale' and 'esprit d'corps' are dirty words, because they cost money. Their theory is keep everybody running scared. When anybody slows down or gets to be surplus, fire his ass! And they do. Some with lots of service. They call it 'cutting out dead-wood.' Well, sure, they've got to do some of that, because a company has to make a profit. But these guys in control now don't think anything about their people. They just think about pushing up the profits and making their personal stock options pay off while they're clawing at one another to see who can get to the very top. It's a new breed. I don't have any confidence at all that they won't can my tail tomorrow. That's a hell of a feeling for a guy with twenty-five years plowed in who doesn't know anything but geology and has a family to feed."

"Sounds like it's been a rough go, Berry," said Jim McNeely sympathetically. "Bison's stock has done real well, though. But I guess they've had their problems."

"Real tough, they've had it," said Wakely sarcastically. "They've got so damn much oil in the ground, old reserves in West Texas and South Louisiana and the Middle East and Indonesia, reserves that other people long-gone found for 'em, that it would be real hard to ruin this company. But this little clique at the head of the company now has come close to doing it. Not financially. Oh no, they're showing bigger profits every year, but at the expense of their people and the company's reputation. And of the reputation of the oil industry and of the whole damn system. They're the best salesmen for socialism we've got. Most everybody that works for the company except those on the stock option list feel like the company don't give a damn about 'em any more. It didn't use to be this way. If you had scratched me twenty years ago I would have bled green, Bison's color.

335

That's all over." He had become quite exercised and realizing it gave an embarrassed laugh and drained his martini. "Old broken-down geologist really sounded off! Enough of that. How're things going with you, Jim? I've been real proud of you, boy. You really made me proud of all the geology I taught you. All forty-five minutes worth."

"Oh, I guess I've done all right," said Jim McNeely feeling the situation develop just as he had hoped it would. "I'm not any Sid Richardson or H. L. Hunt, but I try to pick up my share of the leavings. But I haven't finished about you. What about the family? Gaye? And the kids?" He knew a great deal about Gaye and the kids, having taken the pains to check them out before this meeting. He had met Mrs. Wakely only once, briefly, years ago and had felt sorry for his friend afterwards.

Berry Wakely sighed heavily and shook his head without meaning to. Jim McNeely waved at a waiter and pointed to their glasses for a refill of martinis, their third. The geologist did not object.

"Jim, you may not know it but I have a little boy who is—retarded. Well, goddamit, he's a Mongolian idiot, and that's that. He's just barely able to dress himself, if somebody ties his shoes and buttons his buttons. We should have sent him away when he was born. We knew he wasn't right, but Gaye couldn't bear to do it, and I guess I couldn't either. He's always been a sweet little boy, but a constant care. It's made an old woman of Gaye. And now he's growing up and puberty is on him and he's out and around the block and the neighborhood parents are afraid of him, what he might do. I'm just about wild. Soon we'll have to put him in an institution. Gaye says she'll die first. She never has given up. That's what's taken so much of our money, what little we've had. She'll hear of some quack somewhere that has some treatment for Mongolianism and she won't sleep until she's tried it and been through the wringer of failure and bitter disappointment all over again. Goddammit, I'm a scientist, Jim, and I know a fact when I see it, but Gaye—" He said this tenderly and was suddenly almost distraught. "She's an ordinary woman and mother. She doesn't think, she *feels*, and hopes. She won't consider sending him to a state institution. I haven't got the money, I don't make enough, to hire a tutor or a caretaker to look after him fulltime, and Gaye is killing herself. She weighs about ninety pounds. And little Gaye—she's ten—is a full-time job herself. She's bright as a damn dollar, but so goofed up on account of Billy—ashamed about him in front of the other kids, and jealous, downright neurotically jealous of him because we spend so much time and attention on him and just kind of let her fend for herself, that she's mean and emotional, and well, Christ almighty, there's no way she or *any* of us can have a normal life."

Jim McNeely was really sincerely sorry for his friend, and began to think of his developing scheme as one having roots in justice and humane purpose that would justify and override any questionable aspects of business morality. He also felt that Berry Wakely had shot his wad emotionally this day and that the next move should await another meeting.

"You've had a rough ride, buddy," he said. "I don't think I could have stood up to it the way you have. Waiter, bring on the lunch. Berry, we got to get together more often. I was thinking about flying down to the coast Saturday morning. Got a rig running down close to Matagorda. Come with me. We'll take the little plane and we'll get a boat and just mill around up and down the inter-coastal canal and drink some beer and catch us some reds and unwind a little. Do you good. I'll get you back here Sunday night. How about it?"

"Gosh, I'd like it." The geologist heaved a big sigh. "I'd sure like it."

41

THEY TROLLED ALONG THE INLAND WATERWAY paralleling the coast line, through the marshy flats under a warm blue sky full of big, fat shining clouds. Now and then a water bird, frightened by the boat, would explode upward, shrieking into the sky. It was a good day, and now and then they anchored in a shallow bay and cast for reds. The fish were biting fairly well but the two men didn't work hard at it for they were having too much fun popping another cold can of beer and taking the sun and the soft, salty air off the Gulf.

"Man, this is a treat," said the geologist. "I didn't mean to make you feel sorry for me, shooting my mouth off the way I did the other day. But I'm glad you brought me, anyway. Naw, we all got our work cut out for us, our crosses to bear of one kind or another I guess, and all that stuff. If it wasn't this it'd be something else. Maybe that's why we're put here. To make out the best way we can."

"I don't buy that, Berry," said Jim McNeely, pulling on the beer can then compressing his lips reflectively. "I think we're put here to make out, period. I don't go for this martyr business. You've done your time at that. Somebody somewhere owes you something. I'd be thinking about collecting, instead of being so damn meek and philosophical and long-suffering."

"I'm available," said Berry Wakely, smiling. "I'm standing here with my hand out, waiting for manna to drop in it. Manna must be in short-supply up there."

"I got news for you, buddy." Jim McNeely broke off talking and reeled in his line rapidly as his bright orange cork far out in the gray water bobbed and dove under. The fish got off the hook and he didn't care. He didn't even re-bait for the moment but laid the rod across the gunwale of the boat. "Manna don't drop any more, buddy. You got to reach up and pluck it."

"It sounds easy. It *looks* easy when you do it. But I just don't know how."

"I'm gonna tell you."

"Well, I'm listening."

Jim McNeely crushed his beer can in his strong hands, tossed it out into the water and watched it sink, and without looking, reached into the little ice box for another and punctured its top with a squishing sound, twice, with the sharp beer-opener.

"I've got rigs," he said. "I've got money. I can drill wells. But I got to know where to drill 'em. If I don't know where to drill it's like playing pin-the-tail on the donkey, and I'm the jack-ass. I'm tired of drilling dry holes. You tell me where I can drill and make oil wells, and you'll never draw another poor breath."

The geologist turned his head reflectively but didn't look at him. He just looked at the water as the import of the words sank in. Jim McNeely went on while the thought was hot.

"All the obvious structures, all the easy prospects have been drilled and a lot besides. The whole damn country where there was an easy chance of finding oil has been fairly riddled with holes. And every time a new hole is drilled there's one less place to try. A deep dry hole costs me two hundred thousand dollars and up. I'm tired of drilling blind. You got to have dope to drill on any more, good, solid, scientific dope to get your odds down to a reasonable figure. That means geophysics. Not just any old kind of shooting, but the new super-duper high-fidelity stuff that some of the majors have developed. They're still finding some big deep reserves with it. Hell, one strike like that Smackover discovery that Pan Am just made in East Texas would make a man well. Permanently. But it takes know-how and dope, and I haven't got it."

The geologist ran his hand over his mouth.

"Am I being too subtle for you, buddy?" said Jim McNeely.

"I don't guess you are. We, uh, are about to talk about a little grand larceny, ain't we?"

This was a thought, a problem, a temptation that had confronted, at some time or other in some degree, every geologist or geophysicist who ever worked for a major oil company, and to which, to the lasting credit of those professions, only a miniscule minority ever succumbed. The company spent thousands, millions over a period of time, on geological and geophysical research and exploration and in the process developed equipment and know-how and data that eventuated ill subsurface prospects for drilling-likely places to find oil, centered and pin-pointed in some farmer's cotton field or rancher's pasture. As quickly as the data could be assembled, interpreted, developed, and plotted on a map, a decision was made. Orders were then given to the company's land department to go and sign the owners of the promising land to a lease giving the company the right to drill for and produce any oil or gas that was found. The company acted as swiftly as its technical and administrative procedures would permit, for this top-secret knowledge was highly volatile and had a tendency to leak out even though it was limited to the barest minimum of people necessary to assemble it and act upon it. Those involved were trusted employees, to be sure, but they were still human beings, and an old employee in the inner circle who went bad, who succumbed to temptation and made clandestine arrangements with an outside operator or lease broker, could pass the word quietly as soon as he saw the data developing into a worthwhile drilling prospect. Then, when the company landmen arrived on the scene with their lease forms and check books, they would find that the land had been leased just the week or the day before. Rumors were perennial of ex-company men basking at Mediterranean resorts, who owed their affluence to this interesting and difficult-to-detect way of stealing, or some variation of it. In self-defense the oil companies had tightened their security of information and developed an almost cloak-and-dagger atmosphere in seeking ways of combating the problem. But there was no foolproof defense against a trusted employee who turned crooked on you. Jim McNeely spat over the side of the boat and glanced up at Wakely, studying his face. "You can call things any damn thing you want to, depending on where you sit. The rules of the game were written by a bunch of high-placed thieves to keep anybody else from muscling in on their racket. I happen to know of some top people in your company, now retired and rich, that didn't get that way off what they saved out of their salary. It's only you yard-birds that are supposed to toe the line and keep your noses clean. And work and sweat your guts out all your lives for two hundred and eighty dollars a month retirement pay while your bosses buy stables of race horses. You know it's really amazing to see somebody like you that's so smart—*technically* smart, I mean—who is such a dope when it comes to practical matters."

"Jim, even if I—I mean, even if I could, I mean *would*, I'd be—well, goddamit, I'd be afraid!" The geologist wiped his hand across his face again, become more nervous as the conversation progressed.

"Afraid of what? That you'd get caught? Caught doing what? Stealing? Stealing what? Information? Hell, you can't steal information. You got to steal something tangible, something worth something before they can send you to the pen, even if they could prove it. I've looked into this. So you give me a little map. A piece of paper. What's it worth? Fifteen cents? Who knows whether the well is gonna produce? The damn information might be a liability! You think they can nail you for stealing a possible dry hole?"

"But the cost that went into making that piece of paper might run into thousands, Jim, hundreds of thousands."

"Hell, a piece of paper is a piece of paper. Who can prove that it's worth anything? Anyway, I don't even need a piece of paper. Just *tell* me where to buy and where to drill. Then who the hell can prove anything! You'll end up with a nice chunk of stock in a company that owns a producing lease. The stockholders' names are not on the public records. Who the hell would ever know?"

The geologist sat and thought a long time. He tried nervously and ineffectively to crush his empty beer can and not succeeding threw it in the bottom of the boat and picked up his rod and started to bait the hook with a shrimp and fumbled it and stuck the hook in his thumb. "Nobody would know, I guess," he said, sucking his injured member, "but me."

The task of subverting Berry Wakely was not an easy one, and Jim McNeely was not discouraged when he did not accomplish it overnight. He made a point of calling the geologist for lunch at least once a week, and he even got him out on the golf course for the first time in twenty years. He didn't push him, but he always reminded him.

"Buddy, I've been around some places and seen some things you haven't. You scientific types live in your ivory towers and don't really know how the world runs. The wolves run the world. The business world and the political world. The cold-eyed, smart, ambitious boys that head up the big outfits, in government and business, they all use their leverage to sack it up for themselves. They're not hypocrites because they don't see anything wrong with what they're doing. Oh, they're cagey enough to play it just inside the ragged edge, and only the dumb ones get caught."

"That's not what bothers me, Jim."

"I know what's bothering you. But tell me this. Where does something stop being just smart business and become immoral or unethical? It all depends on how you look at things. There's people in the world that think we're a bunch of criminals because we kill and eat *animals*. Ain't they a bunch of idiots!"

"I don't know whether they are or not," said Berry Wakely.

42

NOT TOO MANY YEARS AFTER DRAKE BROUGHT IN the first dug oil well somebody came up with statistics scientifically proving that the world's supply of crude oil would soon be exhausted. The same cry had gone up from authoritative alarmists periodically ever since.

Now in this time of glut nobody worried much about running out of oil. One industry mogul went so far as to predict that we would *never* run out of oil, meaning presumably that we would either find a substitute for it, or run out of people first, though he didn't say which.

The fact was that we started running out of oil when the first barrel was produced, for no more was being made, unless you could wait a couple of million years for it to brew. And now, given the world population trend and the rising consumption and falling discovery rates, the day was surely coming when we would run slap-dab out of economic oil.

Oh, it probably wouldn't come in our lifetimes, if we'd been shaving long, and something else would surely take oil's place. And the major companies, or whatever they or their successors might then be called, would slide right into the new business without a hiccup. The companies were already beginning to diversify—into uranium mining, chemicals, power generation, and the like, and most had great research organizations probing into the world of the future.

But in the meantime what had the fruit of this iron-tree meant to man? In a hundred short years the graph of oil consumption on the globe had soared to a still climbing pinnacle. In the same hundred years, fueled and lubricated by oil, man's material progress (if it could properly be called progress) had rocketed to the same heights. In that time he had leaped into the air, then leaped into space. Overnight he had developed the technological capability to annihilate himself, and in this brief span it was not surprising that he had shown no really comforting sign that he wouldn't do just that—because his coeval development as a rational creature proceeded at a turtle's pace. If he killed himself off, oil would be a principal villain. It would have made it possible.

In the meantime the independent oil men, the wildcatters, leasebrokers, deal-makers, who were not inclined to worry any more about the Bomb than dentists or bankers or football coaches, would tell you that the oil business had gone to hell. And as far as they were concerned it pretty well had. The golden swashbuckling Age of the Wildcatter was at an end. Oil itself was moving into the final act of its brief, brilliant drama on earth. Oh, it would swing on for a while, but it would never blaze again with the old brilliance. The wane had set in. The beginning of the ending had begun.

Hail, oil! And, a bit forehanded, farewell!

Jim McNeely received a big assist from a circumstance of fate about the time he had decided that the geologist, Wakely, was one of those half-starved, true-blue people who would choose to faint from hunger before he would pick up a crust of bread that wasn't rightfully his. The Wakely boy, the Mongolian, got out of the house one day and wandered into a neighbor's yard where two little girls were playing. He played happily with them for a while though he was eight years older than either, then there was a childish disagreement and a tug-of-war over a sand pail, and the mother of one of the little girls came out of the house just in time to see the boy lock a muscular arm around the neck of one screaming child while he beat the other over the head with the pail, all the while making snorting noises like a young bull at bay.

A great crisis in the neighborhood ensued. The police came, then the juvenile authorities. The Wakelys were handed an ultimatum. Put the boy in a private institution, or he would be taken from them and placed in the State home for mental defectives. Wakely's wife became hysterical. She threatened to kill the boy and herself if her husband didn't take them away, move to another town, another country. She had begged for years to go to Sweden where there was a treatment for Mongolians she had heard about. The geologist was plunged into a frenzy of despair.

Two days later Jim McNeely received a call advising him to buy royalty under a certain section of land that was already under lease to Bison. He promptly dispatched a broker and bought a quarter of the landowner's retained one-eighth royalty for $30 a royalty acre. A week later Bison Oil Company announced that a wildcat well would be drilled on the section and Jim McNeely promptly sold half of his purchase for $100 an acre. He met Berry Wakely at lunch and handed him an envelope containing sixteen one hundred dollar bills.

"That's your part, buddy. I'm holding half of what's left—eighty royalty acres—as trustee for you. If the well hits it'll be worth maybe a thousand an acre. If it doesn't it won't be worth anything. But we've made a small profit and we still have a good shot at a big one. Anything wrong with that?"

These clandestine dealings with the Bison geologist could not be carried on without Dent finding out. Though Jim McNeely did not draw him a picture, Dent, with his sharp, feminine mind, divined both the immediate small maneuver and the grand strategy behind it. He was incensed and deeply depressed and could not hide his feelings.

He confronted Jim McNeely in the big corner office one day behind closed doors.

"This won't wash, Jim. Let's go to peddling marijuana to high school kids. But leave Berry Wakely alone."

"Oh, go tot up your books, sonny boy. You feeling sorry for the poor old Bison Oil Company that's got more money than Uncle Sugar?"

"Listen, I don't care if you steal anything you can from Bison. I'll help you. But leave Berry out of it. Don't ruin him."

"Ruin that poor bastard? You know anything about the trouble he's got?"

"I know enough. I also know he's a good guy. He's human, sure, and he's got a breaking point. But he's fought his battle and stayed true a long time. So don't turn him into a crook. You and I can be crooks, because we don't believe it's crooked. But don't mess up a good simple man. That's all I'm asking. Don't screw up Berry Wakely."

Jim McNeely lost his temper. "You're talking an awful lot like a goddamn preacher lately. You thought about taking early retirement and going out to the Seminary and getting your license? You might do real well. But do your preaching in church, buddy. I'm trying to run an oil business. I can do without it."

345

"OK, OK," said Dent in a sharp voice. "We haven't ever traded in people before. We've run a pretty clean show. That's really all we've got to be proud of. Don't frig it up."

Jim McNeely glared at him. "Why don't you take the afternoon off and go to a picture show?"

It was a day in late winter, a blustery day when low driving clouds alternately slammed cold rain then sleet against the tinted windows of the high office in this building tall above the southwestern prairies.

Dent Paxton entered Jim McNeely's office, his face a mask of tragedy. Jim McNeely had been drinking steadily since ten o'clock. He closed his desk drawer with the glass in it, for he did not like even Dent to know that he was starting his daily intake of alcohol so early.

Dent opened his mouth but before he could speak Jim McNeely cut him off savagely. "I see you got your preacher's suit on again this morning. Fixing to give me hell, aren't you? Because I'm gonna buy up one of Bison Oil Company's little old shooting prospects. Right? You don't mind putting the britches to Bison but you think I'm a no good son-of-a-bitch because I've seduced an old worn-out geologist that Bison has crapped on for over twenty-five years. One that's given the lousy company his life, found millions of barrels of oil for 'em. And hasn't got a dime to show for it! He may not even have a job tomorrow if some sorry bastard in the home office decides he's dead-wood."

Jim McNeely warmed to his subject with growing anger. His gray shot temples fanned out like a porcupine's quills. Dent looked at him helplessly, on the verge of tears.

Jim McNeely said, "Well, let me tell you that Berry Wakely has an idiot boy that is going to wreck him and his wife and their whole life if he doesn't get some money from somewhere, and soon. Money, pal. The hell with good old Berry's integrity that you're so goddamn weepy about. And listen, whether you know it or not, buddy, your ass is in the fire, too. You've gotten pretty damned spoiled working for me, living it up. Oh, you're a real exotic little gentleman with mighty expensive tastes, you are. Well, if this outfit goes bust you'll be out on your ass, and you couldn't make a living anywhere else if you had to. You'd starve to death! So quit acting like a goddamn neurotic woman. I've got three brokers out right now buying leases on a Bison shot-high in East Texas that's liable to solve a lot of things for you and me and Wakely, too. The Bison head office won't even know about it 'til next week because the shot records are just now being plotted. It's a Smackover prospect and I mean it's a big son-of-a-bitch. Looks just like Edgewood and right on trend. When old Bayard Jackson gets all excited next week and sends his lease-hounds out to sack it up they're gonna find that old Jim McNeely done gone and got there first. If it's a gas condensate reservoir like Edgewood, or anything near that good, the wells'll be worth ten million dollars apiece. There's no proration on gas wells, buddy. Good ones over there produce anywhere from five hundred to twenty-five-hundred barrels of natural-gas liquids a day along with the gas. And that's three hundred and sixty-five days a year. You put your pencil to that, sonny boy, and if your sense of integrity is still offended why you just get Mrs. Lukens to make out your time because you won't be any help to me any longer."

Dent Paxton stood before him, looking at him, his slender shoulders drooping as if all the starch of life that held men and even half-men together had been washed out of him. He was almost at the point of tears. He drew a deep, silent breath and steeled himself to the necessity of speaking.

"All right, Jim," he said. "You'll do whatever you want to anyway and I'll go along, because there's nowhere else I can go. Like you said, I'd starve to death. But that's not what I came to say. I came to tell you that Ort Cooley is dead."

Jim McNeely glared at him as if not comprehending. There were seconds of silence. "What do you mean he's dead?"

"I mean he shot himself, and he's dead."

"What?"

"Don't worry. It wasn't suicide. At least—I don't think it was."

In an empty voice Dent unfolded the bare details of Ort Cooley's demise. Ort had been night-watching on a stacked rig out in Ward County, where the rig had been idle a long time. Perhaps the tedium of guarding cold pig-iron had grown too depressing and the long nights under the stars too lonely. For a long time he had been, as he told Dent, mighty "low in his mind." In any event last night he had with great cunning and ingenuity rigged a spring-gun, a cocked doublebarreled twelve gauge shotgun loaded with buck-shot, under the end of the pipe rack at the rig. He had attached a wire to the trigger and stretched it tight across the open space between the rack and the doghouse so that any thieves prowling the premises in his absence would almost certainly trip the wire and blast themselves into perdition, or at least have the daylights scared out of them. Having thus secured his watch he climbed into his old pick-up and drove off to town to have just one beer. Just one, surely. There was no way of knowing how many times he had done this. In any case, sometime in the dark early hours of morning he had returned to the rig, drunk as only Ort could be and still remain on his feet. He had dismounted from the pick-up and staggered straight into his own trap. It was his last act of forgetfulness. Both barrels caught him full in the belly. Cotton, who was pushing tools for the rig, found him just after daylight when he drove by the location.

"Near cut him in two," sobbed Cotton, who called the news to Dent over the long distance telephone. "Blowed the guts clean out of hisself!"

By the time Dent finished his dry-voiced narrative Jim McNeely had begun to shake all over. He clenched his fists and brought them down violently against the desk. "Low-life son-of-a-bitch!"

The slightest shrug rippled Dent's thin shoulders. "He lived happy in the main, and he never knew what hit him." He turned and went silently out of the office and closed the door. Jim McNeely clenched his teeth and hit the desk again, hard, with his fist. Then he sat digging the heel of his hand into the bridge between his eyes. In a little while he put his head down on his arms and cried.

43

JIM MCNEELY KNEW THAT HE NEEDED A PARTNER for this deal. Not just any partner, but one highly respected and financially sound. There would possibly, even probably, be repercussions, and he needed a partner with strength and standing in the industry who could withstand the attacks that almost certainly would come.

For a long, long time he had been holding in the back of his mind an old remembered invitation from a great oil man. Years ago, when he was just an oil field hand trailing around after a queer broker named Hoss Hennery, J. E. (Big Jim) Wilfong had looked him squarely in the eyes and said, "If I can ever help you, boy, come to see me." It was lightly spoken, but the words of a man like Big Jim Wilfong were never lightly taken.

Jim McNeely had watched with awe and envy the rise of Big Jim Wilfong whose holdings had pyramided through the years into an empire. It almost seemed that Big Jim could do no wrong. His people were always at the right place at the right time when a new play broke. Big Jim's churchly contributions had grown apace, and he had become a kind of legendary, secular saint, if a slightly tarnished one, since it was known that his abiding passions were race horses and women.

It was surprisingly easy to get in to see the old man in his tower suite of offices in his Dallas sky-scraper. The motherly secretary took Jim McNeely in and said, "Mr. Big Jim, here's an old friend of yours, Mr. Jim McNeely." She spoke in a loud, penetrating voice. With a little smile and a wink she said *sotto voce* to Jim McNeely, "You'll have to talk right up. His hearing isn't what it used to be."

The old man was sitting in a padded rocking chair in the corner of the great office reading a *Turf* magazine through thick reading glasses set on the end of his big nose. He still made an impressive figure but Jim McNeely was shocked at his frailty. His skin was like a soft mantle of flesh over a great, gaunt bone structure. Jim McNeely had never had any direct oil deals with him but had seen him and visited briefly with him at countless API, IPAA, Texas Mid-Continent, and TIPRO meetings, family conclaves of the great industry. He felt, or at least he hoped, that the old man knew who he was.

"Hello, Mr. Big Jim," he said warmly as he walked across the room.

"Hey, boy!" boomed the old man, still sitting in his chair, wrapping his two old hands about the hand of his visitor. "Glad you could come, glad you could come!"

Jim McNeely felt relieved and nodded his thanks to the secretary who smiled and winked again and left, discreetly closing as she went the door to an adjoining room which looked like a tack room, with racing saddles and racing silks in evidence and many framed photographs on the walls of horses running at great speed or standing lathered in the winner's circle.

"How are things at Hot Springs, boy?" said Big Jim, and Jim McNeely's warm feeling vanished instantly and was replaced by one of distress as he looked searchingly into the old faded blue eyes. He had never been at Hot Springs in his life.

"I'm Jim McNeely, Big Jim," he said, pulling up a chair and sitting down knee-to-knee with the old man. "McNeely Oil Company. Last time I saw you was at API, three years ago in Chicago. I've got a little deal I thought you might be interested in."

"I know who you are, boy. I never forget a face. One time I was in the First National, Chicago, closing up a deal. When I bought out DeSoto. This young man come up to me—he was on the other side and said, 'Mr. Wilfong, you won't remember me.' I said, 'Young feller, I never forget a face.' I knew he worked for DeSoto. How come me to buy that property was I knew the Stanolind was trying to buy it." He was well started into a rambling discourse which went on and on and took him back through this one of many financial triumphs of the past and branched off when something his own words suggested sparked his memory into another entirely unrelated deal, then into still another, and as the words flowed unabated Jim McNeely's heart and hopes sank further. Eventually, after fifteen minutes the old man ran out of wind without ever getting back to the young feller of DeSoto who had challenged his memory, or to Jim McNeely.

He sat puffing and nervously twisting the knob on the hearing aid device clipped to his coat pocket. "What? How're things at Hot Springs, son?"

"Just fine, Big Jim. I didn't know for sure you'd remember me. Once a long time ago when I was a button you told me if I ever needed any help, why, to come see you. Well, I've got a good deal working—I think it's a great prospect—and I need that help. It's a little too big for me to swing by myself. I need a partner to come in for half. If you've got time I'd like to show it to you—"

Big Jim had recovered his breath and was ready to go again. He leaned over and took Jim McNeely's hand and broke in with a fresh bass-horn attack. "Boy, I'm sure glad to see you. An awful lot of the old timers are gone now. An awful lot. I never forget a face. And I'm glad to help a young man on his way up." He gripped the arms of his chair and with an effort struggled to his feet. He towered above Jim McNeely. Gripping the younger man's shoulders in his old hands he talked right down into his face, his old blue eyes blazing. "I'm mighty glad you come to see me. I never yet failed to help my fellow man at any turn of the road. Do you love the Lord, boy? That's the only road and that's the road that Big Jim Wilfong has followed all his life. Love the Lord. Looky here, son." He caught his arm and led him over to the wall of the office on which were hung many pictures of churches, architectural monstrosities in yellow brick, colored architects' elevations with great blooming trees that existed only in the architects' imagination. Brass plaques at the base of the frames commemorated "Wilfong Sunday School Annex—Dedicated May 3, 1957"—"Wilfong Memorial Church-Anno Domini MCMLVI"— "Wilfong Student Center for Seminary Students, Dedicated November 27, 1949."

A wide glass case at the end of the room housed a dozen or more shovels, some plated with silver, some with gold, relics of groundbreakings done for the glory of the Lord and financed with Big Jim Wilfong's oil money.

Big Jim opened the case, took out a silver-plated shovel and read the inscription engraved upon it. He took a spraddle-legged stance with the tool as if posing for cameras. "This here one set me back two hundred and seventy-eight thousand. Right smart shovel, hey boy? You got to give back

351

to the Lord what he giveth thee. That's the best investment in the world." He winked at the younger man. "It cometh back in full measure, tamped down and running over. I'm glad you come to see me, son. Helpin' young people on the way up is one of my greatest pleasures."

Thinking that he wasn't so damned young and that this sure as hell wasn't the help he was looking for, Jim McNeely said with growing impatience, "It's a fine work you've done. Now, Big Jim, I'd like to show you this East Texas Smackover deal—"

At this moment the door opened and the secretary reappeared, announcing loudly, happily, "Time for a little siesta, Mr. Big Jim." She grasped Jim McNeely's arm and steered him firmly toward the door whispering, again *sotto voce*, "He tires so easily now. We're so glad you came to see us, Mr. McNeely. He does enjoy visiting with young people."

That night at bed time Mazie, who knew little or nothing about her husband's business but had heard that he was going to see Big Jim Wilfong and was impressed because of the fabled wealth of the man, inquired about the meeting. Realizing now that he had waited too long to cash in on a long-ago promise, Jim McNeely mumbled, "Aah, the old rooster's made too many trips to the hen-house. He's done blanked his blankin' brains out!"

He was forced to concede, however, and with more than a trace of envy, that anyone who had his name engraved on as many brass plaques in as many Houses of God as Big Jim Wilfong could hardly fail to receive some consideration on the great Day of Reckoning.

44

AND SO BIG JIM WILFONG TURNED OUT TO BE
another dry hole. Yet Jim McNeely knew he desperately
needed morals as well as financial reinforcement for this deal
if he was going to pull it off—this big one of his life. Basically he knew
that he lacked something—he had never been completely accepted. He
had achieved many of the trappings of success, but there was the cloak of
sound moral standing, character success, that he had somehow never put
on. He knew this and it angered him deeply. The cloak of character success
which oil man Boyd Hallam had slipped into so easily.

He knew Hallam better than he did Big Jim and after his first-hand
experience of learning that the old man's brain had softened and begun to
disintegrate he called Hallam on the telephone and flew down to Houston
to see him. The two had become acquainted on a first-name basis in a
rather involved unitization deal in New Mexico several years back. The
acquaintanceship had grown into warm friendship when they later served
together on a committee of the IPAA.

Jim McNeely admired Boyd Hallam and envied him, which wasn't
unusual since Hallam was an admirable and successful man. He was
more typical of the modern independent oil man than Big Jim Wilfong
or any of the other flamboyant big-spenders though he was little known.
There was nothing very newsworthy about a successful, hardworking businessman who had slept with the same woman for twenty years, and that
one his wife, who was a concerned and loving father, who dressed conser-
vatively, who went regularly to church, and who, while a generous giver
to many charities always stipulated that his gifts remain anonymous, and

whose only love outside of his family and his work was birddogs and bird hunting. No mistresses, no scandals, no hundred thousand dollar parties with champagne fountains and orchids in the swimming pool. He made very poor copy for hardworking newspapermen.

Boyd Hallam had been born in the oil business. Son of a successful drilling contractor, he had prepared himself to take up his father's calling by studying petroleum engineering. He was successful from the start. He was a fair example of the better educated young generation: of oil men who used all the leverage that science and engineering and hard work could give them.

He was not a grand-stand wildcatter. Usually he worked in close to where the oil was already coming out of the ground, bought high priced acreage and put together complicated deals that had a margin of profit and return on investment calculated against estimated risk, precisely on a slide-rule. He was one of the first independents to go into secondary recovery, buying up depleted shallow leases and pumping water into selected wells to force much of the remaining oil in the field to come out of other wells.

Through the years Hallam was one of the ones that Jim McNeely had measured his own success by, and he did not fare well in the comparison. He was deeply envious of the prestige and recognition that had come to Boyd Hallam, besides wealth. Two years after they had served together on the minor committee of the IPAA, Boyd was elected to the executive committee of that great organization of oil men. Yet no one even suggested to Jim McNeely the possibility that he might be good executive committee material himself. He passed it off: "Aw, it's a brother-in-law outfit. A little clique runs it, and they're all cronies of Boyd's old man."

He breezed into Hallam's office late in the morning and was greeted warmly. The two men sat with feet on Hallam's desk, talking with pleasure and laughter and animation for an hour about people and deals and committees they had lived through in common, though Hallam noted a brooding nervousness in his friend that he had not seen before. There had always been a real liking between these two robust men, and Jim McNeely did not force an unnatural break in the reminiscing to bring up the business that had drawn him to this city on the coastal plain.

Finally with a bang Hallam put his feet down and said, "Christ, it's twelve o'clock! Time to cook and eat. Let's mosey over to the Petroleum Club. I'll buy you a martini and a piece of bull meat."

"Aw, naw, Boyd," Jim McNeely protested deferentially. "I don't want to take any more of your time. I can tell you my business in fifteen minutes and get the hell out of here."

"The hell with that," said Boyd grinning. "You done screwed up my morning. You might as well screw up the whole day."

They sat in the high-ceilinged opulence of the Petroleum Club amid tables of men who represented the wealth of this great southwestern oil province. High windows looked out across the sprawling, haze-shrouded city. While they drank their martinis Jim McNeely laid out in brief, oil-esoteric terms the outlines of his deal. His first sally was purposely guarded. He had an A-1 Smackover prospect. Positive shot-high based on excellent records. It was too big for him alone. He needed a partner, and he had always wanted to do a deal with Boyd Hallam.

Hallam's interest was whetted. His plain, unhandsome face—the kind Lee had pleased to call *good*-looking—lighted with the true oilman's intensity when fresh oil was on the wind.

"Man, that Smackover is like young pussy," Hallam said. "Nothing I'd like better than tie into another Edgewood. But those features are sharp and hard as hell to find. Who did your shooting?"

Jim McNeely looked at him closely. He said, "There's only two outfits in my judgment that know how to shoot the Smackover." He waited a long second then played his critical card. "Both of 'em are major companies."

Boyd Hallam sat silent for an even longer space. He seemed to be fighting away a frown that kept flickering back across his brow, trying to keep any sign of pre-judgment or disappointment from showing in his face. Finally he said lightly, almost jokingly, "Sounds like somebody's had their hand in somebody's cookie jar."

An appalling feeling of guilt and dirtiness crept upward into Jim McNeely's scalp and he suddenly hated this man. He bulled it through.

"You don't need to know anything about it except that I'm putting my take-home pay into this deal. And you know I'm no fool."

"You're no fool, pardner. I've known that a long time." Boyd Hallam was suddenly terribly ill at ease, embarrassed. He was a man of the world. He didn't want to sound like a prude or hurt his good friend's feelings. "Aw, hell, Jim," he said. "I'm pretty well loaded now. This damn off-shore drilling I've gotten into is about to eat my lunch. God damn, it's expensive! Don't ever let anybody talk you into going off-shore."

Having gone this far Jim McNeely was determined to wring the prospect dry. He said, "This shooting comes straight from a source I'm absolutely sure of. It's not speculative. It's positive. It's there."

Cornered and trapped, Boyd Hallam looked down at his plate and as gently as he could laid his position on the line. He said, "Jim, to tell you the truth, I never have gone in for any of that sort of thing." During the ensuing awkward silence he felt very bad. He winced inwardly for his friend. Then he said with as much warmth and friendship and joviality as he could muster, "Hell, man! Why do you want to fool with anything like that for? There's too many easier ways to make a living. Like selling insurance or ditch-digging!"

As he rode back to Winfield in his airplane Jim McNeely thought grimly, "A lot of ditch that silver-spoon bastard ever dug!"

And so he knew he would have to do the Smackover deal alone, on his own. The hell with all of the old, pussy-addled and young, sanctimonious sons-of-bitches! When the chips were shoved into the middle a man had to play his cards, all by himself.

45

THE FINAL, DECISIVE CONFRONTATION BETWEEN Jim McNeely and Dent Paxton was not long coming after this. The day it happened was after Dent had tossed sleeplessly the night before. His head ached. He rode the elevator up to the office knowing he had reached a crisis in his life, a point in time and space at which he had to quit drifting with the winds and take his stand. If he did not, his life, which was adjectival at best, would be revealed as altogether meaningless.

"You must not do this to Berry Wakely," he said flatly, coming straight to the issue, sitting across the great mahogany desk from Jim McNeely, his face harrowed. "I have no special interest in Berry. But he's a guy who's fought a long, dismal battle and somehow has kept going with his head up. You can't just wreck a man like that and get away with it. It'll wreck you, too, Jim, and everybody that's believed in you. Now undo what you've started and let's go back to West Texas and run our rigs and be poor but honest and happy and all that jazz. I'm serious. We can only eat so much and drink so much, and we all pull our pants on one leg at a time. When it's all said and done we've got to live with ourselves and each other. We've had a good run. So we crapped out. We can still look in the mirror without throwing up. Let's cut it that way. Clean."

Jim McNeely had taken his first drink of the day on awakening from a fevered restless sleep. By the time of this meeting he had had four more. The liquor in his blood stream formed a volatile mixture that now flared into uncontrollable rage.

"All right, you little pissant! I don't need any more preaching from you!"

His voice was cruel, guttural. "I've made it by myself, the hard way, all the way, in spite of your assisting me, you and your asinine philosophy!" He drove his fist against the desk. "You ever stop to think that you're just a little sucker-fish that's been living off a lean, hungry shark all these years? Well, I'm fed up with you. Get out!"

Dent's voice was shaking, unnatural, trying to hold firm. "Jim, this is Dent you're talking to."

"*Yes, Dent.* My little pervert philosopher!"

"Jim, you can't talk to me like that."

The voice of Jim McNeely reverberated dully and brutal. "As far as I'm concerned you're a useless little queer! Now get out of my sight! Get out of my life!"

Dent Paxton put a trembling hand to his forehead. His face was white and bloodless as plaster. He did not look at Jim McNeely but stared unseeing at the top of the desk. When he spoke his words were barely audible.

"I was born the way I am. I've had to live with myself the best way I could. But I never hurt anybody, so far as I know, or corrupted anybody—with my own corruption."

He arose and walked on legs stiff as dry sticks, out of the room.

46

THE DRILLING BLOCK WAS LEASED AND THE WELL spudded, and Jim McNeely went to East Texas to stay for the duration. This was the big one. The big one of all. It would be the deepest and most costly wildcat he had ever drilled, and it would be "heads-up"—just by and for Jim McNeely—all the way. And so it had to go right, and fast, without twist-offs, stuck-pipe, lost circulation, or any other trouble or delay. The mullet money had dried up and his credit was shaky everywhere. With some suppliers he had been put on a strictly cash-in-advance basis. He instructed his bookkeeper and new office manager, Mrs. Lukens, to hold out certain oil-run checks from his West Texas production which were supposed to be endorsed over to the New York bank and applied on his loan, and to forward them to him at a post-office box in Wills Point, Texas. With these checks he figured he could meet the crew's payroll and spread a little cash around among the fuel and mud suppliers if they got nervous.

Yes, this was the big one, the best prospect he had ever drilled, a classic, razor-back seismic structure centering on the Jennie Doolittle farm in the Heirs of Josiah Eddlebrock Survey in southeastern Kyle County. This was the one he had been waiting for, the golden pool. The one that would pay everybody back, in more ways than one. It would slap a lot of people across the mouth like a wet fish soaked in crude oil. It would be a big disappointment to a lot of people who would like to see Jim McNeely broke, and in hell.

The great hundred and thirty-six foot derrick towered above the clearing in the pine and scrub oak that carpeted the rolling countryside. The tremendous engines and draw works and all the supporting machinery, pumps, generators, stacked pipe, sacked mud, fuel, and water tanks clustered about the base of the derrick, gave the impression of a gigantic machine of war. Jim McNeely from the start was on the high derrick floor amid the deafening rumble and the precise ballet of the roughnecks much of every eight hour tour. The men wondered when he slept.

He moved his personal gear into the small tool pusher's trailer parked on the edge of the location under the overhanging branches of an oak tree. Thus began the drilling of the deep test of Jim McNeely's life.

By the end of the third day, before they had drilled out from under the surface string of casing, he had traded his city clothes for a suit of old khakis and a tin hat. He was on the derrick floor every time the crews changed tours and most of the rest of the time as well around the clock. In a few days his face was covered with black stubble and his khakis were mud spattered. To an outsider he would have been indistinguishable from one of the rig hands. He slept in two hour stretches at odd times, when a crew was coming out of the hole to change bits, or going back in with a new one. He left standing orders with the drillers to call him at any time in the event of any occurrence out of the ordinary, no matter how slight.

The days and nights wheeled around and in a while he lost track of their passage as he poured every ounce of his concentration into the drilling of this well, and the drill bit ground steadily deeper without incident through the rock strata. He was a dark and brooding man leaning against the derrick leg an hour at a time, watching the weight indicator and watching the rotary table turn and the square kelly joint inch slowly down through the derrick floor. It was as if he were cast into a deep hypnotic spell by the sight and earth-rumbling sound of the massive machinery grinding its slender hole toward a target over two miles below—a target that might not even be there.

Oh, this one would be there. The little contour map that Berry Wakely had nervously drawn from memory on the back of a menu showed unmistakably that the seismograph had picked out the buried structure clearly and sharply. It was almost a textbook structure in a horizon that was certain to be the Smackover limestone, and it was right on trend, in the same curving band of deep Smackover fields, both to the north and south, that were paying off like slot machines in a broke gambler's dream.

During this time he spoke few words to anyone except the young contract geologist from Geo-Lab, Inc., who was sitting on the well and who worked the samples and plotted the well's progress downward through the rock pages of terrestrial history. The formation markers were coming in just about right. So far the well was correlating perfectly with Edgewood.

Then, without warning, one afternoon in the second week he began to have some highly significant visitors at the well. The first of these was calculated to frighten him and unnerve him, but had, instead, the effect of encouraging him and finning his resolve, though this was already hard as obsidian. In mid-afternoon a new Chevy sedan rolled up the road out of the woods and stopped before the trailer. A muscular youngish man in a business suit and snap-brim hat got out of the car and knocked on the trailer door. Jim McNeely had just awakened from an hour's nap and sat on the edge of his bunk working his toes in his stocking feet and scrubbing his hand over the stubble of his face, trying to bring himself back to the reality of the present. He had been dreaming of Lee and he couldn't get her out of his mind.

The man outside knocked again.

"Come in," growled Jim McNeely.

He looked up unpleasantly as the big man bulked through the narrow door. "James McNeely?"

Jim McNeely nodded and grunted, still half asleep.

"I'd like to talk to you, Mr. McNeely." The man's tone and aspect were firm and confident, like a peace officer's. Jim McNeely nodded to the small chair beside the built-in table. The man sat down and pushed his hat back from his forehead with his thumb.

"I'm Mike Arthur, division attorney for Bison Oil."

Jim McNeely shrugged with his mouth. He had half-expected this visit. He had heard of this Arthur. In fact he had watched him make all-conference full-back in some rugged Texas University games a number of years back. Tough monkey.

"McNeely," said the lawyer, pointedly dropping the "mister" and talking in the hard, uncompromising tones which litigation lawyers reserve for formidable adversaries. "You are drilling on a lease that belongs to Bison Oil Company. You acquired this lease through the defalcation of a trusted Bison employee, a geologist named Berry Wakely. You hold color of title under leases from the land owners. But in the eyes of the law those leases belong to Bison. In order to save embarrassing you my company is willing to take you out, pay whatever out-of-pocket costs you have incurred, provided you assign those leases to us, where they belong. Immediately. No charges will be filed against you or Wakely if you do."

Jim McNeely sat back and scratched his belly under his unbuttoned shirt and studied the lawyer across the narrow aisle and decided it would not be practicable to offer him the choice of leaving quietly or being thrown out. The lawyer was at least ten years his junior and obviously in top physical condition. One of those physical fitness nuts that played handball every day at the "Y." It would not serve his purposes to brain him with the whiskey bottle there on the sink, either. Nothing must interfere with the smooth flowing team-work of men, machinery, and plan working toward the sinking of this hole in the ground.

"You're talking funny talk, Mr. Lawyer," he said mildly. "Did Berry Wakely tell you this bed-time story?"

"Wakely has disappeared," said the lawyer, unwisely. This was just the information Jim McNeely sought and it had not been necessary to give it to him. "He walked off the job and disappeared right after we confronted him with this. It's a clear admission of guilt, though we don't need it. We've got other evidence. We know he's been meeting with you."

"For over twenty years, off and on," said Jim McNeely. "We used to work together for Bison, when you were making mud pies, podner."

"I know all about your record with Bison," said the athletic lawyer in tones that implied that the record was little short of criminal.

"Well, what you don't know, maybe, is that all I've been doing for Berry is helping him out a little now and again with his kid that's not right. His wife's been about to go off her rocker. I'm sorry to hear Berry's taken a powder—that sounds like things are real bad at home. But that hasn't got anything to do with me or this well."

"No? You just happened to lease the exact structure that Bison shot out. It won't wash, McNeely."

"Come on, now, buddy. Half a dozen majors and independents have shot this area in the last six months."

"Bison is the only one besides Pan Am that knows how to shoot this deep Smackover and you know it. You're not kidding us, McNeely." This was something else the lawyer didn't have to say, and Jim McNeely felt almost warm toward him. It confirmed his high hopes for the prospect.

He smiled and said, "Are you guys trying to buy me out? This is a new way to go about it. I've seen a lot of approaches in my time but this one is unique in my experience."

The attorney flushed, seeing his adversary sliding away from his blows. He said what he had left to say: "I won't spar with you, McNeely. We don't kid ourselves. We know we're dealing with an old pro. But I can tell you that you're dealing with a major oil company that has been unscrupulously looted, and we'll spare no time or expense in getting back what is rightfully ours. The law says that if we can prove Berry Wakely gave you the confidential information of his employer, and we can prove it, we can impress a trust on these leases and recover them. I don't have to tell you, either, that there's a new statute that makes it a penitentiary offense to steal valuable geophysical information."

Jim McNeely arose from his bunk and started buttoning his shirt. His manner was almost over-friendly, but there was now shortness and impatience underneath his cordial tone, for he had learned all he wanted to know and he wanted the younger man to pack up and go away and quit bothering him. "Mr. Lawyer, I guess you have to do these things, working for a big company, and I don't take it in bad part. But your folks are way off-base. You just draw up some papers and sue me. I got some lawyers that know how to take care of those things."

Suddenly they were two men, big, strong, ambitious, opportunistic men who understood each other and who, somehow, in a few brief minutes, had developed a healthy respect and even a kind of liking for one another, as formidable adversaries, guard to tackle across the line, in spite of their differences.

The lawyer got up and resettled his hat. "OK, hombre. I've got a one-sixteenth override to give you on top. That's all she wrote. You better take it. Otherwise I'll see you in the courthouse."

"Thanks, podner," said Jim McNeely, smiling. He put out his hand. "If she's dry, I'll buy you a drink, because then nobody'll give a damn but me. If she comes roaring in like a wildcat ought to, then we'll have something worth law-suiting about. I hope we'll both have some work to do."

The lawyer hesitated, shook his head, then took Jim McNeely's extended hand. Then he ducked out through the small door and departed.

47

THE TAXI TURNED OUT OF THE THINNING midnight traffic on Fifth Avenue and drove on to the Carlton House, where Charley Dupre jumped out spry as a goat and helped Mazie to the sidewalk. He paid the fare and stood facing her as the cab pulled away. She looked very lovely in her black velvet evening wrap. A cluster of brilliants sparkled in her blonde hair.

"It was a marvelous evening, Charley. The show was great. You're a love to look after a lonely rig-widow in the big city."

"Pleasure, pure heathen pleasure, oh exotic cactus blossom from the great plains. I was thinking you might invite me up for a nightcap," said Charley Dupre.

In the suite the smiling man with the shiny satyr face brought two brandy globes and sat down on the divan facing the handsome wife of Jim McNeely.

"*Salud, pesetas* and bezazz!" he said, lifting his glass.

"I drink to New York," she replied, her lips sparkling with the volatile Cordon Bleu. "I can go so long, then I have to get to New York."

"You belong here, my lovely."

"Jim has been so damned preoccupied. So nervous and irritable he's been simply impossible to live with. He's literally sleeping with that rig in East Texas now. I told him if he was going to desert me for a pile of clanking machinery I was going to New York."

Charley Dupre sipped his drink and studied her face closely, the satyr's smile twinkling in his eyes.

"You do belong here, chickee. You're not like the people down in Tex-iss.

They've all got egg on their faces. Not you. Class is class. Anywhere. You can go anywhere."

"Aren't you nice."

"I'm your type, chickee. We could go far and ring some new bells together."

"Charley, how bold you are tonight!"

"Brazen. And I'll say more, my sweet. You are approaching the end of the line with your pudgy-boy-oil-magnate. He's in trouble. Big type. I'm not saying he's going to wind up in a stupid suit—with horizontal stripes, if you know what I mean. But he's *had* it with some big people that he didn't perform well for. Fine old gentle aristocratic people who will cut the heart out of anybody that disappoints 'em and tries to double-time 'em. Jim has disappointed some of my friends grievously and they're going to nail his ears to the barn door before they're through." He drew on his cigarette and puffed a ring of smoke blithely into the room. "I couldn't care less but you deserve better. How are you at washing and ironing? Better get in practice. A big blow is coming, chickee. It'll roll you up in a ball, with him and all the debris and baling wire if you aren't wise, and rather quickly."

Mazie listened to him attentively. When she spoke her tone was serious, confiding. "I know that things are not good. Saks refused a charge from me today. I have never been so mortified. I was terribly embarrassed and angry. I asked to see the manager. Some snip of an assistant redit manager informed me that my account of eighteen hundred dollars was five months past due. The bills have always been paid from the office."

"The Rockefellers' account could get a year past due and nobody would give it a thought, chickee," said Charley, smiling. "But credit men have a way of knowing when an account is getting sick. They have a secret fraternity."

"Oh, Charley," Mazie cried, "You don't know how awful it's been lately. When he's sober he's so cynical, and when he's drunk he's a beast. That's the story of my life. Two alcoholics in a row!"

Charley Dupre leaned forward and kissed her, lightly but slowly, on her pouting lips.

"You can do better," he said.

"*Mmmm*," she murmured. "That tastes like more."

The visit from Bison's lawyer made Jim McNeely feel some better. It meant that Bison was really stung about this well and that the seismic picture was valid. It also meant that Berry Wakely hadn't become conscious-stricken and talked. Not yet. He had just become conscious-stricken and lost his nerve and fled. Jim McNeely drove rapidly into the little town of Arondale and called the office in Winfield and talked to Mrs. Lukens, the bookkeeper. She was a mean, close-mouthed woman. He would have to trust her, for there was nobody else to put trust in since he had run Dent off. He told her to take a thousand dollars and give it to a certain private detective, the one he had used a time or two before. The detective was to find Berry Wakely and give him the money and tell him to stay out of sight and keep his mouth shut, and that the well was running high and looking good.

When he got back to the rig at dusk he found one of the lawyers from his retained firm of attorneys in Winfield waiting for him.

"Hello, Scotty," he said, a question mark on his face. "You'll get your britches dirty out here where the work is."

"It's not a pleasure trip, Jim. Things are about to blow up all of a sudden. The New York bank and Oilfield Supply and two or three of the other people that you're into for a few million bucks have formed a creditors' committee. They want to meet with you tomorrow and see what you're going to do about it. They say they're at the end of the line. Your investors sent a lawyer down with 'em. Seems like they think there's been some misrepresentation or something. They say they're entitled to an accounting and some kind of positive action to clean this thing up. Everybody's serious as a bunch of funeral directors."

Jim McNeely took off his tin hat and flipped it angrily into the back of the pick-up beside which they were talking. The twilight air was close and humid and he raked sweat from his brow with a forefinger.

"Tell 'em to go to hell," he said. "I got an oil well to drill."

"I'm afraid it won't be that easy," said the lawyer. He was a slender sharp-faced man with a graying crew-cut. "They want to see you tomorrow. What they really want is for you to shut down and not spend another dime until you settle up with 'em. That means they want you to sell out. Everything. And divvy up. If anything's left, it's yours."

"They're outa their infantile minds! I'm drilling a well right here that's going to pay off *everybody*. And I'll put those lousy New York cry-babies in for an interest that will ease their pain, too. I can't stop *now!* Haven't they got the sense they were born with? This well has got to be drilled!"

"So I told them. They tell me they've heard something like that before. They've also heard that Bison is making some kind of claim to this lease block. I'm afraid you haven't got much choice. If you don't meet 'em they'll file involuntary proceedings and throw you into bankruptcy."

"Which means?"

"Which means the Federal District Court will hold a hearing and under the circumstances will undoubtedly appoint a receiver to seize your assets, including this well and lease block."

"How long can you stall 'em? How long will all of this take?"

"Not long. A few days, maybe. They've got fire in their eyes."

"OK. You tell 'em I'm sick. Tell 'em I'm in the hospital and I'll meet with 'em as soon as I get out."

"I can't do that, Jim. I'm a lawyer, not a shyster. They wouldn't believe it, anyway."

"Everybody gets so goddamn moral when a man gets in a little tight. You lawyers will lie and steal for a rich client, but you run like chickens when a poor bastard gets in a jam."

"Now, wait a minute, Jim. That's not fair. We're not running out on you. *Talk* to these people. You can do a better job of stalling them than I could, anyway. They may let you go on."

"The hell with 'em. You just tell 'em that you have been discharged. You no longer represent me."

"Now wait a minute, Jim," the lawyer said gravely.

"You tell 'em that. Tell 'em to send an emissary down to see me, personally. I'll talk to them here and tell 'em who my new lawyer is."

"Are you serious, Jim?"

"That's all, Scotty. I don't need you people. I don't need anybody. I've made it all the way by myself. I'll make it from here on in."

When his ex-lawyer had left, Jim McNeely took a cold hosing down at the side of the rig and put on his city clothes and drove into Tyler. It was after nine when he arrived. He went into a cafe and called D. Q. Shafto on the telephone and asked him to come down to see him. Shafto was an independent operator in the East Texas field. He had made an offer for an interest in the McNeely block as soon as the leases had been recorded in the county records. He had proposed that he would carry Jim McNeely's part of drilling costs for a three-quarter interest in the block.

Jim McNeely had turned him down, not only because he wasn't about to give the deal away, but also because he didn't like the man, whom he knew to be a crook. Shafto had made a small fortune buying worthless leases on the eastern edge of the East Texas field where, taking a smart crook's advantage of modern drilling technology, he had drilled a dozen or more wells, deviating the bore holes from the vertical so that they ran far to westward, off his leases, and bottomed under the producing part of the field as far as a quarter of a mile from the well head. Not many people knew this, but Jim McNeely did.

"So you got you some hot leases, have you, Jim, old sock?" chuckled D. Q. Shafto, shifting the stump of a cigar in his mouth, then taking it out and spitting a shred of tobacco to the floor beside the booth where they sat.

"Hell, they're not hot. Those bastards can't prove anything. *Nothing!* But they might try to screw me up and I'm not about to stop this hole and fuss with 'em about it. All I want to do is use your name as a delaying action. I'll assign the entire block of leases to you and put the assignment on record. Then from here on, for public consumption, you'll be the owner and driller of this well. You'll assign the leases right back to me, of course, and I'll put the assignment in my pocket and record it when I get ready. For your trouble I'll give you an option to buy a one-sixteenth interest in the well and the block at my cost. In other words, a free ride on a one-sixteenth."

The man from Tyler grinned and shifted his cigar to the other side. "It ought to be worth at least an eighth, Jim old sock."

"Christ Almighty! An eighth! This is not costing you a goddamn thing!"

"Aw, now, Jim—when a man uses his good name to help screw somebody! It's really worth a quarter."

"All right, you thievin' bastard. One-eighth. I almost hope it'll be dry."

"It won't be dry. But it ain't drilled yet, Jim, old sockee. You'll need something else before you're through. This is my kind of deal. My original offer still stands. You can trust old D. Q."

"Yeah," said Jim McNeely. "Just as far as I can throw an anvil."

48

HE WAS BACK AT THE RIG SHORTLY AFTER midnight and went straight up on the floor and told the driller to increase the weight on the pipe and increase the drilling speed and never mind if it caused the hole to veer more than the standard four degrees from the vertical. On his way back he had stopped in Arondale, roused his pilot at the motel and told him to have the plane, the single engine Cessna, waiting at the small air strip near Arondale for take-off at first light. He stayed up on the rig floor watching the flickering hand of the weight indicator and the accelerating feed of the kelly joint through the rotary table until 4 a.m. and was satisfied. The drilling was going much faster. It increased the risk of a twist-off but it wasn't a bad risk, and it was necessary. His mind clicked ahead over the two thousand feet to go and the time he would have to make it in. He went down to the trailer and tried to sleep but only lay sweating in tension for an hour until it began to get gray outside. Then he got up, dressed, had a quick cup of black coffee from the ever-brewing percolator in the dog-house and drove roaring over the dirt lease road and the hump-back farm-to-market road ten miles to the air field where the pilot was waiting. They took off immediately for Winfield.

They were on instruments all the way, bumping around in the dirty ragged clouds and slid in under a three hundred foot ceiling in a driving rain. When they taxied up to the hangar at Municipal Airport the young pilot's shirt was wet, though it wasn't that hot.

"Lucked out again, Mr. McNeely," he said, smiling.

"Stand by in the operations office," said Jim McNeely. "I don't know when we'll go back, but it might be any time. Just stand by."

"I'll be here, Mr. McNeely," the young pilot replied. "But the forecast don't look good. They wouldn't clear us for anywhere right now."

"The hell with 'em. You just stand by."

He went directly to the office of Southwestern Fliers next to the terminal building, a charter, aircraft sales, and maintenance concern. These were the people he had bought both of his planes from. Red Savage, the manager, hadn't arrived yet and he waited a nervous twenty minutes drinking coffee in the terminal coffee shop until Savage came in.

"Hello, Mr. McNeely," said Savage. He was a wiry little man who had flown Jennies and every thing since and traded in airplanes with the cunning of a used car dealer. "How about selling you a jet? Man, you're moving too slow in those old prop jobs."

"You're reading my mind," said Jim McNeely. "Seriously, I'm thinking about an executive jet. Buy my Lodestar and we'll talk about it."

"A trade-in?"

"Nope. I've got a tax problem. I want to sell the Lodestar, first. We'll talk about the jet later."

"That Lodestar is getting pretty antiquated."

"Horse-hockey! When you sold it to me you told me it'd be an airplane in demand for the next twenty years."

"It is a good airplane, but times change. People want to move faster."

"Cut the baloney. How much?"

"You serious? Hell, I haven't got a buyer for a luxury Lodestar."

"Come on. How much?"

"Cash?"

"Cash."

"Oh, I don't know. I'd have to think about it."

"Red, don't horse around with me. You know that plane. You want to buy it? If you don't, say so. I'll go to Dallas."

The old pilot-turned-airplane-trader studied him, frowning. "Somewhere around fifteen thousand is all I could see in it."

"You dried up little crop-duster! Give me a price or I'll go to Dallas. Right now."

"Twenty. That's tops, Jim. Go to Dallas. You'll be surprised."

"It's a lousy steal. But fix up the papers."

"What the hell! Is that plane hot?"

"Hell no, it's not hot. And you've made a ten thousand profit in ten minutes. Now move! I want the money."

"I'll write you a check."

"I want cash. Currency. In my office. In an hour."

"Hell, you know the bank is closed. This is a holiday, man. Where am I gonna get that much cash? Outa my piggy bank?"

Jim McNeely groaned. He had forgotten about the holiday.

"All right, first thing in the morning. We couldn't go back to East Texas in this weather, anyway. But I got a red-hot wildcat grinding over there, so don't be late or I'll change my mind."

Infuriated and disgusted by the necessary delay he told the pilot to be ready for a ten o'clock take-off tomorrow morning and took a taxi to town through the driving rain.

As he sat glumly in the corner of the cab watching the rain slick streets through the half moons made by the windshield wipers, watching the stream of traffic moving in and out of the business district, and the neon signs, still glowing along the streets on the gray overcast morning, refracting red and green lights through the rain streaked windows, he felt a sudden loneliness, a deep loneliness and desolation and homesickness for a home he didn't have. He was tired. It was an effort to breathe. He loosened the collar that suddenly was choking his neck.

He dreaded the thought of having to spend this day and night in Winfield. He hated to be away from the well for an hour, much less a day. But more than that he dreaded the prospect of being alone tonight in the big house. Mazie had come back from New York and gone off with a group on some asinine party to Las Vegas. Charley Dupre had thought it up. That sorry bastard. Jim McNeely had had his fill of him. When this well was done he was going to chop him off, get him off his back, once and for all, him and his high and mighty blue-bloods who were now belly-aching because they hadn't quadrupled their money. Hell, they hadn't lost a dime! The bastards!

And Mazie wasn't treating him right, going off at a time like this. She ought to stay at home and stand by him. Lee wouldn't have done anything like that. But Mazie was restless. Time on her hands seemed to drive her frantic.

No, he couldn't face the thought of going out to that big pink monstrosity and spending the night there alone. He never had felt comfortable there. And he sure wasn't about to call up any of their "friends" to come over and make a party. The grapevine was beginning to whisper things about him, and those Glen View bastards were all plugged in.

He thought about Dent and wondered if he was still in town. One of these days, when the well was in and things were settled down, he'd call him up and make peace with him. Even eat a little crow and tell him he was sorry he had called him a queer. But he couldn't do it today. He couldn't face anybody today. Everything was too much in a state of suspense. Everything hung on this well. It had to be finished. Before anything.

No, he would just spend the miserable day and night at the office. Open a jug and have a few drinks and do a little work, then have some supper sent over from the club this evening, take a shower in his office shower-dressing room which he seldom used, then bed down on his couch. In the morning he would collect twenty thousand in cash from Red Savage, strap it in a money belt and head back for the well. With the cash he could pay the drilling crews, buy fuel and mud and finish the well, and his creditors could file all the bankruptcy suits they wanted, garnishee his runs, impound his bank accounts, and the hell with 'em all. He would finish this well. This was the big one.

When the cab pulled up in front of the building he gave the driver a five-dollar bill and told him to keep the change. Then he ran across the sidewalk, getting soaked in the pouring rain before he made the shelter of the entrance. In the elevator lobby a man with a paunch, wearing a rusty black suit and a stockman's hat and a weary look on his face, stood leaning against the marble wall by the elevators reading a newspaper. He glanced up as Jim McNeely punched the button to call a car. A look of sudden alertness came over the man's heavy features. He quickly folded the newspaper and approached Jim McNeely.

"Mr. McNeely?"

Before he thought, his mind miles away, Jim McNeely said, "Yeah?" and immediately cursed himself for doing so.

The man gave a sigh of satisfaction. "Am I glad to see you. I been waitin' for you for two days." With a practiced motion he pulled a white paper from his side pocket, caught Jim McNeely's unsuspecting hand and clapped the paper in it. A card clipped to the paper said, "Abe Duvall-Deputy Sheriff, Mead County, Texas." The folded paper was imprinted with bold black letters that said CITATION.

"No, you got the wrong feller," said Jim McNeely. "My name's Smith."

The deputy laughed. "My name's Duvall, and your name's McNeely. I seen your pictures." He patted Jim McNeely on the shoulder and started to leave. "Good luck, Mr. McNeely."

"Wait a minute!" Jim McNeely said angrily. "What the hell is this all about?"

"I don't read 'em, I just serve 'em," said the deputy, "And you've been served. From now on it's up to you and the judge and the lawyers."

Raging at his own stupidity and at his unknown assailant who had unleashed the pompous, anachronistic processes of the courts upon him, Jim McNeely let himself into his offices. He went into his own office and turned on the lights in the early gloom. He locked the door for no one would be coming to the office on this holiday. Then he threw himself down at his desk and unfolded the paper which he had crushed in his angry hand.

The legal paper was headed, "In the District Court of Mead County, Texas, 98th Judicial District. Cause No. 38074. Mazie Wales McNeely, plaintiff, vs. James McNeely, defendant. Plaintiff's Original Petition for Divorce.

To the Honorable Judge of Said Court.

Now comes, Mrs. Mazie Wales McNeely, hereinafter called plaintiff, who resides in Mead County, Texas, complaining of James McNeely, hereinafter called defendant, who resides in Mead County, Texas, and praying for a divorce, for grounds therefor would show the Court the following . . ."

49

ON THE GRAY BITTER MORROW JIM MCNEELY WAS shaken, hesitantly, by Mrs. Lukens, who told him that a Mr. Savage and another man were there to see him. They said they had an appointment. At a glance she took in the empty whiskey bottle on the carpet, the overturned glass and empty ice tray on the watery desk top, and the general disarray of the office and set about with cold efficiency tidying up as Jim McNeely roused himself, shuddering up from the depths of a bone-deep hangover. He muttered to her to give him five minutes, then to let them in.

He staggered into the bathroom, avoiding a direct look into the mirror, and sloshed cold water in his face and ran a comb through his matted hair. His head felt as if it would burst with each pound of his heart. His belly was sick and shuddery for he had not eaten in twenty-four hours but had sat alone drinking, rereading the terse, bitter legalese of the divorce petition and cursing the fraudulent, faithless, cowardly nature of this woman that fate and his own unbridled appetites had saddled him to. She had not changed since childhood and youth, when she had rejected him, twice before. Now at the first sign of foul weather she had run out on him for good. Well, the hell with her. He did not need her, either.

The business of the airplane sale took less than fifteen minutes. After the men were gone he counted the money again with shaking fingers. Twenty thousand. Forty five-hundred dollar bills. He fished around in the bottom desk drawer until he found his old money belt, then packed the bills tightly into it, strapped it around his middle under his shirt, and was preparing to tell Mrs. Lukens to order a taxi when the phone rang. It was Jimmy Dale, the pilot.

"Even the ducks are hoofin' it this morning, Mr. McNeely. There's no use to come out here now. Might as well save yourself the trip. The forecast is for this stuff to blow out of here sometime this afternoon. I'll call you the minute I can get take-off clearance."

Jim McNeely sat cursing and fuming and toying with the idea of hiring a car and chauffeur to drive him back to the well, but he felt so sick he could not now face the prospect of the long swaying ride in the back seat of a car. He went into the bathroom, took a couple of Alka-Seltzers and threw up massively, then took a couple more. A warning thought of caution told him he had better leave the office. If word got out he was in town, and it certainly would, he might have other visitors with other pieces of legal paper to slap in his hand. Putting on an old soft felt hat and dark glasses he told Mrs. Lukens to tell any callers that he was ill, at home. Pulling a plastic slicker over his beefy shoulders he went down the elevator and out into the rainy streets.

He first thought of taking a room in a hotel under an assumed name, then decided against it. All the hotel clerks knew him. Anyway, he wouldn't be staying in town that long. As soon as the pilot could get clearance to take-off he would be on his way. And so he went to the Winfield Club, keeping his head down and his collar pulled up, and was glad that he ran into no one he knew and that the Mexican girl operating the elevator was new and didn't know who he was. He got off on the ninth floor and went into the quiet dimness of the reading lounge. The room was little used by the members. It was empty now. He chose a high-backed chair on one side of the room, turning it away from the entrance, then rang for a waiter and sank into its wrinkled leather depths.

The waiter was an old, white-haired Negro retainer who knew him well. Jim McNeely told him to bring him a double Scotch on the rocks and a plug-in telephone, and to check back every fifteen minutes. Then he gave him a ten dollar bill and told him not to let anybody know he was in the club, and not even to turn in his bar checks until he had gone.

When the phone came he called the airport, found the weather still zero-zero, and told the pilot to keep standing by and that he would call him every half hour. He drew a deep draught from the iced glass of liquor, fought for a full half minute until it stayed down and began to work, then settled back to wait.

As he wandered down the wet sidewalk, hands thrust deep in his trench-coat pockets, Dent Paxton window-shopped avidly, compulsively, reading the price tags on all of the cheap ladies' pumps in the windows of the shoe store with an almost frantic interest, as if it kept him in the main current of life and was somehow a tie with sanity to be interested in what it cost a working girl to be fashionably and inexpensively shod these days in Winfield, Texas.

Later he wandered in this same aimless, intense pursuit through the cosmetics and health food departments of Weingart's Department Store and ended up at an old familiar and well-loved spot, the book department. His good friend, Martha Eckman, finished waiting on a customer and came up to him with hands outstretched.

"Dent! I haven't seen you in a hundred years! Where have you been?" Martha Eckman was an attractive, efficient, middle-aged widow with a love for books and a need to make a living. She had a pencil stuck in her brown graying hair.

"Got time for a cup of tea?" Dent said.

"I'll take time. Nobody buys books on a rainy day."

They went into Weingart's nearly deserted tea room and took a small table in a corner. Dent placed the tea bags in the two cups of hot water and covered them with the saucers to steep, his slender fingers working delicately, almost as if this were a ceremonial ritual. It didn't result in good tea, but it was the best he could do with the materials at hand.

"Where have you been, you naughty boy? You've deserted me. Oh, there's a fine new book by Morris West. I thought of you after I'd read the first three pages." Martha Eckman had long had a keen interest in Dent Paxton. He was, she thought, basically a religious person, a person with a latent genius which had never been lighted and which if once touched with just the right spark at just the right time could take fire and glow and burn with a fine and holy light. He was a special person to her and her life's pleasure and satisfaction was picking out the special, super-usual people who swam past her vision, and encouraging them to find their genius.

"I've retired now, you know. I've been in Mexico."

"Oh? No, I didn't know."

"You can't go on slaving all your life. You finally have to make a break and seek your own little garden."

"How nice. If you can do it. Some of us aren't so fortunate. Eating is such a nasty habit."

"I've been in Mexico. But it was so—depressing. The colors have gone out of it. Faded and gone."

"Oh, I can't imagine that. I love Mexico."

"Yes, Martha. They've faded. They were once vivid, clashing, atrocious— but wonderful colors. But they've faded out, almost white. Commercialism, I guess. It made me want to cry when I saw how the colors had faded. So I came back home. Home is where the heart is. Isn't that touching? I thought it up."

"You and Eddy Guest or somebody." He was talking strangely. Not like the old Dent. Her eyes narrowed with concern as she looked at him.

"Life is so simple to live, Martha, really. You have only to breathe, and love, and enjoy it. We make it complicated for no understandable reason. People who have only the wonderful privilege of being alive and the opportunity to love have all there is. We muddy it up so. It's so ridiculous. We have everything! If only we could face away, just this much, just thirty degrees, we could see past this tangled mess we've worked up with our silly, childish fingers. Just out there it's all clear. Clear and serene. Why can't we do that, Martha?"

"You're asking me the riddle of the ages, Denton, my dear friend. But you can solve it. Of all the people I've ever known, you're the one who can solve it."

"Not I, Martha. My neck is paralyzed. I can't turn my head and see—" He pointed obliquely to the right. "Out there where it's clear."

The woman looked at him with real concern now. "Yes, Dent, you can."

"When you have become so entangled in the threads, have woven yourself so deep into the fabric, you lose your identity. You have nothing left of your own."

"But Dent, you have your own fabric. My dear funny friend, I see I'm going to have to give you a good talking to. You come to dinner with me tonight. At the apartment. Seven o'clock. All right?"

"Oh—no—well, all right." He reached across the empty cups and patted her hand. "You're a good gal, Martha. I'll put in a word for you at the head office."

"Seven o'clock," she said, laughing with a strange uneasiness. "You hear?"

"Seven o'clock. I'm deeply grateful. I love you, Martha."

On the street again, Denton Paxton found that he could not read the price tags on the shoes and suits and garden tools in the store windows, and it no longer seemed to matter what they cost. What to do? How to do it? His membership in the Club was still valid. Under the by-laws he was still a member in good standing. The Club had been his symbol of status as well as the next member's. His home away from home, as they say. His carnet of quality and worth in the society of his time. It was his right to go there, and there he would go.

The day dragged itself slowly away toward night and the sky had not lifted. The front had stalled its massive wet grayness athwart the land where Jim McNeely sat in the high, silent gloom of the club reading room. With each call to the airport he promised himself that after the next he would hire a car and a driver, but each time he put off his departure for one more call. It was as if a force of indecision held him there for some dark appointment. His depression had deepened with the swing of the clock hands.

Seated in the high backed chair in the musty, faintly tobacco-ish, faintly leather-scented gloom, he heard the muted hiss-click of the elevator door opening and closing in the foyer. He wondered with annoyance what other homeless bird had made his way to these deserted quarters on this dreary afternoon. He did not turn to look, for he did not want to see or be seen, but presently he heard the quiet noises of someone walking across the deep carpeting near him, the whispers of clothing, the faint sound of breathing. Then he saw the figure of a man passing the magazine-covered table, the leather couch, the dark fluted column that rose to the ceiling. It was Denton Paxton.

Dent did not see him. Jim McNeely caught and held back an old instinctive impulse to call out to him. He had things to make up to Dent for, but not now. This was not the time. What was the silly bastard doing up here, anyway? He scowled at the straight, slender back as his oldest and truest friend moved aimlessly across the room and stopped at a window and stood for a moment looking out.

When Dent raised the window and stood looking out into the misty air, Jim McNeely shrugged. There was nothing unusual in this. The room had not had a breath of unrecirculated, chilled, rebreathed air in months, maybe years. When Dent slipped off his wrist watch, wound it carefully, listened to see that it was ticking, then laid it on the table by the window, Jim McNeely's scowl deepened and to himself he wondered, half angrily, *What is the silly ass doing now?*

The rest came too quickly, with a paralyzing horror of realization, like a vessel breaking in his head. Before his eyes Dent Paxton swung his slender legs over the sill and was sitting in the window. Jim McNeely had only time to throw up his hand and lurch and open his mouth in a wordless, deep-throated cry of anguish. Then the window was empty, and Dent Paxton was gone.

50

THEY SAID THAT AFTER JIM McNEELY RETURNED to the rig, after the funeral, he never slept again. At least no one ever saw him sleep. He never again went to the trailer to catch a few hours nap as he had done before. He stayed in the dog-house off the rig floor, leaning with his hands braced against the knowledge-box, his head down between his shoulders as if he were asleep standing up, but he was not asleep. Or sometimes he would lie on the board catwalk that ran by the shaleshaker and mud pumps, between the derrick and the mud pits, and sometimes he had his eyes closed, but when anyone approached he would open his eyes and look up at them, whoever it was.

The drilling went rapidly and without incident for days, and he scarcely spoke. He seemed to have lost his anxiety about the well, even his interest in it. It was almost as if he were sitting up with it as an obligation he had undertaken long ago and must perform because it was ordained in the pattern and order of his life that he do so.

The great compounded organism of the drilling rig, trembling with deep and deafening power, spiralled its slender wand farther and farther into the cockles of the earth, like the galeae of a butterfly probing for the deep-seated nectars of a flower.

The first trouble came below twelve thousand feet. The mud returns, the flow of drilling fluid carrying the cuttings from the bottom of the bore hole, slackened, then all but stopped. The bit had penetrated a porous formation and the weight of the two mile mud column in the hole forced the slurry out into the porous rock instead of circulating it upwards outside the pipe in the bore hole. Drilling without mud returns would bring sure and swift disaster, for the turning drill pipe would bind in its own cuttings and twist off in the hole.

The driller cut the throttle and stopped the rotary action of the pipe. Then he shifted the controls and touched the throttle again. With a shattering roar the powerful engines lifted the two miles of pipe off bottom and drew the drill-stem fifteen feet up into the derrick. Glancing at Jim McNeely, the driller set the brake and stood waiting for him to say what to do next.

The lost-circulation problem was to continue, off and on, for the next twenty-four hours. A gelatinous lost-circulation material was dumped into the mud pit and pumped into the hole to seal the porous walls of the formation, for the well was still nearly six hundred feet above its objective depth and drilling had to go ahead. Jim McNeely then ordered the mud mixture to be lightened, diluting it with water to lessen the weight of the mud column on the formation. Then drilling was started up again. That was when the well began to kick. The porous formation just penetrated was obviously charged with a tremendous pressure. The mud returns began to come up belching and gassy and Jim McNeely ordered the mud weight increased again by the addition of solids, to hold the pressure down.

Then circulation was lost again. By tense, careful experimentation during the next two eight-hour tours which took him through a yellow dawn into the hot noonday hours, Jim McNeely found that a mud weight of 13.4 pounds per gallon would result in lost circulation and a mud weight of 12.8 pounds would cause the well to start kicking and threatening to blow the confining mud column out of the bore hole. This was the terror, the nightmare of oil men—a blow-out, with fire that almost always followed, destroying well, machinery, and sometimes men when the awakened hydrocarbon giant, pent for millennia in the deep layers of the earth, defied man's best efforts to tame it and reduce it to docile utility.

The record books were filled with accounts of blown-out wells caught fire, cratering, swallowing whole rigs, cars, trucks, burning men to cinders, bankrupting millionaires, raging uncontrolled for weeks and months, burning up millions in the wild escaping blast from high-pressure reservoirs that slipped out of man's control in spite of all his technology and know-how and expensive high pressure apparatus. No pain or expense had been spared to guard against this possibility in Jim McNeely's well.

Heavy blow-out preventers with hydraulic rams had been installed, stacked, and bolted on top of the casing head. When the well first started kicking, Jim McNeely ordered these preventers to be tested to make sure they were working properly. They were. The rams closed around the drill pipe and packed off the upsurging mud column. Then they were released and the drilling proceeded. Everything was OK.

The cuttings floated up in the circulating mud stream, the increased penetration speed of the bit and the high-pressure surging of gas—the hydrocarbon character of which was confirmed by the mud logger—clearly indicated that they had drilled into a well-developed sand body above the Smackover and that it appeared to be a potential pay zone. This was unexpected because the sand had not been productive in other wells in the area. It was a welcome sign, like stumbling onto a vein of silver when you were mining for gold. But the prime objective of the well was still the Smackover limestone of Jurassic age five hundred-odd feet deeper.

Normally Jim McNeely would have ordered the drill pipe to be snaked out of the hole and would then have run in a testing tool to make a drill-stem test to evaluate what this "show" really amounted to. But now he seemed interested only in punching the hole down to its objective depth and finishing it up as rapidly as possible. Besides, a drill-stem test took time and time cost money on a drilling rig, and his money belt was running low. He had paid Dent Paxton's funeral expenses out of it, including the cost of bringing a sister and an aunt from the state of Washington to join the small group of mourners.

The contract geologist from Geo-lab, Inc. was very unhappy, even cross, when Jim McNeely rejected his recommendation to pull out the pipe and test. Geologists like to see what they have found, even when they haven't known they were going to find it.

"If it's a good pay it'll show on the electric log," Jim McNeely said in a low voice, absently, as if he had only half heard the young man. "We can test it later. Drill ahead."

And so the drilling proceeded, cautiously. It was like walking a tightwire, adjusting the mud weight to keep the well from either kicking or losing circulation, and with only a fraction of a pound leeway in between.

The blow-out came at 12:20 a.m., just after the graveyard crew had come on tour. The tri-cone bit on the bottom of the drill-stem had ground its teeth smooth and ceased to cut hole, and it was necessary to make a round trip with the pipe, to pull all two and a quarter miles of it out of the hole, take off the used-up bit, screw on a new one, then run the pipe into the hole again.

As the drill-stem was thunderously drawn from the hole, ninety foot stand at a time and stacked in the derrick, the mud level dropped in the bore hole, for circulation had to be suspended during this operation. Fresh drilling mud was routinely pumped into the hole at intervals to fill it up to the top to keep the pressure down. Perhaps it was the critical pressure balance that made the blow-out inevitable, or perhaps the drilling crew was not on its toes and the filling procedure was slow, or perhaps it was because Jim McNeely was exhausted and despondent beyond caring and sat on a bit-box in the dog-house with his head in his hands when he might have been alert, watching every motion, every action, as he once had done.

It happened so fast there was only time to yell and run. A thribble stand of pipe had just been racked back in the derrick and the huge traveling block was descending from the crown block, dangling its iron elevators which would catch and pull up the next stand. One moment gray viscous mud welled up through and around the rotary table and started to gush over the derrick floor, and the next moment all hell broke loose. With a shattering roar the derrick was filled with vaporized mud, gas, sand, rocks and bits of torn lumber. Reacting with the instinct of men who see and feel in an instant that events are blown beyond their control and that only their lives can be saved, the driller and roughnecks yelled futile warnings, as if from a single throat, and dove for the nearest openings in the derrick. They jumped and hit the ground running, two with broken bones in their legs.

In a daze, Jim McNeely staggered from the dog-house into the choking, deafening, gray cataclysm on the derrick floor. Peering upward in the blinding storm of mud and gas, he yelled to the derrick man high on his monkey board, "Hit the wire!"

In the uproar his cry was unheard, but the derrick man, who wanted to live, saw and felt and smelled the gray gas mist swirling up at him like a rising tornado. Tearing loose from his safety belt he leaped to the guy-wire running from the run-around to the dead-man anchored far out on the edge of the clearing near the trees. Grabbing the escape trolley with both hands he launched himself down the slanting wire, like a circus peformer.

Had he hesitated but seconds he would have burned to a cinder, for some tiny spark—perhaps from the exhaust of the still-running deisels, perhaps from a rock striking metal with bullet-velocity—ignited the roaring gas column that flumed from the well, then the whole heaven seemed to light up in a great terrible twisting, enveloping ball of fire.

Men in shock react strangely. In the woods, in the glaring light of the flames, as near to the well as the heat would allow, the crew gathered. Jim McNeely kept brushing the seat of his pants, as if he could brush away the pain of the smashed coccyx received when he hurled himself down the wooden pipe ramp in his escape from the derrick floor. In the eerie glare and heat and the abrasive, rock-showering roar of the early stages of the blow-out he moved purposefully among the men, now milling about in the underbrush and trees like dazed cattle, and he was once again the man in charge, fatigue forgotten, schemes gone, plan gone, ambition gone, all gone from his heart and mind except the safety of men and the critical necessity of the moment. Quickly he counted heads and found that no injuries were fatal. He heaved a deep groan of relief. "Thank God this long lost son-of-a-bitch didn't kill anybody else."

51

IGHTING AN OIL WELL FIRE IS A CRAFT, A SCIENCE, an art of its own. It is the most hazardous non-wartime occupation of civilized men. When interviewed by a television reporter on the scene of a blazing well the most famous living oil-well firefighter once was asked, "What is it—the thrill of danger that keeps you working year after year in this crazy business?"

The firefighter, a good looking red-head with the build of an athlete and a hard twinkle of savvy in his eyes said, "Oh, I wouldn't say that."

"The challenge of the wild, untamed forces of nature?" the reporter shouted over the roar of the well. "Surely it's not the money. What a way to make a living!"

The firefighter shrugged. "It pays all right."

"Well then what is it?" cried the reporter. "What on earth impels a man like you to travel all over the world seeking out these raging infernos week after week, month after month, year after year, risking your life to tame them, bring them under control? Why do you do it?"

A grin flickered across the firefighter's eyes. "I guess you might say it's all I know how to do."

It was nearing noon before the first shock and the ensuing chaos began to subside and order and plans to emerge. The well, the monumental thing that was the focus of all attention, cleaned itself of mud and rocks and water and settled down to a whistling, deafening roar, sending up a bright yellow-white column of fire that towered and flowered and twisted three hundred feet in the air. It began with the thick column of gas that roared from the casing-head, where the pressure was too great for combustion, then the blast-furnace blaze began and rose in a swirling cone which expanded as it mounted upward through the derrick. It was a malevolent, consuming force, and it quickly burnt out the derrick floor, its heat devouring all wooden walkways, braces, derrick blocks, like chips in a blacksmith's forge. Two cars and a pick-up parked too near the rig had exploded like firecrackers in the first hour. By daylight the trailer near the edge of the clearing had begun to blister and smoke from the heat and the steel derrick itself, under the direct upward blast, had begun to lose its temper and collapse inward like a framework of hot candy.

By noon the rig and derrick and auxiliary equipment lay a crumpled, white hot mass of ruined metal about the belching maw of the well. Sparks from falling debris set grass and brush fires that ate eddies into the woods surrounding the square location clearing.

Volunteers drawn from the hundreds of curious country people attracted to the blaze took wet tow sacks and beat out the fires in the underbrush and kept them from spreading farther.

A command post was set up in the edge of the woods next to the road leading to the highway and as close to the well as the heat would permit.

The young grimy-faced geologist studied the towering column of flame and said, "It's making a hundred and fifty million cubic feet of gas a day, at least. No telling what the pressure is. And it's making some condensate. See there." He pointed upward to the top of the huge torch where in the rolling fire there were red flame tongues licking in the midst of black smoke.

A fire of this magnitude made four alarm news in the industry. It was on all the wire services by afternoon. D. Q. Shafto arrived on the scene shortly before one o'clock. Being the nominal owner of the well and the actual owner of a one-eighth interest, he appeared to be angry and upset, though Jim McNeely knew he was highly pleased.

"I thought you was a well-man. How come you let her get away? Passed out drunk?"

"All right, D. Q., if that's all you got to say you can just haul your ass on back to Tyler."

Jim McNeely was glad, nonetheless, to have the counsel of an experienced well-man, even a crook. The two made plans, what to do, how to go about it. You didn't just sit and watch a well burn when it was your own. It had to be killed and brought under control.

"You put in a call for Red Adair?" said Shafto.

"I thought about it," said Jim McNeely. Red Adair of Houston was the No. 1 wild well man in the world. "He's over in Africa somewhere. Big blow-out in the desert."

"Hell, there's others in his outfit can handle this job," said Shafto. "But that's not the main point. What're you gonna use for money?"

"I figured you could answer that."

"I can. I'll pay you fifty thousand dollars for a half interest in the block. That'll give you fifty to work with and I'll put up fifty for my half. That'll make a hundred thousand to kill her with."

"That won't do it. Anyway this block is worth twenty million dollars."

"Yeah, if you like lawsuits. All right, go somewhere else. I got cash. Call me if you change your mind."

"Hold on, D. Q. I'll take it. But a hundred thousand won't do it."

"When that's used up," said D. Q. Shafto, "we'll take another look. I might just take you clean out and get you out of a jam."

"That's real generous," said Jim McNeely. "But I don't give a damn. I just want to kill the son-of-a-bitch and finish it. Get some money out here. We need water. Lots of it. And pumping equipment and 'dozers and drag-lines. A contractor from Gladewater is on his way with a crew and equipment. There's a river about a mile north. The sheriff has agreed to keep the sightseers back and get us a right-of-way for the water lines. But that contractor is gonna want to see some cash. Get some cash out here."

"I'll get the money, but who's going to put the fire out?"

"Me, that's who," said Jim McNeely. "And Al McKnight. You ought to remember him. He used to be the best in the business. He's seventy-eight years old and retired. But he still knows how to do it. He can tell me. His grandson, Albert, has been working summers for me. Three years now. Goes to college at Texas Tech. I talked to old Al on the phone. He's coming. I sent my plane after him two hours ago."

The effort of saying it all, spelling it out, making the deal he knew he would have to make, was too great for Jim McNeely. He sank down on the ground and leaned back against a tree trunk.

"Looks like we got everything in hand, pardner," said D. Q. Shafto, happily, admiring the distant torch rising from the mass of twisted metal.

"Just get some money out here," said Jim McNeely.

52

I T WAS NIGHT AGAIN BEFORE REAL PROGRESS BEGAN
to be evident. The farm-to-market roads in the area were choked
with cars of curious country folk who had heard of the fire or seen
its flickering glow and rising smoke column and had driven toward it
from miles around, making passage to and from the well difficult despite
the best efforts of the sheriff's men. A guard was posted on the lease
road leading from the black-top to keep out these sightseers who, if not
stopped, would have driven on until they singed their eyebrows.

During this opening phase of driving activity Jim McNeely twice felt
his legs give way under him and both times he sat stupidly on the ground,
fighting sheer animal exhaustion for five or ten minutes before he could
find the will to get up and go again.

By midnight, twenty-four hours after the blow-out, the effort began to
shape up. The contractor from Gladewater had arrived with a full roustabout crew and truck-loaded caterpillar tractors and drag-line. Shafto had
eased the contractor's anxiety about payment, and the roustabouts were
now halfway from the river laying two six-inch water-lines.

Al McKnight, accompanied by his grandson, Albert, arrived early next
morning. Albert greeted Jim McNeely warmly.

"Gosh, Mr. McNeely, this is great! What I mean is, maybe we can do
something for *you*, now. Grandpa—Al—he knows what to do, and I got
the strong back and weak mind to carry it out. I'm sure glad you called on
us, Mr. McNeely."

Old Al McKnight had tamed many a wild well. He had had two little
strokes and his physical appearance was not reassuring, but his mind

seemed to be good as he walked around the perimeter of the fire with Jim McNeely and surveyed the monumental problem before them.

"Looks like you got you a real bitch-kitty here, Jim."

"Yeah. I can pay you, Al. In advance if you want it."

"Let's not worry about that now," said the old man, studying the fire, the glare flickering warmly on his face and lighting an old excitement. "Main thing is to put her out and shut her in. A man works for more things than money."

They sat down on some sacks of mud that had been unloaded from one of the contractor's trucks and set about planning what they would do first.

"It looks like the pipe dropped back in the hole when the rig collapsed. The blow-out preventers probably won't help us, even if we can get to the control console. The mastergate on the casinghead is probably frozen with the heat and nobody could get in the cellar, even in asbestos, anyway. Nope, the only thing to do is blow out the fire. But first all that hot metal has got to be pulled out of there, clean away from the well-head. If we didn't and blew out the fire, it would catch right back from the hot metal. First things first, the fella says. We'll have to pull that hot junk out of there, piece at a time, get everything clean away from the well. Then we'll rig a satchel-charge of dynamite, hang it on a boom on a bull-dozer and run the charge in close to the flame and try to blow the fire out that way. Then we'll flood the damn place with water and maybe somebody can get in there and close the master gate. If the gate won't close we'll have to have a special control-head machined at the Cameron works down in Houston, and try to stab it on top of the blow-out preventers, and then close that. If that don't work we'll try something else. You just keep trying things 'til something works. We'll play it by ear, like always. But first things first. Let's go."

And so began the slow, tortuous process of clearing the well-site. Welders worked around the clock under Al's direction building heat-shields of corrugated iron on the bull-dozers and drag-line, cab-like structures with eye-slits, which enabled the operators to get in close enough to the well base to do their work. The water lines from the river were completed and pumps were set and started and thereafter were kept running twenty-four hours a day, filling the battery of five hundred barrel tanks which had been trucked in and unloaded at the edge of the clearing. A well cementing company had brought out high-pressure pumps and rigged stationary nozzles at two points on the south side of the clearing down-wind from the blaze. These nozzles could be aimed and directed by hand, and two streams of water were kept playing on the caterpillars and drag-line as they moved into and out of the heat. Toward the center of the inferno the streams of water vaporized to steam before they could hit the machinery, but in the approaches they did some good.

Albert rode one of the "cats," and he worked like a demon with a lot of talk and pepper, like a good infielder under a good manager, his grandfather, who strode up and down the sidelines as he directed the other cat and drag-line operators and the support force of roughnecks on the rim on the fire. And so fifty men who yesterday had been strangers, today worked together in this crisis, smoothly, efficiently, uncomplainingly, dedicated and intent, with no thought except to subdue this wild thing of nature run amuck that was somehow threatening man's promised dominion over the earth. And the giant stalk of fire roared stiffly into the sky, white orange by day, a blinding, colorless brilliance by night, and the nights seemed even brighter in its light than the days, though the shadows were a deeper black.

53

SLOWLY THE HERCULEAN TEAM EFFORT BEGAN to take effect. Rigged with special hooks constructed on the spot with welding torch and scrapiron and cable the drag-line rumbled toward the fire and fished for, now missing, now catching and breaking loose, but now hooking firmly onto some piece of white-hot derrick metal or draw works, then backing out, dragging it into the relative cool of the clearing where the bulldozers took over and shoved it to the sidelines where streams of water quenched its imprisoned heat. When a really big piece of iron was caught and dragged away from the fire, the main reel and housing of the draw works or the undergirding of the derrick, the workers and the curiosity seekers around the perimeter sent up a cheer like a football crowd. Albert, drenched in sweat and water, would stand up from his seat on the cat and yell and shake hands with himself over his head and take a bow. It was a great time for him. And slowly he and his teammates literally tore the melted rig apart and dragged it, piece by piece, out of the fire.

Jim McNeely watched it all from the command post at the edge of the clearing where a tarpaulin had been stretched between trees for shade from the sun and protection from the intermittent showers. A telephone line had been run in from the highway and a few canvas cots had been set up and a large wooden table, procured from somewhere, held a coffee urn and cans of coffee and sacked sugar and stacks of paper cups.

The workers came and went in shifts and those who stayed around the clock, Jim McNeely, Al McKnight, and Albert, ate what was brought to them and slept in leaden exhaustion on the cots when they could, except that no one ever saw Jim McNeely really sleep. Sometimes he closed his eyes, but when anyone came up to him his eyes were open looking at them before they spoke.

There wasn't much for Jim McNeely to do as these early days of the fire-fight wore on. Old Al and Albert and the contractor's foreman were specialists doing a specialized work. They knew their business and any advice from him would have been a hindrance more than a help. He disbursed money where it was necessary in order to keep the work going, and then one afternoon he had another visit from the Bison lawyer, this time with two other people, and he got rid of them rather quickly.

"My company claims this well, McNeely. You negligently let it blow out and the company holds you responsible for all damage to the reservoir. We'll give you a full release and take over the job of bringing it under control, if you'll execute an assignment of title." The muscular attorney recited lines he had written out in the office. He had witnesses this time and was building a case.

"Friend," said Jim McNeely wearily. "This well belongs to D. Q. Shafto. Check the county records. I'm just working for him and I'm mighty busy right now. Come see me when we get done here—if we ever do."

"We don't put any stock in that assignment to Shafto. I'm warning you that I intend to get out an injunction to keep you from interfering with the proper salvage of this property," said the attorney.

"Lawyer," said Jim McNeely, "take a look around you. We're doing everything anybody could do. Come back when it's under control and we'll fuss about it."

"You don't leave me any choice but to go the injunction route, McNeely."

"OK," said Jim McNeely. "Go get your injunction, if you can. And while you're at it see if you can't get the judge to enjoin this blazing son-of-a-bitch from burning."

In the light of the towering fountain of fire, as the dwarfed men and machines moved in and out of its consuming heat, dragging away the tumbled wreckage which it had, in minutes, made of the best, the strongest, the most complex and costing drilling machinery and control equipment that man could devise, Jim McNeely sat at the table under the overstretched tarpaulin, his head resting in one grimed hand, watching Al McKnight as the old man explained to the welder the kind of boom he wanted constructed on the front end of one of the bulldozers. Rain from a brief shower dripped from the edge of the tarpaulin overhead. On a large piece of brown paper Al had drawn the crude but practical design of a slender steel proboscis for the caterpillar, long enough to give the driver some protection from the heat of the fire and the blast of dynamite charge which would be mounted at the very tip and strong enough, with welded cantilever braces, to support the weight of the sizeable charge.

He drew an arrow pointing to the end of the snout. "Albert will drive the cat with this charge. When he gets it in place, *he*," he looked significantly at Jim McNeely, "will connect the wires to the detonator. Soon as Albert drops off the cat and scrams out of there I'll set her off. If we're lucky that'll interrupt the gas stream from the fire long enough so it won't catch again. Then we'll pour the water to the hot ground, then Lord willing, we'll shut in our well, or cap it with a new control head if we have to. If we can get a break on the wind so it'll disperse the gas and some damn fool this side of Tyler don't take a notion to smoke a cigarette, we might get her shut in before she catches again. But first things first. Main thing's to get the fire out so we can get in close enough to work. That's the story."

As the wreckage clearing continued, the perimeter around the well began to take on the aspect of a bombed-out city. The twisted, grotesque shapes of fused and oxidized metal reminded Jim McNeely of a graveyard. Good things, good hopes, all gone bad and buried. It remained only to say the final requiem mass. He could not keep his eyes open for very long at a time now, nor could he sleep, either. His heart raced raggedly, as if on a final, frantic mission of its own. He had long forgotten the feeling of relaxation or rest.

Before he realized it had happened, almost before he was ready—for he sensed that this would begin the last act before the final curtain, not just of the fire, or the well but of the wandering tale of his life—the location was cleared and the charge was ready. The caterpillar tractor was welded to its long proboscis and a packet the size of a foot-locker encased in asbestos was clamped by explosives—men gingerly into the bracket at the boom's slender tip.

There was no final ceremony, and this seemed unfitting. There should have been some *kamikaze* invocation of the divine wind, some ritual of purification and sacrifice before men exposed themselves to danger and at least one of them entered upon the stage to perform this final volitional act of his life. But there was nothing. Not even a hitching-up of the pants, no exchange of deep, significant glances between dedicated men. The action flowed in a casual, almost routine sequence. The charge was ready, the caterpillar was thrumming deeply, and Albert, long briefed in his precise role in the unfolding drama, mounted lightly up into the seat of the machine. He received an almost imperceptible nod from his grandfather, then touched the throttle and eased the monstrous contraption slowly toward the geyser of fire.

54

ALBERT'S AIM HAD TO BE PRECISE, EXACT ALMOST to the inch, so he did not hurry his advance toward the well. He had never been this deep into the heat before, heat which intensified with every yard as he drove into its core. He had smeared his face thickly with cocoa butter, had drenched with water the double suit of khakis he wore. His fibre safety hat had been packed with wet towels, and dark goggles shielded his eyes. Perched on the seat of the cat he looked like some Martian character in a TV drama as he maneuvered the machine slowly into the throat of the inferno.

"He's moving too damn slow!" said Al McKnight irritably, standing next to Jim McNeely beside the small detonator box on the edge of the clearing. The bare ends of the unreeling wire leading from the charge on the boom-tip were held tightly in the old man's bare hand. In the final moments of preparation, unnoticed, dusk had faded into darkness. Despite the efforts of the sheriff's patrols hundreds of country folk, oil scouts, news reporters, and the merely sadistically curious from surrounding parts, had come through the woods, over barbed wire fences, evading guards and ignoring danger, to see the free show in which the raging elements would be challenged and there was a chance that somebody might get blown sky-high.

"He's going too slow!" said Al, now clearly agitated. It was useless to shout against the roar of the well but the old man moved forward, out into the heat, still clutching the bare wires, and began waving and pumping his free arm in a motion to hurry. But Albert, intent on doing his job just right, was not looking.

"That damn charge can stand just so much heat. It'll catch fire and burn up, or blow up, before it's in place," said Al. "Boy! Go on!" he cried agonizingly. "He can't take but only so much of that heat himself!"

Deep into the fire now, Albert had decided that he had made a wrong approach, too oblique to the column of fire, not square enough. So he stopped and put the cat into reverse to back up and come in straight. After backing a foot or two he apparently realized that he was going to back directly over and probably cut the trailing detonating wire. That was good thinking, Albert, but not wisdom. The youth, intent on doing the job right, jumped from the cab, out of the protection of the heat-shield onto the sizzling earth where the fire caught him in its dissolving force and drove into the depths of his brain. Stricken, in slow motion, like a man gasping with surprise at his waning strength, he grabbed for the wire on the ground, larruped it out of the way of the cat's backward track, then started to climb back onto the tractor. He did not make it. Heat like this was beyond the ken and experience of ordinary men. He made the step, then reached up his hand toward the seat. Wavering a moment in mid air he fell slowly backward, crumpling onto the burning earth beside the tractor.

"Albert!" Old Al's cry pierced the roar. "Albert!" He dropped the wires and started, instinctively, blindly, running across the open space into the glare toward his fallen grandson.

From a start two paces behind, Jim McNeely caught the old man in ten strides and tackled him like a half-back. Then he wrestled furiously with him on the ground until a dozen men, oblivious to heat or danger, darted from the perimeter and laid hands on the old man and dragged him back toward the trees.

"Let me go!" yelled Al, struggling. "Albert! He'll die!"

"OK, Al," said Jim McNeely, hauling himself to his feet. "We'll get him." He wiped dirt out of one blinded eye, sucked in a deep breath, and started toward the tractor at a run, mumbling, rumbling curses to himself, heedless of the shouted warnings behind him. This son-of-a-bitch was not going to kill anybody else.

As he ran the glare struck into his eyes and narrowed them to slits. The heat—it was incredible—like opening the door of a furnace and forcing yourself into it. He felt the skin of his face pucker. The breath was sucked out of him and he could barely see the black lump of the tractor for the flaring jewel-like blaze. His hair began to curl and it felt as if his lashes were melting into his eyes. His limbs seemed to shrivel and lose power and he had decided he would never cover the remaining distance to the fallen man. Then he ran suddenly, headlong, into the rear of the tractor and fell down bruised and cut on top of the soft fallen form. The shape under him moved and groaned.

"Get up, Albert! Stand up! Let's go, boy!" His shouted words were soundless in the roar of the well. But his touch, the feel of another human being, of hope and a chance for life, stirred the youth so that he struggled, trying to lift himself to his feet. If he had not done so Jim McNeely would never have made it, for Albert was heavy, muscular, and big-boned. Looping one limp arm over his neck Jim McNeely grabbed Albert around the waist and tried to steer him and impel him into motion toward the dark distant ring of safety. But Albert's legs would not function and he began to sag back into the blistering earth. With his last ounce of remaining strength Jim McNeely flexed his knees, half-turned, and put his shoulder into soft belly then lifted Albert like a big baby and began to stagger wobble-legged away from the well. He walked with the same over-burdened intensity of a young man many years ago, staggering under a deadening weight of pipe, determined not to go down.

He did not go down, and when he reached the sheltering spray of water from the fire nozzles his shirt and trousers were smoking. Outstretched arms received his burden and he stood hulking in the drenching spray and heard and saw the darting figures casting fantastic shadows and he felt a cleansing surge of strength as though the heat had reached and burst and let drain away a deep buried sac of pus, close to his heart.

Unnoticed by the knot of men who were preoccupied lift-carrying Albert into the woods he turned and started back toward the tractor at a slow, dogged trot. This time the fire was not so bad. He was used to it, and he had an unfinished job to do. A job, or a life, done in a half-assed fashion was not worth doing at all. There would be no other chances for Jim McNeely. There would be no money or strength or will for another try at making it, in this life. As the heat stacked up on him, geometrically as he advanced, he ran faster, driving into its crystalline glaze.

From the woods a thousand eyes watched in wonder and horror as the tiny blackened figure reached the tractor, then climbed uncertainly, as if in slow motion, into the protecting cab, onto the seat. Then the still-running cat began to inch forward, its slender snout with the satchel charge at its tip trembled and swayed with the lumbering advance. In the very heart of the fire the tractor stopped. The dark figure slid from the seat and came to rest behind the cab, half standing, half leaning. One arm with fingers spread, raised overhead. Alert hands at the campside feverishly bent bare wire ends to detonator posts. Then the arm of the distant figure fell. A firm, grimy hand in the woods grabbed the detonator handle and pressed downward. A splitting report cut like a clean knife through the roar from the well. Shock waves rocketed through the woods as the fire column was blasted in two. The high rolling clouds of flame were disengaged from their source. The mushroom of fire seemed to reel its own stem upward into itself, devouring it. Then, suddenly, the blazing brilliance of the earth was plunged into pitch darkness. The hoarse roaring of the well changed instantly into a shrill blinded whistling. After a breathless moment of suspense the blackness held. The fire did not recatch. It was out.

A wild cheering went up from five hundred throats around the perimeter. Somehow this was victory for even the most uncommitted, uninvolved stranger from seven miles down the road. After minutes that dragged like hours in the drenching blackness tiny probing eyes of light began to wink on in the woods. The beam of a powerful flashlight swept the charred circle of ground around the well. A car's headlights came on deep in the woods. The hand-lantern's beam began to play back and forth across the clearing, searching for the man at the tractor. Finally it found him, a solitary figure, walking as if lost, far off course from his angle of entry. A dozen men sprang into motion and ran for him.

A light shone in his blackened face. Arms reaching out for him were brushed aside as he stalked nearly sightless ahead, as if bound for a destination known only to himself. Almost as if from respect, or fear, the men stopped when they reached him and made way for him as he walked through their midst and headed into the woods, away from the camp, searching for air, and not finding any. Half stumbling over a root he walked straight into a brushy tree trunk. He grasped its thick bole in his arms, as if embracing a long lost friend, then he slid slowly down its bark to the ground.

55

IT WAS MID AFTERNOON. DOWN THE POLISHED VINYL of the hospital corridor the woman walked purposefully beside the nurse. She was bare-headed, and she was no longer young. Threads of gray streaked her short dark hair, but her figure was still trim and firm and youthful.

"He's a very sick fella. I'm glad you're here," said the nurse in a hushed voice, preparing her and silently hoping he would still be breathing when they reached the room.

"I came as soon as I heard. Is he—badly burned?"

"He has second degree burns on his face and hands. But that's not the real trouble. He's had a massive coronary thrombosis. The doctor just left. We've given him anti-coagulents and oxygen. He's under sedation for pain, but he's conscious. I'm certainly glad you're here. You must be—Lee?"

"Yes."

"I thought so. You're the wife?"

"I—yes—I'm the wife."

Lee McNeely's hands were trembling and her heart was beating in her throat as she hesitated, then pushed against the door indicated by the nurse. She dreaded what she would see, but nothing could have kept her from going in.

The heavy form on the high bed lay half enclosed in a clear plastic oxygen tent. Two hands swathed in gauze lay motionless at his sides upon the folded sheet. His breath came and went in short gasps.

At the bedside Lee slipped her hand into one of the gauze swaddled claws that had been a hand. She squeezed gently, firmly and looked at the face behind the plastic window.

"Jim."

A tremor went through him as he looked up and recognized her. His breathing came faster. He pawed at the tent with his free hand, trying to brush it away. His voice was low and raspy, muffled.

"Lee . . . Lee . . . I knew you would come."

"Of course you did." She choked off her words to keep from breaking into tears. His face was puffed, dull red, blistered, and cracked. He had no eyebrows or lashes. He gripped her hand and with his other hand kept trying to paw away the oxygen tent that separated them.

"Mr. McNeely," said the nurse, alarmed. "You must be quiet, fella. You need this oxygen to make you well."

"Get the damn thing off me!" he cried weakly. "Lee. Help me!"

Freeing her hand from his Lee McNeely lifted the corner of the cubicle tent and inserted her head and shoulders under it with him. She embraced him, pressing herself on his chest, smiling down at him, her eyes welling with tears. She kissed him on his cracked, crusted lips.

"Hello, my darling."

"O-oh, Lee." A long, shuddering tension seemed to flow out of him. "I *told* her. I told the nurse you would come. I bet her you would . . . if you knew about it."

"I came the minute I heard. And I'm not ever going to leave you again."

"Oh, Lee—" He began to cry. Big tears began spilling over his raw eyelids. "I've been so terrible. I love you, Lee. I never loved anybody else."

"Nor I, my darling."

"I got to tell you so many things. Help me. I got to tell you."

"Mrs. McNeely," said the nurse, growing frantic. "He mustn't talk. He must be still. He must have all the oxygen he can possibly get."

Lee McNeely half withdrew from the tent, but Jim McNeely held her tightly with two bandaged hands.

"I got to talk to you, Lee," he said in a rasping, imperious voice. "I got to say it before I die!"

"You're not going to die, my dearest," said Lee firmly. "Get that out of your mind right now."

"Mr. McNeely," said the nurse, "You *must not talk* any more. You must be still!"

"I'm going to talk!" said Jim McNeely, rumbling it out between clenched teeth. "I'm gonna talk to her! Get away from me, nurse! I'll get up and walk outa this two-bit hospital and die on the damn sidewalk."

"All right, baby. All right." Lee pressed her face firmly against his cheek. Then she withdrew from the tent and faced the white-lipped nurse.

"Please. Let me handle this. I take full responsibility. I know this man. Please, leave it with me."

"You may be his wife," the nurse said. "But I'm the nurse in charge and I'm trying to save his life. I'll have to tell the doctor about this. This patient must have absolute rest and quiet."

"Yes, nurse. I know. Thank you." Lee touched the nurse's arm, then she turned back to Jim McNeely, putting her head and shoulders again under the tent and pressed her face against his blistered cheek. "Everything is all right, my baby. Everything is *all right*."

The large fallen trunk of a man drew in her warmth and love and breathed out a whimpering infant's sob.

"I'm gonna die, Lee. I got to talk to you before—"

"If you say that one more time I'll leave here, Jim McNeely. You're not going to die. I didn't come here to help you die. Now grab hold! Live! For us! Do it for me, Jim!"

"OK, baby, OK," he whispered.

"Don't OK me. Just hang on. Don't consider *not* living. *You're going to be all right.* And you and I are going to do a lot of things we always needed to do and never did. I won't leave you, ever again. So don't talk about leaving me. Just say what you need to say, and hang on."

"OK . . . baby." His voice was weak and thready and his breathing shallow, but he smiled and his eyes shut and he dozed.

She held him and she did not move, and he awoke in minutes, talking. He talked in mumbling whispers. That is how the day wore out and the night came on. He talked, and dozed, and awoke again, talking. She held his hand and pressed her face against his and he seemed to draw strength from her voice and her nearness and from the vitality in her.

"I killed Dent," he said.

"No, sweetheart."

"He was mine. My crippled boy."

"Jim, don't torture yourself. You're just a human being. We've all made mistakes.

"I'm to blame . . . for Ort, too. I didn't look after him. The Lord gave 'em both to me to look after . . . and I didn't look after 'em."

Awake again, he said, "I did a terrible thing to you, Lee. I messed up your life . . ."

"I made my big mistake, too, sweetheart," she said. "I ran away. I wasn't strong or wise enough to stick and work it out. But that's all gone and forgotten now."

"I wrote a new will last week . . . everything to you. Little to leave but trouble. But some things got to be righted, Lee. I knew you would . . . take care of 'em . . . for me. Berry Wakely. Give Bison their well. But ask 'em to take Berry back. He couldn't help what he did. I trapped him. I'm the only one to blame . . ."

This was a purging of the soul. The cleansing ritual of a scarred and dirty warrior confessing his sins of battle before the gates of Valhalla.

When he awoke his voice was grasping for breath. He mumbled, "What do you reckon I wanted with all . . . that money? All I want right now is a good chestful of . . . air."

"We need something better, something deeper, something more lasting than air, my darling. A little air, more or less—a year or two added to our lives. Sooner or later we come to a place where we have to face the fact of—something bigger than we are. Something bigger than the world is. Sooner or later we reach a point where God is the only possibility left."

She didn't know whether he had heard her or not but in a little while he said, "I'm there. And I got nothin' to trade with. Lee . . . I'm scared."

"Being afraid is a part of it. And the wonderful thing about God is, if you're really ready to trade, your credit is good."

"Not mine, Lee. I been too sorry. And I'm shot."

She clung to him and could almost feel him slipping from her grasp. Suddenly she felt helpless and panicky. She closed her eyes and prayed with all the intensity of her being. *Dear God, tell me how to make this man want to live!*

The doctor came in, making his evening rounds, trailed by the upset nurse. He touched his stethoscope briefly to the stricken man's chest. Then he patted Lee on the shoulder and left without a word. He was an old doctor long in the trade, and he knew that this patient had passed a line beyond which the love and closeness of this woman was a better, kinder medicine than anything the physician had left in his bag.

When Jim McNeely's eyelids fluttered Lee spoke softly, strongly against his ear. "A long time ago an old preacher wrote something that has helped me out of some bad holes, when the past has seemed incredibly bad and wasted and meaningless. 'God requireth that which is past.' I've never been exactly sure what he meant except I feel it must mean that it all wasn't wasted or meaningless, even the worst of it."

He said, "I got a terrible lot of making up to do . . . for what's in my past."

"Everybody has!" she said. "Everybody! And it's got to be done. Here and now or in another world we can only wonder about."

Suddenly it was as if she saw a glimmer of light far ahead, at the end of a long tunnel. Her voice continued steady and clear as she talked to this man she loved, as though to a child.

"You remember the place my daddy had down on the Paluxy? I have it, still. It's not much of a farm but it's pretty, especially in the fall when there's wood smoke in the air. You and I could take that and do something important with it, Jim. Something good, even exciting. Maybe make it into a-a summer camp, for children like the Wakely boy. A place their parents could bring them and leave them a while, when they're worn out and think they can't go on—remember how you used to say there ought to be some way to 'handicap' people in life the way you do in golf, to try to even things up a little for those not as talented or as fortunate as others, through no fault of their own? This could help a little that way."

The planted thought penetrated the deep, inner mind of Jim McNeely and stirred a faint spark of response. He said, "I could do . . . something like that."

The night mounted steadily to its dark crest then slowly glided down the silent hours toward another day. Lee McNeely literally talked her man through those sinking hours, and she prayed in all the ways she knew to pray, and when his breathing faltered she held him tightly and at times shouted at him and shook him. And during the quiet times she heard the soft cry of a water bird, blown in from the coast, through the open window, and the sound, mixed with the faint murmur of the oxygen flow, came to her as the lute voice of the universe, calming her, giving her courage and strength. When the light began to gray in the oleanders outside the window he was still breathing.

When the sun was bright and hot outside, his precarious breathing was deeper and steady. The morning head-nurse came in, fresh and efficient and starched. She took his pulse, studying his color with narrowed, pro-fessional eyes. As the seconds ticked off she slowly pursed her lips and wrinkled her brow. Then she looked at Lee and nodded.

"This boy's trying."

"He's plenty tough. He'll make it," said Lee, her voice suddenly so full of tears that she could hardly speak.

When the nurse had gone Lee wiped her eyes with her fingers and leaned over the big man, smiling.

"If we're going to do all these things together, I guess I'll have to ask you to marry me—again."

Jim McNeely raised one bandaged hand and waved it weakly back and forth. There was a glint of laughter in his eyes. "Quit trying to run things," he said. He tapped himself on the chest. "I'll do the asking."

Then he fell into a deep sleep for the first time in many days.

AFTERWORD

OUT ON THE OLD NANYUKI-MARURA CROSSROADS
I stood sweating as swirls of hot dust blew past. My eyes shifted
from one end of the road to the other as I began to wonder if
a ride would come at all. It was a long way from the Andrews Highway
north of Odessa, Texas, but I'm certain I felt the same uneasiness Jim
McNeely felt out on that desolate road. I had arrived in Kenya days before
looking for work, and with dog luck had connected with a Texas woman
who had a barn full of horses that needed more riding than she could
handle. Not a bad first job out of college and a far cry from the oil fields.

A tan Suzuki Samurai finally slowed for the turn. The driver, David,
offered me a lift as far as Ol' Pejeta. We descended into the Great Rift
Valley drinking lukewarm beer in thick recycled bottles and ate greasy sausage wrapped in newspaper while listening to an original Kenny Rogers
cassette. As the land got flatter (and hotter) I told David how much it
reminded me of the country north of Midland, where the Llano Estacado
runs as flat as the eye can see and the mesquites are tall but still somewhat
sparse. Thousands of miles from home and the Acacia trees, "The Gambler" and "cold" beer were spinning my mind back to West Texas. It was
in Africa that I first saw a glimpse of my future and uncovered a primeval
need to explore and to share my findings with others. All I had to do now
was to transform those findings into compelling cinematic experiences.

A decade (and many film projects) later I got a call from an old friend
of my father's who had bought the movie rights to *The Iron Orchard*. A
former roughneck turned pipe supplier, he had made a buck the hard
way—by ambition and the calluses on his hands, just as Jim McNeely

had done. He needed help getting the film project off the ground, and I seemed to be the filmmaker with the right background to do it. I was living in Argentina at the time but managed to track down an elusive first edition of the novel. Pendleton's prose drew me in with such potency that I quickly connected with Jim McNeely as if he were an old buddy sharing stories of our youth spent on deserted highways. With each turn of the page it was as if a small movie projector was playing a familiar story in my head. Jim's desire to tap the earth's crust in order to extract a primordial substance began to drill deep into my own psyche. No, *this* was not just another great book; this was the ultimate Texas oil field drama, and it would come to occupy a considerable part of my head over the next eight years. With the same determination as McNeely drilling his first well, I set out to make *The Iron Orchard* my first feature film.

As I dug deeper into the novel, I learned that its author, Tom Pendleton, was the pen name for Edmund Van Zandt, a Fort Worth native who as a young man worked in the West Texas oil fields in the last years of the Depression, where he lived with and came to know the roustabouts, wildcatters, and other colorful characters drawn to the Permian Basin in its early boom years. His later career, as a Marine Corps officer, lawyer, and executive of an international oil company, was in a way a long gestation period for the novel, which was published in 1967.

My own connection to this material was, like Tom Pendleton's, as ancestral as it was visceral. McNeely's early days mirrored those of my grandfather, who broke out roughnecking in the 1930s north of Odessa. Just like McNeely, he saved every penny earned until he launched a small oil field service outfit. He sold, rented, and often lent equipment to wildcatters in exchange for a piece of their deal. That's how the small-time, dogged oil men made it—wheeling and dealing, persistence and resourcefulness—exactly how Jim McNeely wrangled his start in Pendleton's novel, the very same manner in which the Permian Basin was leased, drilled, and proliferated into one of the great discoveries of its age.

As McNeely evolved from boll weevil, to contractor, to wildcatter himself, he began to find and drill deals on his own. This was where my father's side of the story came in. An independent oil man for over fifty-five years, my father was a charismatic landman through three decades of boom and bust in Midland, until the First National Bank finally shut its doors and we fled to Austin. A true West Texas gentleman, my father was as comfortable in his M. L. Leddy boots as he was in his penny loafers, and his mood often fluctuated with the price of West Texas Intermediate. From my earliest memories he was always on the hunt for the "next deal," with the same thirst and hope for a new prospect that fueled Jim McNeely.

Failed ambition proved disastrous for the increasingly unstable Jim McNeely. It got its hooks into my father, too, where both dry wells and gushers were celebrated with the same ritual—in the bowels of the 007 Bar, one of downtown Midland's finest watering holes. This was a place worthy of a book itself, a windowless haunt as dark as a well digger's boots, where great oil patch characters would gather, often before lunchtime, to drown their sorrows on deals lost, or toast the ones to come that promised to deliver them from the perpetual precipice of financial ruin. The 007 didn't last long after the bust in the 80s. Another friend of my father's bought it with hopes to resurrect it before the next boom. But its doors never reopened. After living in the 007 a few years, he couldn't afford the utility bills. It's said he died there—perhaps a metaphor for the doomed wildcatters of my father's generation.

These types of eccentrics populate Pendleton's *The Iron Orchard* and were destined for the big screen. But turning a 384-page novel into a two-hour movie is no easy feat. Hollywood had already shelved the project back in the late 60s, even with Paul Newman attached. On an indie budget many would say it's an impossible film to produce. Like all wildcatters, I was often staggered by doubt. The downturns in oil prices didn't help our funding efforts either. But after enlisting screenwriter Gerry De Leon to pen the first script, I finally saw Pendleton's story come to true cinematic life. But a movie about wildcatters refuted the traditional approach. I needed the people of West Texas—*my* people—to share this journey with me. And that's exactly where I turned.

Built in 1930, the lavish Hotel Settles served as an oasis and a beacon of hope for the oilmen of Big Spring. But by the 1970s, the glut had transformed the Settles into an undesirable boarding house, and it slumped downhill from there. In the mid-2000s, Big Spring native Brint Ryan purchased the Hotel Settles and embarked on a historical restoration. In 2017 the hotel not only housed our cast and crew for months, but it was also the centerpiece of our film, taking the place of the now defunct Scharbauer Hotel in Midland, the dealmakers' den in *The Iron Orchard*. The Settles was pivotal in getting our film made, and *The Iron Orchard*'s revival could not have come at a more opportune time.

Many people along the way have asked me if the story represented the oil business in a positive way. All I could say then, and still today, is that it represents how things were. For good or bad, *The Iron Orchard* is real and relatable to anyone who has spent time in the oil patch. It's an ode to times past and the hardships of making it in one of America's toughest industries. I am grateful that Tom Pendleton wrote such an authentic account of the Texas oil culture and its people. The film is my way to memorialize not just the novel, but the special place where it happened, and that tough, resilient, eccentric breed of people who lived through it.

I hope our film honors these men and women of the oil field simply by telling their story. Tom Pendleton did his part; I certainly hope that I have done mine. Jim McNeely left a lesson behind for all of us, and perhaps it's more pertinent today than ever before. The magnanimous spirit and hospitality of West Texas informed Tom Pendleton's epic novel. It seems fitting that it fueled the feature film, as well. And now, it belongs to us all.

I'd like to thank the Van Zandt family for entrusting me to tell their father's story. Without their unending faith this film would have never been made. I'd also like to offer a heartfelt thanks to all our incredible partners who stuck with us through thick and thin during the downturns, upticks, and sidewinding travails of filmmaking. Endless thanks to the good folks of Big Spring, our friends, family, and many partners in Midland, including the Permian Basin Petroleum Museum who met us with open doors. To all our producers, cast, and crew, whose endurance and passion have been unequaled and who remain the best damn crew in the state of Texas. To all the drillers, oil companies, engineers, geologists, and roughnecks who lent us an ear and their ideas for making the best film that we could. Lastly, without the freewheeling wildcatter spirit in both of my parents, Mike and Barbara Roberts, I would certainly not be writing this at all. You both live high in the sky of my heart. Caro, Quino, and Andi, you have tapped the eternal well of my soul and continue to inspire me daily.

Ty Roberts, director, producer,
and coscreenwriter of the feature
films *The Iron Orchard* and
(upcoming) *12 Mighty Orphans*